HOMER

THE ODYSSEY

The Story of Odysseus

TRANSLATED BY
W. H. D. ROUSE

A MENTOR BOOK

NEW AMERICAN LIBRARY

NEW YORK
PUBLISHED IN CANADA BY
PENGUIN BOOKS CANADA LIMITED, MARKHAM, ONTARIO

MENTOR TRADEMARK REG. U.S. PAT. OFF. AND FOREIGN COUNTRIES
REGISTERED TRADEMARK—MARCA REGISTRADA
HECHO EN DRESDEN, TN.

SIGNET, SIGNET CLASSIC, MENTOR, ONYX, PLUME, MERIDIAN AND
NAL BOOKS are published *in the United States* by
NAL PENGUIN INC.,
1633 Broadway, New York, New York 10019,
in Canada by Penguin Books Canada Limited,
2801 John Street, Markham, Ontario L3R 1B4

50   51   52   53   54   55   56   57   58

PRINTED IN THE UNITED STATES OF AMERICA

A Magnificent Saga

The Odyssey was the first and probably the greatest adventure story of all time. Each age has had its translators of Homer, each finding in him the peculiar weather of that age. The Elizabethans found him a Renaissance man, Pope found him an Augustan, Matthew Arnold a Victorian. It was perhaps inevitable that T. E. Lawrence, and W. H. D. Rouse, should have found him the father of the modern novel.

In his preface to this edition Rouse calls *The Odyssey* "the best story ever written . . . it has been a favourite for three thousand years." He goes on: "Indeed it enchants every man, lettered or unlettered, and every boy who hears it; but unless someone tells it by word of mouth, few are likely to hear it or read it unless they know Greek. They cannot get it from any existing translation, because all such are filled with affectations and attempts at poetic language which Homer himself is quite free from. Homer speaks naturally and we must do the same. That is what I have tried to do in this book, and I ask that it may be judged simply as a story."

Of the Rouse translation the *London Times Literary Supplement* said: "His version is always alive and gives us *The Odyssey* as the great and moving story it is, unlittered by the bric-a-brac of scholarship and by the fussiness of scholars anxious to point to its literary merits." And the *Christian Science Monitor* wrote of the American edition: "There can be no doubt that Dr. Rouse has made Homer live, and has compelled us to see that his contemporaries were men and women in all essentials like ourselves. I suppose I have read *The Odyssey* a dozen times; but I never before saw its characters so clearly."

This edition contains an invaluable appendix by the translator on "Homer's Words" and a "Pronouncing Index."

NOTE

I have to thank several friends for reading and commenting upon certain parts of this translation; and particularly Miss A. M. Croft, B.A., whose help has been indispensable.

Four Books were published in the *New English Weekly* (1935), for which I thank the Editor, Mr. P. Mairet.

To guard against possible mistakes I add that the translation was made before T. E. Lawrence's *Odyssey* was published. Whenever I was in doubt as to the meaning I consulted the scholiasts, Merry and Riddell and Munro for the *Odyssey*, Walter Leaf for the *Illiad*, and the most careful and exact translation I know, that of A. T. Murray in the Loeb Library, to all of whom I return my sincere thanks.

Much have I travelled in the realms of gold,
   And many goodly states and kingdoms seen;
   Round many western islands have I been
Which bards in fealty to Apollo hold.
Oft of one wide expanse had I been told
   That deep-browed Homer ruled as his demesne;
   Yet did I never breathe its pure serene
Till I heard Chapman speak out loud and bold:
Then felt I like some watcher of the skies
   When a new planet swims into his ken;
Or like stout Cortez when with eagle eyes
   He stared at the Pacific—and all his men
Looked at each other with a wild surmise—
   Silent, upon a peak in Darien.

JOHN KEATS

PREFACE

THIS IS THE BEST STORY EVER WRITTEN, AND IT HAS BEEN A favourite for three thousand years: not long since I heard its far-off echo in a caique on the Ægean Sea, when the skipper told me how St. Elias carried an oar on his shoulder until some one called it a winnowing-fan.[1] Until lately it has been in the mind of every educated man; and it is a thousand pities that the new world should grow up without it. Indeed it enchants every man, lettered or unlettered, and every boy who hears it; but unless some one tells it by word of mouth, few are likely to hear it or read it unless they know Greek. They cannot get it from any existing translation, because all such are filled with affectations and attempts at poetic language which Homer himself is quite free from. Homer speaks naturally, and we must do the same. That is what I have tried to do in this book, and I ask that it may be judged simply as a story. If the names are odd, they are not more so than what people are content to swallow in their Tolstoy or Dostoyevsky or Turgeniev. They are less so, indeed; for readers will soon become familiar with the Greek surnames and even welcome their musical cadences as Homer's audience did. Those who like thrillers and detective novels will find excitement enough here, and nothing they can find elsewhere will be as good as the fight with Penelope's pretenders. Those who like fairy tales will find nothing better than Polyphemos the Goggle-eye. Those who like psychology will find plenty to entertain them in the characters, both gods and men, and particularly in the wonderful picture of Odysseus himself: as he grows from the gay prattling child and the merry young husband to the grim dispenser of vengeance, patient, untiring, unfailing, and within as tender-hearted as Nausicaä herself. Those who like delicacies of deep feeling will find it in Penelope and her husband, whose meeting is one of the supreme scenes of human life.

But I have to think also of scholars, although the book is not addressed to them in the first place. If they have studied Homer only in the library they may be apt to worry more than I do about the digamma, and recensions, and interpo-

[1] *The Adventures of Ulysses*, page x, published by Macmillan, London.

vii

lations. But if they have heard, as I have, the whole *Iliad*
and *Odyssey* read aloud in Greek by intelligent readers a
dozen times from beginning to end, they will be able to test
what I say in the Appendix, about stock epithets and tradi-
tional tags. Nor will they be shocked when I speak of
Homer as a man, and not as a syndicate. But I foresee that
some will be shocked at the simple words which I put into
the mouths of Homer's characters. Then I will ask them to
consider what I have said below on that matter. And if they
can bring themselves not to regret the affectations of the
so-called "poetic style," they may compare Homer's words
with what they know of the Greek language, and they will
find that Homer uses what people did use in daily life and
did not reject blunt words or even invented words.

They will see also how this simple style brings out the
characters of the speakers and the real meaning of what
they say. They will see also how Homer uses the domestic
scenes of Olympos as a comic relief against the grim reali-
ties of the world; and they will see how he dots in touches
of comedy amid the battles, a scene here or a phrase there.
His hearers, remember, were in rollicking mood after a
good dinner. They do not mind having their feelings har-
rowed, but you can't keep always on that level. Nestor's
son says to Menelaos, "Don't think me rude, sir, but I don't
like crying over my supper," and after a bit of bloodshed,
cheerfulness keeps breaking in. If Homer bores his audience
he will not be invited to dinner again. The passages of po-
etry, again, are beautiful by their own merits, even in Eng-
lish prose; and they come breaking in of themselves in the
middle of everyday sayings and doings just as such things
do in human life. They do not try to be poetic, they are
poetic in the true sense.

The manners and thoughts of the heroic age are illumi-
nated by the Icelandic sagas, such as Dasent's *Burnt Njál*
and Morris's *Grettir the Strong*. Many references to the
great hall and the home-buildings can be understood by the
help of the figures in Dasent's book; and the judgment scene
on the shield of Achilles might have been taken from the
Althing.

W. H. D. ROUSE

CONTENTS

THE STORY OF ODYSSEUS

BOOK I

What Went On in the House of Odysseus

THIS IS THE STORY OF A MAN, ONE WHO WAS NEVER AT A loss. He had travelled far in the world, after the sack of Troy, the virgin fortress; he saw many cities of men, and learnt their mind; he endured many troubles and hardships in the struggle to save his own life and to bring back his men safe to their homes. He did his best, but he could not save his companions. For they perished by their own madness, because they killed and ate the cattle of Hyperion the Sun-god, and the god took care that they should never see home again.

At the time when I begin, all the others who had not been killed in the war were at home, safe from the perils of battle and sea: but he was alone, longing to get home to his wife. He was kept prisoner by a witch, Calypso, a radiant creature, and herself one of the great family of gods, who wanted him to stay in her cave and be her husband. Well then, the seasons went rolling by, and when the year came, in which by the thread that fate spins for every man he was to return home to Ithaca, he had not yet got free of his troubles and come back to his own people. The gods were all sorry for him, except Poseidon, god of the sea, who bore a lasting grudge against him all the time until he returned.

But it happened that Poseidon went for a visit a long way off, to the Ethiopians; who live at the ends of the earth, some near the sunrise, some near the sunset. There he expected a fine sacrifice of bulls and goats, and there he was, feasting and enjoying himself mightily; but the other gods were all gathered in the palace of Olympian Zeus.

Then the Father of gods and men made them a speech; for his heart was angry against a man, Aigisthos, and Agamemnon's son Orestês, as you know, had just killed the man. So he spoke to the company as follows:

"Upon my word, just see how mortal men always put the blame on us gods! We are the source of evil, so they say— when they have only their own madness to thank if their miseries are worse than they ought to be. Look here, now: Aigisthos has done what he ought not to have done. Took Agamemnon's wedded wife for himself, killed Agamemnon when he came home, though he knew quite well it would be his own ruin! We gave him fair warning, sent our special messenger Hermês, and told him not to kill the man or to make love to his wife; their son Orestês would punish him, when he grew up and wanted his own dominions. Hermês told him plainly, but he could do nothing with Aigisthos, although it was for his own good. Now he has paid the debt in one lump sum."

Then up spoke Athena, with her bright eyes glinting:

"Cronidês our Father, King of Kings and Lord of Lords! I have nothing to say for Aigisthos, he richly deserved his ruin. So perish any one else who does a thing like that! But what about that clever Odysseus? I am anxious about him, poor fellow, kept from his friends all this while, in trouble and sorrow, in that island covered with trees, and nothing but the waves all round it, in the very middle of the sea! It is the home of one of ourselves, the daughter of Atlas, you remember, that creature of mischief, who knows all the depths of the sea; you know, he holds up the pillars which keep earth and heaven apart. It is his daughter who keeps the wretched man a prisoner. She is always coaxing him with soft deceitful words to forget Ithaca; but Odysseus would be happy to see as much as the smoke leaping up from his native land, and then to die. And you cannot spare him a thought, Olympian. Don't you owe him something for all those sacrifices which he used to offer in their camp on the plain of Troy? Why have you such an odd grudge against him, Zeus?"

Then Zeus Cloudgatherer answered:

"My child, what a word to let out between your teeth! How could I forget that fine fellow Odysseus, after all! He is almost one of us. Wise beyond mortal men, ready beyond all to offer sacrifice to the lords of the broad heavens. But Poseidon Earthholder bears him unrelenting hatred, because of the Cyclops whose eye he put out; I mean Polyphemos, who has our blood in his veins, the most powerful of all the Cyclopians.

"Thoösa was his mother, the daughter of Phorcys prince of the barren brine; Poseidon possessed her in a hollow cave. Ever since then, Poseidon has kept the man wandering about, although he does not kill him outright. Come now, let us all try to think how we can persuade Poseidon to abate his anger and let him go home to his native land. Surely he will not be able to stand out against all the immortals, and keep up a quarrel all by himself!"

Then Athena said:

"Cronidês our Father, King of Kings and Lord of Lords! If all the gods now agree that Odysseus shall return to his own home, then let us dispatch our messenger Hermês Argeiphontês to the island of Ogygia; and let him announce forthwith to the nymph our unchangeable will, that Odysseus, after all he has patiently endured, shall return home. And I will myself go to Ithaca, to put heart into his son and make him do something. He shall call the people to a meeting, and speak his mind to all the would-be bridegrooms who have been butchering his sheep and his cattle in heaps. And I will send him to Sparta and to sandy Pylos to inquire about his beloved father, if he can hear that he is on his way home. That will be some credit to him in the world."

So saying, she fastened under her feet those fine shoes, imperishable shoes of gold, which used to carry her over moist and dry to the ends of the earth, quick as the blowing of the breeze; down she went shooting from the peaks of Olympos, and stood in the town of Ithaca against the outer gates of Odysseus upon the threshold of the courtyard. In her hand she held a spear of bronze, and she took the form of a family friend, Mentês, the chief man of the Taphians.

So there she found those high and mighty gallants. Just then they were amusing themselves with a game of draughts in front of the door, sitting on the skins of the cattle which they had killed themselves; and their orderlies and servants were all busy, some mixing wine and water in the great bowls, some wiping up the tables with oozing sponges and laying the dishes, some serving the meat, and there was plenty of it.

Telemachos saw the visitor long before the others. He was a fine-looking boy; and he sat there among the intruders in deep distress, with his heart full of his noble father. He wondered if his father would suddenly appear and make a clean sweep of them all, and take his own honourable place again, and manage his property.

These were his thoughts as he sat among them, and saw some one at the door. He went straight to the porch, indignant to think that a visitor should be left standing at the door. He took the visitor's right hand, and relieved him of the spear, and spoke to him in words that wing like arrows to the mark:

"Good day to you, sir. You will be welcome in our house.

Refresh yourself, and after you have eaten and drunk you shall say what you have come for."

So saying, he led the stranger in. Then as soon as they were within the lofty hall he carried the spear to a tall pillar, and set it in a polished spear-stand in which other spears were standing: the spears of Odysseus, that patient man, a whole lot of them. Then he led his visitor to a seat and bade him be seated. He threw a rug over it, a beautiful rug, an artist's work; and there was a footstool ready at his feet. Beside him he placed an armchair of carven work, apart from the rest of the company; for he did not wish the visitor to be disgusted by the noise, and to lose all relish for his food as he found himself amongst a rabble of bullies. He wanted also to ask about his lost father. A servant brought the hand-wash for the visitor, and poured it over his hands from a jug all made of fine gold into a silver basin. He drew up to the seat a polished table, a comely maid brought in the vittles and put them on the table—all sorts of things, she did not spare her store; the carver added plates of all sorts of meat, and set beside them cups of gold; an orderly kept their cups filled with wine.

In came the gallants, full of pride. They flung themselves down at once into chairs or settles, one after another, and the orderlies poured water over their hands, while the women piled up heaps of rolls in the baskets, and the boys filled the mixing-bowls with drink to the brim. Then they put out their hands to take the good things that lay ready. At last, when they had eaten and drunk till they wanted no more, their fancies turned to other things, singing and dancing: for these are the graces of a feast. An orderly brought a beautiful harp, and put it in the hands of Phemios, who used to sing for them because he could not help it. So he struck up a prelude for his song. Then Telemachos spoke to Mentês, who was really Athena, and he brought his head close, that the others might not hear;

"Kind sir, will you think me rude if I say something to you? You see what these fellows care about, music and song—easy enough, when some one else pays for the food they eat, a man whose white bones are lying on the ground and rotting in the rain, no doubt, or rolling about in the salt sea. That man! if they only caught sight of him here in Ithaca once more, they would gladly give a fortune of gold for a light pair of heels! But he is dead and gone in this miserable way, and there is no comfort for us, even if there are people in the world who say he will come back. No, the day of his return will never dawn.

"Well now, please tell me this: I want to know all about you. Who are you, where do you come from? Where is your country, what is your family? What ship carried you here? I don't suppose you walked all the way! How was it those sailors brought you to Ithaca? Who did they say they were? And another thing I want you to tell me: Is it your first visit, or are you a friend of our family? For a great many other men used to come to our place, since that man also was a traveller in the world."

Athena answered him, with her bright eyes glinting:

"Very well, I will tell you all about it. My name is Mentês; I am the son of a clever father, Anchialos, and I rule over a nation of seamen, the Taphians. I have come here now with ship and crew, voyaging over the dark face of the sea to places where they speak other languages than ours; just now to Temesê for bronze, and I have a cargo of shining steel. My ship came to land some way from your town, and she lies in the harbour of Rheithron, under woody Neïon. Let me say that we are family friends from long ago, if you will only go and ask that fine old gentleman Laërtês; they say he does not come to town any more, but keeps far away in the country in a miserable plight, with one servant, an old woman who gives him something to eat and drink when his poor limbs are tired out with stumbling over the slopes of his vine-plot. And now here I am. They did say he was come home from his travels—your father I mean, but I suppose the gods have put something in his way. I tell you he is not dead yet, that grand man Odysseus, but he is still alive—a prisoner somewhere in the broad sea, in an island amid the waters; and dangerous men hold him fast, savages, who are keeping him no doubt against his will.

"Well, now, I will play the prophet, and tell you what is in the mind of the immortals, and what I think will come to pass; although I am no prophet really, and I do not know much about the meaning of birds. I tell you he will not long be absent from his dear native land, not if chains of iron hold him fast. He will find a way to get back, for he is never at a loss.

"Come now, please tell me this; I want to know all about you. Are you really his son—a boy as big as you the son of Odysseus? You seem terribly like him, that head and those fine eyes of yours—I can see him now! for we used to meet ever so often in the old days, before he embarked for Troy, when so many of the best men of the nation sailed away in that fleet. Since then I have not seen Odysseus, and he has not seen me."

The boy answered politely:

"Very well, sir, I will tell you all about it. My mother says I am his son, but I don't know myself; I never heard of any one who did know whose son he was. I only wish my father had been a man who lived to grow old upon his own rich acres! But now!—there never was mortal man more unlucky than the man whom they call my father, since you ask me the question."

Then Athena said, with her bright eyes glinting:

"I tell you one thing: the breed will not be inglorious in time to come, when you are what I see and your mother is Penelopeia; thank God for that. But come now, please tell me this. Feasting—company—what does it all mean? What has it to do with you? Banquet or wedding? It is clear that this is no bring-what-you-like picnic! It seems to me they are making themselves very much at home. Lords of all they survey! It is enough to make a man angry to see all this rough behaviour, if he had any decent feeling."

The boy answered once more:

"Sir, since you ask me the question, this house might have been wealthy and beyond reproach, so long as that man was at home; but now the gods have willed otherwise. They have chosen to send trouble upon us. That man they have picked out of all the men in the world, and they have made him vanish out of our sight. If he were dead, it would not hurt me so much; if he had fallen before Troy among his comrades, or if he had died in the arms of his friends, after he had wound up the war. Then the whole nation would have built him a barrow, and he would have won a great name for his son as well in days to come. But now, there is not a word of him. The birds of prey have made him their prey; he is gone from sight, gone from hearing, and left anguish and lamentation for me.

"And that man is not all I have to mourn and lament, since the gods have sent other sorrows to trouble me, in this way: All the great men who rule in the islands, in Dulichion, and Samê, and woody Zacynthos, and all those who are lords in rocky Ithaca, one and all they want to marry my mother, and here they are, wasting our wealth. She hates the thought of it, but she neither denies nor dares to make an end of the matter, while they eat me out of house and home. Like enough they will tear me to pieces myself as well."

"Insufferable!" was the thought of Pallas Athena; and she said, "What a shame! It's clear you do need Odysseus to lay hands on these heartless men who pester his wife! And he is so far away! If only he would come at this moment, and stand right in the doorway of this hall, with helmet and shield and a couple of spears; looking as he did when I first set eyes upon him in our house, while he drank his wine and enjoyed himself, on his way back from Ephyra, from the house of Ilos Mermeridês! He had been all that way in a fast ship, Odysseus I mean; he was looking for a deadly poison to smear on the barbs of his arrows. The man would not give him any, for fear of the everlasting gods; but my father did give him some, for he was terribly fond of him. May he be like what he was then when he comes upon these rioters! Quick death would be theirs, one and all! They would be sorry they ever wanted to marry! Ah, well, of course all that lies on the knees of the gods—whether he will come back or not, and punish them in his own house. But you had better think how to get them out of the place, that is my advice.

"Look here now, just listen to me. To-morrow call together all the great men of the nation to a meeting, make them a speech, protest before all the gods. Tell the intruders to make themselves scarce and go home, and your mother—if she has a mind to marry again, let her first go back to her father's house; he is a man of influence, they will arrange the marriage, and see that the bridegroom makes a handsome provision for her, such as a beloved daughter ought to have.

"My advice to you is this, if you will let me advise you. Get the best ship you can find, put twenty oarsmen aboard, go and find out about your father and why he is so long away. Perhaps some one may tell you, or you may hear some rumour that God will send, which is often the best way for people to get news.

"First go to Pylos, and ask that noble prince Nestor; then to Sparta and Menelaos (good old red-head!), for he was the last to come home of all the army. Then, if you hear that your father is alive, and on his way back, for all your wearing and tearing you can bear up for another year. But if you hear that he is dead and no longer in this world, come back yourself to your own home, and build him a barrow, and do the funeral honours in handsome style, as you ought, and give away your mother to some husband.

"When at last all this is finished and done, collect your wits and make a good plan to kill these hangers-on, either by craft or by open fight. Indeed, you ought not to play about in the nursery any longer; your childhood's days are done. Haven't you heard what a great name Orestês made for himself in the world, the fine young fellow, when he killed the traitor Aigisthos who had murdered his famous father? You, too, my dear boy, big and handsome as I see you now, you too be strong, that you may have a good name on the lips of men for many generations.

"Now I will go back to my ship and my crew, for they will be tired of waiting for me. It is your own business, so don't forget what I say."

Telemachos answered with his usual good manners:

"Sir, I thank you for your kindness; you might be a father speaking to his own son, and I will not forget one word of what you say. But do stay a little, even if you are in a hurry. Let me offer you a bath, rest and refresh yourself, and take back to your ship a gift from me—something precious, a real good thing, to be an heirloom, from me, such as a friend gives to a friend."

Then the goddess Athena answered:

"Don't keep me longer, I want to be off. As to any gift which your kind heart bids you offer, when I come back you may give it me to take home. If you choose me a good one, you shall have as good in return."

When Athena had said this, away she went like a bird, up through the luffer in the roof. In the spirit of the boy she left courage and confidence, and he thought of his father even more than before. He understood what it all meant, and he was amazed; for he believed her to be a god. At once he went back to that rough crew, looking more like a god than a man himself.

He found the minstrel singing to them in fine style, while they sat all round in silence, listening. He sang of the lamentable return of the Achaians from Troy which Pallas Athena had laid upon them.

In the upper chamber the wonderful sounds fell on the ears of Penelopeia the daughter of Icarios, the wise and faithful wife. She came down the high staircase out of her room; but not alone, two waiting-women went with her. And when this lovely creature came amongst the men who would have her for a wife, she stood by the doorpost of the great hall, with its massive walls, and drew the soft veil over her cheeks. There she stood, with one honest waiting-woman on each side. Tears were in her eyes, as she spoke to the singer of that divine song:

"Phemios, you know many other songs fit to charm the ear,

great deeds of men and gods, which singers are used to noise
abroad. Sing one of those to the company, and let them drink
their wine in silence; but make an end to this piteous song,
which tears the heart-strings in my breast, since I beyond all
have had to suffer grief intolerable. So dear is he that I long
for and never forget—my husband, whose fame is known
over the length and breadth of the land."

Telemachos answered her with good sense: "My dear
mother, why won't you let the worthy minstrel entertain us as
he likes? Don't blame the minstrel, blame Zeus, who makes
men work hard for their living, and then gives them just what
he chooses for each! As for the minstrel, there is no harm in
his singing the bad luck of the Danaans; the song people
praise is always the latest thing. You should brace up your
heart and mind to listen. Odysseus was not the only one who
never saw the day of return from Troy; many other good fel-
lows were lost too. Go to your room and see about your own
business, loom and distaff, and keep the servants to their
work; talking is always the man's part, and mine in particular,
for the man rules the house."

She was astonished to hear him, and went back to her room,
but she noticed how sensibly her son had spoken. When she
was upstairs with the servants she wept for Odysseus her be-
loved husband, until Athena laid sweet sleep upon her eyelids.

But the pretenders made quite an uproar in the shadowy
hall, and each one might be heard praying loudly that she
might share his bed. Then Telemachos made them a speech:

"Gentlemen, you pretend to marry my mother, but you are
behaving in a most outrageous fashion. For this once, let us
eat and drink and be merry, but let there be no shouting, for
it's a fine thing to hear a man sing when he has a heavenly
voice like this. Then to-morrow let us hold session in the
market-place, for I wish to tell you in plain words that you
must go from my house. Lay your dinners elsewhere, and eat
your own food in your own houses, change and change about.
—Well, if you think it meet and right to consume one man's
goods without paying, carve away. I will appeal to the ever-
lasting gods, and see if Zeus may one day grant me vengeance!
There would be no ransom then: in this house you should
perish!"

As he said this they all bit their lips; they were surprised
to hear how boldly Telemachos spoke.

Antinoös rose to answer him—his father was the soft-
spoken Eupeithês:

"Why, Telemachos, you must have gone to school with the

gods! They have taught you their fine rhetoric and bold style! I do hope Cronion will never make you king in our island of Ithaca, to sit in the seat of your fathers!"

Telemachos took him up neatly, and said:

"I dare say it might annoy you, Antinoös, but I should be glad to accept the gift. Do you think it the worst thing in the world to be a king? It is not a bad thing at all. He gets plenty of wealth, he is highly honoured. But of course there are other kings in our nation, not a few in this island young and old, and one of them might perhaps have the place of that great man Odysseus as he is dead. But then I will as least be master of my own house and my own servants, which my great father won for me."

Now Eurymachos o' Polybos answered him:

"Telemachos, it lies on the knees of the gods, you may be quite sure, who is to be king over the people in our island of Ithaca; but your property I hope you may keep for yourself and be master in your own house. I pray that no man may ever come to force you against your will, and rob you of your property, so long as Ithaca is a place to live in.

"But I do beg you, my good sir, tell me about that stranger, where the man came from, what country he claims, where he was born, who in the world he is. Does he bring a rumour of your father's return? Did some private business send him here like this? How he jumped up! Gone in a moment, and did not wait for us to make his acquaintance! Certainly he did not look a bad sort of fellow."

Telemachos answered him:

"Eurymachos, I am sure my father will never see home again. I believe no rumours any more, wherever they come from; I take no notice of any divinations, if my mother calls in a diviner and asks him questions. That is an old family friend from Taphos; he says he is Mentês, the son of a clever father Anchialos, and prince of the seafaring Taphians." That is what he said, but in his heart he knew the immortal goddess.

So they turned to dancing and joyous singing, and made merry. They were still at it when the darkness of evening came on them; then off they went, each to his home and bed.

And Telemachos went up to bed in his room, which was built high up over the wide courtyard, with a view all round, and his heart was full of thoughts. To light him on the way a faithful old servant carried a blazing torch. She was Eurycleia, daughter of Ops Peisenoridês; Laërtês had bought her long ago at his own cost, when she was in her first youth, and he gave twenty oxen for her. He treated her as well as he did his own faithful wife; but he did not lie with her, for he wanted to avoid any quarrel with his wife.

This was the woman who carried the torch for Telemachos; she loved him more than any other of the household, and she had been his nurse when he was a little tot. He opened the door of the handsome room and sat down on the bed, and stript off his soft shirt, which he gave into the wise old woman's hands. She folded it up and smoothed it out, and hung it on a peg beside the bed-frame, and left the room, pulling the door to by the silver crow's-beak, and ran home the bolt by pulling the strap.[1] There all night long, covered up with a soft fleece of wool, he thought over the journey which Athena had told him to go.

---

[1] The bolt was inside, with a strap fastened to the end, which passed through a hole to the outside; pull the strap and the bolt runs home inside. The door-handle is the crow's-beak; the islanders still use the term crow (koráki) for a drop-catch at the top of a casement window.

BOOK II

*How the Council Met in the Market-place of Ithaca;
and What Came of It*

DAWN CAME, SHOWING HER ROSY FINGERS THROUGH THE
early mists, and Telemachos leapt out of bed. He dressed
himself, slung a sharp sword over his shoulder, strapt a
stout pair of boots on his lissom feet, and came forth from
his chamber like a young god. He called the criers at once,
and told them to use their good lungs in summoning the
people to Council.

The criers did their part, and the people came. As soon
as they were assembled, he went down to the Council him-
self, with a strong spear in his hand, and a couple of dogs
for company, which danced round him as he walked. He was
full of enchanting grace, and the people stared at him in ad-
miration. Not for nothing Athena was his friend.

He took his seat in his father's place, and the reverend
seniors made room.

The first speaker was Aigyptios, a great gentleman, bent
with age and full of ripe wisdom. He also had lost a son,
who had sailed with Prince Odysseus in the fleet to Ilios,
Antiphos the lancer; the savage Cyclops had killed him in
the cave, in fact he was the monster's last supper. Three other
sons the old man had. One of them, Eurynomos, was among
the wooers, and two kept their father's farms; but he could
not forget the other, whom he mourned unceasingly, and
now there were tears in his eyes for his son's sake as he began
to speak:

"Listen to me, men of Ithaca, for I have something to say
to you. There has been no session of our Council since the
time when Prince Odysseus sailed with the fleet: and now
who has summoned us? Is it a young man or one of the
elders? Was it some private need that moved him? Or has
he news of some threatening raid, and now wishes to report
what he was the first to hear? Or is there some other public
matter which he wishes to bring before us? He has done
well, I think, and deserves our thanks. I pray Zeus may grant
him that blessing which his heart desires."

These words seemed a good omen to Telemachos, and en-
couraged him. He made no delay, for he was eager to speak,

22

so he stood up before the Council. The speaker's staff was put in his hand by Peisenor, the public crier. Then Telemachos first addressed himself to the old Councillor:

"The man you call for is not far away, reverend Sir, who summoned the people together, as you shall soon know—I am that man, and I am in great trouble of my own. There is no news of a threatening raid to report; I have no advantage of you there, and there is no other public matter which I wish to bring before you. This is my own private need, trouble which has fallen upon my house—two troubles, indeed: first, I have lost a good father, who once was king over you that are present here, and he was like a kind father to you; and now again there is something much worse, which I tell you will soon utterly tear to pieces my whole house, and destroy my whole living. My mother is besieged by those who would marry her against her will, own sons to those men who are chief among you here; they will not go near her father's house, and lay a formal proposal before Icarios—the thought makes them shiver!—for then he might collect the bridal gifts for his daughter, and give her to the man of his choice, the one he likes best. No! it is our house they visit regularly every day, kill our cattle and sheep and fat goats, hold high revel and drink my sparkling wine, quite reckless: that is the way it all goes. For there is no man at the head, no one like Odysseus, to drive this curse from the house. You see, we are not able to drive it away ourselves. Sorry champions we shall prove, if we try; we have little skill for the combat.

"Indeed I would defend myself if I had the strength! What they have done is quite intolerable, there is no decent excuse for the ruin they have made of my house. *You* ought to be ashamed in your own hearts, you ought to think what others will say about it, our neighbours, who live all round us; you should fear the wrath of the gods, who may be provoked by such wickedness to turn upon you. I appeal to Olympian Zeus, and Themis, who dissolves the parliaments of men, and summons them! Let me be, my friends! leave me alone to be worn out by my bitter sorrow—unless I must suppose that my father Odysseus, my good father, was a cruel man and ill-treated the nation, and that is why you are cruel and ill-treat me, out of revenge—why you encourage these men.

"I should like it better if *you* would eat up my treasures and my flocks. If *you* would eat them up, perhaps there might be some redress. Then we might go round the town, dunning you, imploring, demanding our goods again, till you should give all back. But now! I am helpless, all I can do is to suffer the humiliations which you heap upon me!"

He spoke angrily, and now he dropt down the staff on the ground and burst into tears. All the people were sorry for him, and they all sat silent, not one had the heart to say an unkind word in reply; only Antinoös answered and said:

"You are a boaster, Telemachos, and you don't know how to keep your temper! What a speech! Cry shame on us, fasten the blame on us, that's what you want to do! Blame us indeed! Your own mother is at fault. You cannot find fault with *us* for paying court to your mother. She is a clever piece indeed! It is three years already, and the fourth will soon go by, since she has been deluding the wits of the whole nation. Hopes for all, promises for every man by special messenger—and what she means is something quite different. Here is the latest trick which came out of her meditations.

"She set up a great warp on her loom in the mansion, and wove away, fine work and wide across, and this is what she told us: 'Young men who seek my hand, now that Odysseus is dead I know you are in a hurry for marriage; but wait until I finish this cloth, for I don't want to waste all the thread I have spun. It is a shroud for my lord Laërtês, against the time when all-destroying fate shall carry him away in dolorous death. I should not like the women of our nation to cry scandal, if he should lie without a winding-sheet when he had great possessions.'

"That is what she said, and we swallowed our pride, and consented. There she was all day long, working away at the great web; but at night she used to unravel it by torchlight. So for three years she deluded the whole nation, and they believed her. But the seasons passed on, and the fourth year began, and a time came when one of her women told us, one who knew the secret; we caught her unravelling that fine web! So she had to finish it, because she must, not because she would.

"And as for you, this is the answer of those who pay court to your mother, a plain answer to you and to all the nation: Send your mother out of the house, tell her to marry whichever her father says, whichever she likes herself; but if she will go on and on teasing the young men of our nation—with her head full of pride to think how Athena has been generous to her beyond all others, given her skill in beautiful work, and good intelligence, and cleverness such as never was heard of, even in the old stories—those women of our nation who lived long ago, with their lovely hair, Tyro, Alcmenê, Mycenê with her fine coronals—not one of them had the clever wits of Penelopeia: but this clever turn was a wicked trick. To put it plainly, we will go on eating up your living and substance just so long as God allows her to keep the mind she has now. She is making a great name for herself, but for you—good-bye to a great fortune! As for us, we will not go to our lands or anywhere else, before she marries whoever may please her best out of the nation!"

The boy stood up to him, and said:

"Antinoös, it is impossible for me to turn out of doors the mother who bore me and brought me up; my father is somewhere in the world, alive or dead, and it is a hard thing for me to pay back all that dowry to Icarios, if I send away my mother of my own will. Her father will be bad enough, but heaven will send me worse, for my mother will call down the dread Avengers upon me, if she leaves home; and men will reproach me—so I will never say that word. And if your own minds have any fear of such a reproach, go out of my house, get your dinners elsewhere, eat your own food turn by turn in your own houses. But if you think it meet and right to consume one man's goods without paying, carve away; I will appeal to the everlasting gods, and see whether Zeus may not one day grant me vengeance. There would be no ransom then, in that house you should perish!"

So spoke Telemachos: and Zeus, whose eye can see what is far off, sent him a pair of eagles, flying from a lofty mountainpeak. On they flew down the wind awhile, side by side, soaring on wide-stretched sails; but when they came right over the place of debate, they took a turn round; then hovering with quick-beating wings they stared down on the heads of all, with death in their eyes; and tearing at their cheeks and necks with their talons, away they darted to the east across the houses of the town. The people were amazed, when they saw this sight with their own eyes; and they pondered in their hearts what was to come of it.

Then up and spoke a noble old man, Halithersês Mastoridês; for there was no man of his day who came near him in the knowledge of birds or in telling what omens meant. He spoke to them in this fashion, out of an honest heart:

"Hear me now, men of Ithaca, for I have something to say. I speak especially to those who would wed, for upon them a great woe is rolling; Odysseus will not long keep away

from his friends, but I think he is already near, planting the
seed of death and destruction for all these men. Trouble
there will be also for many others of us who live in the island
of Ithaca. But let us consider in good time how we can stop
these men; or let them stop themselves—indeed, the sooner
the better. I am no novice in prophecy, that is something
I understand. As for that man, I declare that all has been
fulfilled as I told him, when our people embarked for Ilios
and with them went Odysseus, the man who is ready for
anything and everything. I said he would have many trou-
bles, and lose all his companions, and after twenty long
years, unknown, he would come home again: and see now,
all is being fulfilled."

Then another man got up, Eurymachos, and he said:

"Off with you, old man, go home and prophesy to your
children, or they may come to grief sometime! In this mat-
ter I am a better prophet than you are. Any number of birds
are flying about under the sun, and not all of them are birds
of omen. At any rate, Odysseus is dead, far away from this
place, and I wish you had died with him! Then you would not
be here making a long speech as God's mouthpiece; you
would not unleash this angry Telemachos! No doubt you
expect to find something from him when you get home, if he
doesn't forget it. But I tell you this, and I will do it too: he
is a young man, and you are full of antediluvian wisdom, but
if you cajole him and inflame his passions, he shall be the
first to suffer.

"As for you, sir, there will be damages which you will be
sorry to pay; a heavy burden shall be yours. For Telemachos,
this is my advice which I give before you all: Let him tell
his mother to go home to her father's house; they will ar-
range a marriage, and collect the bridal gifts, plenty of
them, as many as there ought to be for a beloved daughter.
For I do not think the young men will cease their importu-
nate wooing until that is done, since we fear no one in
any case—not Telemachos, certainly, for all his flood of
words, and we care nothing for your prognostications,
respected sir; they will come to nothing, and only make you
more of a nuisance than you were. Yes, his wealth shall be
wasted and consumed, and there shall be no retribution, as
long as that woman keeps putting off her wedding and
wasting our time! Here we are, waiting day after day, rivals
for a great prize, never look at another woman, when you
would expect each man to go a-wooing for himself!"

But Telemachos still kept his wits about him, and he replied:

"Eurymachos, and all you other gentlemen who pay court to my mother, I make no more appeal to you, I have no more to say: for now the gods know, and all the nation.—But I beg you to lend me a swift ship and twenty men, to carry me there and back. For I am going to Sparta and sandy Pylos, to find out about my father and why he is so long away; perhaps some one may tell me, or I may hear some rumour that God will send, which is often the best way for people to get news. Then if I hear that my father is alive and on his way back, for all my wearing and tearing I can bear up for another year; but if I hear he is dead, and no longer in the world, I will come back to my own home and build him a barrow, and do the funeral honours in handsome style, as I ought, and give away my mother to another husband."

He said his say and sat down; then up rose Mentor, friend and comrade of the excellent Odysseus, to whom Odysseus had entrusted his whole house when he sailed away; they were to obey the old man, and he was to keep all safe. This is what he said, and very good sense it was:

"Listen to me, men of Ithaca, and hear what I have to say. Let no man henceforth take the trouble to be kind and gentle, no sceptred prince; let none try to be fair and right, but let him be always harsh and do what he ought not to do: since no one remembers the noble Odysseus, not one out of all the people he ruled like a kind father. I do not grudge at the proud men who pay their court, if they act with violence in the mischievous bodgery of their minds: they stake their own heads when they devour the house of Odysseus with violence, and think he will never come back. But now it is you, the others, who make me ashamed; how you all sit mum, when you ought to denounce them and hold back a few young men when you are many."

Leocritos Euënoridês answered him:

"Mentor, you mischief-maker, you madman! What a thing to say! drive them on to stop us! One against many is done, a many's too many for one, in fights for a supper! Why, even Odysseus himself, if he came back to Ithaca and found a sturdy company feasting in his own house, and thought of driving them out of hall—his wife would have little satisfaction, however much she may have missed him, but then and there he would die an ugly death, if he's one against many! What you say is all wrong. Come now, men, make yourselves scarce, away to your lands every one. As for

this fellow, Mentor shall help him with his voyage, and
Halithersês, since they have been friends of the family for
ages. But I think he will have to sit here for a good long
time and wait for his news in Ithaca; he will never bring off
that voyage."

With these words he broke up the assembly forthwith. They
all made themselves scarce and went each to his own house,
and the pretenders went back to the house of Odysseus.

But Telemachos went by himself to the seashore. There
he washed his hands in the grey brine, and offered a prayer
to Athena:

"Hear me, thou who yesterday didst come a god into our
house, who didst bid me take ship over the misty sea, and
inquire if my father is coming home, and why he is so
long away: all this the people prevent, but most of all my
mother's wooers, men full of wicked pride!"

Such was his prayer; and Athena came to his side, like
Mentor in shape and voice; she spoke to him, and the words
were plain and pointed:

"You will not lack either courage or sense in the future,
Telemachos, for we can see now that there is a drop in you
of your father's fine spirit. What a man he was to make
good both deed and word! I tell you your journey shall not
be hindered or stopped. But if you are not his son and
Penelopeia's, then I do not expect you to succeed in what
you wish to do. Few sons, let me tell you, are like their fa-
thers; most are worse, a few are better. But since you will
lack neither courage nor sense in the future, and since the
mind of Odysseus has not wholly failed in you, there is hope
for the future, and I tell you that you will succeed.

"Think no more now of the plots and plans of those who
woo your mother, for there is neither sense nor justice in
them. They know nothing of the death and destruction
which is near them, so that in one day they shall all perish.
But the journey which you desire shall not be long delayed,
when you have with you such an old friend of your father
as I am; for I will provide a swift ship and go with you my-
self. You must just go home, and mingle with the company;
get provisions ready, and put them all up in vessels, wine
in jars, and barley-meal, which is the marrow of men, in
strong skins; I will go at once and collect volunteers among
the people. There are many ships in the island of Ithaca, both
new and old; I will look round and find you the best, and we
will make all ready and launch her upon the broad sea."

So spoke Athena daughter of Zeus; and Telemachos did not

stay long after he heard what the goddess said. He set out for the house, with a heavy heart; and he found the proud pretenders there, skinning goats and singeing fat pigs in the courtyard. Antinoös laughed, and made straight for Telemachos and grasped his hand, and called him by name, and said:

"You are a boaster, Telemachos, and you don't know how to keep your temper! Do not trouble your head about plots and plans, but just go on eating and drinking as usual. Our people will manage all you want, I am sure, a ship and the best crew to be found; they will give you a quick passage to sandy Pylos, if you want to hear news of your father."

Telemachos pulled his hand from the hand of Antinoös, and said:

"Antinoös, with your friends rioting all round it is impossible to enjoy a meal in peace and quiet. Is it not enough, men, that you have been carving up a good portion of my possessions all this time, while I was still a boy? But now you see I am grown up, and I hear every one talking about it, and so I find things out; now I feel my own strength, and I mean to do my best to bring retribution upon you when I come back from Pylos, or now in this country! I mean to go, and no one shall prevent me, even if I must go as a passenger, since I am not to have my own ship and crew: I suppose that suited you better."

When he said this the others mocked and jeered at him, and you might hear one of the young bullies saying, "Clear enough, Telemachos has murder in his mind! He will bring help from Pylos, or may be from Sparta, since he is so terribly set on it. Or perhaps he wants to go as far as Ephyra, to bring some deadly poison from that rich land, and put it in the cup, and kill us all."

Another of the young bullies would say, "Ah, but who knows? Once aboard ship he may be carried far from his friends, and perish just like Odysseus! That would double our trouble, for we should have to divide all his goods among us! But we would give the house to his mother, for herself and the man who would marry her."

So much for them. But Telemachos went down to his father's storehouse, a room lofty and wide where heaps of gold and bronze were kept, with clothes in coffers and plenty of fragrant oil: jars of delicious old wine stood there, full of that divine drink without a drop of water; there they stood in rows along the wall, ready for Odysseus when he should come home again after all his troubles. The place was closed in by double doors, right and tight. The house-keeper was on the spot day and night, and she took care of everything; and a very clever woman she was, Eurycleia the daughter of Ops Peisenoridês. Telemachos called her to the storehouse, and said:

"Come, Nanny, draw me some kegs of this fine wine, the nicest you have, next to that which you keep so care-fully for your noble master, unhappy man! all reàdy in case he should come from somewhere or other, if he can get clear of death and ruin.—Fill me a dozen, and put a stopper on each. And a few skinfuls of barley-meal, good skins properly stitched, twenty measures of good barley-meal ground in the millstones. Keep this to yourself, and let all the stuff be put ready together. This evening I mean to fetch it away as soon as mother has gone upstairs to bed. For I am off to Sparta and sandy Pylos, to see if I can hear any news of my father."

When he said this, his dear old nurse cried aloud in dis-tress, and said in her downright way:

"Eh, what on earth put that into thi head, love? Why wilta go to foreign parts, and tha an only son, and reet well loved? He's dead, far away from home, my blessed Odysseus, in some foreign land! Aye, and if tha goes, they'll up and plot mischief against tha by and by, to murder thee by some trick, and all that's here they will share among 'em. Stay thee where tha bist, sit down on thi property; what's the sense of wanderen over the barren sea and maybe hap-penen an accident?"

Telemachos only said, "Cheer up, Nanny, this is God's will, let me tell you. Now promise me on your oath not to say a word to mother for ten or twelve days, unless she asks herself and hears I have gone, or you'll have her crying and spoiling her pretty skin!"

When he said that, she took her oath; and this done with all due solemnity, she wasted no time—drew off the wine into kegs, packed the barley-meal in the skins right and tight; then Telemachos went off and joined the roysterers.

Meanwhile the goddess Athena was doing the rest. She took on the form of Telemachos, and tramped the length and breadth of the city, took aside each of the men and told her tale, then directed them to meet in the evening beside the cutter. The boat itself she begged of Noëmon, the sturdy son of Phronios, and he agreed with all his heart.

The sun went down, and the streets were all darkened. Then Athena ran the boat down into the sea, and put in all the gear that ships carry for sailing and rowing; she moored her at the harbour point, and the crew assembled, fine young fellows all, and she set them each to work.

But she had something else to do. She made her way to the house of Odysseus, and there she distilled sweet sleep upon them all, and dazed them as they drank, until they let the cups drop out of their hands. So they got up and went to find sleep, dispersing all over the city, for they did not sit long after sleep fell on their eyelids. Then Athena called out Telemachos in front of the great hall, taking the shape and voice of Mentor, and said to him:

"Telemachos, your men are all ready and furnished cap-a-pie, sitting at the oars, waiting for you to start. Come, let us go, and waste no time about it."

With these words she led the way briskly, and he followed in her footsteps. And when they came to the ship and the seaside, there he found the bushy-headed boys on the beach, and he spoke to them, full of dignity and strength:

"This way, friends, let us fetch the provisions; they are all ready and waiting in the house. My mother knows nothing about it, nor any of the servants, but only one single soul has heard our plan."

So he led the way, and they went with him. They carried all the stuff down to the ship and put it on board, as Telemachos told them to do. Telemachos himself went on board following Athena; she took her seat on the poop, and he sat beside her. The others cast off the hawsers, and themselves came on board and sat down on the benches. Athena with her bright eyes glinting sent them a following wind, right from the west, piping over the purple sea. Then Telemachos called to the men, and told them to put a hand to the tackling. They lifted the mast and stept it in its hollow box, made it fast with the forestays, hauled up the white sail by its ropes of twisted leather. The wind blew full into the bellying sail, and the dark wave boomed about the stem of the ship as she went; so on she sped shouldering the swell, travelling steadily on her way. When they had made snug all the tackle about the ship, they set before them brimming bowls of wine, and poured libations to the gods immortal and everlasting, but most of all to the bright-eyed daughter of Zeus. So all night long and in the dawning the ship cut her way.

BOOK III

What Happened in Sandy Pylos

THE SUN LEAPT OUT OF THE LOVELY BAY, HIGH INTO the brazen sky, to give light to the deathless gods and to mortal men all over the fruitful earth; and they came to Pylos, the stately city of Neleus. The people were on the shore, sacrificing jet-black bulls to the blue-crested god who shakes the earth. There were nine messes, five hundred sitting in each mess, and nine bulls were laid out before each. They had already distributed the tripes, and they were burning the thigh-pieces for the god, when the ship came sailing in. The crew brailed up the sail and trussed it, and moored ship, and went ashore; Telemachos came ashore too, after Athena, who broke the silence by saying:

"Telemachos, there is no need to be shy, not a bit. You know why you have come on this voyage: to ask news of your father, how he died, and where he was buried. Come along, then, straight to Nestor; let us learn what he really thinks and knows about it. You must speak to Nestor yourself, and ask him to tell you the whole truth; he has too much good feeling to deceive you."

Telemachos answered:

"Mentor, how can I go, how can I greet him? I have no practice in polite speeches; then again, a young man must be shy when he addresses an older man."

Athena with a glance of her keen eyes replied:

"Some things you will think of yourself, Telemachos, some things God will put into your mind. Not without the blessing of heaven were you born and bred, I think."

With these words, Pallas Athena led the way briskly, and he followed. They came to the place where the Pylians were all gathered in their messes; there was Nestor, sitting with his sons, and all around were his companions preparing the feast, with meat broiling and grilling on the spits.

When they saw strangers, they came up in a body and welcomed them, and bade them be seated. Nestor's son Peisistratos reached them first; he grasped both their hands, and seated them in front of the spread, upon soft fleeces laid on the sands beside his brother Thrasymedês and his father. Then he gave them their plates of tripe and chitterlings and

32

poured wine into a golden cup; he raised his cup and called upon Pallas Athena, daughter of Zeus Almighty, and said:

"Pray, now, sir, to Lord Poseidon, who owns this feast which you have happened to join. When you have poured your drops [1] and offered your prayer as usual, pass on the cup to your friend. He too, I think, will join our prayer to the immortals: for all men need the gods. But he is younger, he is of my own age, so I will give you the golden chalice first."

So saying, he put the cup full of delicious wine in her hands; Athena was pleased that he knew what was proper, and gave her the golden goblet first. At once she prayed earnestly to Lord Poseidon:

"Hear me, Poseidon Earthshaker, and grudge not to accomplish these things for us who pray to thee! To Nestor first and his sons vouchsafe renown; and next, to all the Pylians besides grant a gracious requital for this splendid sacrifice! And grant that Telemachos and I may have a safe return, when we have done that for which we came hither with our swift black ship!"

And while she prayed, she was doing her part to fulfill it. Then she passed the fine two-handled cup to Telemachos, and the son whom Odysseus loved made his prayer. The others took the broiled meat off the spits, and distributed the portions, and all had a famous feast.

But when they had taken as much as they wanted, the old cavalier Nestor addressed them:

"That is better; and now I may be allowed to put a few questions to my guests, and ask who they are, since they have enjoyed their meal in peace. Who are you, sirs? Where do you come from over the waters? Is it business, or are you voyaging at random, like the sea-robbers who voyage about and risk their lives to bring trouble in foreign parts?"

Telemachos now plucked up courage; for Athena herself gave him the courage to ask about his father's delay, that he might show he knew how to behave in society. He said:

"May it please your Majesty, Nestor Neleïadês! You ask where we come from, and I will answer. We come from Ithaca, and the town under Mount Neïon; my business is private, not public. I seek any news I can hear anywhere in the wide world of my father, the noble Odysseus, the ever-patient man,

[1] The libation of "grace before drink." The attendant poured a few drops in the cup, the drinker spilt them upon the ground with a prayer; then the attendant filled the cup, and he drank.

who they say fought by your side when you took Troy. We have heard about all the others who were in the war, we know where each of them died, to our sorrow; but as for that man, we have not even heard that he is dead; such is the will of Cronion. For no one can tell us for certain when he died, whether he was brought low on land by his enemies, or at sea amid the billows of Amphitritê. That is why I am here to appeal to you.

"Tell me, if you please, of his lamentable fate, if you saw it with your own eyes, or if you have heard any one speak of him on his wanderings: for he was born to sorrow if any man ever was. And do not soften your words out of pity, to spare me, but tell me plainly what you saw of him. I beseech you, if ever in word or deed my honourable father made you a promise and did it before Troy, where you Achaians suffered so much, remember that now for my sake, and tell me truth."

"My dear boy," answered the fine old cavalier, "how you bring it all back to me! what we reckless fellows did go through! How we ranged over the misty seas in our ships for plunder, wherever Achillês led us, how we fought round the great city of King Priam—ah! there and then all our best men were slain! There lies Aias, the man of war, there lies Achillês; there is Patroclos, prudent as a god in counsel; there is my own dear son, a man strong and without blemish, Antilochos, swift of foot beyond all, and a fighter; and what a world of troubles we suffered besides these—what mortal man could tell them all? Not if you would stay here five long years, or six long years, could you hear the whole story of the troubles which the brave Achaians there endured—you would soon be tired and go back to your own country!

"Nine long years we were busy, scheming and plotting and planning in every possible way, and only just managed it, thanks be to God! All that time no one came near Odysseus in resource, for that grand man was first by a long way in all plots and plans and schemes, your father, I say, if you are really his son—if! you amaze me, young man: when I hear you speak, I might be hearing him, you could not imagine a young man *could* speak so like him! All that time I and Odysseus never took different sides, either in parliament or in council: we were of one mind; with good sense and wisdom we advised the people always that which promised the best success. Again, when we had sacked the tall city of Troy, and embarked, and God scattered the fleet, ah, then

Zeus ordained a lamentable home-coming for us; for not all were sensible and fair-minded, and so a great many of them drew upon themselves an evil fate, from the destroying wrath of the Bright-eyed Daughter of the Thundering Father, who made a quarrel between the two princes of the house of Atreus.

"When these two called the people to parliament—quite wrong, most improper, at sunset of all times—and they all came heavy with wine—the two of them explained why they had summoned the people. Then Menelaos advised them to see about the return voyage, and Agamemnon did not like it at all. He wanted to keep the people back and to make solemn sacrifice, hoping to calm the dire anger of Athenaia; poor fool, he did not know that she was not likely to yield, for the mind of the everlasting gods is not quickly turned. So there the two stood, bandying angry words! All the men-at-arms jumped up, and there was the devil of a noise in the place, as each backed his own opinion.

"All through the night there was a lull; but the angry passions remained, for Zeus was preparing an unhappy issue from this trouble. Then at dawn, some of us launched our ships, and put our goods on board with the captive women drest in their best. About half stayed on shore with King Agamemnon; half of us embarked and rowed away.

"Quickly the ships ran on, for God made smooth the great billows of the deep. We came to Tenedos, and offered sacrifice there to the gods, longing to get home; but Zeus had no thought yet of home for us—hard god! to put a quarrel among us again for the second time! There some turned back their ships—a fine trim-built lot they were, led by Prince Odysseus; for that deep and clever man wished to take the side of Agamemnon once more. But I went on with all the ships that were left, since I knew that providence had trouble in store for them. With me went the warrior Diomedês, and he brought his companions; then, better late than never, Menelaos came after us, and caught us up at Lesbos, while we were hesitating about the long voyage straight across; whether to go seaward of rocky Chios close along the island of Psyria, keeping the island on our left, or inside of Chios, past windy Mimas.

"We prayed God to show us a portent; and he showed us one, and told us to cut straight across the sea to Euboea that we might escape our troubles the quickest way. A whistling wind began to blow; the ships ran at a great rate over the

water, and in the night they put in at Geraistos.[1] There we
sacrificed many rump-slices of bulls to Poseidon, in thanks
for traversing that long stretch of sea. It was the fourth day
when the party of Diomedês Tydeidês brought their fine
ships to harbour in Argos; but I held on for Pylos, and the
wind never fell from the time when the god first let it out to
blow.

"So I came home, my dear boy, without news; and I know
nothing of the others who were saved of the army, or those
who were lost. But all the news I get while I sit in my hall,
you shall hear, as is right and proper, and I will not hide
anything. There was a good return for the Myrmidons, they
say, those champion spearmen, who were led by the doughty
son of proud Achillês; a good return for Philoctetês, the
famous son of Poias; all the company of Idomeneus were
brought back safe to Crete, all who survived the war, and the
sea did not take one of them. But Agamemnon you have
heard of yourselves, although you live far away; how he
came back, and how Aigisthos plotted a pitiable death for
him. Well, he paid for it, sure enough, in horrible fashion.
What a good thing it is that a son should be on the spot
when a man is dead! That son, you see, took vengeance
upon his father's murderer, the traitor Aigisthos, who killed
his famous father. You too, my friend, be brave, for I see
you are handsome and tall; and then those to be born in fu-
ture generations will praise you."

Telemachos answered:

"May it please your Majesty, Nestor Neleïadês! He did
indeed take his vengeance, and his fame shall be carried
down in the world for many generations to come. How I
wish that the gods would invest me with power as great as
his, to take vengeance on the men who woo my mother, for
their outrageous violence, for the intolerable insults of their
scheming brains! But no, the Spinner has spun me no such
happiness for my father and me: we must just be patient,
come what may."

Then Nestor answered:

"My friend, since you have spoken of it yourself and re-
called it to my memory, they do say that there are a great
number of men in your house, seeking your mother's hand in
marriage against your will, full of evil schemes. Tell me, do
you submit willingly to this? Do all the people dislike you
because of something said by the voice of God? Who knows

---

[1] The south promontory of Euboea.

if some day he may come and take vengeance for their violence, whether alone, or all the people with him! If only Athena Brighteyes would choose to show her love to you, as she used to care for that glorious man Odysseus in the Trojan land, among all those hardships which our nation had to suffer!—for never have I seen the love of the gods so manifestly shown as when Pallas Athena stood manifestly by his side: if only she would show love to you like that, and care for you, many a one of them would have something else than weddings to think of."

Telemachos answered:

"Sir, I do not think that will happen yet; what you say is too great; it amazes me. Never could I hope for that, even if it should be the will of God!"

Then Athena said:

"Telemachos, what words you have let slip between your teeth! It is easy for God to bring a man safely home if it be his will, even from a long way off. I would choose to suffer great tribulations, and then live to return home, rather than to return safely, and then die beside my hearth; as Agamemnon died, by the treachery of Aigisthos and his own wife. But death is the common lot, which not even gods can keep from a man they love, as soon as the lamentable fate of dolorous death gets hold of him."

Then Telemachos answered:

"Let us say no more of this, Mentor, although we are not free from sorrow. The day of his return can never dawn, but the immortals have already ordained death for him and a black fate.

"Now there is something else I want to ask Nestor, since he knows men's manners and minds better than others do; they say he has been King through three generations of men, so that he has quite the look of an immortal to me—Nestor Neleïadês, tell me the truth: how came my lord King Agamemnon to die? Where was Menelaos? How did the traitor Aigisthos manage to murder him, since the murdered man was far stronger? Was he not in his own city of Argos? or was he somewhere else, and so the man took courage and killed him?"

Nestor answered him:

"Indeed I will tell you the whole truth, my boy. Surely you can surmise yourself what would have happened if Aigisthos had been found in the place by King Menelaos when he came from Troy? Dead he would have been, not a clod of earth dropt upon him, but dogs and vultures would have torn his corpse to pieces, thrown on the ground outside the city walls: not a woman in the whole nation would have wept for him; for it was a monstrous crime he plotted.

"We were over there doing our arduous duties, firmly fixed; he at his ease in a corner of that land of horses, bewitching Agamemnon's wife for ever with his talk. At first she would have nothing to do with the shameful business, I mean Queen Clytaimnestra; for she was not really a bad woman. And there was that singing-man by her side, who was put in full trust by Agamemnon when he went to Troy, to look after his wife. But when the chains of fate bound her fast and she must needs be mastered, then the man took his minstrel to a desert island, and left him prey and plaything for the carrion birds; and the woman he took to his own house, one as willing as the other. Many thank-offerings he burnt on the gods' holy altars, many precious things he cast into the fire, woven stuffs and gold, for success in a great enterprise which he had never in his heart expected to carry out.

"Well then, we both set out from Troy, Menelaos and I, in great contentment together; but when we came to holy Sunion the headland of Attica, Phoibos Apollo attacked the helmsman of Menelaos and slew him with his gentle shafts, while the man held the steering-oar between his hands and the ship was running free; that was Phrontis Onetoridês, champion of the world when the stormy winds do blow. So for all his haste to go on he stayed there until he could bury his comrade and perform the funeral rites.

"But when he followed us over the purple sea, and the ships came in their course to the steep cliff of Malea, Zeus Almighty decreed a hard road for him to travel: he poured out a hurricane of whistling winds and monstrous swollen waves mountain-high. Then he cut the fleet in two, and brought part of them to Crete, where the Cydonians are settled about the stream of Iardanos. There is a smooth cliff running down steep into the sea at the verge of Gortyn, over the misty deep, where the wind from the south-west drives a great wave against the western headland up towards Phaistos, and a little bit of stone keeps off the great wave. So far they came, and then the men escaped death with great trouble; but the ships were all smashed to pieces on those rocks by the sea.

"The other ships, five in number, were driven to Egypt by wind and water. While Menelaos was there, collecting a heap of gold and commodities, and sailing his fleet about into foreign parts, that was the time when Aigisthos was making his murderous plans at home; and after he killed Agamemnon he reigned seven years in all the wealth of Mycenê, while the people were cowed under his rule. But in the eighth year came his ruin; Prince Orestês came back from Athens, and killed his father's murderer, the traitor Aigisthos, because he had killed his famous father.

"When Orestês had killed him, he gave a funeral feast to the people over his hateful mother and Aigisthos the coward: and on that very day arrived that stout champion Menelaos, with a heap of wealth filling his ships. Now my friend, don't go a-roaming too long far away from home, and desert your property, and leave those blustering fellows in your house like that; or they will eat up everything and share your wealth among themselves, and your journey will end in nothing. Go to Menelaos, that is my advice and bidding. He has lately come from abroad, from such places as he could never really expect to return from, when you think how at first the storms drove him astray over all that expanse of sea; even the birds take more than a year to cross it, for it is wide and dangerous too. Off with you at once, ship and crew and all; or if you prefer the land, horses and car are at your service, my sons are at your service, and they shall be your guides to lovely Lacedaimon, and there you will find Menelaos. Beg him yourself to tell you the truth; but he will not deceive you, for he knows what is right and proper."

When he finished, the sun set and darkness came. Then Athena spoke, with her bright eyes glinting:

"Sir, you have told your tale well. Now then, cut the tongues of sacrifice, and mix the wine, that we may pour libations to Poseidon and the other immortals, and think of our rest; it is high time now, for the light has gone down into the west, and it is not fitting to sit long at a feast of sacrifice, but to pass on."

The others listened, and did as she said. Attendants poured water over their hands; boys filled the mixing-bowls to the brim, and served wine to all after pouring in the first drops; they cast the tongues on the fire, and the company standing poured out one after another the first drops in honour of the gods. And when the libation was done and they had drunk as much as they wished, Athena and the handsome lad made as though to return to their ship; but Nestor would not have it: he said at once:

"Zeus and all the immortal gods forbid that you should leave me and go off to your ship, as if I were a pauper without a rag, as if I had not plenty of blankets and rugs in the

house, nothing for myself to sleep soft on, nothing for my
guests! Come, come, I have blankets and rugs of the best.
No, no, that man's son shall not lie on a ship's deck, his very
own son, so long as I am alive, and while children are left
after me to entertain the guests who may come to my house!"

Athena answered him:

"That is well said, dear and reverend sir! It is yours to
command, and Telemachos must obey, as is right and proper.
Well, he shall stay with you and sleep in your mansion; but I
will return to our ship, to hearten the men and make them
do their duty. You see I am the only man of full years
among them; the rest are all of an age with our brave young
Telemachos, and come as volunteers out of affection for him.
So I will just lie down in the old black ship for this night;
but to-morrow I mean to visit the Cauconians. Those good
fellows owe me a claim, no new thing and no small thing.
And our friend here—since he has come to your house, lend
him your son and a carriage, and let him go on; and lend
him horses, the fastest and strongest you have."

With these words, Athena departed, taking the shape of a
sea-osprey. All that saw it were amazed; the old man was
amazed, when he saw this with his own eyes, and he grasped
Telemachos by the hand and said:

"My friend, I do not think you will turn out a coward or
a craven, if in your young days you have gods to escort you!
For this is one of those who dwell in Olympos, none other
than the very daughter of Zeus, most glorious Tritogeneia,
the same who used to honour your father amongst our peo-
ple.—O Queen, do thou be gracious and grant me an hon-
ourable name, myself and my children and my beloved wife!
And I in my turn will sacrifice to thee a yearling cow, broad-
browed, unbroken, which no man has ever brought under the
yoke: such a one I will sacrifice to thee, and cover the horns
with gold."

Thus he prayed, and Pallas Athena heard his prayer. Then
Nestor led them all, sons and godsons, to his fine mansion-
house. And when they came to the King's house, they sat
down in order upon chairs and settles. Then the old King had
a mixing-bowl filled with delicious wine, eleven years old
when the cellarer cut the cap and opened it. Such was the
wine which the old King sent for; and as he sprinkled the
sacred drops, he prayed earnestly to Athena daughter of
Zeus Almighty.

They poured their drops, and drank, and separated, each

to his own room to sleep. But royal Nestor took Telemachos in hand, and left him to sleep there in the echoing gallery; and by his side the famous lancer Peisistratos, a born leader of men, one of his sons who lived in the mansion still unmarried. The king slept himself in a recess of the lofty hall, and there the Queen his wife prepared bed and bedding.

Dawn showed her rosy fingers through the mists of the morning; King Nestor arose from his bed, and went out to the smooth stone benches which were before his lofty doors, all white and brightly polished. There in former days had sat Neleus his father, wise as a god in counsel; but he long since had yielded to fate and gone down to Hadês, and now Nestor sat there as warden of the nation, holding the royal sceptre. About him gathered all his sons as they came from their rooms: Echephron and Stratios, Perseus and Aretos, and the young Prince Thrasymedês. Last came the sixth, Peisistratos, a fine young fellow; and they led out Telemachos to a seat, looking like a young god. Then Nestor addressed the company:

"Quickly, my dear boys, carry out my wish, that I may find favour with Athena first of all the gods, who showed herself manifestly at our rich sacrifice yesterday. Be quick! let one go into the country for the heifer, and let the herdsman in charge drive her in; one go to the ship of brave Telemachos, and bring up all his companions, leaving only two; one summon Laërcês the goldsmith, that he may cover the heifer's horns with gold. The rest of you stay here together, and tell the women indoors to get ready a good meal in my house and set the places and collect the firewood and bring clean water."

Then they all bustled about. The heifer came from the country; the companions of Telemachos came from their ship; the smith came with all his tackle, the tools of his trade, anvil and hammer and handy tongs, which he used to work the gold: and Athena came to receive the offering. Old King Nestor provided the gold, and the goldsmith covered the horns, fitting the gold neatly to please the goddess with a handsome sight. Stratios and young Echephron led the heifer by the horns. Aretos came out of his room, bearing in one hand the jug of water in a bowl worked with a flower-pattern, and in the other hand a basket with the sprinkling-meal. Thrasymedês the young soldier was there, holding a sharp axe to cut down the heifer. Perseus held the bowl for the blood. Old King Nestor began the rite with hand-wash and barley-meal, and as he did it he prayed earnestly to Athena, while he cast the forelock into the fire.[1]

When they had prayed and sprinkled the barley-meal, at once Thrasymedês approached and struck the blow; the axe cut through the sinews of the neck, and the strength went from her. Then all the women raised their alleluia, daughters and sons' wives and Nestor's honoured consort Eurydicê, eldest of the daughters of Clymenos. The other sons lifted up the victim from the ground, and held it on their shoulders; Peisistratos cut the throat. Then the red blood flowed and life left the body. So they broke her up forthwith, and cut out the rump-slices in proper form, and wrapt them one slice between two pieces of fat, and laid other slices of raw flesh upon these. The old King burnt them upon the faggots, and poured over them sparkling wine; the young men stood by his side, holding their five-prong forks in their hands. Then, after the rump-slices were burnt, and they had divided the tripes, they chopt up the rest and ran the pieces on spits, and grilled them holding the ends of the spits in their hands.

Meanwhile Telemachos had been bathed by Polycasta, the youngest daughter of Nestor Neleïadês. And when she had bathed him and rubbed him with olive oil, she gave him a wrap and a tunic to wear; then he stept out of the tub, as handsome as a young god. He came to Nestor's side, and sat him down by the King.

The others had now roasted the fleshy parts and taken them off the spits, and they were sitting down to their meal; good men looked after them, pouring out the wine into golden cups. And when they had eaten and drunk all they wanted, old King Nestor addressed them:

"My boys, hurry up with the horses and put them under the yoke, that he may get on his way."

They did as they were told, with a will; quickly they put the swift horses under the yoke. And the housekeeper packed in bread and wine, and meat such as kings eat by the grace of heaven. Up climbed Telemachos into the splendid car; beside him was Peisistratos Nestoridês, who got into the car and took hold of the reins. He whipt up the horses, and they left the tall castle of Pylos, and flew on nothing loath into the plains. So all day long they shook the yoke up and down.

The sun went down, and all the ways became dark; and

---

[1] The barley-meal was sprinkled on the victim's head; a few hairs were plucked from the head and cast into the fire.

they came to Pherai, to the house of Dioclês the son of Ortilochos, whose father was the river-god Alpheios. There they rested for the night, and he gave them the gifts that were a guest's due.

But when dawn showed her rosy fingers again out of the mists, they put the horses to and mounted the car; he whipt up the horses, and the pair flew along. By and by they came to a plain full of growing wheat, and there at last they were near the end of their journey: so well did the swift horses carry them on. The sun went down, and all the ways became dark.

BOOK IV

What Happened in Lacedaimon

So NOW THEY WERE IN THE DEEP VALLEY OF LACE-
daimon, and drove up to the gate of the illustrious King
Menelaos. They found him holding a feast with a large com-
pany of friends, for his daughter and for his admirable son at
the same time, in his own house. He was giving his daughter
to the son of Achillês the invincible; he had promised to
give her first in Troy, and now the gods were bringing off the
match. He was sending her with horses and chariots to the
far-famed city of the Myrmidons, where the young man was
king. He was bringing from Sparta the daughter of Alector
for his son; a fine young man, called Megapenthês, the son
of sorrow,[1] late-born and the son of a slave-woman; for the
gods had given Helen no more children after her first daugh-
ter Hermionê, a girl as lovely as golden Aphroditê.

And so there was feasting in the lofty hall, all the neigh-
bours and friends of Menelaos, enjoying themselves mightily.
In the company was a minstrel, playing divinely upon the
harp; and as he struck up his tune, a couple of tumblers
were making wheels all over the place.

The two young men stopt their horses before the gateway
of the mansion; and out came my lord Eteoneus, one of the
king's men-in-waiting. When he saw them, he went into the
house to tell the news to the king, and as he reached him
he said in plain words:

"Here are two strangers, your majesty. They look like young
princes. Tell me if we are to put up their horses, or send
them to find entertainment elsewhere."

This made Menelaos very angry, and he said:

"I didn't know before that you were a fool, Eteoneus Boë-
thoïdês! but what you say now is a child's foolish prattle.
How often have we eaten the food of a stranger, you and I,
in other parts of the world, on our long journey home, pray-
ing that Zeus might somewhere give us rest and peace at
last. Go and take out their horses, and bring the men in to
share our feast."

The man shot out of the hall, and called the others to lend

---

[1] So named from the faithlessness of Helen.

him a hand. They took the horses from under the yoke, all in a sweat, and tied them up at the stalls, and gave them a feed of spelt mixed with white barley. Then they tilted the car against the inner wall of the doorway, and led the men into the stately hall.[1]

How astonished the strangers were at what they saw round them in this royal house! for a brilliance like the light of sun or moon filled the lofty rooms. When they had gazed in delight at everything, the servants took charge of them and led them to the bathroom, bathed them and rubbed them with oil, dressed them in woollen robes and tunics, and conducted them to seats besides Menelaos. A maid poured the handwash out of a golden jug over a silver basin, and set a smooth table by their side. A dignified housewife brought them bread, and laid ready all sorts of vittles, for she did not spare her store. A carver set out plates of all sorts of meat, and put golden cups ready at hand. There stood their host, with his golden-brown hair piled in a glossy mass upon his head, and falling in a thick bush over his shoulders. He received them with the words:

"Break your bread, and be welcome. After you have dined, you shall tell us who you are, for you do your parents credit: you must come of a line of princes ruling by divine right, since no bad stock would produce men like you."

As he said this, he set before them a good juicy chuck from the roast sirloin with his own hands, the portion of honour which had been set before himself; and they helped themselves to the good things that lay ready. Then after they had taken all they wanted to eat and drink, Telemachos moved his head close to Nestor's son, that the others might not hear, and said,

"Just look, Nestoridês, dear old boy. Look at the bronze gleaming all over these resounding halls! the gold, the amber, the silver, the ivory! I think Zeus must have a palace like this in Olympos, when I see all these treasures that no tongue could tell! I am fairly amazed!"

Menelaos overheard this, and said:

"My dear boys, no one can be compared with Zeus, let me tell you. His halls are imperishable, and so are his treasures. But there may be a man to match me, or there may not. I offer no opinion.

"Ah, yes, I have suffered much and wandered far, while

---

[1] The body of the car was lifted off the wheels, and each part put away conveniently.

I collected my treasures in my ships, and came home after seven long years. I went to Cyprus, Phoenicia, Egypt; I saw the Ethiopians, the Sidonians, the Erembans; I went to Libya, where the lambs are born with horns ready made! Yes, the ewes wean their lambs three times every blessed year! There neither prince nor shepherd lacks cheese or meat, or fresh milk, the ewes always have milk in their dugs all the year round!

"And while I was in those parts and collecting all this wealth, a man was murdering my brother, who looked for anything but that—by the machinations of his accursed wife. So you see not for nothing I got my royal state (you will have heard all this from your fathers, whoever they may be)—since I had very much to suffer, and left a fine domain to be ruined; well laid out indeed it was, and full of excellent stuff. I wish I had kept only one-third of it and stayed at home, and saved all those lives which were lost on the wide plains of Troy, far from Argos and the fine horses that Argos breeds!

"But however, although I mourn for them all and often sit brooding in my mansion—sometimes I weep outright, and so ease my heart a bit, sometimes again I stop—a man soon has enough of groans, which fairly freeze him to the bones! However, I do not mourn so much for the whole lot of them, though I really am sorry for them, as for one man, who keeps me awake at night and will not let me eat, because I miss him so; for not one man of the nation worked so hard as Odysseus worked and laboured. Well, trouble was to be his portion, it seems, and mine to be sad on his account, never to be consoled, wondering how he can delay so long, and we don't know whether alive or dead. Surely they will all be mourning for him at home, the old man Laërtês, and discreet Penelopeia, and Telemachos, whom he left a new-born babe in the house."

Now the young man could not restrain himself; tears dropt from his eyes to the ground as he heard his father's name, and he held up the purple robe before his eyes with both hands. Menelaos noticed this, and he considered whether he should leave him alone to think of his father, or if he should first ask him about everything.

But while he was pondering things over in his mind, Helen appeared from her fragrant room upstairs, looking like Artemis of the golden arrows. Adrestê came with her, and moved up a handsome couch; Alcippê brought a rug of soft wool; Phylo carried her silver basket.

This was the gift of Alcandrê, whose husband Polybos was a great nobleman in the Egyptian Thebes, with a palace full of treasures. He had given Menelaos two bathing-tubs of silver, a couple of tripods and ten talents' weight of gold; besides this, his wife had given fine gifts to Helen, a golden distaff, and a basket with wheels underneath, made of silver and the edges finished off in gold. This basket the attendant Phylo brought and placed near her, stuffed with dressed yarn; and the distaff was laid across the top with dark-blue wool upon it.

Helen sat on the couch and put her feet on a footstool. She began at once, and asked her husband about everything in plain words:

"Do we know, my dear, who these gentlemen are who have come to our house? Can I be wrong? Can it be true? I think it is. I declare I never saw any one so like, man or woman—it amazes me quite, how this young man looks exactly like the son of Odysseus! I mean Telemachos whom Odysseus left a new-born babe behind him, when the whole nation invaded Troy on my account, I am ashamed to say, and began that cruel war."

Menelaos answered at once:

"I think so too, my dear, now you mention the likeness. That man had feet just like that and hands just like that, and the way his eyes go, and a head and hair on him just like that. Just a moment ago I was describing Odysseus as I remember him, what hard work he did for me and all his distresses, when the young man burst into sobs and put up the purple cloak in front of his eyes!"

Then Prince Peisistratos said:

"Your Majesty, that man's son he is in truth, as you say; but he is modest, and he feels shy, on his first visit like this; he would not thrust himself forward or put in any remarks of his own, in your presence, sir, when your speech delights us both as if it were a voice from Heaven. And my royal father has sent me with him as his escort; for he desired to see you, in case you might offer some advice or help. There are always troubles in a house when the father is away and the son is alone, and there are no others to stand up for him; so now with Telemachos, his father is away, and there are no others in the town who will protect him from injustice."

Menelaos answered:

"Dear me, I did love that man, and here is his son in my house! Many a hard labour he wrought for me, and I made sure he would come here and let me show how I loved him beyond any man of the nation, if only we two had come speeding home over the sea in our ships, if Zeus Olympian in his infinite wisdom had granted that! Yes, I would have given him a city and house in Argos to live in, and brought him from Ithaca with his goods and his son and all his people —I would have cleared one of those cities which are all round here, part of my own domain. Yes, we should have always been in and out with each other, and nothing should ever have parted us or put an end to our happy friendship, until the black cloud of death should have swallowed us up. But I suppose that must have been too much happiness for God to grant, since he is the only one to whom return is denied."

This made them all seek relief in tears. Argive Helen wept, Helen the daughter of Zeus; Telemachos wept, and King Menelaos; tears also were in the eyes of Nestor's son, for he thought of the admirable Antilochos, who was killed by the glorious son of Eos; but as he thought of him he said plainly:

"My lord King, my honoured father would always say that you were courteous above all men, we've often talked of you at home together; so now if it is possible at all, let me persuade you, for I do not enjoy crying over my supper; besides there will be to-morrow for that, when daylight doth appear. Not that I grudge sorrowing for the dead, when a mortal man meets his fate. Indeed, this is the only tribute we can pay to unhappy mankind, to cut the hair and to let the tears run over the cheeks. I know, because a brother of my own is dead, by no means the least valiant of our army; you must have known him. I never saw him myself, but they say that Antilochos was in the first rank, both as a sprinter and as a fighter."

Menelaos answered:

"My friend, you speak like a man of sense, you are older than your years; your father is just the same, you get it from him. It is easy to know a man's breeding, when Cronion spins out happiness for him in birth and marriage; just as now we see he has been gracious to Nestor, always and all his days, so that he grows old in plenty and comfort, and his sons are men of sense and excellent spearmen. We will leave the lamentation which we had begun, and turn our thoughts to supper; let them swill our hands. Stories may wait for to-morrow, when Telemachos and I will have something to say to each other."

Then Asphalion poured water over their hands, and they

helped themselves to the food which lay ready before them.

But the admirable Helen had a happy thought. She lost no time, but put something into the wine they were drinking, a drug potent against pain and quarrels and charged with forgetfulness of all trouble; whoever drank this mingled in the bowl, not one tear would he let fall the whole day long, not if mother and father should die, not if they should slay a brother or a dear son before his face and he should see it with his own eyes. That was one of the wonderful drugs which the noble Queen possessed, which was given her by Polydamna the daughter of Thon, an Egyptian. For in that land the fruitful earth bears drugs in plenty, some good and some dangerous; and there every man is a physician and acquainted with such lore beyond all mankind, for they come of the stock of Paiëon the Healer. She dropt in the drug, and sent round the wine, and then she said:

"My lord King Menelaos, and you sons of honourable men who are here—but God gives good fortune or bad fortune to this man or that man when he pleases, for he can do all things—sit there now in our hall, eat and drink and enjoy yourselves with talk; for I have something to tell in the same mood.

"I am not going to tell you everything, all the long tale, all the labours of Odysseus, that indomitable man; but one daring deed which he did in the land of Troy where you Achaians had so many hardships. He had allowed himself to be cruelly scored with lashes; and with a ragged old wrap over his shoulders, like a menial, he entered the streets of the enemy town; he pretended to be a beggar, when he was anything but that in the Achaian fleet. In this disguise he entered the city of Troy, and they were all taken in; I was the only one who knew him in that shape, and I questioned him, but he was clever enough to evade me. However, I gave him a bath and a good rubbing with oil, and swore a solemn oath never to let out the secret before he returned to the camp; and then he told me the whole plan of the Achaians.

"He killed many a Trojan with his own spear before he got back again, and he brought away many secrets. There was loud lamentation among the women of Troy, but my own heart was glad. For I was already longing to come home again, and I mourned the infatuation which Aphroditê brought upon me; when she carried me away from my native land, and parted me from my daughter and my home and husband, although there was no fault in him either of mind or body."

When he heard this, Menelaos answered:

"Upon my word, my dear, that is quite right and proper. I have heard tell of many heroes and their intelligence and their prudence, and I have travelled much in the world; but never did I set eyes on a man like Odysseus for patience and pluck.

"See now what the bold man did and dared in the Wooden Horse, where we all were hidden, the best men of the army, to bring death and ruin upon Troy! You came there, my dear, on that occasion; some divine power must have sent you who wished to give triumph to the Trojans; and that fine fellow Deïphobos came with you. Three times you walked all round our hiding-place, feeling over it with your hands, and you called out the names of the best men in the army, mimicking the voice of each man's wife! I was there, and Diomedês, and Odysseus, sitting among the rest, and we listened to your calls. Both of us wanted to jump up and get out, or to answer at once from within; but Odysseus prevented us and kept us back, although we wanted to do it very much. So nobody uttered a sound; only Anticlos would have made you some answer, but Odysseus held his two hands tight over the man's mouth, and saved the whole nation—and there he held them firmly until Pallas Athena led you away!"

Then Telemachos said, quite to the point:

"Your Majesty, that is only so much the worse; all this did not save him from a lamentable fate, nor would it even if the heart within him had been made of iron. But let us go to our beds, that sleep may give us pleasure and peace for the time being."

As he said this, Helen directed her maids to lay the beds under the open gallery, gay blankets of purple with coverlets upon them and woollen gowns for them to put on. So the maids took torches out of the hall and laid the beds; and a marshal led out the guests. Telemachos and Nestor's son lay down to rest in the gallery before the hall-door; but the King lay in a closet of the hall, and beside him the beautiful Helen in her long robe.

When dawn showed her first gleams, Menelaos leapt out of his bed, and put on his clothes, and slung a sharp sword over his shoulder, and put on his shoes, and went out of his chamber. He sat down by Telemachos, and said to him:

"What business brought you here to Lacedaimon, brave Telemachos, over the broad back of the sea? Public or private? Tell me, and conceal nothing."

Telemachos answered him:

"Your Majesty, I came to learn if you could tell me any news of my father. My house is being eaten up, my rich estate is ruined, the place is full of malicious men, who kill my sheep for ever and my crumple-horn skew-the-dew cattle; they want my mother as a wife, but all they do is outrage and violence. And so I come to your knees as a suppliant that you may tell me of that man's lamentable fate, whether you have seen it with your own eyes in any place or heard from another the story of his wanderings; for he was born to sorrow if any man ever was. Do not soften your words out of pity, to spare me, but tell me plainly what you saw of him, I beseech you, if ever in word or deed my father, your faithful friend, made you a promise and did it before Troy when you suffered all those hardships, remember that now for my sake, and tell me the truth."

Menelaos in hot anger said to this:

"Bless my soul! I declare they are a lot of cravens, who wish to lie in the bed of a mighty man! Imagine a deer in the jungle, which has laid her suckling fawns just born to sleep in the den of a strong lion, while she goes over the hillocks and into the grassy dells to seek her food: then the lion comes back to his lair, and deals death on the lot of them, dam and fawns, and tears them to pieces! So Odysseus will deal death on these, and tear them to pieces!

"Oh Father Zeus, Athenaia, Apollo! could he but appear before them as he was in the pleasant island of Lesbos, when he up and wrestled a match with Philomeleïdês, and threw him by main force, and the whole nation was delighted! If he could be as he was then, and grapple with these men as they gaily go awooing! Quick would be their death, more rueing than wooing! But as to your prayer and petition, I'll not misguide you along, I will not deceive you, but what the Old Man of the Sea told me (and he speaks the truth), that I will tell you and hide nothing.

"In Egypt, when I wished to return here, the gods kept me back because I had not performed the proper sacrifices to them. For the gods are always determined that we shall remember their claims. Well then, there is an island in the open sea before Egypt; they call it Pharos, as far off as a sea-going ship makes in a whole day when a whistling wind blows abaft. In this there is a capital harbour, where voyagers take in fresh water before they push off again. There the gods kept me back for twenty days; never a good wind blew over the brine, none of those which speed a ship over the broad back of the sea. All our provisions would have been used up, and the spirit of the men gone, if a divine being had not pitied me and saved me; a daughter of mighty Proteus the Old Man of the Sea, one Eidothea.

"I must have touched her heart, when she met me wandering alone without companions; for they used to go about fishing with hook and line, since famine tore at their bellies. She came up and spoke to me, and said, 'Are you a fool, stranger, just slack and lazy? or do you prefer to let things slide, and do you enjoy hardships? Here you are all this long time stuck in this island, and you cannot find any way out, while the heart of your men is fainting!'

"I answered, 'I tell you plainly, divine being, whoever you are, it is no wish of mine that I am stuck here; but I must have offended the deathless gods who rule the broad heavens. Do tell me, I pray, for the gods know all things, which of the immortals chains me here, which has tied me back from my way; tell me how I shall make my journey over the fish-giving sea.' That is what I said, and the divine being answered: 'Well, then, stranger, I will tell you exactly what to do.

"'This place is frequented by the Old Man of the Sea, immortal Proteus the Egyptian, a servant of Poseidon; who always tells the truth, who knows all the deep places of the sea. They say he is my father and begetter. If you could lie in wait for him, and catch him, he would tell you your way and the measure of your homeward path, and how you may pass over the fish-giving sea. Yes, and he would tell you, sir, if you wish, what has been done at home and both good and bad, while you were travelling on your long and painful road.'

"I answered her: 'Give me a plan yourself to catch the Old Man divine, or he may see me first, and forewarned is forearmed: the gods are kittle cattle for mortal men to tackle.'

"Then she said: 'Very well, stranger, I will tell you exactly what to do. When the sun mounts to mid-heaven, that is the time when the Old Man of the Sea comes up out of the brine, under the breath of the west wind, hidden by the dark ripples; and when he comes out, he lies to rest in a hollow cave. All round him sleep the seals, in a shoal, the brood of Halosydnê, breathing out the rank scent of the briny deep. You must choose three comrades with care, the best you have in your company. I will lead you to the place in the light of dawn, and lay you all in a row. And now I will tell you all the Old Man's tricks. First, he will inspect the seals and count them. When he has seen them and reckoned them up, he will lie down among them, like a shepherd among his sheep. As soon as you see him safe in his bed, that is the time for brawn and muscle: catch him fast and hold him, however he may struggle and fight. He will turn into all sorts of shapes to try you, into all the creatures that live and move upon the earth, into water, into blazing fire; but you must hold him fast and press him all the harder. When he is himself, and questions you in the same shape that he was when you saw him in his bed—then no more violence, but let the Old Man go; and then, sir, ask which god it is who is angry, and how you shall make your way homewards over the fish-giving sea.'

"When she had spoken, she dived into the waves. But I went back to my ships on the sands, all in a brown study. When I reached the seaside, we prepared our meal, and holy night came on. Then we slept upon the sea-shore.

"But when dawn showed the first streaks of red, I walked along the shore of the sea, earnestly praying to the gods; and I took three comrades, men whom I trusted most for every enterprise.

"Meanwhile, she had dived into the broad bosom of the sea, and brought out four seal-skins newly flayed. It was a little dodge of her own she had made to take in her father! She had hollowed out beds in the sandy beach, and there she sat waiting. When we came near she made us lie down in a row in these beds, and threw a skin over each. That would have been a most trying wait for us, for we were terribly tormented by the horrible stink of the seals from the salt sea. Who would like to lie beside a monster of the salt sea? But she had thought of this without our asking and made it all right. She had brought some ambrosia, and now she put a plug of it into each man's nose, smelling O so sweet! which quite drowned the stink of the monsters.

"All the morning we waited patiently; then the seals came out of the sea in a body. They soon lay down in rows on the sand; and at noon the Old Man came out of the sea, and found his fat seals, and went his rounds, counting the number: counted us first among the monsters, and never dreamt of the trick! Then he lay down himself in the count. At once we rushed on him with yells, and seized him—the Old Man did not forget his arts! First he turned into a bearded lion, then into a serpent, then a leopard, then a great boar; he turned into running water, and a tall tree in full leaf, but we held fast patiently.

"At last the Old Man grew tired of the tricks he knew so well, and questioned us in proper speech: 'Which of the gods devised this plan for you, Prince Atreidês, and helped you to catch me like this against my will in your trap? What do you want?' I answered: 'You know, sir; why do you ask, and try to put me off? You know I am kept back in this island, and cannot find a way out, so that my heart fails within me. I pray you to tell me—for the gods know all things —which of the immortals chains me here, which has tied me back from my way, how I shall make my journey over the fish-giving sea.' He answered me at once: 'Why, of course you ought to have made a handsome sacrifice to Zeus and the other immortals before you embarked, if you wanted a quick passage to your native land over the purple sea. So it is not your lot to see your friends and to return to your fine house and your native land, until you go back to the waters of Aigyptos, that river which is fed from the sky, and perform a solemn sacrifice to the immortal gods who rule the broad heavens: then and not before the gods will open the road which you desire.'

"When I heard this, my heart was broken within me, that he commanded me to go a long and dangerous journey back to Egypt over the misty sea. Nevertheless I said to him: 'This I will surely do, reverend sir, as you command me. But please tell me really and truly; did all our people come home safe in their ships, those who were left by Nestor and me when we set out from Troy? Did any one perish by some unkind fate in his own ship, or with friends around him after we had wound up the war?'

"He answered at once: 'My lord, why do you ask me that? You ought not to know or to learn my mind: you will not long be tearless, when you hear all that happened. Many of them were lost, and many were left, but only two captains of the armed host perished by the way; at the fighting you were present yourself. And one still lives, kept a prisoner somewhere in the broad sea. Aias was lost, with his galleys. First Poseidon wrecked him on the Gyraian rocks, but he was saved from the sea; and indeed he could have escaped death, although Athena was his enemy, if he had not uttered a boastful speech in his blindness—for he declared that he had escaped the devouring gulf "God willing or not!" But Poseidon heard his wicked boast; then and there he lifted the trident in his strong hand, and struck the Gyraian rock, and split him off—the rock remained where it was, but the splinter fell in the sea, the part on which Aias was sitting at first when his heart was blinded, and this carried him with it into the bottomless deep. So there he perished with a mouthful of salt water.

" 'Your brother managed to escape the dangers of the sea; he was saved by Queen Hera. But when he was just coming to the steep cliff of Malea, a storm caught him and carried him over the sea in great distress, to the headland of that country where Thyestês ruled long ago, and then ruled his son Aigisthos. Even then he found a safe voyage, as the gods turned back the wind and home they came. Full of joy he set foot on his native soil, and touched the ground, and kissed it, while the tears ran down his cheeks at the welcome sight of his own country. But a watchman spied him from his look-out; Aigisthos the traitor had placed him there, and promised him two nuggets of gold as a wage. The man had been watching for a year, that the King might not land and pass unseen and be able to defend himself. He hastened with the news to the prince in his palace. At once Aigisthos arranged his plot. He chose the best fellows in the town, twenty of them, and posted them ready; at the other side of the house he ordered a feast to be prepared. Then he went down, with murder in his heart, bringing chariot and horses to invite King Agamemnon; and so he brought him up suspecting nothing, and feasted him, and killed him, as one might kill an ox at the manger. And not one of the King's escort was left, and not one of Aigisthos' men, but all were killed in the place.'

"When he had finished, my heart was broken within me; I sat weeping and rolled my body on the sand, and cared no longer to live and see the light of the sun. When I could weep no more, the truthful Old Man of the Sea said to me, 'My lord, do not go on weeping so long, since there is no help for it; but lose no time in trying to make your way back to your native land. Either you will find him alive, or Orestês will have caught him and killed him, and then you will come in for the funeral feast.'

"This gave me heart and courage, and comforted me in spite of my grief, so I said to him: 'So much then for these; but there is a third I would ask you to name, who is still held prisoner somewhere in the broad sea, or he may be dead; but I want to hear, though it may hurt me.' At once he answered: 'Odysseus Laërtiadês, the man of Ithaca! I saw him in an island weeping hot tears, in the house of Calypso the nymph who holds him by force; and he cannot get away to his native land, since he has neither men nor galleys to take him over the broad back of the sea. But your

fate, royal Menelaos, is not to die and meet your end in
Argos. The immortals will convey you to the Elysian plain at
the end of the earth, where golden-headed Rhadamanthys
dwells. That is the place where life is easiest for mankind:
no snow, no stormy wind or rain, but Zephyros with his
gentle whistling breeze ever comes up from the Ocean to
refresh mankind. For you are Helen's husband, and they
look on you as one of the family of Zeus.' With these words,
he dived into the billowy deep.

"Then I returned to the ships, all in a brown study,
with my loyal comrades. When we reached our ships, we
made our meal, and as soon as sacred night came on we laid
us to rest on the sea-shore. But when dawn came again rosy
through the mist, first of all we launched the ships, then we
set up masts and sails; then the men embarked and took
their seats on the benches, and paddled away over the sea.
Back we went to Aigyptos, that river which is fed from the
sky; and there I stayed the ships, and performed the solemn
sacrifice. When I had thus allayed the resentment of the ever-
lasting gods, I built a barrow for Agamemnon, that his name
might not be forgotten. This done, I set out, and the im-
mortals gave me a fair wind and brought me very soon to
my native land.

"So come now, stay here in my mansion for ten or twelve
days, and then I will give you a good send-off and a
handsome gift, three horses and a chariot; I will give you a
fine chalice too, that when you pour your drops to the im-
mortal gods you may think of me all your days."

But Telemachos knew better, and said:

"My lord, do not keep me here long. It is true I could stay
here a whole year with you, idle, and I should not miss
home or parents; for I am terribly in love with your stories
and your conversation: but my companions are bored already
in Pylos, and I am staying here a long time. If you should
offer me a gift, let it be something for me to treasure; but
horses I will not take to Ithaca. I will leave them for you to
enjoy; for you are lord of a broad plain, in which is plenty
of clover, here is galingale and wheat and spelt and broad-
eared white barley. But in Ithaca we have neither wide roads
nor meadows; it is a goat-country, much pleasanter than a
horse-country. None of the islands in the sea is good for
driving or good for meadows, and Ithaca least of all."

When he said this, the great champion smiled, and stroked
him with one hand, and said to him:

"You come of good blood, dear boy, to hear you speak.

Then I will give you something else, that will be easy enough. You shall have the best and most precious of the treasures which lie in my house. I will give you a mixing-bowl finely wrought; it is all silver, but the lips are finished off with gold. It is a genuine work of Hephaistos; the noble Phaidimos presented it to me. He is King of Sidon, and his house gave me shelter on my homeward journey; now it shall be yours."

As they were thus conversing, the banqueters arrived at the King's mansion. They drove sheep with them, and carried wine that makes glad the heart of man, and their wives at home were sending on the bread.

While these were busy about the feast in Lacedaimon, the others in front of the house of Odysseus were enjoying their game with quoits and javelins upon the paved space as usual, full of riotousness. Antinoös was sitting there, and the handsome Eurymachos, the two leaders among them, who excelled in all their feats. Just then the young man Noëmon appeared, and asked a question of Antinoös:

"Do we know, or don't we, Antinoös, when Telemachos is coming back from Pylos? He took my boat with him, and I want it. I want to cross over to the lowlands of Elis, where I have a dozen mares, with as many hardy mules at foot, unbroken. I want to drive off one of them to be broken in."

These words struck amazement into their hearts; for they did not think he had gone to Pylos—they supposed he was somewhere about the farms, with the sheep, or with the swineherd. Antinoös answered:

"Tell me the truth about it: when did he go, what lads went with him? The pick of Ithaca, or his own serfs and servants? He might do that, of course. Tell me, I want to know the truth; did he steal your boat against your will, or did he beg and pray until you consented?"

Noëmon said:

"I consented all right; what could any one else have done, when a man like him has something in his mind and asks a favour? It is hard to say no to a borrower. The best lads in the town went with him; and I noticed their leader going aboard, Mentor it was, if he wasn't a god, but he was the very spit of Mentor. What does surprise me is, that I saw the very man himself here yesterday morning. But by that time he was on board ship on his way to Pylos!"

He said his say, and off he went to his father's house; and the two were left behind thunder-struck. They made the others stop playing and sit down together; then Antinoös spoke to them in high displeasure, while the dark places of his heart were full of rage and his eyes flashed fire:

"Damn it all, this is a monstrous piece of defiance, this journey of Telemachos! we never expected him to manage it. Off he goes, with all this crowd against him, a young boy like that, launches a ship, picks and chooses the best of the whole town! First score to him! and more trouble to follow; but I pray Zeus may destroy his power first. Come along, get me a fast boat and twenty men, that I may lie for him on his way back, and watch in the strait between Ithaca and the cliffs of Samos; then he shall finish his filial expedition in anything but shipshape fashion!"

They all applauded, and told him to go ahead; then they got up and repaired to the dining-hall.

But Penelopeia did not remain long unacquainted with what they said and what they were scheming in the depths of their hearts; for Medon the marshal told her. He overheard them from outside the courtyard, while they were weaving their scheme inside. He went into the house to inform her, and as he stept over her threshold Penelopeia said to him:

"Marshal, why have these people sent you out? To order the servants of my noble husband to drop their work and get dinner ready for them? If only they might woo no more and visit no more in this world, if only this dinner here this day might be their latest and their last! Here you come constantly in crowds, and you have wasted a heap of wealth, the possessions of Telemachos my clever boy! Did you never hear from your own fathers, when you were children long ago, how Odysseus behaved towards them? never one unjust thing did he say or do among his people like the common run of princes, who hate one and favour another! That man never did a cruel thing in his life. But your way of thinking is as clear as your ugly doings; there is no gratitude in the world for good deeds done."

But Medon answered respectfully:

"I only wish, my lady, that this were the worst; but there is something still worse and still more dangerous which they are plotting, and I pray that Cronion may not bring it to pass! They want to murder him with cold steel on his way home; he has gone to Pylos and sunny Lacedaimon to inquire news of his father."

When she heard this, her knees gave way and her heart fainted, and for a long time she could not utter a word; her eyes filled with tears, and her soft voice was choked. But at last she found words and was able to say:

"Marshal, why has my boy gone? He need not have any-thing to do with seafaring ships, which carry men over the wide waters as horses over the wide world! Did he wish to leave not even his name in the wide world?"

Medon answered as before:

"I do not know whether some god sent him, or if it was his own notion to go to Pylos; but he did go to get news of his father, whether he is on his way home, or what fate has be-fallen him."

This said, he went back through the house. But she was plunged in heart-burning grief. She could not bring herself to sit upon a chair, and there were plenty in the room; but she sat upon the floor near the doorway, bitterly lamenting, while the maids all whimpered, young and old, all through the house. Amid her sobs Penelopeia said to them:

"Listen, my dears! The Olympian has allotted to me sor-rows above all women who were bred and born with me. Long ago I lost a good husband, a man with a lion's heart, first in the whole nation for every noble gift. Now again my beloved son has been torn away by the tempests, without a word, from our house, and I never heard of his going. Hard women you are,—not even you, not one of you could find it in her heart to awake me from my bed, though you knew quite well when he went away to his vessel! If I had only heard that he was planning this voyage, I declare he should never have gone, however much he wanted to go, or he should have gone over my dead body! Go some one, hurry up, and call old Dolios, the man my father gave me when I came here, the man who keeps the garden with all those trees,—tell him to go quickly and find Laërtês and tell him the whole story. Perhaps he can think of some plan; he may come out and complain to the people how these men wish to wipe out his whole race and the family of the noble Odysseus!"

Then Eurycleia the nurse said in answer:

"Dear lass, kill me with cruel steel, or let me be in the house, but I will hide nowt from thee. I knowed the whole thing, I gave all a told me, bread and meal of the best, but a made me swear a gurt oath not to breathe one word to thee till twelve days pass or tha'st ask thysen about his goen away. He was afeared tha might spoil thi pretty skin wi' weepen. Come now, tak' a bath, put on clean linen, go up to thi chamber wi' the maids, and pray to Athenaia the daughter of Zeus Almighty; maybe she'd howd him safe even from death. And donta worret the poor old man who has worrets enough. I make sure the Lord God do not hate the kin of Arceisadês,

but there will be summon yet left i' the world to own the tall
house and all the fat farms out younder."

With these words, the old woman calmed the grief of her
mistress and wiped away her tears. Then the lady bathed and
put on clean linen, and went up to her chamber with the
maids. She filled a basket with the sacred barley-groats, and
prayed to Athena:

"Hear me, daughter of Zeus Almighty, Atrytonê! If ever
my undaunted Odysseus burnt for thee the fat thigh-slices in
this house, remember that for me now, and keep my dear son
safe, and defend me against these proud and riotous men!"

Then she cried aloud the women's alleluia; and the goddess
heard her prayer. But the pretenders applauded in the gloomy
hall when they heard her cry; and you might hear one say to
another of these violent men:

"Sure enough after all our courting my lady is going to
marry again—and she does not know that death is ready for
her son!"

That is what they would say, for they did not know what
the cry meant. But Antinoös warned them, and said:

"Now then, you fellows, no bragging, not a word of any
sort must pass your lips, if you please! Some one may tell
tales inside. Come along, just let us get up quietly and carry
out the plan we thought so good."

Then he chose out twenty, the best fellows there, and they
set out for the ship on the seashore.

The ship first of all was launched into deep water, the
mast and sail set up in the dark hull, the oars hung to the
thole-pins [1] by their leathern loops, arms and armour were
all brought by eager attendants. Well out in the water they
anchored her, and left her there, while they ate their meal on
shore and waited for evening to come.

But there in the upper chamber lay true-hearted Penel-
opeia, without food, touching neither meat nor drink, won-
dering whether her innocent son would escape death or
whether he would be brought low by the men of violence.
Even as a lion is baulked and helpless with fear, when they
put a circle of hunters round him, so she lay troubled in
mind until she fell into a deep sleep. Then she sank down
and slept, and her weary frame had rest.

Now Athena Brighteyes had a thought. She made a phan-
tom in the shape of a woman, Iphthimê, another daughter of
Icarios, and the wife of Eumelos who lived in Pherai; she

[1] Each oar had one thole-pin and a loop attached, as the Greek
boats have still.

sent it to the house of Odysseus, that Penelopeia might have peace from her tears and lamentable grief. It came into the room along the keyhole strap, [1] and spoke to her, leaning over her head.

"Are you asleep, Penelopeia, with your heart full of sorrow? Nay, the gods who live in quiet and peace will not have you weep and mourn, since your boy will yet return; for he has not offended the gods in any way."

Penelopeia answered, as she slumbered sweetly within the gates of dreams:

"What brings you here, sister? You never paid me a visit before, living all that way off. Now you tell me to cease from my mourning and all the pains which trouble me in heart and mind. Long ago I lost a good husband, a man with a lion's heart, first in the whole nation for every noble gift; and now again my beloved son has gone on board ship, a mere child, who knows nothing of plots or parliaments. I am really more grieved for my boy than for the other. For him I am all of a tremble, and I fear what may happen to him in the place where he is gone, or on the sea; for enemies many are planning and plotting against him, determined to kill him before he can return to his native land."

Then the dim phantom answered:

"Take courage, let not your heart fear too much; for one is near to guide him whom others have often prayed to stand by their side, Pallas Athenaia, and she pities you in your grief. She it is who has sent me now to tell you this."

Penelopeia the true-hearted answered:

"If you are really divine and a god sent you here, tell me also about that unhappy man: is he still alive anywhere, does he see the light of the sun, or is he already dead and within the house of Hadês?"

Then the dim phantom answered and said: "I may not tell you for certain whether he is alive or dead; it is a bad thing to babble like the blowing wind."

As she said this she slipt along the bolt of the door into the outer air: Penelopeia leapt up, and her heart warmed within her, that this phantom had appeared so clearly in the dark night.

But the plotters embarked and sailed over the waters, with foul murder in their hearts for Telemachos. There is a rocky islet between Ithaca and the cliffs of Samos, quite a small one, called Asteris, and harbours in it for ships on both sides; there they lay in wait for him.

[1] See note on p. 21.

BOOK V

*Hermês is Sent to Calypso's Island; Odysseus
Makes a Raft and is Carried to the Coast of Scheria*

DAWN ROSE FROM HER BED BESIDE OLD TITHONOS,[1]
bringing light for mortals and immortals both; and the gods
came to their morning session. There in his place was Zeus
Almighty, Thunderer in the heights; and Athena made them
a speech about Odysseus and his troubles, for she was con-
cerned that he still remained in captivity:

"Father Zeus, and all you gods everlasting and blessed!
From this time forth let no sceptred king be kind and gentle,
let none have justice in his heart! Let him always be harsh
and act the tyrant! For none of his subjects remembers that
noble prince Odysseus, who ruled them like a kind father.
Now he lies wretched and miserable, Calypso's prisoner in
her island, and he cannot return to his native land; for he
has no men and no galleys to carry him over the broad back
of the sea. And now again they want to murder his beloved
son, who has gone to Pylos and to Lacedaimon to find out
news of his father. They are only waiting for his return."

Zeus Cloudgatherer answered:

"My dear child, what in heaven do you mean by that? Was
not the whole thing your own notion? Didn't you want him to
come home that way and take your vengeance? As for Tele-
machos, you can easily manage to bring him back safe and
sound, and let the plotters just sail home again."

Then he called to his son Hermês, and said:

"Hermês, you are my messenger, and here is an errand
for you. Go and declare to Calypso our unchangeable will,
that Odysseus shall return after all his troubles. But no god
shall go with him, and no mortal man. He shall build a raft,
and a hard voyage he shall have, until after twenty days he
shall come to land on Scheria, the rich domain of our own
kinsmen the Phaeacians. They shall honour him like a god
in the kindness of their hearts, and they shall escort him in
one of their ships to his native land. They shall give him
plenty of gold and bronze and heaps of fine clothing, more

---

[1] Eos, or Dawn, fell in love with Tithonos, and made him immortal;
but although he did not die, he grew older and older forever.

indeed than he could have brought from Troy as his share of the spoils if he had come home without mishap. For this is how he is destined to return to his tall house and his native land, and to see his friends once more."

The King's Messenger was ready, as he had been when he brought death to the watcher Argos.[1] He put on his fine shoes, those golden incorruptible shoes which used to carry him over moist and dry to the ends of the earth, swift as the breath of the winds. He took up the staff which lays a spell on men's eyes if he wills, or wakens the sleeping. Holding this, Argeiphontês flew away swift and strong. One step on Pieria, and he swooped from the upper air upon the deep; then he skimmed the waves like a seagull, which hunts fish in the dangerous inlets of the barren sea, and dives into the brine with folded wings. Such was the shape of Hermês as he rode on the rippling waves.

When at last he came to that far-off island, he left the blue sea and passed over the land until he reached the great cave where Calypso lived. He found her in the cave, with her beautiful hair flowing over her shoulders. A great fire blazed on the hearth, and the burning logs of cedar and juniper wafted their fragrant scent far over the island. Calypso sat within by her loom, singing in a lovely voice, and shooting her golden shuttle to and fro. A thick coppice of trees grew round the cave, alder and aspen and sweet-smelling cypress. There the birds would sail to rest on their outspread wings, owls and falcons and long-tongued sea-ravens who busy themselves about the waters. Over the gaping mouth of the cave trailed a luxuriant grape-vine, with clusters of ripe fruit; and four rills of clear water ran in a row close together, winding over the ground. Beyond were soft meadows thick with violets and wild celery. That was a sight to gladden the very gods.

King's Messenger Argeiphontês stood still, and gazed about him with deep content. Then he went into the cave, and Calypso knew him as soon as she saw him; for all those of the divine race know one another when they meet, even if they live a long way off. But Odysseus was not there. He was sitting in his usual place on the shore, wearing out his soul with lamentation and tears.

[1] Zeus had fallen in love with a girl, Io; Hera turned her into a heifer, and put her in the charge of Argos, who had eyes all over his body. Zeus sent Hermês to get Argos out of the way. He charmed Argos with his magic staff, and put all his eyes to sleep; then killed him. Hence he is called Argeiphontês.

Calypso gave him greeting:

"My dear Hermês, this is an honour! with your golden rod and all! What has brought you here? You do not often pay me a visit, but you are heartily welcome. Tell me what you want: I am glad to do it if I can, and if it is doable. But do come in, and let me entertain my guest."

With these words, she led him to a seat that shone with diligent polishing, and set a table beside him with a dish of ambrosia and a cup of red nectar. The royal messenger ate, he drank, he enjoyed a hearty meal, and then he answered her question:

"You ask me what brings me here, as one god to another. Very well, I will tell you the whole history, as you ask. Zeus sent me here. I did not want to come here; who would want to travel all that distance over the salt water, no end to it? and no city of mortals anywhere near to provide a god with sacrifice and a handsome feast! But no god can shirk or baffle the will of Zeus Almighty; that is quite impossible. He says there's a man here, one of those who were nine years fighting before Priam's town, and the most unlucky of them all. It took them ten years to capture that city: then they set out for home, but on the way they offended Athena, and she raised a bad wind and a heavy sea against them. All his good comrades were drowned, but he as it seems was carried here by winds and waters.

"That's the man, and the orders are to send him away at once; for it is not his fate to perish in this place far from his friends. It is decreed that he shall see his friends again, and return to his tall house and his native land."

Calypso shivered, and she spoke her mind plainly:

"A hard-hearted lot you are, you gods, and as jealous as jealous can be! Why are you shocked if a goddess sleeps with a man and makes no secret of it, when she happens to find one she could love as a husband? It is always the same. When blushing Dawn chose Orion, all you gods were shocked. You live as you like yourselves, but you would not rest until Artemis let fly one of her gentle bolts and killed him in Ortygia. Her Holiness on that golden throne! Then Demeter had a fancy for Iasion, and pleased herself, made her love-bed on the furrows of the plowland. Zeus heard of it in no time, and killed him dead with a fiery thunderbolt.

"So you gods are all shocked at me now, because there's a mortal man with me. I saved the man when he was straddling across a ship's keel, all by himself, after Zeus had sent another fiery thunderbolt at him and smashed the ship to pieces

in the middle of the sea. All his crew were drowned, and
the winds carried him here. I loved him and cherished him,
and I did think I would make him immortal like myself. But
since it is impossible for any god to shirk or baffle the will of
Zeus Almighty, let him go to the devil over the barren sea,
if that is the command of his Mightiness. I will not give him
a passage home; I have no ships and no sailors to carry him
over the broad back of the sea. But I will gladly advise him
and help him to get home.

Hermês answered:

"All right, let him go now, and don't forget the wrath of
God, or he may be angry with you one fine day."

So Argeiphontês departed, having delivered his message,
and Calypso went in search of Odysseus. She found him sit-
ting upon the shore. The tears were never dry in his eyes;
life with its sweetness was slowly trickling away. He cared
for her no longer; at night he was forced to sleep by her side
in the cave, although the love was all on her part, and he
spent the days sitting upon the rocks or the sands staring at
the barren sea and sorrowing.

Calypso came up to him and said:

"Poor old fellow! please don't sit here lamenting any more,
don't let yourself pine away like this. I'm going to send you
off at once, and glad to do it. Come along, cut down trees,
hew them into shape, make a good broad raft; you can lay
planks across it and it shall carry you over the misty sea! I
will provide you with bread, water, red wine, as much as you
like, you need not starve. I'll give you plenty of clothes and
send a fair wind behind you to bring you home safe and
sound—if it so please the gods who rule the broad heavens,
who are stronger than I am both to will and to do."

As she said this, the ever-patient man shivered, and he said
plainly:

"I am sure there is something else in your mind, goddess,
and no kind send-off for me, when you tell me to cross the
great gulf of the sea on a raft. That is a difficult and dan-
gerous thing even for well-built ships, although they sail
swiftly enough when they are blessed with a good wind from
heaven. And I should not care to embark on a raft without
your goodwill: not unless you could bring yourself to swear
a solemn oath that you will not work some secret mischief
against me."

The beautiful goddess smiled, and stroked him with her
hand, saying:

"Ah, you are a wicked man! always wide awake! or you

would never have thought of such a thing. Now then: I swear
by heaven above and by earth beneath and the pouring force
of Styx—that is the most awful oath of the blessed gods:
I will work no secret mischief against you. No, I mean what
I say; I will be as careful for you as I should be for myself
in the same need. I know what is fair and right, my heart is
not made of iron, and I am really sorry for you."

Then she led him briskly to the great cave. They went in
together, the goddess and the man. He took the seat which
Hermês had just left; she laid the table with food and drink,
everything which mortal man can eat, and sat opposite while
the maids brought her nectar and ambrosia. They took what
they wanted, and when they had had a good meal the beauti-
ful Calypso spoke first:

"Prince Odysseus Laërtiadês, now is the time to show your
famous cleverness! So you want to go home at once? Well,
I wish you luck all the same. If you knew what troubles you
will have before you get to Ithaca, you would stay where you
are and keep this house with me, and be immortal, however
much you might want to see your wife whom you long for
day in and day out. Is she prettier than me? I think not. I
don't think it likely that a mortal woman would set herself
up as a model of beauty against a goddess!"

Odysseus knew what to say to that, and he answered at
once:

"Gracious goddess, don't be cross with me! I know all that
as well as you do. My wife is nothing compared to you for
beauty, I can see that for myself. She is mortal, you are im-
mortal and never grow old. But even so, I long for the day of
my home-coming. And if some god wrecks me again on the
deep, I will endure it, for I have a patient mind. I have suf-
fered already many troubles and hardships in battle and
tempest; this will be only one more."

As he spoke, the sun went down and the darkness came;
and these two lay down in the corner of the lofty cave, and
enjoyed their love together.

When Dawn showed her rosy fingers through the mists,
Odysseus put on tunic and cloak, and the nymph a silvery
wrap, with a golden girdle under it round the hips and a veil
over her head. Then she began to help Odysseus in his work.
She gave him a good handy axe of bronze, double-edged,
with a well-fitted handle of olive-wood, and an adze with a
smooth shaft, and led him to the end of the island. There
was a coppice of tall trees, long since dry and sapless and
easy to float, alder and aspen and pine-trees high as the sky.

When she had shown him the trees, Calypso went back and he began to fell them. He worked fast, and soon cut down twenty trees, then trimmed them with the axe, shaped them neatly, and made them true to the line. Then Calypso brought him a boring-tool, and he bored holes and fitted the spars together, making them fast with pegs and joints. He made his craft as wide as a skilful shipwright would plan out the hull of a bluff ketch. He fixed ribs along the sides, and decking-planks above, and finished off with copings along the ribs. He set a mast in her, and fitted a yard upon it, and he made also a steering-oar to keep her straight. All round he ran bulwarks of wattle to keep the water out, and threw brushwood into the bottom. Then Calypso brought him cloth to use for a sail, and he made that too. Stays and halyards and sheets he made fast in their places, and dragged her down to the shore on rollers.

In four days he had finished the whole; and on the fifth Calypso saw him off, after she had bathed him and clothed him in garments scented with juniper. She did not forget a skin of red wine, and another large one full of water, with provisions in a bag, tasty stuff and plenty of it; and she sent with him a fair wind, friendly and soft. Odysseus was glad of that wind as he set his sail, and sat by the stern-oar steering like a seaman. No sleep fell on his eyes; but he watched the Pleiades and the late-settling Wagoner, and the Bear, or the Wagon, as some call it, which wheels round and round where it is, watching Orion, and alone of them all never takes a bath in the Ocean.

Calypso had warned him to keep the Bear on his left hand as he sailed over the sea.

Seventeen days he sailed over the sea; and on the eighteenth day he approached the nearest point of the Phaiacian Country, with its shady uplands. The island looked like a great shield lying upon the misty deep.

But the Earthshaker was now on his way back from the Ethiopians, and caught sight of him in the distance from the Solyman Hills. He fell into a royal rage, and shook his head, as he cried out:

"Damn it all, the gods have changed their minds about Odysseus, as soon as I was out of the way! And there he is close to Phaiacia, where he is fated to find the end of the tribulations which afflict him. But I promise that I will yet give him a good run of bad luck!"

Then he gathered the clouds, and stirred up the deep with his trident: he roused all the tempestuous winds, and cov-

ered in clouds both land and sea; night rushed down from
the heavens. East wind and South wind dashed together,
West wind blowing hard and North wind from the cold
heights, rolling up great billows. Odysseus felt his knees
tremble and his heart fail, and in despair he spoke to his own
strong spirit:

"How unlucky I am! What will be the end of all this? I
fear what the goddess said was true: she said I was to have
trouble in full measure, before I could see my native land,
and here it is all coming true. What clouds are these that
Zeus has brought over the broad heavens! How he has stirred
up the deep, how all the winds come sweeping upon me!
Now my destruction's a safe thing! Thrice blessed were my
countrymen, four times blessed indeed, who perished on the
field before Troy to please the royal house of Atreus. I wish I
had died there, and found my fate on that day when a host
of enemies were casting their sharp spears at me over the
dead body of Achillês! Then I should have had burial, and
my countrymen would have spread my fame; now I am
doomed to die an ignominious death."

As he said this, a great wave rolled up towering above
him, and drove his vessel round. He lost hold of the steering-
oar, and fell out into the water; the mast snapt in the middle
as the fearful tempest of warring winds fell upon it; sail and
yard were thrown from the wreck. He was kept long under
water, and he could not get clear, for his clothes weighed
him down. But at last he came up, spitting the bitter brine
out of his mouth, while it ran down streaming off his head.
For all this he did not forget his raft, exhausted as he was,
but he made a dash after it through the seas, and caught
hold, and sat in the middle to save his life if he could. Round
and round it went on the waves. As the North wind in Au-
tumn rolls up lumps of thistles and carries them over the
fields, so that winds blew the raft round and round over the
water; [1] now the South wind tossed it to the North wind,
now the East wind passed it to the West wind in turn.

But Ino saw him. She was a daughter of Cadmos, and a
beautiful creature; once a mortal who spoke with human
voice, now she is Leucothea the White Sea Goddess, to whom

[1] "Over the harvested fields grew thistles tall as a child, but now
yellow and dried and dead. The wind snapt them off at the hollow
root, and pitchpolled their branching tops along the level ground,
thistle blowing against thistle and interlocking spines, till in huge
balls they careered like runaway haycocks across the fallow."—
Seven Pillars of Wisdom, page 626.

the gods have given that honour in the salt deeps. She pitied Odysseus, as he was buffeted about in this miserable way; like a great shearwater she rose on the wing from the waves, and perching on the wreck she said:

"Poor Odysseus! You're odd-I-see, true to your name![1] Why does Poseidon Earthshaker knock you about in this monstrous way, and persecute you so much? But he will never destroy you, although that is what he wants to do. Well, this is my advice, and I think you have sense enough to take it. Strip off your clothes, and let the raft go roaming; take to the sea and swim, and you may get your grip on Phaiacian land, since it is ordained that you shall find safety there. Here, take this veil and stretch it under your chest: it is a divine thing, and while you have it there is no fear that you will drown or come to any harm. When you have your hands fast on the land, take it off and throw it back into the sea as far as you can, but turn your face away as you do it."

Then the goddess gave him the veil, and dived back herself into the sea, like a great shearwater, and the dark waves covered her. But Odysseus was left in doubt. How much he had endured patiently already! and he was angry as he said to himself:

"More trouble for me! I can't help thinking that some god or other is weaving another snare, when she tells me to leave the raft. At all events I won't do it yet; she said I should get ashore there, but the land was a long way off when I caught sight of it. Well, I know what I'll do; this seems the best thing. As long as these sticks hold together, I'll stick to them, and make the best of my hard luck; but if the sea smashes them up, I'll swim for it, since I cannot see anything better to do."

While these thoughts were passing through his mind, Poseidon Earthshaker brought up another great wave, a terrible great mass that curved over him, and drove him along. Planks and spars were scattered as a strong wind catches a heap of dry straw, and scatters it over the ground. Odysseus straddled across one spar, as if he were riding a horse, and stript off his clothes, all he had left of the gifts of kind Calypso. He fastened the veil under his chest, and fell flat on the water, with arms spread abroad to swim. The mighty Earthshaker saw him, and nodded his head as he said to himself:

"That's right! You have had a good lot of troubles already,

[1] There is a pun on Odysseus and ὠδύσατο.

and now you may go tossing about on the water and get
ashore if you can. Even if you get there, I don't think you
will be able to complain of having less than your share of
trouble!"

With these words he whipt up his horses; they shook their
manes, and carried him to Aigai, where his famous palace
was.

Now it was the turn of Athenaia the daughter of Zeus, and
this was her plan. She tied up the courses of all the other
winds, and commanded them to rest and be quiet; but she
sent a steady wind from the north, and broke down the waves
in front of Odysseus, that he might make his way to Phaiacia
and save himself alive.

After that, he tossed about for two nights and two days on
the rolling waves, always looking for death. But the third day
broke with rosy streaks of dawn, and when the light was full,
the wind fell and there came a breathless calm. Odysseus
lifted high on a great swell, took a quick look forward, and
there close by he saw the land. As a father's life is welcome
to his children, when he has been lying tormented by some
fell disease, and in his agony long drawn out the hateful
hand of death has touched him, but God has given relief
from his troubles; no less welcome to Odysseus was the sight
of earth and trees, and he swam on, longing to feel his feet
on solid ground.

When he came near enough for a man's voice to carry, he
could hear the dull sound of the sea breaking upon the rocks.
The great waves were crashing against a rough coast, and
belching up terrific showers of spray which covered the cliffs
in a mist; for there was no harbour for a ship, and no road-
stead, nothing but bluffs and crags and headlands along that
shore.

Then Odysseus felt his limbs grow weak, and his heart
failed within him; dauntless though he was, he was disturbed
and said to himself:

"My trouble is not over yet! Zeus has granted me to see
the land, which I never hoped to see; now I have come to the
end of my journey over all that immeasurable gulf, but there
is no way to get out of the water. Sharp reefs outside, roaring
surges all round, a smooth cliff running up straight with deep
water along the shore: nowhere to stand on my two feet and
find safety. If I try to get out, I suppose the swell will catch
me and dash me on the sharp teeth of some rock; then much
good will it do me to try. If I swim along the coast on the
chance of finding a bay and a sloping beach, I am afraid the

gale may catch me again and carry me out into the deep sea, and that will be a bad job; or luck may send me a monster out of the sea; Amphitritê is famous for monsters. I know the Earthshaker has an odd dislike for Odysseus!" [1]

As these thoughts passed through his mind, the swell carried him against the rocky shore. Then his skin would have been torn off and all his bones broken, if Athena had not put a thought into his mind; he flung himself upon a rock and caught hold with both hands, and clung there groaning, until the wave had passed on. That time he saved himself; but the backwash rolled upon him again, and carried him far out into the sea. When you drag a squid out of its hole, you may see a lot of little stones sticking to the suckers; that is what his strong hands looked like, with rags of skin and flesh, and bits of rock along the fingers, when the wave swallowed him up.

And then Odysseus would have perished, fate or no fate, if Athena had not put prudence into his mind. He got clear of the line of breakers foaming upon the shore, and swam along outside, keeping his eye on the land, in case he could see a bay and a sloping beach. On he swam until he came opposite the mouth of a river, and glad he was to see it. That seemed a good place, as there were no rough stones, and it gave some shelter from the wind. He saw the river pouring into the sea, and prayed to the river-god in his heart:

"Hear me, Lord, whoever thou art! How I have longed for thee, and now I pray to thee, save me from Poseidon's threats! Pity a homeless man! even the immortal gods might pity one who comes, as I come now, to thy stream and thy knees, after much tribulation! Have mercy upon me, Lord, I throw myself upon thee!"

Then the river stayed his flowing, and held back the wave and made calm before him, and brought him safe into the mouth. He sank on his two knees, and let his strong arms fall, for the sea had worn him out. All his body was swollen, and the salt water bubbled from mouth and nostrils; breathless and voiceless he lay in a faint, and awful weariness overcame him. When his breath came back by and by, and his spirit rallied again, the first thing he did was to unwind the goddess's veil: he dropt it into the river, as it ran murmuring seawards, and the swell carried it back, until Ino quickly received it into her kind hands. Odysseus crawled up out of the

[1] Another pun on his name. Odysseus speaks all through with a grim humour, and never loses his self-possession.

river, and sank down on the rushes, and kissed mother earth. Then, deeply moved, he spoke to his own brave heart:

"And now what will become of me? What will be the end of all this? If I keep watch all this wretched night by the riverside, I think hard frost and drenching dew together may be too much for me after that fainting fit; and the wind blows cold towards dawn. If I should climb the hill into the dark forest, and lie down in a clump of bushes, to have a good sleep and get rid of this chill and weariness, I am afraid I may be just something for wild beasts to eat and play with."

But after thinking it over, the last plan seemed the best. So he entered a coppice which he found close to the river, with a clear space round it: there he crawled under a couple of low trees which were growing close together out of one root, a wild garden olive and a blackthorn. So thick and close they grew that no damp wind could blow through, nor could the sun send down his blazing rays, nor could rain penetrate. Odysseus crept into this thicket, and found there was plenty of room for a bed; so he scraped up the leaves with his bare hands, for there were plenty there, enough to shelter two or three men in the wildest winter weather. Imagine the delight of Odysseus when he saw this place, after all his troubles! Down he lay in the middle, and heaped the leaves over his body. So there was Odysseus lying under the leaves, like a smouldering brand which some one has buried under black ashes far away in the country, with no one living near: that is how he keeps the seed of fire, or else he would have to go elsewhere for a light. And Athena shed sleep upon his eyes, and closed the two eyelids, that he might quickly rest from his weariness after sore tribulation.

BOOK VI

*How Odysseus Appealed to Nausicaä, and She
Brought Him to Her Father's House*

So THERE HE LAY IN HIS THICKET, WORN OUT AND
heavy with sleep; but Athena made her way to the Phaiacian
town. Formerly this people had lived on the plains of Hypereia, near the savage Cyclopians, who did them great damage,
being stronger than they were. Afterwards they migrated, led
by their great king Nausithoös; and he settled them in Scheria, far from the world of men who earn their bread in the
sweat of their brows. Nausithoös ran a wall round the city,
and built houses, and made temples for the gods, and divided
the fields among the people. But by this time he had yielded
to fate and gone to Hadês, and the king was now Alcinoös,
a man full of inspired wisdom.

To the house of Alcinoös Athena made her way, with her
grey eyes glinting, as she planned the home-coming of Odysseus. She entered a splendid chamber where the king's daughter lay asleep. This was Nausicaä, a girl tall and divinely
beautiful; and in the same room were two attendants, graceful girls, one beside each doorpost; the gleaming doors were
shut. Like a breath of wind Athena passed to the girl's bed,
and stooping over her head spoke to her; she had made herself look like the daughter of that famous seaman Dymas, a
girl of her own age and her particular friend. In this shape
Athena spoke:

"Why are you so lazy, Nausicaä, and with such a mother
as you have? There is all the fine linen lying soiled, and it is
high time for you to marry; you will want a nice frock then
for yourself, and the same for your wedding company. That
is the kind of thing which gives a girl a good name in the
world, and pleases her father and mother. Let us go out and
wash the linen as soon as day dawns. I will lend you a hand
myself, that you may get it done quickly, for you will not remain a maiden long; you have plenty of admirers, the finest
young men in all the nation. Get up and persuade your good
father as soon as the morning dawns to get ready the mules,
and a wagon to carry sashes and robes and sheets all glossy
and shining. Better for yourself to drive rather than walk,
for the washing-tanks are a good way off from the town."

When she had said this, Athena sped to Olympos, where as they say is the gods' abiding-place, unshaken for ever. There are no beating winds or drenching rain; no snow falls there, but the clear sky spreads cloudless, over it a white radiance floats; there the blessed gods are happy all their days. To that place went Athena, when she had spoken to the girl.

In a moment, there was Dawn on her golden throne; and Nausicaä in her dainty robe awoke. She was excited by the dream, and went straight through the house to tell her mother and father. She found them indoors; her mother sat by the hearth with her attendant women, twisting the purple yarn; her father she met just going out to attend a council of the chief princes, to which he had been summoned. She came close to him, and said:

"Daddy dear, couldn't you let me have a good big cart with plenty of room? because I want to take our best clothes to the river and give them a wash; they are all lying in a dirty heap! You know what is proper for yourself when you are with their worships passing resolutions, you must have clean clothes. And you have five sons in the house, two married and three spruce young bachelors; they always demand everything fresh from the wash when they are going to a dance, and only my poor brains to manage it all!"

That is what she said, for she was too shy to mention her happy dreams in her father's presence; but he saw through it, and answered at once:

"Take the mules and welcome, my child, and anything else you want. Go ahead; the servants shall get you ready a good big cart with plenty of room, and a tilt over the top."

Then he called to the servants, and gave his orders. They got ready the mule-cart outside, and fitted it upon a fine set of wheels, and brought up the mules and yoked them in; and a house-maid brought a handsome cloak from her chamber and laid it in the cart. Her mother packed a hamper full of eatables, everything the heart could desire and plenty of it, not forgetting the meat, and a goatskin full of wine. Then the young girl got into the cart, and her mother handed her a golden flask of olive oil to use after the bath with her attendant women. Then the girl picked up the whip and reins, shining with polish, and whipt up the team: the mules went rattling along and did not shirk the pull, so on went load and lady together—but not alone, for the maids were trotting by her side.

In due time they reached a noble river. The washing-tanks were there, never empty, for the water came bubbling up and running through them enough to cleanse the dirtiest stuff. There they took out the mules and let them go free, driving them down to the eddying stream to browse on sweet clover. Then the maids unloaded the wagon and carried the clothes into the deep water, where they trod them out in the pits, all racing for first done. And when the washing was over, and all was spotless, they flew in a long string to the seashore, choosing a place where the sea used to beat upon the beach and wash the pebbles clean. There they bathed, and rubbed themselves all over with olive oil. After that they took their meal on the river-bank, while they waited for the clothes to dry in the sun.

When they had all had enough, both maids and mistress, they threw off their veils and began playing at ball, and Nausicaä led the singing, with her white arms flashing in the sunlight as she threw the ball. She looked like Artemis, when bow in hand she comes down from the mountains, over lofty Taïgetos or Erymanthos, to hunt the boars and fleet-footed deer: round about her the nymphs make sport, those daughters of Zeus who frequent the countryside; and her mother is proud indeed, for she lifts head and brow above all the troop, and she is preeminent where all are beautiful. So shone the fresh young maiden among her girls.

But just as she was about to yoke the mules, and fold up all the fine clothes, and set out for home, Athena decided that Odysseus should awake and see the lovely girl, and let her take him to the city.

So then, the princess threw the ball to one of the maids; the ball missed the maid, and fell in the eddies, and they all shouted at that. The noise wakened Odysseus, and he sat up and began to think:

"What next, I wonder! what sort of people live in this land? Violent, savage, lawless? or kindly men who know right from wrong? I seemed to hear something like women's voices, the cry of girls. Perhaps they are nymphs; there are plenty of them on the mountains; the dells and springs and brooks are full of them. But these seem to be using human speech. Well, I'll just go and see."

So saying, he crawled out of the bushes. He broke off a branch thick with leaves, and held it before him in his hand, to hide his naked body. Then he strode along like a lion of the mountains, proud of his power, who goes on through wind and rain with eyes blazing, as he pounces on cattle and sheep, or chases the wild deer; indeed he is ready to follow belly's bidding, and to invade even a walled close in search of the bleaters. Odysseus felt just as desperate when he resolved to join a party of pretty girls without a rag upon him; but he could not help it. What a vision they saw! Something filthy and caked in sea-salt which fairly terrified them: away they scampered in all directions, to hide behind hillocks of sand. Only the young princess stood her ground; for Athena took all fear away.

So she halted and stood firm; and Odysseus was uncertain what to do. Should he throw his arms round her knees, and crave mercy of the lovely girl? or should he stand where he was, and ask her politely to give him some clothes, and to tell him the way to the city? When he thought over the matter, it seemed best to stand where he was and to speak politely and quietly, in case he might give offence to the girl by embracing her knees. He lost no time, but spoke to her in gentle and persuasive words:

"I kneel to thee, Queen!—Art thou goddess? Are you mortal? If you are a goddess, one of those who rule the broad heavens, I would liken you most to Artemis the daughter of Zeus Almighty, so tall and beautiful and fair. If you are a mortal and one of those who dwell upon earth, thrice blessed are your father and your gracious mother, thrice blessed are your brothers; their hearts must be warm for your sake, when they see such a fresh young creature trippling over the green. But most blessed beyond all these in his heart of hearts is he who shall come laden with bridal gifts and take you to his home. Never in all my life have I seen such another, man or woman: I am amazed as I look upon you. In Delos once I did see something like you, a young palm-spire springing up beside Apollo's altar. For I have travelled even so far; and there were many others with me on that voyage which was to bring me so much tribulation. Even so when I saw that sapling my spirit was dumbfounded for a long time, for no other trees like that grow out of the earth; and so, my lady, I am amazed and dumbfounded at seeing you, and I am awestruck at the thought of touching your knees.

"But I am in deep distress. Yesterday after twenty days on the dark sea, I escaped; all that time sea and storms had been carrying me away from the island of Ogygia; and now fate has cast me ashore here. No doubt I am to suffer more troubles here; I do not think the gods will give over yet, for they have much to work off on me still. Pity me, Queen, I pray; to you first I appeal, after so much misery; not another soul do I know of all those who live in this country. Show me the way to your town, give me a rag to cover me, some wrapper you may have brought with you for the clothes. And may the gods give you the dearest wish of your heart, husband, and home, and one heart between two; for nothing is better and more precious than when two of one heart and mind keep house together, husband and wife. That is a sight to make their friends happy and their enemies miserable; but they know it best themselves."

Nausicaä stood her ground, and replied:

"Stranger, you do not seem like a bad man or a foolish man; but happiness is something which Olympian Zeus above allots to men, whether good or bad, to each according to his will. Your fortune is what he has given you, and you must endure it in any case. But now that you have come to our country, you shall not lack for clothes, or anything else which it is proper that any forlorn wanderer may have for the asking. I will show you the way to town, and I will tell you what this nation is called. This is the country of the Phaiacians: I am the daughter of Prince Alcinoös, their king and ruler."

Then she called to her maids, and said:

"Stand still, my girls! Why do you run off at the sight of this poor fellow? You don't think he's an enemy, do you? There is no man living upon the earth, and never shall be, who would come into the Phaiacian land to do harm to its people; for they are dear to the immortals. Our home lies far away in the sea, out of sight of land, at the end of the earth, and no other mortal men visit us. But here is a poor homeless man, and you must look after him. God sends the stranger and the beggar man; we gladly give, not much, but all we can. Come along, girls, give this stranger something to eat and drink, and a bath in the river, where he can find shelter from the wind."

The girls stood still, calling to one another, and then they brought Odysseus to a sheltered place, as the princess told them to do. They laid a wrap beside him and a tunic, and gave him the golden flask of olive oil, and bade him go into the river for his bath.

Then Odysseus said to the maids, "Just stand a little way off, good maids, while I wash the salt off my shoulders by myself, and give them a rub with the oil: it is long since my skin knew what oil feels like. I will not wash before you, for I am too shy to show myself naked before a lot of pretty girls."

Accordingly they went and told the princess all about it. Then Odysseus waded into the river, and washed himself clean from the salt which covered his back and broad shoul-

ders, and wiped off the scruff of brine from his head. When
he had washed all clean and rubbed himself with oil, and put
on the clothes which the princess had provided, Athenaia
daughter of Zeus made him taller and stronger to look at,
and gave him a crop of bushy hair, like a cluster of hyacinth
flowers. As when a plating of gold is laid over silver by some
clever craftsman, who has learnt all the secrets of his art
from Hephaistos and Pallas Athena, and knows how to make
works full of grace, so Athena covered his head and shoul-
ders with beauty.

Then he walked away to the seashore, shining with comeli-
ness and grace; and the girl gazed at him. She turned to her
attendants, and said:

"Listen to me, pretty ones, I have something to say. The
hand of the gods is in this; they who rule Olympos have sent
this man to visit the Phaiacians, who are of their own kin-
dred. When I saw him I thought him an ugly creature, but
now he is like one of the gods who rule the broad heavens.
I only wish that I might have one like him for my husband! I
wish it might please him to stay here and live with us! Come,
my girls, give him something to eat and drink."

They hastened to obey, and set food and drink before
Odysseus; and Odysseus ate and drank heartily after all his
tribulations, for it was long since he had had anything to eat.

But Nausicaä had other things to think of. She folded up
the clothes, and packed them into the wagon, and yoked the
sturdy mules, and got in herself. Then she called to Odysseus
that they must be going. She said:

"Now then, stranger, up with you and let us go on to the
town. I will take you to my wise father's house, where I
promise you shall become acquainted with all the best men
of the nation. But this is what you must do: you seem to have
your share of good sense. So long as we are still in the coun-
try among the farms, you must follow smartly with the maids
behind the cart, and I will lead the way. But when we reach
the city,—which has a lofty wall round it, with a fine har-
bour on each side, and only a narrow approach: the galleys
are drawn up there along the road, and each man has a slip
for his own: there is their meeting-place, round about the
precinct of Poseidon, and it is full of great blocks of stone
bedded in the earth. There the men are busy about the tackle
of their black ships, making ropes and sails, and planing down
their oars. For the Phaiacians care nothing for bow and
quiver, but only masts and oars and the ships with their fine
lines, these are their delight as they cross the hoary sea.

"Well, I want to avoid any unkind gossip among the people, or some one might blame me afterwards. They are very high and mighty in our town; some evil-minded person might say, if he met us, 'Who is this fine big stranger with Nausicaä? where did she pick him up? Will be a husband for her, no doubt. Some wandering soul she has brought from his ship, must be a foreigner from a distance, for there is nobody near us. Perhaps she had tired out some god with her prayers, and down he comes from heaven to have her for ever more! A good job, if she has gone herself and picked up a husband from somewhere else, for she only turns up her nose at the young men of our nation, who are all after her, and good men too!' That's what they will say, and it might bring me into disgrace. Indeed, I should not approve of any girl who did such a thing, flying in the face of her friends, with father and mother to teach her better, if she has anything to do with men before it comes to marriage open and above-board.

"Now then, sir, be quick and understand what I say, if you wish to have escort and safe conduct from my father. You will find a fine grove of Athena close to the road, poplar trees, with a spring bubbling up inside and a meadow all round. There is my father's park, and the orchard, full of fruit, as far from the city as a man's voice will carry. Sit down there and wait long enough for us to get into the city and reach my father's mansion. When you think we have got there, enter the city yourself and ask the way to the mansion of Prince Alcinoös. It is easy to know it, a little child could lead you; for the other houses are not like the house of the royal prince Alcinoös.

"When you are within the house you must enter the hall, and pass along quickly until you come to my mother; she is a sight worth seeing! There she sits at the hearth in the fire-light, twisting her purple yarn, close up to a pillar, and the serving-women sit behind. My father's throne is placed near to hers, and there he sits quaffing his wine like a god! Pass him by, and lay your hands on my mother's knees, that you may see the day of your home-coming, and be happy soon, even if you come from a long way off. If she is pleased with you, there is good hope that you will set eyes on your friends, and come to see your own fine house and your native land."

When she had said this, she touched up the mules with her shining whip, and they soon left the river behind them. Quickly they trotted along, quickly their toes went weaving, but she drove just so fast that Odysseus and the maids could follow on foot: she flicked the lash with judgment.

The sun went down, and they came to the famous grove sacred to Athena, and there Odysseus took his seat. Then he prayed to the daughter of great Zeus:

"Hear me, daughter of Zeus Almighty, Atrytonê! Hear me now at least, since formerly thou didst not hear what a blow I had, when the famous Earthshaker struck me! Grant me to come among the Phaiacians as a friend and one worthy of compassion!"

Thus he prayed, and Pallas Athena heard him. But she did not show herself to him face to face; for she stood in awe of her father's brother Poseidon, and he was furiously angry with the hero Odysseus until he reached his own land.

BOOK VII

*What Happened to Odysseus in the
Palace of Alcinoös*

WHILE ODYSSEUS WAS PRAYING TO HIS GUARDIAN GOD-dess, the girl drove her mules into the city at a brisk trot, and drew up at her father's door. There her brothers met her, and fine young fellows they were; they soon unhitched the mules and carried in the clothes. She went up to her own room, and found the waiting-woman lighting the fire. This was the nurse of her childish days, Eurymedusa, who had been cap-tured long ago after a raid on Apeira, and she had been chosen then out of the spoil as a special prize for the King whom the people loved to honour and obey.

Soon the fire was lit, and the supper coming; at the same moment Odysseus set out for the city. A thick mist hid him from sight, for Athena did not wish any one to meet him and provoke him, or ask him who he was. But just as he was about to enter the city, Athena met him herself in the shape of a young girl carrying a pitcher. Odysseus said to her:

"My dear child, could you show me the way to the mansion of King Alcinoös? I am a stranger from foreign parts, and I have come a long way, so I know not a soul in this country."

Athena said:

"Indeed I will, father, and welcome; my own father lives close by. But just follow me quietly, and don't look at any one or ask any questions. People here simply will not stand strangers, they are not glad to see any one who comes from abroad. Ships are what they believe in, fast cutters that travel about the open sea; this is the Earthshaker's gift to them. Their ships fly quick as a bird, quick as a thought!"

So Athena prattled on as she led the way briskly. Not a man of them noticed Odysseus as he passed through the people along the street; for Athena had him in her care, and she covered him in a thick mist by her divine power. But Odysseus could see the wonderful sight—the harbours and fine-run ships, the people's meeting-places, the long high walls with their palisade.

When they reached the place, Athena said:

"There is the mansion you asked for, sir. You will find the royal princess feasting away at their feast. Go in and don't

81

be frightened. Dogged does it every day, though you come
from far away. Look for my lady first in the hall. They call
her Arêtê, and she has the same parents as the king.

"You see there was first Nausithoös, the son of Poseidon
Earthshaker and the lovely Periboia, youngest daughter of
Eurymedon king of the furious Giants. Eurymedon destroyed
his own wild people, and he was destroyed with them. But
Poseidon lay with Periboia, and their son was Nausithoös,
King of the Phaiacians. Nausithoös, had two sons, Rhexenor
and Alcinoös. Rhexenor was killed in his own hall by Apollo
with a silver bolt, while he was a young bridegroom and had
no son as yet; but he left an only daughter Arêtê, and Al-
cinoös married her. Alcinoös honoured her as no woman in
the world is honoured by her husband. So she is honoured
still by her husband and children, and the people think her
divine, and cheer her loudly whenever she passes through
the city. Aye, indeed, she has plenty of good sense. If her
friends quarrel, she makes it up, even for men! If she likes
you, there's good hope you may come safe to your tall house
and your native land, and see your own friends at last."

And with these words away went Athena over the barren
sea, and left lovely Scheria behind; to Marathon she passed,
and Athens with its broad streets, and entered the strong
house of Erechtheus.

But Odysseus approached the great mansion. Again and
again he stood still in wonder, before he set foot on the
brazen threshold. For a brightness as of sun or moon filled
the whole place. Round the courtyard, walls of bronze ran
this way and that way, from the threshold to the inner end,
and upon them was a coping of blue enamel; golden doors
and silver doorposts stood on a threshold of bronze, with
silver lintel and golden crowlatch. Golden and silver dogs
were on either side, which Hephaistos had made by his clever
brain to guard the mansion of proud Alcinoös; they were
immortal, and never grew old as the days went by. Within the
hall were seats fixed along the wall on both sides, from the
threshold right to the inner end; and spread over these were
soft coverings of fine-spun stuff which the women had made.
There the leaders of the Phaiacians used to sit, eating and
drinking, for they had plenty which never failed. Golden boys
stood on pedestals of masonry, and held blazing torches in their
hands, which gave light by night in the hall for the feasting.
There were fifty serf-women about the place, some grinding the
apple-yellow grain on the millstone, some weaving their webs
or twisting their yarn as they sat, all a-flutter like aspen leaves

on a tall tree; and there was fine close-woven cloth, with olive oil dripping from it.[1] As much as the Phaiacians surpass other men in skill to drive a swift ship over the deep, so much their women surpass in making of cloth; for Athena has granted them excellent knowledge of fine work and good intelligence.

Outside the courtyard was a great orchard near the gates, four acres; a fence ran round it in both directions. There were tall trees in full luxuriance, pears and pomegranates and apple-trees with glorious fruit, sweet figs and olives. Their fruit never fails or comes to an end all the year round; but the same west wind ever blowing buds one crop and ripens another. Pear after pear grows mellow, apple after apple, fig after fig, vintage after vintage. There was a flourishing vineyard full of fruit. One part of it was a level plot for warming and drying the grapes in the sun; in another part grapes were being gathered, in another men were treading. In front were unripe grapes just shedding the bloom, others were beginning to colour. Beyond the last row of vines were neat beds of all kinds of garden-stuff, ever fresh and green. There were two springs of water; one was led in rills all over the garden, the other ran opposite under the threshold of the courtyard, and came up near the high house; from this the townspeople used to draw their water.

Such were the gods' glorious gifts in the palace of Alcinoös. There Odysseus stood gazing, after all his tribulations. When he had taken it in he crossed the threshold with brisk steps, and entered the hall. He found the lords and rulers of the Phaiacians dropping the libation out of their cups in honour of Hermês Argeïphontês, whom they used to honour the last of all before they went to rest. Odysseus passed through the hall hidden in the mist which Athena spread about him. When he came up to Arêtê and King Alcinoös, he threw his arms about the knees of Arêtê, and in a moment the mist faded away. All fell silent throughout the hall when they saw him, and they stared in surprise, while Odysseus put his petition to the queen:

"Arêtê, daughter of divine Rhexenor! I come in my distress, a suppliant to your husband and to your knees. Yes, and to these who sit at meat; may the gods grant them to be happy while they live, and may each have children to inherit his wealth and the honourable place which the people has given him. Now I beseech you to send me home to my native land without delay, for I have long suffered tribulation far from my friends."

[1] The oil was applied as a part of the finishing.

This said, he sat down upon the hearth in the ashes beside the fire, and silence fell upon all. At last a noble old man spoke, Echeneos, one of the elders of the nation, a notable speaker and one who knew well the traditions of ancient days. In kindness and friendship he spoke:

"Alcinoös, it is not right and proper that a stranger should sit on the ground amid the ashes of the hearth: but we must all wait for you to speak first. Come now, sir, take him by the hand, and raise him up, and lead him to a seat of honour; bid the ushers mix wine, and let us pour our drops to Thundering Zeus, who is always beside a suppliant to win him respect: and let the housewife give the stranger food."

There they were, face to face: the King in his majesty, and the castaway with only his knowledge of man and his ready wit. Alcinoös held out his hand to Odysseus and led him from the hearth to a high seat, where his own son was sitting, near himself, for he loved the courteous Laodamas best of all his sons. He moved his son out of that seat, and placed Odysseus there. A servant brought the handwash, and poured it from a golden jug over a silver basin to rinse his hands; then set a table beside him. A dignified housewife brought bread and laid the table with all sorts of food, and plenty of it. Then the strong man ate and drank after all his troubles. Meanwhile the King called to an usher:

"Pontonoös, mix a bowl, and serve all who are in the hall; and we will pour our drops to Thundering Zeus, who is always beside a suppliant to win him respect."

So Pontonoös mixed the honey-hearted wine, and went round the company pouring the first drops into their cups, which they then poured out on the ground; after this they drank what they wanted, and Alcinoös addressed them.

"Listen to me, my lords and princes of the nation, and let me tell you what I think. You have finished your feasting; now go home to rest, and early in the morning we will call the older men to a full meeting, and entertain the visitor in my hall. We will offer a handsome sacrifice to the gods, and then we will consider his send-off. We must escort him home without trouble or annoyance, and bring him to his native land in contentment without delay, even though it may be far off. On the way we must see to it that he meets no hurt or misfortune until he sets foot in his own country. But after that he will have to suffer whatever his lot may be, whatever the stern spinners spun off their thread for him on the day when his mother brought him forth.

"Or if he is one of the immortals come down from heaven,

then we may take it that this is something new in the gods'
dealings with us. For in time past they have always been in
the way of showing themselves to us face to face when we
perform our solemn sacrifices, dining with us and sitting
along with us in the same place. And even if some solitary
wayfarer meets them, they make no concealment, since we
are very near akin to them, like the Cyclopians and the
savage tribes of Giants."

Odysseus answered readily:

"You need not be anxious about that, Alcinoös. I am not
at all like the immortals who rule the broad heavens, either in
stature or feature, but I am just a mortal man. Those men
whom you know most ridden with affliction would be most
like myself. Aye indeed, I could tell you of more sorrows
than theirs, which I have borne from first to last by the will of
God. Well now, let me dine, in spite of my troubles; for there
is nothing in the world more shameless than this cursed belly!
forces a man to remember it, in spite of dire distress and sorrow
of heart such as the sorrow which is in my heart; yet the belly
commands me to eat and drink, and makes me forget all that I
have suffered, and bids me fill it up. Do your best, I pray you,
early tomorrow, that an unhappy man may return to his own
country after so much suffering. Let me once set eyes on my
lands and my men and my great house, and then let me die."

"Excellent!" they all said, "couldn't be better put! We must
see our visitor safely home." Then they poured out their last
drops, and when they had drunk all they wanted, they went
home to bed.

Now Odysseus was left in the dining-hall, and beside him
sat Arêtê and King Alcinoös; the attendants cleared away
the trappings of the feast. Then Arêtê asked him a question;
for she had recognized the fine tunic and the wrapper which
he wore as soon as she saw them—she had made them herself
with her women, and now she came to the point at once:

"Now, my guest, I will ask the first question myself. Who are
you, and where do you come from? Who gave you these clothes?
Didn't you say you had been drifting about on the sea?"

Odysseus answered readily:

"A hard task, my Queen, to tell the whole story of my
troubles, since the gods who dwell in heaven have given me
many; but I can answer this question easily enough. There is
an island called Ogygia, lying far away in the sea. There lives
the daughter of Atlas, the scheming witch Calypso with her
lovely hair, a terrible being! No one ever visits her, neither
god nor mortal man. But I was her guest, unhappily, as

fortune would have it; all alone, for Zeus had struck my ship with a fiery thunderbolt, and smashed it to pieces on the dark sea. Then all my companions were drowned; but I straddled across the ship's keel and tossed about for nine days. On the tenth black night, the gods brought me to Ogygia, where beautiful Calypso lives, and a terrible creature she is! She rescued me and treated me kindly, loved me and fed me, and promised to make me immortal and never to grow old all my days. But she could not win my heart.

"There I remained seven long years on end, and the imperishable clothes which Calypso gave me were always wet with my tears. But when the eighth year rolled round, she told me to go in a hurry; some message from Zeus, or perhaps she had changed her mind. She sent me off on a raft which I put together, and gave me all sorts of things, bread and delicious mead, and imperishable clothes which she had woven, and sent behind me a warm soft wind. Seventeen days I sailed over the deep; on the eighteenth appeared the shadowy hills of your land, and glad my heart was to see it.

"But bad luck was still to come from Poseidon Earthshaker. He drove the winds against me, and barred my course, and stirred up the infinite sea, so that the waves would not let me get on; and there I sat despairing on my raft. Then the tempest broke it to pieces; and I went swimming across yonder gulf, until wind and water drove me near to your coast. If I had tried to get ashore there, the waves would have crushed me against the face of the cliff, and dashed me upon the rocks in a most unpleasant place; but I sheered off, and went on swimming until I reached a river, which seemed to me a good place to land, with some shelter from the wind and no jagged rocks. I was thrown up gasping for breath, and night came on. Then I got away from the swollen river, and sank down in the bushes, where I scraped up the leaves over me, quite worn out, and God let me fall into a deep sleep. So there under the leaves I slept all night long and through the dawn past midday; sunset hour was coming when sleep left me. Then I noticed your daughter's maids playing about on the beach, and herself with them, like some goddess come down from heaven. I made my prayer to her; she had no lack of good sense, indeed, she had such as you would not expect a young person to show—the young are thoughtless one and all! She gave me bread enough and sparkling wine, and a bath in the river, and she gave me these clothes. There is the true story of an unhappy man."

Alcinoös answered, "I will say this, sir. My girl did not

show good sense at all that she did not bring you home with the waiting-maids. You appealed to her first, after all."

Odysseus had his answer ready:

"My lord, do not blame your girl for that, I pray you; it was not her fault. She did tell me to follow with the maids, but I would not. I was afraid, and bashful too, in case you might be offended to see me there. We men that walk the earth are a touchy generation."

Alcinoös answered:

"Sir, I am not the kind of man to be put out for nothing; it is better to have everything done fairly and squarely. I could wish—if only ye would grant it, Father Zeus and Athenaia and Apollo! I could wish that you, just as you are, with such sympathy between us, would agree to take my daughter and become my son, and stay here! I would give you house and estate, if you would stay willingly—for against your will no one of our nation will keep you: Father Zeus forbid! Do not be anxious.

"You shall have an escort, and I will fix the time for to-morrow. Then you shall just sleep soundly while they row you over the calm sea, until you reach your native land and your home, or anywhere you like, even if it be farther off than Euboia; which our people say is the most distant place there is, those who saw it, when they took golden-head Rhadamanthys to visit Tityos the son of Gaia. They went there, let me tell you, and did the journey without trouble, and came all the way back on the same day! You shall see and know for yourself that my ships and my lads are the best in the world to splash up the brine with their blades!"

Odysseus was glad indeed to hear this, and he prayed aloud, and said:

"Father Zeus, may Alcinoös do all as he has promised! Then his fame would be spread over the whole earth never to be extinguished, and I should come home to my native land."

While they conversed in this manner, Queen Arêtê directed her maids to prepare a bed under the open gallery, to lay upon it fine purple blankets with coverlets, and to provide fleecy wraps for clothing. The maids went out of the hall, torch in hand; and when they had done their task and the bedstead was ready furnished, they came to Odysseus and invited him to go: "Come now, sir; your bed is made." He was quite ready, and glad at the thought of rest.

And so Odysseus slept after all his troubles; but Alcinoös lay down in a recess of the lofty hall, where his lady prepared their bed and lay down by his side.

BOOK VIII
How They Held Games and Sports in Phaiacia

As soon as the first gleams of dawn appeared, King Alcinoös sprang out of bed, and up rose Prince Odysseus. Alcinoös led the way to the parliament square by the quay; and there they sat down on the seats of polished stone, side by side. Meanwhile Pallas Athena took the form of the King's herald, and went up and down in the city to arrange for the convoy of Odysseus; and to every soul she met she spoke, and said, "This way, lords and princes of the nation! To parliament, and you shall hear about the stranger who has lately come to the palace of your wise King, after long travel on the sea, a man who seems like a visitor from heaven!"

This made them all eager and curious to hear. Soon every corner and every seat was full of the gathering people; crowds were there gazing at the stranger. Great dignity was about his head and shoulders, and he looked taller and stronger than before; this was the grace of Athena, who wished that all beholders might fear and respect him, and that he might be ready to do the many feats which the Phaiacians tried him with. When they were all there, Alcinoös addressed the assembly.

"Lend me your ears, my lords and princes of the nation! I have something which I wish to lay before you. The stranger beside me (I do not know who he is), has come in his travels to my house, whether from the east or from the west. He asks us to help him on his way, and begs for a sure promise. Then we, as our ancient manner is, must help him on his way. That is a matter of course, for no one who comes to my house has ever to complain of delay as far as that goes. Very well, we will launch a new ship and choose two-and-fifty of our best oarsmen. Sling the oars ready beside the thwarts and then come ashore, and you shall find a meal ready for you in my house. I will see about that, and there shall be plenty for every one. So much for the lads. You, my lords, all who are here, come up to my house now, and we will entertain our visitor: I will take no denial. And send for the minstrel Demodocos; there is no one like him to make us merry if he is in the mood to sing: a divine gift that is indeed!"

So the King went home with the princes, and a herald summoned the minstrel. Two-and-fifty picked men launched the ship, and put mast and sails aboard, and ran the oars into the leathern thole-slings, all shipshape; then they hoisted the white sail, and moored her in deep water. This work done, they made haste to the palace. All the open galleries, all the courtyards and rooms were full of men. Alcinoös had killed a dozen sheep for them, and eight tusker boars, and two oxen; these were skinned and got ready, and the cooks prepared a most inviting meal.

Now Pontonoös the herald arrived with the minstrel. This man was the Muse's darling, but she had given him evil mixed with good: she took away the sight of his eyes, but she gave him the lovely gift of song. The herald placed a chair of state for him against a tall pillar, and hung up the well-tuned harp on a peg over his head, guiding his hand to touch it. Then he set out a table beside him, with a bread-basket and a cup of wine upon it, in case he wanted a drink.

The guests fell to, and when they had had enough, the spirit moved the minstrel to sing the stories of famous men. He began with that lay which had already become famous all over the world, the quarrel of Odysseus with Achillês; how they wrangled with hot words at a banquet, and how King Agamemnon was delighted; and this was the reason why.

Before the war began, when the storm-clouds were beginning to roll up over Trojans and Danaän by the ordinance of Zeus, Agamemnon had visited the sanctuary of Pytho to inquire of Apollo; and the god had told him that the best men of the army must quarrel, "and then he would take the city of Troy." He thought this was the quarrel, and so he was glad.[1]

So this was the song the minstrel sang. But Odysseus when he heard it caught up his purple robe in his hands, and drew it down over his head, hiding his face; for he was ashamed to let the company see the tears in his eyes. Whenever the singer paused, he would wipe his eyes and throw back his robe, and pour out a few drops to the gods from his cup; but the diners enjoyed it too much to let the singer stop, and as soon as he went on, Odysseus would cover his head again and give way to sorrow. No one noticed him but

[1] This happened at Tenedos before the landing; but the prophecy pointed to the quarrel between Achilles and Agamemnon himself, which is the subject of the *Iliad*.

Alcinoös; but he was sitting next to him and saw what he did, and heard his groans. So at last he spoke:

"Look here, gentlemen! We have had enough of our feast now, enough of banquet's bosom-friend the harp! Let us go out and try our luck at games and sports, that our guest may report to his friends when he gets home how we beat the world at boxing and wrestling and jumping and running!"

At this hint they all got up and went out after him. The herald hung up the harp on its peg, and led our Demodocos after the others. All made haste to the ground, and a huge crowd followed, thousands of them. Young champions were found in plenty [1]: Topship and Quicksea and Paddler, Seaman and Poopman, Beacher and Oarsman, Deepsea and Lookout, Goahead and Upaboard; there was Seagirt the son of Manyclipper Shipwrightson; there was Broadsea, the very spit of bloody Arês himself, and Admiraltidês, the finest man in stature and strength after the admirable Laodamas. And there were three sons of Alcinoös, Laodamas, and deep-sea Halios, and Clytoneos of naval renown.

The first contest was a foot-race. The running was fast from scratch to finish. They went tearing along over the course all in a bunch, except Clytoneos; he was far and away the best, and beat the field by the breadth of the mule's daywork [2] on fallow land.

Next came wrestling, and Broadsea won. At jumping Seagirt was first, the rest nowhere; Paddler was easily first at putting the weight, and in the boxing Laodamas the King's son.

After that good sport, Laodamas said:

"I say, you fellows, let's ask the stranger what he has learnt of games in his schooldays. He is not bad to look at, good thighs and calves and a good pair of arms on him, a strong neck, hefty and not too old, but he's broken down with hardships. I declare there's nothing worse than the sea to wear a man out, however strong he may be."

Broadsea answered, "Excellent! You go and make the proposal, challenge him yourself."

So Laodamas went forward, and said to Odysseus:

"Come along, father, have a try at the games yourself, if you ever learnt 'em. A man ought to know about games. Game is the best way to fame while you're still alive—

_____
[1] All these names are invented to suit the seafaring islanders.

[2] The furrows were of one length; but mules did more than oxen, so the headland, or breadth of the plowed piece, was longer.

what you can do with your arms and legs. Come along, have
a try; begone dull care! You haven't long to wait now, your
ship is afloat and the crew ready."

Odysseus answered:

"Why do you say that, Laodamas? You are all making fun
of me. My mind is more set on troubles than on games.
Suffering and sorrow is what I have had so far; I am here in
your gathering only as a suppliant to your King and people,
and all I want is to get home."

But Broadsea thought he would get a rise out of him, and
said:

"Ah well, sir, I would not put you down as a fellow who
goes in for games, though that is the way of the world,
you know; skipper of a trading crew is what you look like,
plying in a broad hooker, thinking of cargo, keeping an
eye on the goods and grabbing what profits you can. You
certainly have not the look of a sportsman."

Odysseus said with a frown:

"Sir, I do not like your way of speaking. We know the gods
do not grant all the graces to any man, handsome looks
and good sense and eloquence together. One man is not much
to look at, but God crowns his words with beauty, so that all
may listen to him with delight; he speaks in a steady voice
with winning modesty, he is notable where men gather to-
gether, and as he walks through the streets all gaze upon him
as one inspired. Another, again, may be handsome as a young
god, but there is no crown of grace upon his words. So you
are as handsome as God could make a man, but your mind
is empty. You have made me angry by your bad manners.
I am no duffer in sports, as you say, but I think I was among
the first while I could trust in my youth and my hands. Now
I am tired and worn out with perils in battle and perils of
the sea. Well, never mind that; I will try my hand. You
have cut me to the quick, and I cannot sit still any longer."

He sprang up, cloak and all, and seized a huge big weight,
far heavier than any the young men had been using, and
with one whirl round his head he cast it strongly. The stone
went whizzing through the air, and all the stout seamen
standing by crouched down as they felt the wind of it. Over
all the marks of the others it flew like a bird. The man
marking the throws was really Athena, and she called out:

"A blind man could find your mark, stranger, by fumbling!
It's a long way out of the crowd. You need not worry—no
one will reach it, much less beat it!"

Odysseus was pleased to find a real friend on the ground. So he said gaily enough:

"Touch that if you can, young men! If you do, I think I'll follow it up with another as good or better. Has any one else a mind for something? Out with you then, and take me on. You have put my back up, and I don't care what it is —box, wrestle, run, any one you like except only Laodamas. He is my host, and who would fight with a kind friend? I call that man a good-for-nothing fool, who would set up to rival his host at a game in a foreign land; he is docking his own tail. Any one else, I say, no one barred, any one is good enough—I'll try a bout with him, man to man. I am not a bad hand at any game that's going. I know well how to handle a smooth bow; I can pick off my man first out of the enemy ranks, if there are heaps of my comrades shooting at the fellows. Only one man beat me before Troy with bow and arrows, and that was Philoctetês. As for all the men who now eat bread on the face of the earth, I say I am better than any of them. But not the characters of ancient history; I should not care to match myself against Heraclês, or Eurytos the Oichalian, who dared to stand up to the immortals. That is why Eurytos never lived to grow old. He challenged Apollo to a shooting-match, and Apollo was angry and killed him. As for javelins, I'll throw one as far as you can shoot an arrow. I am afraid of nothing but the foot-race. Some one might beat me there, for the sea has been too much for me; there is no great comfort aboard ship, and my sinews are all slack."

All were silent at this; but after a while Alcinoös spoke for the rest.

"My dear sir, you do not offend us by your frankness. You are quite right to stand up for yourself when some one sneers at you as this man did. You make it quite clear that no one who can talk sense could ever question your powers. But now let *me* say a word, please. We are anxious that you should take away a pleasant memory of our performances; we have our own powers, you know, which Zeus graciously gave to our fathers, and they handed down to us. When you are at home again and sitting at dinner in your hall with your wife and children, we hope you will remember us and tell them the story. The truth is, we are not first-rate boxers or wrestlers, but we are fine oarsmen and the best of seamen; our delight is in feasting, in music, and dancing, plenty of clean linen, a warm bath, and bed! Come now, out with the best of our dancers! Let our friend have something to tell his friends when he gets home—how we beat the whole world at shipwork and footwork, dancing and song! Fetch the harp, some one, off with you on the spot, and give it to Demodocos! It is somewhere in the house."

No sooner said than done: away went the herald to fetch the harp. The stewards appeared, nine men appointed to be masters of the ceremonies: they cleared the ground and made a good tidy ring. Then the herald brought the harp for Demodocos, and he stept into the middle. Groups of blooming boys circled about him, footing it round and tapping the ground. Odysseus was fairly amazed to see their twinkling feet.

The harper struck up a tune, and sang the loves of Arês and Aphroditê. He told how first they lay secretly in the house of Hephaistos himself. Arês brought her many gifts, and dishonoured the bed of Lord Hephaistos; but before long Helios the sun came and told him that he had seen them lying in a loving embrace. Hephaistos heard the cruel tale, and straight to the smithy he went with a plan of vengeance in his heart.

He set the great anvil on the stand, and forged chains that could not be broken or loosed, to hold the pair immovable. When he had fashioned this net for Arês in his hot anger, he took it to the bedchamber, and fastened the meshes over the bedposts and down from the roof-beams, network fine as a spider's web, which no eye could see, not even the blessed gods themselves; a masterpiece of clever work.

As soon as he had draped the cunning net to perfection, he made as if he were going to Lemnos, for he loved that noble city best of all. But Arês kept no blind man's watch. He saw the mastercraftsman going away; he made haste to the house of the famous smith, eager for the love of garlanded Cythereia.

She had just come in from Almighty Cronion her father, and there she was sitting in the house when he entered. He clasped her hand, and said:

"Come, my love, let us to bed and take our joy! Hephaistos is not in the place, but I think he is gone already to Lemnos, to hear the barbarous talk of those Sintians!"

She was filled with joy at the thought, and they lay down on the bed. Then the craftsman's clever net closed round them, and they could neither move nor lift a limb: at last they knew there was no chance of escape. Hephaistos was close by all the time, and now he came hobbling along; he had turned back before he came to Lemnos, for Helios had been on the look-out and told him what had happened. He stood in the doorway, with fury in his heart; he roared aloud and called to the gods one and all:

"Father Zeus and all you blessed gods who live for ever! come this way, and see a fine joke! an intolerable piece of impudence! Because I am lame, this daughter of Zeus, this Aphroditê, for ever treats me with contempt; she loves this murderous Arês because he is handsome and has two sound feet on him, and I was born a cripple! Why blame me? It is my parents' fault, not mine, and I wish I had never been born at all! But you shall see where the loving pair are sleeping, on my own bed! It makes me sore to see that. Well, I don't think they will care to lie like that one little minute more, fond lovers though they are. Before long they won't want to sleep, neither one nor the other; but there my ingenious arts will keep them, until her father pays back my marriage gifts, every jot, all I paid for the sake of this bitch because she was a pretty girl! But she does not know how to behave herself."

At this call the gods crowded to the smith's house; up came Earthshaker Poseidon, up came Hermeias Eriunios, up came Apollo, Prince of Archers; but the goddesses were too modest and stayed at home. There stood the Dispensers of all Blessings at the door; a roar of unquenchable laughter rose from the blessed gods to see the skill of Hephaistos the master-craftsman.

You might have heard them say to one another, "Honesty is the best policy! Slow catches quick, as now slow old Hephaistos has caught Arês, the quickest god in Olympos; the lame dog wins by his wits. Now there's damages due to the cuckold!"

Amid this kind of banter, Prince Apollo son of Zeus said to Hermês:

"My dear Hermeias son of Zeus, King's Messenger, Dispenser of blessings! Would you like to sleep with golden Aphroditê and have that strong net smothering you close all round?"

King's Messenger Argeiphontês answered:

"I only wish I could, my dear Lord Apollo Prince of Archers! Wrap round me three nets like that, with no way out, all you gods look on and all the goddesses too, I would sleep with golden Aphroditê!"

The gods burst into laughter at this. Only Poseidon did not laugh, but just begged the famous craftsman to let Arês go. "Let him go," he said, "and I give you my word, as you ask, that he shall pay all that is justly due in the presence of the immortal gods."

But the famous Crookshank God answered him: "Do not ask me that, Poseidon Earthshaker. Go bail for a cheat, and he'll cheat you out of your bail! How can I put *you* in the net, if Arês gets out of net and debt together?"

To this Poseidon Earthshaker made reply:

"Hephaistos, if Arês gets out of his debt and shows a clean pair of heels, I will pay you the debt myself."

Then the famous Crookshank God gave answer, "I cannot and I must not refuse your offer."

So Hephaistos, angry still, undid the net. Once free from the inextricable bonds, the two were off like a shot—he to Thrace, and she to Cyprus, smiling broadly, away to Paphos and her temple and altar of incense. There the Graces bathed her and rubbed her with oil divine, such as the deathless gods refresh themselves with; and they clothed her in lovely garments, a wonder to behold.

So sang the famous singer; Odysseus was delighted as he listened, and no less that whole nation of seafaring men.

Alcinoös next told Halios and Laodamas to dance alone, since no one wished to compete with them. So they took in hand a fine purple ball, one of the clever works of Polybos. One of them would bend his body backwards and throw up the ball into the clouds; the other would jump high and catch it lightly in the air before his feet touched the ground again. After throwing it straight up in this way, they danced on the level ground, throwing the ball one to the other again and again: the lads beat time standing round the ring, with clapping hands. At this Odysseus said to Alcinoös:

"My lord Alcinoös, you boasted that your artists of the dance were the best, and here it is really before us! I am amazed at the sight of them!"

This delighted the royal prince, and he called out at once to the company:

"Do you hear that, my lords and gentlemen all? Our guest seems to be a man of mighty good sense! Come now, let us give him the stranger's due as is right and proper. We have twelve distinguished princes who rule over our people, thirteen with myself. Each of you bring him a mantle newly washed and a tunic, and a nugget of fine gold. Let us make haste and get these together, that our guest may have them in hand and go in happy to his dinner. And Broadsea must

make his peace with a gift and an apology, since he was rude
to him just now."

The princes applauded this; each did his part and sent
his marshal to fetch the gifts. Broadsea too said:

"My lord Alcinoös, surely I will make my peace with our
guest, as you bid me. I offer him this sword of bronze with a
silver hilt, and a new sheath of ivory to hold it: this ought
to make amends for a good deal."

Then he placed in the stranger's hand the sword with its
knobs of silver, and said simply, "I salute you, father! If
I have blurted out an ugly word, may the winds carry it
away! May the gods grant you to come safe to your native
land, and see your wife, after all your long sufferings far
from your friends!"

Odysseus answered, "I wish you well also, my friend. May
the gods give you happiness, and may you never miss the
sword which you have given me with this handsome speech."

Saying this he slung the sword over his shoulder.

The sun went down, and the gifts were all there. The serv-
ants carried them in, and the King's sons laid the magnificent
gifts before their honoured mother. Soon the others came in
led by Alcinoös and took their seats. Then Alcinoös said
to Arêtê:

"My dear, bring out the best coffer we have, and lay in
it a newly-washed mantle and a tunic. Warm a copper over
the fire and get hot water for him to bathe: after that he
may see all the gifts of our excellent princes laid neatly out,
and have a good dinner with music and song. And I offer
him this goblet of wine, a real beauty, pure gold, that he
may remember me all his days, as he pours the sacred drops
in his hall to Zeus and All Gods."

Accordingly Arêtê directed her women to set a large
tripod over the fire at once. They put a copper over the
blazing fire, poured in the water and put the firewood under-
neath. While the fire was shooting up all round the belly of
the copper, and the water was growing warm, Arêtê brought
out a handsome coffer from her room and laid all the gifts
in it, clothes and gold, which had been collected: and she
added, a mantle and a fine tunic, and said to Odysseus:

"Look to the lid yourself, and fasten it quickly, that no
one may do any damage on the way while you are sleeping
soundly on board ship!"

Odysseus at once fitted on the lid, and fastened it up with
an intricate knot which Circê had taught him. Then the
housewife told him his bath was ready. Glad indeed he was

to see the warm water, for he had had little comfort since he left the house of beautiful Calypso, but there he was treated right royally and lived like a god. So the woman bathed him and rubbed him with oil, and put a tunic and a fine robe on him, and he passed from the bath to the feasting company.

As he went in, by the doorpost of the hall stood Nausicaä, looking as lovely as if she had stepped down from heaven. She gazed with admiring eyes at Odysseus, while she said:

"I wish you a happy voyage, sir, and I hope you may sometimes remember me when you are in your native land, since you owe me first the ransom of your life."

Odysseus answered: "Princess Nausicaä, the sea-king's daughter! If only Zeus Thunderer will grant me once more to see my home and my native land, then be sure I will ever remember you in my prayers, for you gave me life, dear girl."

He passed on and found his seat by the side of King Alcinoös. They were already serving out the portions and mixing the wine. A marshal led in Demodocos, their excellent minstrel whom the people honoured: he placed his seat in the midst of the guests, with its back to a tall pillar. Then Odysseus called to the man, as he cut out first a piece of boar's chine which had been given to him (and more was left behind with plenty of fat on both sides), "Here, marshal, take this to Demodocos, and give him my kindest wishes. For in every nation of mankind upon the earth minstrels have honour and respect, since the Muse has taught them their songs, and she loves them, one and all."

The marshal took the slice and set it before Demodocos, who accepted it with great satisfaction. Then they all fell to. When they had eaten and drunk as much as they wanted, Odysseus called out:

"Demodocos, I commend you above all mortal men! You must have been taught by the Muse, the daughter of Zeus, or by Apollo, his son. For you sing only too well the fate of the Achaians, all they did and suffered and the hardships they went through, just as if you had been there yourself, or heard it from one who had. Now change the tune, and sing the contrivance of the Wooden Horse; how Epeios made it with the help of Athena, and Odysseus brought it into the citadel by way of stratagem, full of the men who sacked Ilion. Then if you tell the story aright, I will declare at once to all the world that God has been generous to you and inspired your song."

Then the inspired minstrel delivered his song. He began

where the Achaians embarked in the fleet and sailed away, after setting fire to their encampment: but by that time the illustrious Odysseus, and those with him, hidden in the Horse, were in the market-place of the city, for the Trojans themselves dragged it into their citadel. There stood the Horse, there stood the people all round, doubtful what to do. Three plans found some favour: to break up the wood with axes; or to drag it away and cast it down from the rock; or to leave it as an offering to appease the gods. This last plan was taken in the end; for it was their fate to perish when the city should admit that great Wooden Horse, with all the best men of the invading host within it to bring ruin and destruction upon Troy. He sang how the sons of Achaia left their lair and poured out of the Horse and laid waste the city. He sang how they went this way and that way sacking the place, and Odysseus came to the house of Deïphobos like another god of war, along with royal Menelaos. That was the most dangerous of all his battles, so the minstrel said, and won after all by the help of Athena.

So sang the famous minstrel. Odysseus was melted, and tears ran over his cheeks. He wept as a woman weeps with her arms about a beloved husband, who has fallen in front of his people, fighting to keep the day of ruin from city and children; when she sees him panting and dying, she throws her arms around him and wails aloud, but the enemies behind her beat her about the back and shoulders with their spears, and drag her away into slavery, where labour and sorrow will be her lot and her cheeks will grow thin with pining. No one else noticed his tears, but Alcinoös saw clearly enough, sitting by his side, and heard his sobs. At once he called out to the company:

"Listen to me, my lords and gentlemen. It is time for Demodocos to quiet his harp. Not every one is pleased by the song. Ever since he began to sing at this supper, our guest has been grieving: his heart must be full of sorrow. Well then, let the man stop, that we may all be merry, host and guest alike, which is much the best thing. All this has been arranged in honour of our guest, food and escort and friendly gifts, which we offer in good will. Stranger or suppliant stands in a brother's place to any man who has a touch of good feeling.

"And you too, sir, don't be so reserved, don't try to hide what I ask you; to speak out is the best thing. Tell me what name you go by at home, what your mother and father call you, and the people of your town, and your neighbours all around. No one on the whole world is without a name, high or low; his parents give him some name as soon as he is born. Tell me your country and people, and your city, that our ships may aim at the right place in their minds. For we Phaiacians have no pilots; our ships have no steering-gear, like other ships, but they understand of themselves the thoughts and intentions of the seamen; they know all the cities and countries in the world, and cross the gulf of the sea at full speed, hidden in clouds and mist. There is no fear they will ever come to harm or be lost.

"I will tell you what I heard from my father Nausithoös. He said that Poseidon would be jealous of us one day, because we give safe convoy to all. One day, he said, Poseidon would smash one of our ships coming back from convoy in a fog, and he would throw a high mountain round our city. So the old gentleman said: 'God can do it or not do it as it shall please him.'

"Now tell me all about your travels, what countries you have visited, what cities of civilized men; tell us who are savages and lawless men, who are hospitable and godfearing. And tell us why you are so unhappy when you hear the fate of Argives and Danaäns and the fall of Troy. All that was the gods' doing; their thread of destruction which they spun for men, to make songs for future generations. Perhaps a kinsman of yours died before Ilion, some good man and true, your goodson or your goodfather, who come closest to us after our own blood. Or perhaps a friend, a man dear to you, a good man? For a comrade and a decent fellow is indeed no less than a brother."

BOOK IX

How Odysseus Visited the Lotus-eaters and the Cyclops

Then Odysseus began his tale:

"What a pleasure it is, my lord," he said, "to hear a singer like this, with a divine voice! I declare it is just the perfection of gracious life: good cheer and good temper everywhere, rows of guests enjoying themselves heartily and listening to the music, plenty to eat on the table, wine ready in the great bowl, and the butler ready to fill your cup whenever you want it. I think that is the best thing men can have.— But you have a mind to hear my sad story, and make me more unhappy than I was before. What shall I begin with, what shall I end with? The lords of heaven have given me sorrow in abundance.

"First of all I will tell you my name, and then you may count me one of your friends if I live to reach my home, although that is far away. I am Odysseus Laërtiadês, a name well known in the world as one who is ready for any event. My home is Ithaca, that bright conspicuous isle, with Mount Neriton rising clear out of the quivering forests. Round it lie many islands clustering close, Dulichion and Samê and woody Zacynthos. My island lies low, last of all in the sea to westward, the others away towards the dawn and the rising sun. It is rough, but a nurse of good lads; I tell you there is no sweeter sight any man can see than his own country. Listen now: a radiant goddess Calypso tried to keep me by her in her cave, and wanted me for a husband; Circê also would have had me stay in her mansion, and a clever creature she was, and she also wanted me for a husband, but she never could win my heart. How true it is that nothing is sweeter than home and kindred, although you may have a rich house in a foreign land far away from your kindred! Ah well, but you are waiting to hear of my journey home, and all the sorrows which Zeus laid upon me after I left Troy.

"From Ilion the wind carried me to Ismaros of the Ciconians. There I destroyed the city and killed the men. We spared the women and plenty of cattle and goods, which we divided to give each man a fair share. I told the men we must show a light heel and be off, but the poor fools would not listen.

Plenty of wine was drunk, plenty of sheep were killed on that beach, and herds of cattle! Meanwhile some of the enemy got away and shouted to other Ciconians, neighbours of their inland, more men and better men, who knew how to fight from the chariot against a foe, and on foot if need be.

"A multitude of these men swarmed down early in the morning, as many as leaves and flowers in the season of the year. Surely Zeus sent us a hard fate that day, to bring trouble on a lot of poor devils! They drew up near the ships, and then came volleys on both sides. All through the morning while the day grew stronger we stood our ground and held them off, although they outnumbered us; but when the sun began to change course, about ox-loosing time,[1] the Ciconians got the upper hand and bent our line. Six men-at-arms from each vessel were killed; and the rest of us were saved alive.

"From that place we sailed onward much discouraged, but glad to have escaped death, although we had lost good companions. Yet we did not let the galleys go off, until we had called thrice on the name of each of our hapless comrades who died in that place. But Zeus Cloudgatherer sent a norwester upon our fleet with a furious tempest, bringing clouds over land and sea; and night rushed down from the sky. The ships were blown plunging along, the sails were split into shreds and tatters by the violence of the wind. We let down the sails in fear of death, and rowed the bare hulls to shore. There we lay two days and two nights on end, eating out our hearts with hardship and anxiety. But when the third day showed welcome streaks of light, we stept the masts and hoisted new sails, and sat still, while the wind drove us on and the steersman held the way. Then I might have come safe to my native land, but the sea and the current and the north-west wind caught me as I was doubling Cape Malea, and drifted me outside Cythera.

"Nine days after that I was beaten about on the sea by foul winds, and on the tenth day we made land in the country of the lotus-eaters, who get their food from flowers.[2] We went ashore and took in water, and the men made their meal on the spot close to the ships. When we had eaten and drunk, I sent some of them to find out who the natives were: two picked men with a speaker. Before long they came across some of the lotus-eaters. However, they did no harm to the

---

[1] About noon, when the day's plowing is done.

[2] Not the lotus grass, but some kind of berry like a small date or poppy-pod.

men, only gave them some of their lotus to eat. As soon as they tasted that honey-sweet fruit, they thought no more of coming back to us with news, but chose rather to stay there with the lotus-eating natives, and chew their lotus, and good-bye to home. I brought them back to the ships by main force, grumbling and complaining, and when I had them there, tied them up and stowed them under the benches. Then I ordered the rest to hurry up and get aboard, for I did not want them to have a taste of lotus and say good-bye to home. They were soon on board and sitting on their benches, and rowing away over the sea.

"From that place we sailed on in low spirits. We came next to the Cyclopians, the Goggle-eyes, a violent and law-less tribe. They trust to providence, and neither plant nor plow, but everything grows without sowing or plowing; wheat and barley and vines, which bear grapes in huge bunches, and the rain from heaven makes them grow of themselves. These Cyclopians have no parliament for debates and no laws, but they live on high mountains in hollow caves; each one lays down the law for wife and children, and no one cares for his neighbours.

"Now a low flat island lies across their harbour, not very near the land and not very far, covered with trees. In this are an infinite number of wild goats, for no man walks there to scare them away, and no hunters frequent the place to follow their toilsome trade in the forests and the hills. So it has neither flocks nor tillage; but unsown and unplowed, un-trodden of men, it feeds the bleating goats. For the Goggle-eyes have no ships with their crimson cheeks, and no ship-wrights among them, to build boats for them to row in and visit the cities of the world, like men who traverse the seas on their lawful occasions. Such craftsmen might have civi-lized the island: for it is not a bad island. It could produce all the kindly fruits of the earth; there are meadows along the shore, soft land with plenty of water; there might be no end of grapes. There is smooth land for the plow; the soil is very rich, and they might always stack a good harvest in the season of the year. There is a harbour with easy riding; no cable is wanted, no anchor-stones or stern-hawsers. You just beach your ship, and stay till the sailors have a fancy to go and the wind blows fair. Moreover, at the head of the har-bour there is glorious water, a spring running out of a cave, with poplars growing all round.

"Some providence guided us in through the dark night, with not a thing to be seen; for a thick mist was about our ships, and the moon showed no light through the clouds. At that time we did not catch a glimpse of the island: indeed we saw no long breakers rolling towards the land, before our ships ran up on the beach. When they were safe there, we lowered the sails and got out on the shore, and slept heavily until the dawn.

"As soon as dawn gleamed through the mist, we roamed about and admired the island. Then those kindly daughters of Zeus, the Nymphs, sent down goats from the hills to give us all a good meal. We lost no time, got our bows and long spears out of the ships, divided into three bands, and let fly at the quarry. Very soon God gave us as much as we wanted. I had twelve ships with me, and nine goats were given to each by lot, but ten were picked out for me alone. So all day long we sat there feasting, with plenty of meat and delicious wine. For the good red wine was not all used up yet, but some was left; when we took the Ciconian city, each crew had supplied themselves with plenty in large two-handled jars. We gazed at the country of the Goggle-eyes, which was quite close; we could see the smoke and hear the bleating of sheep and goats. When the sun set and darkness came, we lay down on the beach to sleep.

"But with the first rosy streaks of the dawn, I called a meeting and made a speech to the men. 'My good fellows,' I said, 'the rest of you stay here, while I take my ship and crew and see who these people are; whether they are wild savages who know no law, or hospitable men who know right from wrong.'

"So I went aboard and told my crew to cast loose; they were soon in their places and rowing along. The land was not far off, and when we reached it we saw a cave there on a headland close by the sea, high and shaded with laurels, in which numbers of animals were housed by night, both sheep and goats. Outside was an enclosure with high walls round it, made of great stones dug into the earth and the trunks of tall pines and spreading oaks. These were the night-quarters of a monstrous man, who was then tending his flocks a long way off by himself; he would not mix with the others, but kept apart in his own lawless company. Indeed he was a wonderful monster, not like a mortal man who eats bread, but rather like a mountain peak with trees on the top standing up alone in the highlands.

"Then I told the rest of my men to wait for me and look after the ship, but I picked out twelve of the best men I had, and we set out. I took with me a goatskin of ruby wine, de-

licious wine, which I had from Maron Euanthidês, priest of
Apollo who was the protecting god of Ismaros. We had saved
him and his wife and child out of reverence, because he
lived in the sacred grove of Phoibos Apollo. I had glorious
gifts from him: he gave me seven talents' weight of worked
gold, he gave me a mixing-bowl of solid silver, but besides
that, he gave me great jars of wine, a whole dozen of them,
delicious wine, not a drop of water in it, a divine drink! Not
a soul knew about this wine, none of the servants or women,
except himself and his own wife and one cellarer. When
they drank of this wine, he used to pour one cup of it into
twenty measures of water, and a sweet scent was diffused
abroad from the mixer, something heavenly; no one wanted
to be an abstainer then! I had filled a skin with this wine,
and brought it with me, also a bag of provisions; for from
the first I had a foreboding that I should meet a man of
mighty strength, but savage, knowing neither justice nor
law.

"We walked briskly to the cave, but found him not at
home; he was tending his fat flocks on the pasture. So we en-
tered the cave and took a good look all round. There were
baskets loaded with cheeses, there were pens stuffed full of
lambs and kids. Each lot was kept in a separate place; first-
lings in one, middlings in another, yeanlings in another.
Every pot and pan was swimming with whey, all the pails
and basins into which he did the milking. The men begged
me first to let them help themselves to the cheeses and be off;
next they wanted to make haste and drive the kids and lambs
out of the pens and get under sail. But I would not listen—
indeed it would have been much better if I had! but I wanted
to see himself and claim the stranger's gift. As it turned out,
he was destined to be anything but a vision of joy to my
comrades.

"So we lit a fire and made our thank-offering, and helped
ourselves to as many cheeses as we wanted to eat; then we
sat inside till he should come back with his flocks. At last in
he came, carrying a tremendous load of dry wood to give
light for supper. This he threw down inside the cave with a
crash that terrified us, and sent us scurrying into the corners.
Then he drove his fat flocks into the cave, that is to say, all
he milked, leaving the rams and billy-goats outside the cave
but within the high walls of the enclosure. Then he picked
up a huge great stone and placed it in the doorway: not two
and twenty good carts with four wheels apiece could have

lifted it off the ground,[1] such was the size of the precipitous rock which he planted in front of the entrance. Then he sat down and milked the goats and ewes, bleating loudly, all in order, and put her young under each. Next he curdled half of the white milk and packed it into wicker baskets, leaving the other half to stand in bowls, that he might have some to drink for supper or whenever he wanted. At last after all this busy work, he lighted the fire and saw us.

" 'Who are you?' he called out. 'Where do you come from over the watery ways? Are you traders, or a lot of pirates ready to kill and be killed, bringing trouble to foreigners?'

"While he spoke, our hearts were wholly broken within us to see the horrible monster, and to hear that beastly voice. But I managed to answer him:

" 'We are Achaians from Troy, driven out of our course over the broad sea by all the winds of heaven. We meant to sail straight home, but we have lost our way altogether: such was the will of Zeus, I suppose. We have the honour to be the people of King Agamemnon Atreidês, whose fame is greatest of all men under the sky, for the strong city he sacked and the many nations he conquered. But we have found you, and come to your knees, to pray if you will give us the stranger's due or anything you may think proper to give to a stranger. Respect the gods, most noble sir; see, we are your suppliants! Strangers and suppliants have their guardian strong, God walks with them to see they get no wrong.'

"He answered me with cruel words: 'You are a fool, stranger, or you come from a long way off, if you expect me to fear gods. Zeus Almighty be damned and his blessed gods with him. We Cyclopians care nothing for them, we are stronger than they are. I should not worry about Zeus if I wanted to lay hands on you or your companions. But tell me, where did you moor your ship—far off or close by? I should be glad to know that.'

"He was just trying it on, but I knew something of the world, and saw through it; so I answered back, 'My ship was wrecked by Poseidon Earthshaker, who cast us on the rocks near the boundary of your country; the wind drove us on a lee shore. But I was saved with these others.'

"The cruel monster made no answer, but just jumped up and reached out towards my men, grabbed two like a pair of

[1] This is a parody of the common phrase which describes how "two good men" could not have lifted a certain stone. So with "precipitous rock," used of cliffs and mountains.

puppies and dashed them on the ground: their brains ran out and soaked into the earth. Then he cut them up limb by limb, and made them ready for supper. He devoured them like a mountain lion, bowels and flesh and marrow-bones, and left nothing. We groaned aloud, lifting our hands to Zeus, when we saw this brutal business; but there was nothing to be done.

"When Goggle-eye had filled his great belly with his meal of human flesh, washed down with a draught of milk neat, he lay and stretched himself among the sheep. But I did not lose heart. I considered whether to go near and draw my sharp sword and drive it into his breast; I could feel about till I found the place where the midriff encloses the liver. But second thoughts kept me back. We should have perished ourselves in that place, dead and done for; we could never have moved the great stone which he had planted in the doorway. So we lay groaning and awaited the dawn.

"Dawn came. He lit the fire, milked his flocks, all in order, put the young under each, then he grabbed two more men and prepared his breakfast. That done, he drove out the fat flocks, moving away the great stone with ease; but he put it back again, just as you fit cover to quiver. With many a whistle Goggle-eye turned his fat flocks to the hills; but I was left brooding and full of dark plans, longing to have my revenge if Athena would grant my prayer.

"Among all my schemes and machinations, the best plan I could think of was this. A long spar was lying beside the pen, a sapling of green olive-wood; Goggle-eye had cut it down to dry it and use as a staff. It looked to us about as large as the mast of a twenty-oar ship, some broad hoy that sails the deep sea; it was about that length and thickness. I cut off a fathom of this, and handed it over to my men to dress down. They made it smooth, then I sharpened the end and charred it in the hot fire, and hid it carefully under the dung which lay in a great mass all over the floor. Then I told the others to cast lots who should help me with the pole and rub it into his eye while he was sound asleep. The lot fell on those four whom I would have chosen myself, which made five counting me.

"In the evening, back he came with his flocks. This time he drove them all into the cave, and left none outside in the yard; whether he suspected something, or God made him do it, I do not know. Then he lifted the great stone and set it in place, sat down and milked his ewes and nannies bleating loudly, all in order, put her young under each, and when all this was done, grabbed two more men and made his meal.

"At this moment I came near to Goggle-eye, holding in my hand an ivy-wood cup full of the red wine, and I said:

"'Cylops, here, have a drink after that jolly meal of mans-mutton! I should like to show you what drink we had on board our ship. I brought it as a drink-offering for you, in the hope that you might have pity and help me on my way home. But you are mad beyond all bearing! Hard heart, how can you expect any other men to pay you a visit? For you have done what is not right.'

"He took it and swallowed it down. The good stuff delighted him terribly, and he asked for another drink:

"'Oh, please give me more, and tell me your name this very minute! I will give you a stranger's gift which will make you happy! Mother earth does give us wine in huge bunches, even in this part of the world, and the rain from heaven makes them grow; but this is a rivulet of nectar and ambrosia!'

"Then I gave him a second draught. Three drinks I gave him; three times the fool drank. At last, when the wine had got into his head, I said to him in the gentlest of tones:

"'Cyclops, do you ask me my name? Well, I will tell you, and you shall give me the stranger's due, as you promised. Noman is my name; Noman is what mother and father call me and all my friends.'

"Then the cruel monster said, 'Noman shall be last eaten of his company, and all the others shall be eaten before him! that shall be your stranger's gift.'

"As he said this, down he slipt and rolled on his back. His thick neck drooped sideways, and all-conquering sleep laid hold on him; wine dribbled out of his gullet with lumps of human flesh, as he belched in his drunken slumbers. Then I drove the pole deep under the ashes to grow hot, and spoke to hearten my men that no one might fail me through fear.

"As soon as the wood was on the point of catching fire, and glowed white-hot, green as it was, I drew it quickly out of the fire while my men stood round me: God breathed great courage into us then. The men took hold of the stake, and thrust the sharp point into his eye; and I leaned hard on it from above and turned it round and round. As a man bores a ship's timber with an auger, while others at the lower part keep turning it with a strap which they hold at each end, and round and round it runs: so we held the fire-sharpened pole and turned it, and the blood bubbled about its hot point. The fumes singed eyelids and eyelashes all about as the eyeball

burnt and the roots crackled in the fire. As a smith plunges
an axe or an adze in cold water, for that makes the strength
of steel, and it hisses loud when he tempers it, so his eye
sizzled about the pole of olive-wood.

"He gave a horrible bellow till the rocks rang again, and
we shrank away in fear. Then he dragged out the post from
his eye dabbled and dripping with blood, and threw it from
him, wringing his hands in wild agony, and roared aloud to
the Cyclopians who lived in caves round about among the
windy hills. They heard his cries, and came thronging from
all directions, and stood about the cave, asking what his
trouble was:

" 'What on earth is the matter with you, Polyphemos?' they
called out. 'Why do you shout like this through the night
and wake us all us? Is any man driving away your flocks
against your will? Is any one trying to kill you by craft or
main force?'

"Out of the cave came the voice of mighty Polyphemos: 'O
my friends, Noman is killing me by craft and not by main
force!'

"They answered him in plain words:

" 'Well, if no man is using force, and you are alone, there's
no help for a bit of sickness when heaven sends it; so you had
better say your prayers to Lord Poseidon your father!'

"With these words away they went, and my heart laughed
within me, to think how a mere nobody had taken them all
in with my machinomanations! [1]

"But the Cyclops, groaning and writhing in agony, fumbled
about with his hands until he found the stone and pushed it
away from the entrance. There he sat with his hands out-
spread to catch any one who tried to go out with the animals.
A great fool he must have thought me! But I had been casting
about what to do for the best, if I could possibly find some
escape from death for my comrades and myself. All kinds of
schemes and machinations I wove in my wits, for it was life
or death, and perdition was close by. The plan that seemed
to me best was this. The rams were well grown, large and fine,
with coats of rich dark wool. In dead silence I tied them
together with twisted withies, which the monster used for his
bed. I tied them in threes, with a man under the middle one,
while the two others protected him on each side. So three

---

[1] There is a subtle punning not only with οὔτις and οὔτις, which
differ by accent alone (of course this was clearly distinguished in
speech), but with μῆτις and μῆτις.

carried each of our fellows; but for myself—there was one great ram, the finest of the whole flock; I threw my arms over his back, and curled myself under his shaggy belly, and there I lay turned upwards, with only my hands to hold fast by the wonderful fleece in patience. So we all waited anxiously for the dawn.

"At last the dawn came. The rams and billies surged out to pasture, but the nannies and ewes unmilked went bleating round the pens; for their udders were full to bursting. Their master still tormented with pain felt over the backs of all the animals as they passed out; but the poor fool did not notice how my men were tied under their bellies. Last of all the great ram stalked to the door, cumbered with the weight of his wool and of me and my teeming mind. Polyphemos said as he pawed him over:

" 'Hullo, why are you last to-day, you lazy creature? It is not your way to let them leave you behind! No, no, you go first by a long way to crop the fresh grass, stepping high and large, first to drink at the river, first all eagerness to come home in the evening; but now last! Are you sorry perhaps for your master's eye, which a damned villain has blinded with his cursed companions, after he had fuddled me with wine? Noman! who hasn't yet escaped the death in store for him, I tell him that! If you only had sense like me, if you could only speak, and tell me where the man is skulking from my vengeance! Wouldn't I beat his head on the ground, wouldn't his brains go splashing all over the place! And then I should have some little consolation for the trouble which this nobody of a Noman has brought upon me!'

"So he let the ram go from him out of the cave. A little way from the cave and its enclosure, I shook myself loose first from under my ram; then I freed my companions, and with all speed we drove the fat animals trotting along, often looking round, until we reached our ship. Glad indeed our friends were to see us, all of us that were left alive; they lamented the others, and made such a noise that I had to stop it, frowning at them and shaking my head. I told them to look sharp and throw on board a number of the fleecy beasts, and get away. Soon they were in their places paddling along; but when we were about as far off from the shore as a man can shout, I called out in mockery:

" 'I say, Cyclops! He didn't turn out to be such a milksop after all, did he, when you murdered his friends, and gobbled them up in your cave? Your sins were sure to find you out, you cruel brute! You had no scruple to devour your guests in your own house, therefore vengeance has fallen upon you from Zeus and the gods in heaven!'

"This made him more furious than ever. He broke off the peak of a tall rock and threw it; the rock fell in front of the ship; the sea splashed and surged up as it fell; it raised a wave which carried us back to the land, and the rolling swell drove the ship right upon the shore. I picked up a long quant and pushed her off, and nodded to the men as a hint to row hard and save their lives. You may be sure they put their backs into it! When we were twice as far as before, I wanted to shout again to Goggle-eye, although my comrades all round tried to coax me not to do it—

" 'Foolhardy man! Why do you want to provoke the madman? Just now he threw something to seaward of us and drove back the ship to land, and we thought all was up with us. And if he had heard one of us speaking or making a sound, he would have thrown a jagged rock and smashed our timbers and our bones to smithereens! He throws far enough!'

"But I was determined not to listen, and shouted again in my fury:

" 'I say, Cyclops! if ever any one asks you who put out your ugly eye, tell him your blinder was Odysseus, the conqueror of Troy, the son of Laërtês, whose address is in Ithaca!'

"When he heard this he gave a loud cry, and said, 'Upon my word, this is the old prophecy come true! There was a soothsayer here once, a fine tall fellow, Telemos Eurymedês, a famous soothsayer who lived to old age prophesying amongst our people. He told me what was to happen, that I should lose my sight at the hands of Odysseus. But I always expected that some tall handsome fellow would come this way, clothed in mighty power. Now a nobody, a weakling, a whippersnapper, has blinded my eye after fuddling me with wine! Come to me, dear Odysseus, and let me give you the stranger's gift, let me beseech the worshipful Earthshaker to grant you a happy voyage! For I have the honour to be his son, and he declares he is my father. He will cure me, if he chooses, all by himself, without the help of blessed gods or mortal man.'

"I answered at once, 'I wish I could kill you and send you to hell as surely as no one will ever unblind your eye, not even the Earthshaker!'

"At this he held out his hand to heaven, and prayed to Lord Poseidon:

" 'Hear me, Poseidon Earthholder Seabluehair! If I am truly thy son, and thou art indeed my father, grant that Odysseus the conqueror of Troy—the son of Laërtês—whose address is in Ithaca, may never reach his home! [1] But if it is his due portion to see his friends and come again to his tall house and his native land, may be come there late and in misery, in another man's ship, may be lose all his companions, and may be find tribulation at home!'

"This was his prayer, and Seabluhair heard it. Then once again he lifted a stone greater than the other, and circled it round his head, gathering all his vast strength for the blow,[2] and flung it; down it fell behind our ship, just a little, just missed the end of the steering-oar. The sea splashed and surged up as it fell, and the wave carried her on and drove her to shore on the island.

"When we came safe to the island, where the other ships were waiting for us, we found our companions in great anxiety, hoping against hope. We drew up our ship on the sand, and put the sheep of old Goggle-eye ashore, and divided them so as to give every one a fair share. But by general consent the great ram was given to me. I sacrificed him on the beach to Zeus Cronidês; clouds and darkness are round about him, and he rules over all. I made my burnt-offering, but Zeus regarded it not; for as it turned out, he intended that all my tight ships and all my trusty companions should be destroyed.

"We spent the rest of the day until sunset in feasting, eating full and drinking deep; and when the sun set and darkness came on, we lay to rest on the seashore. Then at dawn I directed the men in all haste to embark and throw off the moorings. They were soon aboard and rowing away in good fettle over the sea.

"So we fared onwards, thankful to be alive, but sorrowing for our comrades whom we had lost.

---

[1] Odysseus introduced himself in the proper Greek way, name, family, and address (see page 282); the reader will notice how carefully the Cyclops repeats it to his divine father, that there may be no mistake. Yet our editors call line 531 spurious.

[2] The movements of putting the weight.

BOOK X

The Island of the Winds; the Land of the Midnight Sun; Circê

"WE CAME NEXT TO THE ISLAND OF AIOLIA. THERE lived Aiolos Hippotadês, a friend of the immortal gods, in a floating island: right round it was built a brazen wall unbreakable, and the rock ran up smooth and straight. Aiolos had a family of twelve children, six daughters, and six sons in their prime: the daughters he had given to the sons as wives. All these live together, and dine with their father and their excellent mother; there is always a fine spread of vittles in infinite variety. All day and every day the house is full of the steam of cooking, and the courtyard resounds with busy noise: all night they sleep beside their faithful wives on bedsteads of neat joinery, covered with blankets and rugs.

"We entered this city with its fine houses, and there spent a whole month as guests. Aiolos wanted to know all about Ilion, and the Achaian fleet, and how they returned home; and I told him the whole history from beginning to end.

"When at last I spoke of leaving, and asked him for help on our way, he was glad to consent, and did everything he could. He gave me the skin of a nine-year ox, which he flayed for us and made into a bag; and in this he bottled up the blustering winds. For Cronion had appointed him to be manager of the winds, to hold them or to let them go as he liked. On board my ship he tied up the bag with wire of shining silver, so tight that not a breath could blow out: but he left the west wind free to blow, that it might carry our ships along. As it turned out this was of no use, for we spoilt all by our own folly.

"Nine days we sailed all day and all night: on the tenth day our native land came in sight. We came so close that we could see them tending their fires. All that time I had held the sheet in my hand and let no one else touch it, to make sure of a quicker passage home; but when I saw the island I fell into a deep sleep, for I was tired out.

"Then the men began to talk to one another, said there must be gold and silver in that bag, presents from the gen-

112

erous Aiolos Hippotadês; and this is the sort of thing they
were whispering:

" 'Upon my word, the man is a prime favourite wherever
he goes! Plenty of treasures from the spoils of Troy, and we
who travelled the same road come home with empty hands!
Now again here is Aiolos obliging him with more generous
gifts. Here, quick, let's look and see what he has got, how
much gold and silver there is in this bag!'

"A scandalous motion, but it was passed. They opened
the bag, the winds leaped out; at once a gale caught them,
and carried them off to sea tearing their hair as they left
their native land behind. This waked me up; I did not know
what to do, whether to throw myself overboard and be
drowned, or grin and bear it in the land of the living. Well, I
just bore it and stayed where I was. I covered my head and
lay down, while the ships were driven by the gale back to the
Isle of Aiolos, amid the lamentations of my companions.

"So we went ashore, and took in fresh water, and the men
had their meal beside the ships. When we had finished, I took
with me a herald and one other, and went on to the house of
Aiolos. We found him feasting with his wife and children.
When we entered the hall, and sat on the threshold near the
door, they called out in great astonishment:

" 'What has brought you here, Odysseus? What ill luck has
touched you? Surely we did everything we could to help you,
that you might return safely to your native land, or any-
where else you wanted to go?'

"I answered sorrowfully, 'Everything has been spoilt by
the fault of my men, and sleep on the top of that, confound
it! Do help us, friends: you have the power.'

"My coaxing was of no use: they were dumbfounded, and
the father said, 'Get out of this island at once, you miserable
sinner! It is not permitted to comfort the enemy of the blessed
gods! Get out of this! You are the gods' enemy come to my
doors!'

"Thus he turned me out of his house in deep distress.

"From that place we sailed on disheartened. The spirit of
the men was worn out by the labour of rowing, all their own
fault! for there was no wind to help us now.

"Six days we carried on, all night and all day. On the sev-
enth we reached the lofty stronghold of Lamos, Laistrygonian
Telepylos, where herdsman hails herdsman as one brings in
his droves and the other answers as he drives out his. There
a man who could do without sleep, could earn double wages,

one by minding cattle, one by pasturing sheep: for the paths of day and night are close together.[1]

"We entered a fine harbour, with percipitous cliffs running all round. At the mouth are two headlands projecting front to front, and the entry is narrow. All the others steered their ships in, and moored them inside the harbour close together (for there were no waves rising inside, large or small, only white calm all round); but I alone made fast my ship outside, at the very end of the point, hitching ropes over the rocks.

"Then I climbed the cliff and stood still to get a good view. There was no arable land or garden to be seen, but we saw smoke rising in the air. So I sent some men to find out who the natives were, two picked men with a third as their spokesman. They went ashore, and proceeded along a levelled road which was used by carts to carry down wood from the hills into the city. They came across a girl close to the city, drawing water, the sturdy daughter of Laistrygonian Antiphatês. She had come down to a running spring named Artaciê, from which they used to get water for the city. The men stopt and asked who was king in those parts, and who the people were. She answered at once, and pointed out her father's lofty roof.

"When they entered the house, there they found his wife, a woman as big as the peak of a mountain, and they hated her at sight. She sent at once to summon her husband Antiphatês from the town-meeting. He gave them a murderous reception: one he grabbed at once and prepared for supper, the other two ran away and managed to get back to the ships. But the monster made a hue-and-cry through the city. Out came the Laistrygonians rushing from every direction in thousands, great inhuman wretches like giants. They threw showers of stones from the cliffs, each as big as a man could lift, and a mighty din there was, smashing of ships and crushing of men; the giants speared them like fishes and carried them home for a horrid supper.

"While this massacre was going on in the deep harbour, I drew my sword and cut the hawsers of my ship, and told my men to put their backs into if they wanted to save their lives; then row they did, with the fear of death to help them. We blessed the open sea when we got clear of those grim rocks; my ship was the only one which escaped, all the rest were lost.

"From that place we sailed on, glad enough to have come

[1] This picture suggests rumours of the land of the midnight sun.

off with our lives, but sad to lose our companions. Next we reached the island of Aiaia. There Circê lived, a terrible goddess with lovely hair, who spoke in the language of men, own sister to murderous Aietas; their father was Helios, who gives light to mankind, and their mother was Persê, a daughter of Oceanos. We brought our ship to the shore in silence, and some providence guided us into a harbour where ships could lie. There we spent two days and two nights on shore, eating out our hearts with weariness and woe.

"On the third day, as soon as dawn showed the first streaks of light, I took spear and sword and climbed to a high place, where I had a look round to see if there was any one about or any voice to be heard. Standing on the top of a rock, I saw smoke rising into the air from the house where Circê lived in the middle of thick bushes and trees.

"When I saw the smoke glowing, I considered whether I should go and inquire. The best plan seemed to be that I should return first to our ship on the shore and give the men something to eat, and then send out to inquire. Just as I came near to the ship, some god must have pitied me there so lonely, and sent me a stag with towering antlers right on my path: he was going down to the river from his woodland range to drink, for the sun's heat was heavy on him. As he came out, I struck him on the spine in the middle of the back, and the spear ran right through: down he fell in the dust with a moan, and died. I set my foot on him and drew out the spear from the wound. Then I laid the body flat on the ground, and pulled a quantity of twigs and withies, which I plaited across and twisted into a strong rope of a fathom's length: with this rope I tied together the legs of the great creature, and strung him over my neck, and so carried him down to the ship, leaning upon my spear; I could not have carried him on the shoulder with one hand, for he was a huge beast.

"I threw him down in front of the ship, and cheered up my friends with encouraging words as I turned from one to another. 'We are not going to die yet, my friends, for all our troubles: we shall not see the house of Hadês before our day comes. While there's food and drink in the ship, don't let us forget to eat! we need not die of starvation, at all events!'

"They were all sitting about with their faces muffled up in their cloaks; but at my words they threw off the cloaks, and got up quickly to stare at the stag lying on the beach; for he was a huge beast. When they had feasted their eyes on the welcome sight, they began to think of another kind of feast;

so they swilled their hands in due form, and got him ready. All day long until sunset we sat enjoying ourselves with our meat and wine; and when the sun went down and the darkness came, we lay down to sleep on the seashore.

"As soon as morning dawned, I called my companions together and addressed them:

" 'My friends, we do not know east from west, we don't know where the sun rises to give light to all mankind, and where he goes down under the earth. Well, then, what are we to do? We must try to think of something at once, and for my part, I can't think of anything. I have just been up on the cliffs to look around. We are on some island in the middle of the sea, with no land in sight. The island is flat, and I saw smoke rising in the air above a coppice of bushes and trees.'

"When I said this, their hearts were crushed with foreboding: for they remembered the doings of Laistrygonian Antiphatês, and the violence of that audacious cannibal the goggle-eye Cyclops. The tears ran down their cheeks, and much good it did to weep!

"However, I divided them into two parts of equal number, and chose a captain for each: one I took myself, the other I gave to an excellent man, Eurylochos. Quickly then we shook lots in a helmet, and out leapt the lot of Eurylochos. Off he went, with his two-and-twenty men, groaning and grumbling, and we were left groaning and grumbling behind.

"They found in a dell the house of Circê, well built with shaped stones, and set in a clearing. All round it were wolves and lions of the mountains, really men whom she had bewitched by giving them poisonous drugs. They did not attack the men, but ramped up fawning on them and wagging their long tails, just like a lot of dogs playing about their master when he comes out after dinner, because they know he has always something nice for them in his pocket. So these wolves and lions with their sharp claws played about and pawed my men, who were frightened out of their wits by the terrible creatures.

"They stopt at the outer doors of the courtyard, and heard the beautiful goddess within singing in a lovely voice, as she worked at the web on her loom, a large web of incorruptible stuff, a glorious thing of delicate gossamer fabric, such as goddesses make. The silence was broken by Politês, who was nearest and dearest to me of all my companions, and the most trusty. He said:

" 'Friends, I hear a voice in the house, some woman singing

prettily at the loom, and the whole place echoes with it. Goddess or woman, let's go in and speak to her.'

"Then they called her loudly. She came out at once, and opened the shining doors, and asked them to come in; they all followed her, in their innocence, only Eurylochos remained behind, for he suspected a trap. She gave them all comfortable seats, and made them a posset, cheese and meal and pale honey mixt with Pramneian wine; but she put dangerous drugs in the mess, to make them wholly forget their native land. When they had swallowed it, she gave them a tap of her wand at once and herded them into pens; for they now had pigs' heads and grunts and bristles, pigs all over except that their minds were the same as before. There they were then, miserably shut up in the pigsty. Circê threw them a lot of beechnuts and acorns and cornel-beans to eat, such as the earth-bedded swine are used to.

"But Eurylochos came back to the ship, to tell the tale of his companions and their unkind fate. At first he could not utter a word, he was so dumbfounded with this misfortune; his eyes were full of tears, his mind foreboded trouble. At last when we were fairly flummoxed with asking questions, he found his tongue and told us how all his companions had come to grief.

"'We went out into the wood, as you told us, most renowned chief; found a well-built house in a dell, and there some one was singing loudly as she worked the loom, goddess or woman: they called to her. She came out at once and opened the doors and asked them in: they all followed in the simplicity of their hearts, but I stayed behind because I suspected a trap. They all disappeared at once, not a soul was to be seen, and I stayed there a long time to spy.'

"When he said this, at once I slung my sword over my shoulders, the large one, bronze with silver knobs, and the bow with it, and told him to go back with me and show me the way. But he threw his arms about my knees and begged and prayed without disguise—'Don't take me there, my prince; I don't want to go. Let my stay here. I am sure you will never come back again, nor will any one who goes with you. Let us get away with those who are here while we can: we have still a chance to escape the day of destruction!'

"But I answered, 'Very well, Eurylochos, you may stay here in this place, eat and drink beside the ship. But as for me, go I must, and go I will.'

"So I made my way up from the sea-side. But just as I was on the point of entering the sacred dell and finding the house of that mistress of many spells, who should meet me but Hermês with his golden rod: he looked like a young man with the first down on his lip, in the most charming time of youth. He grasped my hand, and said:

" 'Whither away again, you poor fellow, alone on the hills, in a country you do not know? Your companions are shut up yonder in Circê's, like so many pigs cosy in their pigsties. Are you going to set them free? Why, I warn you that you will never come back, you will stay here with the others.— All right, I will help you and keep you safe. Here, take this charm, and then you may enter the house of Circê: this will keep destruction from your head.

" 'I will reveal to you all the malign arts of Circê. She will make you a posset, and put drugs in the mess. But she will not be able to bewitch you for all that; for the good charm which I will give you will foil her. I will tell you exactly what to do.

" 'As soon as Circê gives you a tap with her long rod, draw your sword at once and rush upon her as if you meant to kill her. She will be terrified, and will invite you to lie with her. Do not refuse, for you want her to free your companions and to entertain you; but tell her to swear the most solemn oath of the blessed gods that she will never attempt any other evil against you, or else when you are stript she may unman you and make you a weakling.'

"With these words Argeiphontês handed me the charm which he had pulled out of the soil, and explained its nature. The root was black, but the flower was milk-white. The gods call it moly: it is hard for mortals to find it, but the gods can do all things.

"Then Hermês departed through the woody island to high Olympos; but I went on to Circê's house, and I mused deeply as I went. I stood at the doors; as I stood I called loudly, and the beautiful goddess heard. Quickly she came out and opened the doors, and I followed her much troubled.

"She led me to a fine carven chair covered with silver knobs, with a footstool for my feet. Then she mixt me a posset, and dropt in her drugs with her heart full of wicked hopes. I swallowed it, but it did not bewitch me; then she gave me a tap with her wand, and said:

" 'Now then, to the sty with you, and join your companions!'

"I drew my sharp sword and leapt at Circê as though to kill her. She let out a loud shriek, and ran up and embraced my knees, and blurted out in dismay:

" 'Who are you, where do you come from in the wide world? Where is your city, who are your parents? I am amazed that you have swallowed my drugs and you are not bewitched. Indeed, there never was another man who could stand these drugs once he had let them pass his teeth! But you must have a mind that cannot be bewitched. Surely you are Odysseus, the man who is never at a loss! Argeiphontês Goldenrod used to say that you would come on your way from Troy in a ship. Come now, put up your sword in the sheath, let us lie down on my bed and trust each other in love!'

"I answered her, 'Ah, Circê, how could you bid me be gentle to you, when you have turned my companions into pigs in this house? And now that you have me here, with deceitfulness in your heart you bid me to go to your bed in your chamber, that when I am stript you may unman me and make me a weakling. I will not enter your bed unless you can bring yourself to swear a solemn oath that you will never attempt any evil thing against me.'

"She swore the oath at once; and when she had sworn the oath fully and fairly, I entered the bed of Circê.

"Meanwhile, the four maids who served her had been doing their work in the house. These were daughters of springs and trees and sacred rivers that run down into the sea. One of them spread fine coverings upon the seats, a linen sheet beneath and a purple cloth upon it. The second drew tables of silver in front of the seats, and laid on them golden baskets. The third mixt wine in a silver mixer, delicious honey-hearted wine, and set out cups of gold. The fourth brought water and kindled a great fire under a copper. The water grew warm; and when it boiled in the glittering cauldron, she led me to the bath, and bathed me with water out of the cauldron, when she had tempered it to a pleasant warmth, pouring it over my head and shoulders to soothe the heart-breaking weariness from my limbs. And when she had bathed me and rubbed me with olive oil, she gave me a tunic and a wrap to wear.

"Then she led me to the fine carven seat, and set a footstool under my feet, and invited me to fall to. But this displeased me; I sat still half-dazed, and my heart was full of foreboding.

"When Circê noticed that I sat still and did not touch the vittles, when she saw how deeply I was troubled, she came near and spoke her mind plainly:

" 'Why do you sit there like a dumb man, Odysseus, and

eat your heart out instead of eating your dinner? I suppose you expect some other treachery! You need not be afraid; I have sworn you a solemn oath.'

"I answered, 'Ah, Circê! What man with any decent feeling could have the heart to taste food and drink, until he should see his friends free and standing before his eyes? If you really mean this invitation to eat and drink, set them free, that I may see my friends before my eyes!'

"Then Circê took her wand in hand, and walked through the hall, and opened the doors of the sty, and drove them out, looking like a lot of nine-year hogs. As they stood there, she went among them and rubbed a new drug upon each; then the bristles all dropt off which the pernicious drug had grown upon their skin. They became men once more, younger than they were before, and handsomer and taller.

"They knew me, and each grasped my hand; they sobbed aloud for joy till the hall rang again with the noise, and even the goddess was touched. She came close to me, and said:

" 'Prince Laërtiadês, Odysseus never at fault! Go down to the seashore where your ship lies. First of all draw up the ship on the beach, and stow all your goods and tackle in a cave; then come back yourself and bring the rest of your companions with you.'

"So I went; and when I reached the shore, I found my companions sitting beside the ship in deep distress. But as soon as they saw me, they were like so many calves in a barnyard, skipping about a drove of cows as they come back to the midden after a good feed of grass; they cannot keep in their pens, but frolic round their dams lowing in a deafening chorus. So the men crowded round me, with tears running down over their cheeks; they felt as glad as if they had come back to their native land, to rugged Ithaca, their home where they were born and bred; and they cried out from their hearts:

" 'You are back again, my prince! How glad we are, as glad as if we had come safe home to Ithaca! Now do tell us what has become of our companions!'

"I answered gently, 'First of all we will draw up the ship on shore, and store the tackle and all our belongings in some cave. Then bestir yourselves and come with me, all of you, and you shall see your companions in the sacred house of Circê, eating and drinking. They have enough and to spare.'

"At once they set about the work. And now what should I

see but Eurylochos alone trying to stop them! He made no
secret of his thoughts:

" 'Oh, you poor fools!' he cried out, 'where are we going?
Do you want to run your heads into trouble? Go to Circê's
house, and let her turn you all into lions or wolves to keep
watch for her whether we like it or not? Just Cyclops over
again, when our fellows went into his yard, and this same
bold Odysseus with them! It was only his rashness that
brought them to destruction!'

"When I heard this, I thought for a moment that I would
draw my sword and cut off his head, and let it roll on the
ground, for all he was my near relation. But the others held
me back and did their best to soften me:

" 'Let us leave the man here, prince, if you please, let him
stay by the ship and look after the ship. Lead the way! We
are going with you to Circê's house!'

"Then away they went up from the shore. Indeed, Eury-
lochos would not be left behind; he came too, for he had a
terror of my rough tongue.

"Then Circê gave a bath in her house to my companions,
and had them rubbed with olive oil, and gave them tunics
and woollen wraps. We found all the others feasting merrily
in the hall. When they saw one another face to face, and
knew one another, their feelings were too much for them;
they made such a noise that the roof rang again. And the
radiant goddess came up to me, and said:

" 'No more lamentations now, Odysseus! I know myself
how many hardships you have suffered on the seas, and how
many cruel enemies have attacked you on land. Now then,
eat your food and drink your wine until you become as gay
as when you first left your rugged home in Ithaca. Just now
you are withered and down-hearted, you can't forget your
dismal wanderings. Your feelings are not in tune with good
cheer, for assuredly you have suffered much.'

"We took her advice; and there we remained for a whole
year, with plenty to eat and good wine to drink.

"But when the year was past and the seasons came round
again, my companions called me aside, and said:

" 'Good heavens, have you forgotten home altogether? Do
remember it, if it is really fated that you shall have a safe
return to your great house and your native land!'

"And so when I came to Circê's bed, I entreated her ear-
nestly, and she listened to what I had to say: 'Keep the prom-
ise you made me, Circê, that you would help me on my
homeward way. My mind is set upon it, and my companions'

too. They were worrying about it, and grumbling all round me when you are not by.'

"She answered: 'Prince Laërtiadës, never baffled Odysseus! I would not have you remain in my house unwillingly. But there is another journey you must make first. You must go to the house of Hadês and awful Persephoneia, to ask directions from Teiresias the blind Theban seer. His mind is still sound, for even in death Persephoneia has left him his reason; he alone has sense, and others are flitting shadows.'

"This fairly broke my heart. I sat on the bed and groaned, and I no longer cared to live and see the light of the sun. But when I had worked off my feelings by groaning and writhing, I said to her:

"'Oh Circê! Who will be our guide to that place? No one has ever travelled to Hadês in a ship!'

"The beautiful goddess answered, 'You need not hang about the ship and wait till a guide turns up. Set your mast, hoist your sail, and sit tight: the North Wind will take you along.

"'When you have crossed over the ocean, you will see a low shore, and the groves of Persephoneia, tall poplars and fruit-wasting willows; there beach your ship beside deep-eddying Oceanos, and go on yourself to the mouldering house of Hadês.

"'There into Acheron the river of pain two streams flow, Pyriphlegethon blazing with fire, and Cocytos resounding with lamentation, which is a branch of the hateful water of Styx: a rock is there, by which the two roaring streams unite. Draw near to this, brave man, and be careful to do as I bid you. Dig a pit of about one cubit's length along and across, and pour into it a drink-offering for All Souls, first with honey and milk, then with fine wine, the third time with water: sprinkle over it white barley-meal. Pray earnestly to the empty shells of the dead; promise that if you return to Ithaca you will sacrifice to them a farrow cow, the best you have, and heap the burning pile with fine things, and to Teiresias alone in a different place you will dedicate the best black ram you have in your flocks. After that, when you have made your prayers to the goodly company of the dead, sacrifice a black ram and a black ewe, turning their heads down towards Erebos, then turn back yourself and move towards the ocean shore; the souls of the dead who have passed away will come in crowds.

"'Then call your companions, and bid them flay and burn the bodies which lie slaughtered, and pray to the gods, to mighty Hadês and awful Persephoneia. Draw your sword and sit still, but let none of the empty shells of the dead approach the blood before you ask Teiresias what you want to know. The seer will come at once, and he will tell you the way and the measure of your path, and how you may return home over the fish-giving sea.'

"Even as she spoke, the Dawn came enthroned in gold. Circê gave me tunic and cloak to wear, and herself put on a white shining robe, delicate and lovely, with a fine girdle of gold about her waist, and drew a veil over her head. I went through the house and aroused my companions, speaking gently to each man as I stood by him:

" 'Sleep is sweet, but now, no more drowsy slumber! Let us go! Circê has told me what to do.'

"They obeyed me, full of courage. But even there we had trouble before we left. One of us, Elpenor, the youngest of all, one not so very valiant in war or steady in mind, had been sleeping by himself on the roof to get cool, being heavy with wine. He heard the noise and bustle of the men moving about, and jumped up in a hurry, but his poor wits forgot to come down again by the long ladder. He fell off the roof and broke his neck, and his soul went down to Hadês.

"When the men had all come, I said to them, 'No doubt you think we are going straight home; but Circê has marked out another road for us, to the house of Hadês and awful Persephoneia.'

"When I said this it fairly broke their hearts; they sat down where they were, and groaned and tore their hair. But it did them no good to lament.

"While we were on the way to our ship in sorrow and mourning, Circê had got there before us and left fastened near the ship a black ram and ewe. She slipt past us easily. Who could set eyes on a god if he did not wish it, going this way or coming that way?

BOOK XI

How Odysseus Visited the Kingdom of the Dead

"WHEN WE REACHED OUR SHIP LYING ON THE BEACH, the first thing we did was to launch her into the sea; then we set up mast and sail, and taking the ram and ewe we embarked in no happy mind. The radiant goddess Circê sent a sail-filling wind behind us, a good companion for a voyage. We made all shipshape aboard, and sat tight: wind and helmsman kept her on her course. All day long we ran before the wind, with never a quiver on the sail; then the sun set, and all the ways grew dark.

"We came at last to the deep stream of Oceanos which is the world's boundary. There is the city of the Cimmerian people, wrapt in mist and cloud. Blazing Helios never looks down on them with his rays, not when he mounts into the starry sky nor when he returns from sky to earth; but abominable night is for ever spread over those unhappy mortals. There we beached our ship and put the animals ashore, and we walked along the shore until we came to the place which Circê had described.

"Perimedês and Eurylochos held fast the victims, while I drew my sword and dug the pit, a cubit's length along and across. I poured out the drink-offering for All Souls, first with honey and milk, then with fine wine, and the third time with water, and I sprinkled white barley-meal over it. Earnestly I prayed to the empty shells of the dead, and promised that when I came to Ithaca, I would sacrifice to them in my own house a farrow cow, the best I had, and heap fine things on the blazing pile; to Teiresias alone in a different place I would dedicate the best black ram among my flocks.

"When I had made prayer and supplication to the company of the dead, I cut the victims' throats over the pit, and the red blood poured out. Then the souls of the dead who had passed away came up in a crowd from Erebos: young men and brides, old men who had suffered much, and tender maidens to whom sorrow was a new thing; others killed in battle, warriors clad in bloodstained armour. All this crowd gathered about the pit from every side, with a dreadful great noise, which made me pale with fear.

"Then I told my men to take the victims which lay there

slaughtered, to flay them and burn them, and to pray to mighty Hadês and awful Persephoneia; I myself with drawn sword sat still, and would not let the empty shells of the dead come near the blood until I had asked my questions of Teiresias.

"First came the soul of my comrade Elpenor, for he had not yet been buried in the earth. We had left his body at Circê's house, unmourned and unburied, since other tasks were pressing. I was moved with pity for him, and my tears fell as I asked him simply:

"'Elpenor, how came you to the gloomy west? You have beaten our ship with only your feet to walk on!'

"He answered with a groan:

"'I was done for by bad luck and a mort of drink! I slept on Circê's roof, and forgot to climb down by the long ladder, fell head over heels off the roof, broke my neck, and my soul came down to Hadês. Now I beseech you by those who are not here, those you left behind you, by your wife and your father, who cared for you as a child, by Telemachos your only son, whom you left at home—remember me, my prince, when you reach Aiaia, for I know you will touch there on your way back from Hadês. Do not leave me unmourned and unburied; do not desert me, or I may draw God's vengeance upon you! Burn me with all my arms, and pile up a barrow on the shore of the grey sea, that in days to come men may hear the story of an unhappy man; do this for me, and plant my oar on the mound, the same oar which I used when I rowed with my companions.'

"I heard, and answered, 'Be sure I will do this for you, my unhappy friend.'

"As we exchanged these sad words, I stood on one side holding my drawn sword over the blood, and my friend's phantom on the other, telling his long story.

"Then came the soul of my dead mother, Anticleia daughter of the brave Autolycos; she was alive when I left Ithaca on my voyage to sacred Ilion. My tears fell when I saw her, and I was moved with pity; but all the same, I would not let her come near the blood before I had asked my questions of Teiresias.

"Then came the soul of Theban Teiresias, holding a golden rod. He knew me, and said, 'What brings you here, unhappy man, away from the light of the sun, to visit this unpleasing place of the dead? Move back from the pit, hold off your sharp sword, that I may drink of the blood and tell you the truth.'

"As he spoke, I stept back from the pit, and pushed my sword into the scabbard. He drank of the blood, and only then spoke as the prophet without reproach: [1]

" 'You seek to return home, mighty Odysseus, and home is sweet as honey. But God will make your voyage hard and dangerous; for I do not think the Earthshaker will fail to see you, and he is furious against you because you blinded his son. Nevertheless, you may all get safe home still, although not without suffering much, if you can control yourself and your companions when you have traversed the sea as far as the island of Thrinacia. There you will find the cattle and sheep of Helios, who sees all things and hears all things.

" 'If you sail on without hurting them you may come safe to Ithaca, although not without suffering much. But if you do them hurt, then I foretell destruction for your ship and your crew; and if you can escape it yourself, you will arrive late and miserable, all your companions lost, in the ship of a stranger. You will find trouble in your house, proud blustering men who devour your substance and plague your wife to marry and offer their bridal gifts. But you shall exact retribution from these men.

" 'When you have killed them in your hall, whether by craft or open fight with the cold steel, you must take an oar with you, and journey until you find men who do not know the sea nor mix salt with their food; they have no crimson-cheeked ships, no handy oars, which are like so many wing-feathers to a ship. I will give you an unmistakable token which you cannot miss. When a wayfarer shall meet you and tell you that is a winnowing shovel on your shoulder, fix the oar in the ground, and make sacrifice to King Poseidon, a ram, a bull, and a boar-pig [2]; then return home and make solemn sacrifice to the immortal gods who rule the broad heavens, every one in order. Death shall come to you from the sea, death ever so peaceful shall take you off when comfortable old age shall be your own burden, and your people shall be happy round you. That which I tell you is true.'

"I answered him, 'Ah well, Teiresias, that is the thread which the gods have spun, and I have no say in the matter. But here is something I want to ask, if you will explain it to

---

[1] He had his full powers before, but the draught of blood was a pleasure to him, as wine would be to a man, and he repays Odysseus by telling him what he wants.

[2] Thus he is to be reconciled with Poseidon, after he has proclaimed the god's majesty in a place which knew him not, and left the oar as a symbol.

me. I see over there the soul of my dead mother. She remains in silence near the blood, and she would not look at the face of her own son or say a word to him. Tell me, prince, how may she know me for what I am?'

"He answered, 'I will give you an easy rule to remember. If you let any one of the dead come near the blood, he will tell you what is true; if you refuse, he will go away.'

"When he had said this, the soul of Prince Teiresias returned into the house of Hadês, having uttered his oracles. But I stayed where I was until my mother came near and drank the red blood. At once she knew me, and made her meaning clear with lamentable words:

" 'My love, how did you come down to the cloudy gloom, and you alive? It is hard for the living to see this place. There are great rivers between, and terrible streams, Oceanos first of all, which no one can ever cross by walking but only if he has a well-found ship. Are you on your way from Troy, have you been wandering about with ship and crew all this time? Haven't you ever been back to Ithaca, and seen your wife in your own house?'

"I answered, 'Dear mother, necessity has brought me to the house of Hadês, for I had to consult the soul of Teiresias the Theban. I have not been near Achaia nor set foot in our country. I have been driven about incessantly in toil and trouble, ever since I first sailed with King Agamemnon for Troy, to see its fine horses and to fight with its people.

" 'But do tell me, really and truly, what was the cause of your death? how did you die? Was it a long disease? or did Artemis Archeress kill you with her gentle shafts? And tell me about my father and the son I left behind me: do they still hold my honours and my possessions, or have they passed to some other man because people think I will never return? And tell me of my own wedded wife, what she thinks and what she means to do. Does she remain with the boy and keep all safe, or has she already married the best man who offered?'

"My beloved mother answered at once, 'Aye indeed, she does remain in your house. She has a patient heart; but her nights and days are consumed with tears and sorrow. Your honours and your possessions have not yet been taken away by any man, but Telemachos holds your demense and attends the public banquets as a ruling prince ought to do, for they all invite him.

" 'But your father stays there in the country and never comes to town. His bedding is not glossy rugs and blankets on a bedstead, but in winter he sleeps among the hinds in the house, in the dust beside the fire, and wears poor clothes: when summer comes and blooming autumn, he lies on the ground anywhere about the slope of his vineyard, on a heap of fallen leaves. There he lies sorrowing and will not be comforted, longing for your return; old age weighs heavy upon him.

" 'And this is how I sickened and died. The Archeress did not shoot me in my own house with those gentle shafts that never miss; it was no disease that made me pine away: but I missed you so much, and your clever wit and your gay merry ways, and life was sweet no longer, so I died.'

"When I heard this, I longed to throw my arms round her neck. Three times I tried to embrace the ghost, three times it slipt through my hands like a shadow or a dream. A sharp pang pierced my heart, and I cried out straight from my heart to hers:

" 'Mother dear! Why don't you stay with me when I long to embrace you? Let us relieve our hearts, and have a good cry in each other's arms. Are you only a phantom which awful Persephoneia has sent to make me more unhappy than ever?'

"My dear mother answered:

" 'Alas, alas, my child, most luckless creature on the face of the earth! Persephoneia is not deceiving you, she is the daughter of Zeus; but this is only what happens to mortals when one of us dies. As soon as the spirit leaves the white bones, the sinews no longer hold flesh and bones together— the blazing fire consumes them all; but the soul flits away fluttering like a dream. Make haste back to the light; but do not forget all this, tell it to your wife by and by.'

"As we were talking together, a crowd of women came up sent by awful Persephoneia, wives and daughters of great men. They gathered about the red blood, and I wondered how I should question them. This seemed to be the best plan. I drew my sword and kept off the crowd of ghosts; and then I let them form in a long line and come up one by one. Each one declared her lineage, then I questioned them all.

"Tryo came first, that noble dame. She said she was daughter of Salmoneus, and wife of Cretheus Aiolidês; but she was in love with Enipeus the river-god, most beautiful of all the rivers that flow on the earth, and she used to frequent the banks of this river. Poseidon Earthshaker took on him the shape of this river-god, and lay with her at the mouth of the eddying stream: a dark purple wave made an arch over them like a mountain cave, to shelter the god and the mortal woman. He loosed her maiden girdle, and made her fall into a deep sleep. When their love was fulfilled, he took her by the hand, and said:

" 'A blessing on your love, my dearest; when the year has rolled round, you shall bring forth glorious children, for a god's embrace is not barren. Nurse the boys and rear them with loving care. And now, return to your home, keep it to yourself and say nothing; but know that I am Poseidon Earthshaker.'

"Then he dived into the billows of the deep.

"She conceived, and brought forth Pelias and Neleus, who both became mighty servants of Zeus. Pelias dwelt in the broad spaces of Iolcos, rich in countless flocks of sheep; the other in sandy Pylos. She bore other sons as queen of King Cretheus, Aison and Pherês and Amythaon, so famous with chariot and horses.

"Next to her I saw Antiopê, the daughter of Asopos, who could boast that she had slept in the arms of Zeus; and she bore two boys, Amphion and Zethos. These two first founded the stronghold of Thebes with its seven gates and fortified it; since without walls and towers they could not live in spacious Thebes, mighty though they were.

"After her I saw Alcmenê the wife of Amphitryon, who brought forth Heraclês the indomitable lion-heart, when she had lain in the arms of mighty Zeus; and the daughter of proud Creion, Megara, who became the wife of Amphitryon's son, the hero whom no labour could weary.

"I saw the mother of Oidipûs, fair Epicastê, who did a monstrous thing in the innocence of her heart; for she married her own son, and he had slain his own father first. But the gods kept it from people's knowledge for a time. So he continued to be king in his lovely Thebes, but full of misery himself, by the god's cruel will; and she went down to the strong prison of Hadês the warder of the gates. Her grief was too great for her, and she hanged herself from a lofty roof-beam; but she left him misery enough and to spare, which the avenging spirit of his mother brought to pass.

"And I saw beautiful Chloris, whom Neleus married for her beauty, bringing magnificent gifts. She was the youngest daughter of Amphion Iasidês, the powerful King of Minyeian Orchomenos. She thus became Queen of Pylos, and bore him glorious sons, Nestor and Chromios and lordly Periclymenos. Besides these she was the mother of buxom Pero, the admiration of all beholders, wooed by every man within reach. But Neleus would give her to no man, unless he would carry off the cows of Iphiclês from Phylacê—a dangerous task! Iphiclês was a mighty man, the cows were all guarded, crumple-horned, broad-browed beauties. A certain admirable seer promised to drive them off all by himself, but hard fate caught him fast—there were the savage herdsmen and prison walls! Days and months went by, the year rolled round again and the seasons came back to their places, and then King Iphiclês let him go after he had uttered his oracles. So the will of Zeus came to pass.

"I saw Leda also, the wife of Tyndareos, who brought him two stout-hearted sons, Castor the horse-master and Polydeucês the great boxer. These two are both buried in mother earth, and both alive; even deep in the earth they have a special privilege from Zeus, one day living, and the next day dead, so they have the gods' own privilege.[1]

"After her I saw Iphimedeia, the wife of Aloeus, who could say she had lain with Poseidon. She bore him two sons, but they had only a short time to live. These were the famous Otos and Ephialtês, the biggest creatures the fruitful earth ever bred, and the most handsome next after famous Orion. At nine years old, they were nine cubits across the chest and nine fathoms high. They threatened to set up a horrible civil war against the immortals in Olympos. Their plan was to pile Ossa upon Olympos, and Pelion with its forests upon Ossa, and so to climb into heaven. Indeed they would have done it if they had lived to grow up; but they were killed by Apollo, the son of Zeus and Leto, before the down began to grow under their temples and the hair upon their chins.

"I saw Phaidra, and Procris, and fair Ariadnê, the daughter of grim-hearted Minos, whom Theseus carried off from Crete; he was taking her to Athenian soil, but he had no joy of her, for Artemis slew her first in the island of Dia because Dionysos told tales.[2]

"Maira too I saw, and Clymenê, and accursed Eriphylê, who accepted gold as the price of her own husband. I will not stay to name all I saw, wives or daughters of heroes, or night would end before I had done. It is time to sleep now, either here or on board the ship; and to-morrow, please God, you will arrange for my homeward voyage."

---

[1] Zeus granted them the privilege of living on alternate days, so one was always in Olympos, and one in the grave.

[2] Dionysos saw Theseus and Ariadnê in his sacred cave, and told the tale.

When he had done, there was silence in the shadows of the hall, for they were all enchanted by the story. After a while Arêtê began to speak:

"What do you think of him now, gentlemen?" she said. "Isn't he a fine figure of a man, and clever enough for anything? Now he is *my* guest, but you all have your share of the honour, so don't be in a hurry to let him go, and don't stint your gifts which he needs so much. You have plenty of good things in store, thanks be to heaven."

Echeneos followed up, and said:

"My friends, what our wise queen says is not far from the mark; just what we might expect. You should do as she bids you. But here is Alcinoös, and all that we say or do depends on him."

Alcinoös answered at once:

"Well, this shall certainly be done, if I am still alive and king over the sea-faring Phaiacians. But let our guest make up his mind to stay at least over to-morrow, however anxious he may be to get home, and that will give me time to bring all our gifts together. To give him a safe journey is the concern of the whole nation, but mine most especially, since mine is the chief power in the land."

Odysseus answered readily:

"Most illustrious prince, if you should bid me to stay here for a twelvemonth, while you are making full preparations for the voyage and heaping your bounty upon me, that is just what I should choose: the fuller my hands, the better welcome I should find when I came home. They would all think the more of me and love me better when they saw me in Ithaca safe and sound."

To this Alcinoös replied:

"My dear Odysseus, to see you is quite enough to show that you are no cheat or impostor, like so many others. There is a rich crop of such men flourishing on the fat soil of this world, who dress up fabulous tales about what no eye could ever see. But there is the spirit of honest truth about your story, as well as the artist's finish, and you have told it like a poet who understands his craft. What a sad story of your own travels and the whole Argive nation!

"But now be so kind as to tell us something more; did you see any of your noble comrades who were at Ilion with you and there met their fate? There is any amount of this long night before us, it is not time for bed yet; please go on with your tale of marvels. I could listen till daylight shall appear, if you would have the patience to finish your touching story under this roof."

Odysseus was ready to play up to him, and answered:

"Most illustrious prince, there is a time for long stories, and there is a time for sleep; but if you wish to hear I would not grudge you a story even more touching—the misfortunes of those who perished afterwards, when they had come safe out of the perils of the battlefield, and returned home only to fall by the treachery of a woman.

"Very well, then. As soon as dread Persephoneia had dispersed the ghosts of the women, the ghost of Agamemnon Atreidês came near full of sorrow: there was a crowd of others round him, those who died with him in the house of Aigisthos. The king knew me as soon as he had drunk the red blood; he cried aloud and wept, stretching out his hands towards me and trying to reach me. But there was no strength or power left in him such as there used to be in that body so full of life. I shed tears of pity myself when I saw him, and spoke plainly as I called him by name:

" 'My lord Atreïdês, Agamemnon king of men! What fate of dolorous death brought you low? Did Poseidon raise a terrible tempest and drown you in the sea? Or did the hand on an enemy strike you down on dry land, in some foray or cattle-raid, or fighting for conquest and captives?"

"He answered, 'Prince Laertiadês, Odysseus ever ready! Poseidon did not drown me in the sea, no enemy struck me down on dry land; but Aigisthos plotted my death with my accursed wife—invited me to his house, set me down to a banquet, butchered me as if I were an ox at the manger! That was how I died, and a shameful death it was: my friends were falling, falling all round me, like a lot of tusker pigs that a rich man slaughters for a wedding or a banquet or a butty-meal! You have seen men fall in battle often enough, killed man to man or in the thick melée; but you never saw a sight so pitiable as that, as we lay about the winebowl, and the tables were piled with meats, and the floor running with blood.

" 'Most frightful of all was the shriek of Cassandra, and she a king's daughter! I heard it when the traitress Clytaimnestra killed her over my body. I tried to lift my hands, but dropt them again on the ground, as I lay dying with a sword through my body: the bitch turned her back, she would not take the trouble to draw down my eyelids or to close my mouth in death.

" 'True it is, there is nothing so cruel and shameless as

a woman: that woman proved it to be true, when she plotted that shameful deed and murdered her lawful husband. Ah me, I did think to find welcome with my children and household when I came back to my home; but she had set her mind upon outrageous wickedness, she had brought shame on herself and all women for ever, even if one of them is honest.'

"I cried out:

" 'Mercy upon us! Indeed there is no doubt that Zeus Allseeing has been the deadly foe of the house of Atreus from the beginning, and he has always used the schemes of women. For Helen's sake how many of us fell! and for you, Clytaimnestra was laying her plot while you were far away!'

"He answered:

" 'Then take warning now yourself, and never be too kind even to your wife. Never tell her all you have in your mind; you may tell something, but keep something to yourself. However, *you* will not be murdered by your wife, Odysseus. She is full of intelligence, and her heart is sound, your prudent and modest Penelopeia.

" 'Ah, she was a young bride when we left her and went to the war; there was a baby boy at her breast, and I suppose by this time he counts himself a man. Happy boy! His father will see him when he comes, sure enough, and he will give his father a kiss as a good boy should. But my wife would not even let me delight my eyes with the sight of my son; she killed the father first.

" 'But there is something I want very much to know. Have you heard anything about my son's being alive somewhere in Orchomenos, or in sandy Pylos, or perhaps with Menelaos in Sparta? My Orestês is certainly not dead yet.'

"I said, 'Why do you ask me that, Atreïdês? I know nothing, whether he is alive or dead; and it is a bad thing to babble like the blowing wind.'

"As we two stood talking together of our sorrows in this mournful way, other ghosts came up: Achillês and Patroclos, and Antilochos, the man without stain and without reproach, and Aias, who was most handsome and noble of all next to the admirable Achillês. The ghost of Achillês knew me, and said in plain words:

" 'Here is Prince Odysseus who never fails! O you foolhardy man! Your ingenious brain will never do better than this. How did you dare to come down to Hadês, where dwell the dead without sense or feeling, phantoms of mortals whose weary days are done?"

"I answered him, 'My lord Achillês Peleïdês, our chief and our champion before Troy! I came to ask Teiresias if he had any advice or help for me on my way to my rugged island home. For I have not yet set foot in my own country, since trouble has ever been my lot. But you, Achillês, are most blessed of all men who ever were or will be. When you lived, we honoured you like the gods; and now you are a potentate in this world of the dead. Then do not deplore your death, Achillês.'

"He answered at once, 'Don't bepraise death to me, Odysseus. I would rather be plowman to a yeoman farmer on a small holding than lord Paramount in the kingdom of the dead.

" 'But do tell me something about that fine son of mine. Did he go to the war and take a leading place, or not? And tell me of my noble old father—have you heard anything of Peleus? Does he still hold his honourable place among the Myrmidons, or have they lost respect for him throughout the land because his hands and feet are stiff with age? For I am no longer under the sun to help him, strong as I once was on the battlefield of Troy, when I struck down the best of them and defended our people. Let me be for a short time in my father's house strong as I once was, and I would make not a few fear my anger and my invincible hands, if they are keeping him by force from his honour due!"

"I answered, 'I have nothing to tell you of your noble father Peleus, but I can tell you about your beloved son Neoptolemos, and there is nothing to hide. In fact I brought him in my own ship from Scyros to join the Achaian army. When we held a council of war, he was always the first to speak, and always found the right thing to say. Only Nestor and I were superior. When we met our enemies in battle, he did not lag among the crowd or in the scrimmage, but showed himself well in front, the bravest of the brave: many a man he killed in fair fight.

" 'I will not name all those he killed on the field, but what a man was brought low when he ran his sword through Eurypylos Telephidês, that young hero! and many others of his people fell by his side that a woman might enjoy her gewgaws![1] That was the handsomest man I ever saw, ex-

[1] His mother was bribed by Priam, who gave her a golden vine to let her son join the Trojans.

cept Memnon the magnificent. And when the best men of
our army were about to enter the Wooden Horse which
Epeios made, and I was put in charge to open and close
the door as I thought fit, the other captains were wiping
tears from their eyes and trembling in every limb, but I
saw no pallor on his cheeks and no tear in his eyes. Again
and again he begged me to let him out, and handled his
sword-hilt and heavy spear, eager to have at his enemies.

" 'When at last we had sacked the city, he took his share of
the spoil and a special prize, and embarked unwounded, with
never a scratch from sword or spear, although there are
plenty of those in war. You take your luck when war runs
amuck.'

"When I told him this, the ghost of clean-heeled Achillês
marched away with long steps over the meadow of asphodel,
proud to hear how his son had made his mark.

"The other ghosts of the dead halted in turn, and each
asked what was near to his heart; but alone of them all the
soul of Aias Telamoniadês [1] kept apart, still resentful for
my victory over him when there was question about the arms
of Achillês. The goddess his mother set them up as a
prize for the best man. How I wish I had never won such
a prize! What a life was lost for that! Aias, first of all the
Danaäns in noble looks and noble deeds, except Achillês
the incomparable. And so I addressed him in gentle words:

" 'Aias, great son of a great father! were you never to forget
your anger against me for those accursed arms, not even in
death? That prize was a disaster, seeing that we lost a tower
of strength like you. Our whole nation mourns your loss
continually, no less than we mourn Achillês Peleïadês.
Zeus alone is to blame and no one else, because he hated
the Danaän host so vehemently, and brought fate upon you.
Nay, come this way, my lord, and listen to my pleading:
master your passion and your proud temper.'

"He replied not a word, but moved away into Erebos
after the other ghosts of the dead. Then in spite of all, he
should have spoken to me, or I to him; but I wished to see
the souls of the others who were dead.

"There I saw Minos the glorious son of Zeus, holding a
golden rod and giving sentence upon the dead. He was
seated, and the dead were around him in the house of Hadês
with its wide portals, some seated and some standing, as
each asked the judge for his decision.

---

[1] Aias the Less died on page 54.

"After him I noticed the huge figure of Orion driving the beasts in a mass over the meadow of asphodel, the game which he had killed himself when he was alive on the lonely hills; his hands held a cudgel of solid bronze, unbroken for ever.

"And I saw Tityos the son of Gaia most majestic, lying upon the ground; nine roods he covered, and two vultures sat, one on each side, and tore his liver, plunging under the skin: he could not defend himself with his hands. This was his punishment because he had laid violent hands on Leto, the famous consort of Zeus, when she was passing through the beautiful grounds of Panopeus on her way to Pytho.

"Tantalos also I saw in his misery, standing in a lake up to his chin, always thirsty, but try as he would, not a drop could he lap up: for as often as the poor old man dipt his head to take a drink, the water was sucked back and disappeared, until the dark earth showed under his feet as fate dried it away. Tall trees in full leaf dangled their fruit over his head, pears and pomegranates and fine juicy apples, sweet figs and ripe olives; but as often as the poor old man reached out a hand to catch one, the wind tossed them all up to the clouds.

"Sisyphos also I saw and his tedious task, as he held up a monstrous stone with both hands. Scrambling with his feet, and pushing with his hands, he heaved the stone up the hill; but just as he was about to topple it over the crest, the weight was too much for him, and turned it back: down-along to the ground rolled the stone pitiless. Then he would push again, stretching and struggling, with sweat pouring off every limb and the dust rising from his head.

"After him I saw mighty Heraclês, his phantom that is: but Heraclês himself is with the immortal gods, as happy as the day is long, with graceful Youth for his bride. Around this phantom the ghosts were gibbering and twittering like a flock of birds, and scattering hither and thither; he stood holding his naked bow with arrow on string, looking as black as night, and casting dreadful glances round, for ever as if just about to shoot. A terrible, baldric was round about his chest, a golden strap covered with wonderful work, bears and wild boars and glaring lions, battles and conflicts and bloody death. May the artist never invent another work of art who made that terrible baldric by his genius! The hero knew me when he caught sight of me, and sped his words straight to the mark:

" 'Prince Laërtiadês, Odysseus never failing! I pity you,

for you are dogged by an evil fate, as I was, under the light of the sun! My father was Zeus Cronion, yet I had infinite tribulation to endure; for I was bound to a contemptible fellow who set me dangerous labours. Once he sent me here for the Dog, because he thought he could find no more dangerous labour than that. I brought him up, I got him from Hadês sure enough, under conduct of Hermeias and Pallas Athena.'

"With these words he strode back into the house of Hadês; but I remained where I was, in case any other of the heroes of past times should appear. And indeed, I should have seen others of those ancient men whom I wished especially to see, as Theseus and Peirithoös, those famous sons of gods; but before I could see them, the innumerable hosts of the dead gathered together with deafening cries, and I grew pale with fear that awful Persephoneia might send out of Hadês upon me a Gorgon-head of some dreadful monster. Then I went back at once to the ship, and told my men to loose the hawser and get away. They were soon rowing steadily on their benches, and the current bore us steadily down the ocean stream; oars at first, afterwards a following breeze.

BOOK XII

The Singing Sirens, and the Terrors of
Scylla and Charybdis

"OUR SHIP LEFT THE STREAM OF OCEANO, AND PASSED into the open sea. Soon it came to the island of Aiaia, where Dawn has her dwelling and her dancing lawns, and Helios his place of rising. We ran up the ship, and went ashore to sleep on the beach.

"As soon as the next day dawned, I sent my companions to Circê's house to bring the body of Elpenor. We cut chunks of wood for a pyre, and buried him on the end of the foreland, mourning for our dead friend. And when the body was burnt with his arms, we raised a barrow with a large stone upon it and set up his own oar on the summit.

"While we were busy there, Circê did not fail to learn that we had come back from Hadês. She soon came down well provided; the servants brought a load of bread and meat and sparkling red wine. Then standing among us, she said:

" 'You men stick at nothing! So you went down to Hadês alive? Double-diers, when other people are content to die once! Come now, eat and drink once more, all the day is before you; and to-morrow at dawn you shall sail. I will describe the way, I will tell you every single thing, that you may not make mischief for yourselves and come to grief by land or sea.'

"We were quite ready to comply. So all the day long till sunset we enjoyed our feast of good things. When the sun set and darkness came, they all lay down where the ship was moored; but Circê took me apart, and made me tell the story of our voyage as we sat together. I told her everything just as it happened, and at the end she said:

" 'Very well, all that is finished and done with. Now listen to what I have to say, and you will not forget it, please God.

" 'First you will come to the Sirens, who bewitch every one who comes near them. If any man draws near in his innocence and listens to their voice, he never sees home again, never again will wife and little children run to greet him with joy; but the Sirens bewitch him with their melodious song. There in a meadow they sit, and all round is a great heap of bones, mouldering bodies and withering skins.

Go on past that place, and do not let the men hear; you must knead a good lump of wax and plug their ears with pellets. If you wish to hear them yourself, make the men tie up your hands and feet and fasten your body tight to the mast, and then you can enjoy the song as much as you like. Tell them that if you shout out and command them to let you loose, they must tie you tighter with a few more ropes.

" 'When you have got clear of them, there is a choice of two courses, and I will not lay down for you which to take; use your own judgment. I will just say what they are. One course will bring you to a pair of precipitous rocks, washed by the boisterous breakers of dark-eyed Amphitritê; the gods call them the Moving Rocks. Not a bird can pass between them, not even the timorous doves which carry the ambrosia to Father Zeus; one of these is always caught between the towering rocks, and the Father sends in another to keep the number right. No ship sailed by men that came that way has ever escaped, but timbers and dead bodies are all carried away by the rolling seas and tempests of blazing fire. Only one ship ever sailed through, the well-known *Argo*, on her voyage to Aiëtas; and she also would have been wrecked on the rocks, but Hera took her safely through because Jason was her friend.

" 'The other course leads between two cliffs. One drives a sharp peak high into the heavens, and black clouds are round about it; the clouds never disperse, and that peak is never clear either in summer or in autumn. No mortal man could climb up, no man climb down, not if he had twenty hands and twenty feet; for the stone is smooth as if it had been polished. But in the side of the cliff is a dark gloomy cave, facing the west towards Erebos, just where you will steer your ship, Odysseus. There Scylla dwells, and yelps in her dreadful way; the cave is so high that the strongest man could not reach it with an arrow shot from the ship. It is true her voice is no louder than a puppy-dog new-born, but she is a horrible monster! Such a sight could give pleasure to no one, not even one of the immortal gods.[1] She has twelve flapping feet, and six necks enormously long, and at the end of each neck a horrible head with three rows of teeth set thick and close, full of black death. She is hidden in the cave as far as the waist, but she pokes out her heads from the gloomy depths; and there she fishes, hunting all round for

---

[1] A proverbial superlative, used by the poet in sly mischief.

dolphins and swordfish, or any of those leviathans of the deep which Amphitritê breeds in thousands. No seamen can boast that they have escaped scot-free from her: she grabs a poor wretch with each head out of the ship as it sails along.

" 'The other cliff is lower, as you will see, Odysseus. They are not far from one another; you could shoot an arrow across. There is a wild fig-tree growing from it, a tall tree covered with leaves; and Charybdis underneath swallows down the black water. Three times a day she spouts it out, three times a day she swallows it down: she is a terror—don't you be there when she swallows! No one could save you from destruction, not Earthshaker himself! You had much better go by Scylla's rock, keep close, and be quick about it. To lose six of your crew is much better than to lose them all at once!' "

"I answered, 'What do you say to this, my goddess—Suppose I slip away from Charybdis, and show fight when the other attacks my men?'

"She answered at once, 'You hot-head! fighting and asking for trouble is all you care about! Will you stand up even to the immortal gods? She is no mortal, I tell you, but an immortal fiend, dangerous, deadly, savage, invincible! There is no help for it; flight is better than fight. If you stay too long near the rock while you put on your armour, I am afraid she may shoot out another half-dozen heads and catch another half-dozen fellows! No, no, row as hard as you can, and call for help on Crataiïs—that is Scylla's mother, she produced that abomination! Crataiïs will stop her from trying again.

" 'You will come next to the island of Thrinacia, where the herds of Helios feed. There are his cattle and great sheep, seven herds of cattle and seven fine flocks of sheep, fifty in each. These never have young, and never die. Their shepherds are two goddesses, nymphs with lovely hair, shining Phaëthusa and bright Lampetiê, daughters of Helios Hyperion by divine Neaira ever young. When the mother had brought up her children, she sent them away to that far-off island, to look after their father's cattle and sheep. If you leave these unharmed and attend to the business of getting home, you may yet reach Ithaca, although not without suffering; but if you do any damage, then I foretell destruction for ship and men. You may save your own life, but if you do, you will reach your home late and miserable, and all your companions will be lost.'

"As she said these words, the Dawn rose enthroned in gold.

Circê went away up the island; and I to the ship, where I awakened my companions, and bade them embark and cast off the moorings. They were soon on board and in their places. Circê our beautiful goddess, who could speak to us men in our own language, sent us the best of companions, a fair wind to fill our sails: all was snug and ship-shape, we sat still and let the wind carry us on while the steersman kept the course.

"I was anxious enough, of course, and so I spoke to the men. 'My friends, the divine Circê has told me all about what is going to happen; and I do not think it right that only one or two should know, so I will tell you all, and when we all know, we may die or escape as the case may be. First, she bids us keep away from the Sirens with their wonderful voices and their flowery meadow I alone must hear them, so she said; but you are to bind me with strong ropes and fasten me upright against the mast, so that I shall not be able to move. If I implore you and order you to set me free, you must tie me up tighter than ever.'

"So I explained everything to my companions; and by this time the ship was drawing near to the Sirens' isle, travelling briskly, for there was no fault to be found with the wind. Then the wind fell all at once, and there was a dead calm, not a ripple on the water. My men rolled up the sail and stowed it below, and they were soon rowing away, white foam and splashing oars. Then I took a thick round of wax, and chopt it up with my sword into pellets, and moulded the bits in my fingers. The wax grew soft, as it was warmed by the effulgence of my lord Helios Hyperionidês, and I plugged up the ears of all the men one after another. Then they bound me hand and foot and fastened me upright against the mast, took their places and paddled on. But when she was as far off the land as a voice could carry, and going at a good pace, the Sirens saw us coming and raised their melodious song:

" 'Come this way, most admirable Odysseus, glory of the nation! stay your ship, and listen to our voice! No man ever yet sailed past this place, without first listening to the voice which sounds from our lips sweet as honey! No, he has a great treat and goes home a wiser man. For we know all that the Argives and Trojans endured on the plains before Troy by the will of Heaven; and we know all that shall come to pass on the face of mother earth!'

"So they sang in lovely tones. From the bottom of my heart I longed to listen, and I ordered the men to set me free, nodding my head and working my brows; but they simply went on pulling with a good swing. Perimedês and Eurylochos at once got up, and put more ropes round me and fastened me tighter. But when we had gone a long way past the Sirens, so that we could hear them no longer, my companions took out the wax from their ears and untied my ropes.

"At last we left the island behind; and suddenly I saw smoke, and a great rolling wave, and heard a loud noise. The men were terrified, the oars flew out of their hands and fell in the sea with a splash, dragging down at the ship's sides by their loops; she made no way, now the oars drove no longer. I walked down the whole length of the ship, pausing by each man, and coaxing them not to lose heart:

" 'My friends, we are not unacquainted with trouble. This is no greater danger than when the Cyclops imprisoned us in his cave by brute force; we escaped from that place, thanks to my courage and my ingenious plan, and I think we shall live to remember this no less. Now then, attend to my instructions. Keep your seats and row away like men, and then we may hope that Zeus will save and deliver us out of this danger. Now for you, steersman, pay careful heed, for you hold our helm in your hands. Keep her well away from the smoke and surge, and hug the cliffs; whatever you do, don't let her run off in that direction, or we shall all be drowned.'

"They did my bidding at once. But I took care not to mention Scylla and the peril we could not avoid; I thought they would be likely to leave the oars in a panic and huddle down below. At that moment I quite forgot Circê's injunction, when she told me not to arm myself. I put on my armour, and caught up a couple of spears, and took my stand on the foredeck; for that was where I thought Scylla would show herself on the rock, bringing death for my companions. But I could not see her anywhere, though I dazed my eyes with staring about me through the clouds at the rock.

"We passed up the strait, groaning loudly; for on one side was Scylla, on the other Charybdis swallowed up the salt water in terrible fashion. When she spouted, like a cauldron over a great fire she seethed up in a swirling mess, and the spray rose high in the air till it fell on the tops of the two cliffs: when she swallowed up the salt sea, she showed deep down in her swirling whirlpool black sand at the bottom, and the rocks all round echoed a bellowing boom. Every man was pale with fear. As we gazed in our fear at the death on this side, at the same moment Scylla grabbed six of my men out of the ship, the best and strongest of the crew. I turned, took a glance at the ship, looked for my men, saw their hands and feet already in the air swinging aloft in the clutches of Scylla; while they called aloud on my name, for the last time, in despair. As a fisherman stands on a projecting rock with a long rod, and throws in ground-bait to attract the little fishes, then drops in hook and line with its horn-bait, and at last gets a bite and whips him out gasping, so Scylla swung them gasping up to the rock; there in the cave she devoured them, shrieking and stretching out their hands to me in the death-struggle. That was the most pitiable sight my eyes ever beheld in all my toils and troubles on the weary ways of the sea.

"When we were past the rocks, and away from the terrors of Charybdis and Scylla, immediately we reached a delectable island; in that place were the fine cattle with broad brows and the great sheep which belonged to Helios Hyperion. While we were still a long way off I heard the lowing of the cattle penned for the night, and the bleating of sheep; and I remembered the warning of the blind prophet, Theban Teiresias, and of Aiaian Circê, and how they strictly forbade me to land on the island of Helios the joy of man. At once I said to my companions, with my mind full of foreboding:

"'Men, you are having a hard time of it, I know that, but listen to me a moment; I want to tell you a warning of Teiresias and of Circê also. They strictly forbade us to land on the island of Helios; for there they said an awful danger awaits us. You had better give the island a wide berth and row on.'

"This fairly broke them down, and Eurylochos answered at once angrily:

"'You are a hard man, Odysseus, never downhearted and never tired! You must be made of iron! Here are your men, tired to death and scarce able to keep awake, and you won't let us go ashore on this island and cook a square meal. No, you make us go trapesing along the whole blessed night. We must give the island a wide berth and toss about in the dark! Night is the time for dangerous squalls, that's the way ships are lost! How can we expect to get off with our lives if a sudden squall comes out of the south or west? Damned bad winds, that send a ship to the bottom, God willing or not! I vote we take our orders from black Madam Night, pull up the vessel and cook a meal. Then in the morning in we get, and it's over the sea we go!'

"That was the proposal of Eurylochos, and the others applauded. Then I understood that heaven had trouble in store for us, and I gave it him straight:

" 'Eurylochos, I must give way to force. I am one against many. But you must swear a solemn oath, that if we find a herd of cattle or a flock of sheep no one shall dare to kill one cow or one sheep. You must keep quiet, and eat the food that Circê gave us.'

"They all swore the oath accordingly; and when that business was done, we brought the ship into a land-locked harbour close to a spring of sweet water. They all went ashore, and prepared their meal in proper style. When they had taken all they wanted, they had time to remember their lost comrades, whom Scylla had caught and eaten out of the ship; and they lamented their dead until welcome sleep overcame them. But when it was the third watch of the night and the stars had moved south, Zeus Cloudgatherer sent out a furious wind in a regular tempest, and covered earth and sea with clouds; night rushed down from the heavens. As soon as the dawn showed ruddy through the mist, we hauled the ship ashore into a cave, in which the Nymphs had their thrones and dancing-rings. Then I called the men together and addressed them:

" 'My friends, we have food and drink in the ship, so we must keep our hands off these cattle or we may suffer for it. For an awful god is the owner of these cattle and great sheep—Helios, who sees all and hears all.'

"They were quite willing to agree. But the south wind blew for a whole month without changing, and after that, never a breath of any wind we had but east and south. So long as the food and red wine lasted, they kept their hands off the cattle, for they did not want to die; but when all the provisions on board were consumed, and they had to go about hunting for game, birds, or fish, or whatever fell to their hands or their hooks, and they were half starved, I made my way up into the island to offer prayer to the gods and try whether one would help us. I slipt away from the men and found a place with shelter from the wind; there I washed my hands, and prayed to all the gods who dwell in Olympos, but they made me fall into a deep sleep.

"Meanwhile Eurylochos was making a fatal speech to his companions. 'My friends,' he said, 'you are in a bad way; but let me say a word to you. All deaths are hateful to miserable mortals, but the most pitiable death of all is to starve. Come along, let us drive off the best of these cattle, and sacrifice

them to the immortal gods who rule the broad heavens. If
we ever return home to Ithaca, we will build a rich temple to
Helios Hyperion, and set up there many handsome offerings;
but if the god is angry about his straightthorns, and wants to
destroy our ship, and if the other gods agree, I choose rather
to die once with a mouthful of salt water than to be slowly
squeezed out in a desert island.'

"The others applauded this speech. They wasted no time,
but drove off the best of the cattle of Helios close by, for the
fine beasts with their wide foreheads and crumpled horns[1]
used to graze not far off. The men stood round the cattle
and prayed to the gods, but they had no barley-meal to
sprinkle upon their victims, so they used tender young oak-
leaves which they picked from a tree. They had no wine to
pour over the burnt offering, but they sprinkled water before
they cooked the tripes. Then they chopt up the rest and put
the pieces on spits.

"At that moment I awoke and came back to the seashore.
As I came near to the ship a sweetish odour of burning fat
was diffused around me. I cried aloud in horror and prayed
to the immortal gods:

"Father Zeus, and all ye blessed gods that live for ever!
You meant my ruin when ye made me fall into that cruel
sleep! My men whom I left behind have committed a mon-
strous crime!"

"A messenger took the news quickly to Helios Hyperion,
Lampetiê in her flowing robe, and she told him we had
slain his cattle. In great anger he called out to the immortals:

"'Father Zeus and all ye gods that live for ever! Punish
those men of Odysseus Laërtiadês! They have brutally killed
my cattle, which were my great delight when I climbed into
the starry sky, and when I turned back to earth from heaven.
If they do not pay me a fitting compensation, I will just go
down to Hadês and show my light among the dead!'

"Zeus Cloudgatherer answered him, 'Now then, Helios, you
just go on showing your light to us immortals and to mortal
men upon mother earth. I will soon strike the ship with a
thunderbolt, and smash it into smithereens in the middle of
the sea!'

"I was told this later by Calypso; she said she heard it her-
self from Hermês King's Messenger.

---

[1] This is the stock epithet, but Eurylochos called them "straight
horns" just now. Both his speeches (beginning 279 and 340) sound
like a real man speaking, with the natural phrases and the careless-
ness of every day.

"As soon as I came down to the seashore, I reproached them one and all, though we could do nothing to help it now: the cattle were already dead. But awful portents were seen in that place: the skins crawled, the meat bellowed on the spits, both raw and roast; it was like the noise of cattle.

"Six days my companions feasted on the best of the cattle of Helios; but when the seventh day came, the furious tempest ceased; we embarked and went sailing away over the sea.

"When the island was far astern and no other land to be seen, nothing but sea and sky, Cronion brought a black cloud over our ship and darkened the deep. Then she did not run long, for suddenly came the west wind screeching and blowing with a furious tempest, the gale broke both the forestays, the mast fell aft, and all the tackle tumbled into the hold, the mast hit the steersman's head and crushed the skull to splinters, he took a header from his deck and was drowned. Zeus at the same time thundered and struck our ship with his bolt; she shivered in all her timbers at the blow, and the place was full of sulphur. The men were cast out, there they were bobbing up and down on the waves like so many crows. So God ended the homeward voyage for them.

"I kept pacing up and down the ship, until the sea tore the sides from the keel. A rolling wave carried her along dismantled, and snapt off the mast close to the keel, but the backstay had fallen upon it; this was made of stout oxhide, so I used it to lash together keel and mast, and I rode upon these drifting before those terrible winds.

"Now the furious tempest of the west wind was lulled, and the south quickly followed, bringing anxiety for me, for it was sure to carry me back again to the terrors of Charybdis. All night long I drifted, and by sunrise Scylla and dreadful Charybdis were before me. Charybdis swallowed up the salt water; but I had been carried high up, and caught the wild fig-tree; and I stuck to it like a bat and held tight. I had nothing to plant my feet upon for support and no way to climb; for the roots were far below, and the branches far above, those thick long branches which overshadowed Charybdis. But I held tight without slackening until my mast and keel should be spouted up again. How I longed for them! and they came at last. At the time when a judge gets up from court for his dinner, after settling the morning's disputes among quarrelsome young men, just at that time my spars appeared out of Charybdis. I spread out hands and feet and let go, and came down plump in the water alongside the spars, and then clambered up and lay on them, paddling with my hands. What of Scylla? The Father of gods and men would not allow her to set eyes on me, or I should not have escaped with my life.

"From that place I drifted for nine days, and on the tenth at night the gods brought me to the island of Ogygia. There dwells Calypso, that goddess so beautiful and so terrible, who can speak the language of man; and she loved me and cared for me. But why go on with my story? I have told it already, and no one cares for a twice-told tale."

BOOK XIII
How Odysseus Came to Ithaca

HE FINISHED, AND ALL WERE SILENT AS IF SPELLBOUND in the shadowy hall. At last Alcinoös spoke:

"Well, Odysseus, since you have come as far as my brazen walls and lofty roof, I don't think you will look a foiled adventurer when you get home,[1] even if you have had plenty of trouble.

"And now, gentlemen, I have a bolt in my quiver for you, who have always been welcome to drink my best company-wine and to hear my musician. The clothes are all packed in that coffer for our guest, with the fine gold plate and all the other gifts which our councillors have brought. I propose now that we offer him a large tripod and a cauldron apiece. We will collect the cost afterwards in the town: it would be too bad to let each man bear it all himself."

They were quite content with this proposal, and dispersed to their homes for the night.

As soon as the first rosy fingers of Dawn appeared, they made haste to the ship with the useful brass-ware. Alcinoös was careful to stow away these things with his own royal hands, packing them under the benches, so that the men might not damage them in rowing. Then the givers went on to the royal mansion and made ready for their banquet.

The King's Grace sacrificed an ox to our Lord Zeus Cronidês, who dwells in clouds and darkness. When they had burnt the thigh-slices, they had a famous feast and enjoyed it mightily, while Demodocos made music for them such as they always loved to hear.

Odysseus turned his head ever and anon to the shining sun, impatient for his setting, for he was eager to be gone. As a man longs for his meal when all through the day his brown oxen draw the plow over the fallow field, until his knees fail under him while he plods along, and he is glad to see the sun set and leave him to his dinner, so Odysseus was glad to see the sun set. At once he addressed the company, Alcinoös in particular, and said:

"My lord Alcinoös, most illustrious prince! now pour out

[1] See *Iliad* i 59, where Achilles invents this expression.

your libations and let me go in peace, and good be with you all. For what my heart desired has been now brought to pass, a friendly escort and friendly gift; which may the gods in heaven bless! May I return to my home and find my faithful wife and my dear ones safe and sound! May you who remain make happy your own wives and children, and may the gods grant you success of every sort, and may no evil thing befall your people!"

All applauded this prayer, and urged the King to speed their guest on his way after his admirable words. Then King Alcinoös said to the herald:

"Pontonoös, mix a bowl and serve round to all in hall, that every one may offer a prayer to Father Zeus, and speed our guest on his way to his native land."

Then Pontonoös mixed the honey-hearted wine, and served it to all in turn: they poured the sacred drops to the blessed gods who rule the broad heavens, each man from his own seat. But Odysseus rose, and passed the two-handled cup to Arêtê, saying to her:

"May it be well with you, Queen, for ever, until old age and death shall come, as they come to all men. Now I depart: a blessing on you in this house, and your children, and your people, and their King Alcinoös!"

With these words Odysseus stept over the threshold. King Alcinoös sent the herald with him to lead him to the seashore where the ship lay; and Arêtê sent with him three of her women, one bearing a tunic and a robe newly washed, another to convey the coffer, a third with a supply of bread and red wine.

At the seaside where the ship lay, the young men of his escort received all this and stowed it away on board with the food and drink; and they laid a blanket and sheet on the deck of the poop for Odysseus, that he might sleep soundly. Odysseus went on board in silence and laid himself down, while the crew took their places, and cast off the hawser, drawing it through the hole in the stone pillar. Then they paddled away with a good swing back; blessed sleep fell on his eyelids, deep, sound and most sweet, the very image of death. And the ship!—As four fine stallions in a team leap like one, when touched up with the whip, and gallop along the road with bounding paces, so her stern bounded aloft on the purple wave which followed big over the sounding sea. Steady and straight she ran: not even the peregrine falcon could have kept up with her, and he is the most rapid of all winged things. So she cut swiftly through the waves, and she carried a man whose mind was as wise as the gods: long years he had suffered great tribulation and sorrow of heart, wars on land and voyages over the stormy seas, and now he slept quietly forgetting all his troubles.

When that brightest of stars rose, which comes to tell us that the dawn is near, the travelling ship was drawing close to an island.

There is a harbour of Phorcys, the Old Man of the Sea, in the island of Ithaca. Two headlands enclose it, with steep sides sloping down to the harbour mouth, to shelter it from the waves which boisterous winds may raise outside: once inside, ships of good size can lie without mooring when they come within mooring-distance. At the head of this harbour is an olive tree covered with its long leaves, and near the tree is a beautiful dusky cave, sacred to the nymphs who are called Naiads. In the cave are great bowls and two-handled jars of stone, and in these the bees hive their honey. There are also tall poles of stone like the beams of a loom, where the nymphs weave webs of sea-purple wonderful to behold; there are springs of water never dry. It has two doors; one turned to the north, by which mortal men may descend; one on the south, meant rather for gods, by which men do not enter, but this is the road of the immortals.[1]

In that harbour they sailed, for they knew it well. The ship ran up on the beach half her length with a dash—for the oarsmen put a good pace on her; the men leapt on the shore, and carried Odysseus out rolled up in his blanket and white sheet, and laid him down on the sand still heavy with sleep. All his goods were brought out by the sturdy fellows from the places where they had been packed by the forethought of Athena. These were piled in a heap under the olive tree, off the road, so that no chance wayfarer might pilfer before Odysseus awoke. Then the ship went home again.

But the Earthshaker did not forget his threats of long ago against Odysseus, and he asked Zeus what he meant to do:

"Father Zeus, I shall never have any respect in our world, now mortal men pay me none! I mean the Phaiacians who actually belong to my own family. Here's an example. I thought Odysseus was to reach home in all sorts of misery and tribulation: I did not bar his return altogether, because you had solemnly promised him that he should return.

"And now here are these people, bringing him over the sea

---

[1] That is, a hole towards the top, such as there is in the Cave of the Nymphs in Ithaca to-day.

in a fast cruiser, planting him down in Ithaca, giving him any amount of presents, bronze and gold in plenty and woven stuffs, more than he could have collected from the spoils of Troy if he had come home with his share intact!"

Zeus Cloudgatherer answered: "Bless my soul, my good Earthshaker, you mustn't say that. There is no disrespect for you among us gods; it would be a great shame to bombard out eldest and best with insults. If a man thinks himself strong enough to refuse you proper respect, you can pay him out some time yourself. Do as you like about it; what pleases you, pleases me."

Poseidon Earthshaker answered: "That is what I should have done on the spot, Thundercloud, but I always have a wholesome fear of your temper and I do my best to avoid it. Now then, what I should like to do is, to smash that fine ship on the way back from their convoy, that they may stop at once and convoy no more men over the sea, and then I will raise a ring of high mountains about the city."

Zeus Cloudgatherer answered: "Gentle creature! My temper thinks the best thing to be this. Wait till the ship is running in, and the whole city gazing at the sight, and turn it into stone close to the shore, and let the stone keep the shape of a ship that all the world may wonder; then raise a ring of high mountains about the city."

So Poseidon Earthshaker went straight to Scheria, and there he waited. As the ship came sailing in at full speed, the Earthshaker turned it into stone, and rooted it firmly to the bottom by a blow from the flat of his hand. Then he went away.

There was something for those people to talk about, the nation of seamen with their long oars! They spoke out their minds plainly; a man would stare at his neighbour and say: "Mercy on us, who has shackled our ship in full course? I saw her clearly just now." For they did not know what had happened.

But Alcinoös called them together and spoke:

"Ah me, I see now the ancient oracles come true, which my father told me. He used to say that Poseidon was jealous of us, because we gave safe convoy to all men over the sea. He said that one day the god would smash a ship on the water after it had just returned from convoy and would raise mountains about our city. And now what the old man said is all coming to pass. Now then, take my advice, and let us all do as I shall say. Give no more convoy to strangers who shall come to our city: let us sacrifice twelve choice bulls to

Poseidon, and then perhaps he may have pity, and raise no lofty mountains about our city."

Accordingly the people in great fear prepared the bulls: and the lords and princes of the nation offered prayer to Poseidon standing about the altar.

Odysseus awoke. He lay on his native soil, and knew it not, since he had been long absent. For Pallas Athena herself, that divine daughter of Zeus, had covered the place with mist, that she might tell him everything first and disguise him. She wished that his wife and friends might not know him until he had punished the wooers of his wife for their outrageous violence. For that reason she made him find the whole place unfamiliar, the long roads, the wide harbours, the sharp rocks, the growing trees.

He leapt up and stood looking round on his native land. Then he slapt his two thighs with his open hands, and cried aloud in perplexity:

"More trouble for me! What kind of men live in this country where I find myself? Men of violence, savages who know not justice? or kind people that know right from wrong? Where can I bestow these goods? Where can I go myself? I wish they had stayed in Phaiacia; I might have gone on to some other powerful king, who would have entertained me and helped me on my way. Now I do not know where to bestow all this, and I cannot leave the stuff here or some one may come and steal. Ah well, those Phaiacian gentlemen were not altogether just and right-minded men, or they would not have brought me to a strange country, when they promised to take me to Ithaca and did not do it. May Zeus who hears the suppliant's prayer requite them, he that beholds the doings of men, and punishes sinners! I will just count up and see if they have taken anything away with them."

He counted the tripods and cauldrons, and the gold and all the woven stuffs, and missed nothing: then he paced along the seashore, thinking with sorrow and grief of his native land. But now came Athena towards him, in the shape of a young shepherd, but some one who seemed to be delicately nurtured, like a gentleman's son: a cloak was folded about her shoulders, boots were on her feet, and she carried a javelin. Odysseus was glad indeed to see her, and moved to meet her, and he spoke out plainly:

"Welcome, my friend! you are the first I meet in this place. I beg you to do me no wrong, but save me, and save all this. I implore you as if you were a god and embrace your knees! Answer me truthfully, what is this place? What country is it, and what men live here? Is it some bright island, or the mainland shore sloping down to the sea?"

Athena answered with her bright eyes glinting:

"You are foolish, sir, or you have come from a long way off, if you ask questions about this land. It is not so very nameless in the world: many men know it, both those who dwell towards the east and the rising sun, and those who dwell westwards towards the misty gloom. I grant it is rugged and no place for horses, but it is not a bad place, although no one could call it broad. It grows a terrible lot of corn, and makes its own wine: there's plenty of rain and luscious grass; good food for goats and good food for cattle: trees of all sorts, and plenty of water that never fails. Therefore, good stranger, the name of Ithaca has reached as far as Troy, which they say lies far away from the Achaian land."

This made Odysseus glad indeed, after all his sufferings; full of joy to be on his native soil he heard the words of Pallas Athenaia daughter of Zeus, and his answer was plain enough: but he did not tell her the truth, which he was careful to keep back, for he had always a good store of clever fables:

"Yes, I have heard of Ithaca even in the broad island of Crete far over the sea. And now I have come here myself with all these goods. I left as much again for my sons, when I had to get away, a banished man, because I killed a son of Idomeneus,—I mean Orsilochos the sprinter, who beat every living soul in the island with those quick feet of his. He wanted to rob me of all my Trojan booty, which I had won by such toiling and moiling, wars on land and voyages over the sea: the fact was I would not be a servant to please his father, but kept a company of my own men. I ran him through with a spear as he was coming down from the country, where I waited for him off the road with a friend.

"It was a dewy night, and not a soul saw us, nobody knew that I had killed him. When I had finished the business I applied to some honest Phoenicians who were there with a ship, and I paid them a handsome fee out of my booty, to take me on board for Pylos or the fair land of Elis, where the Epeians are in possession. But the wind drove them away from those parts: they could not help it, they had no wish to deceive me. From there we were carried out of our course to this place in the night. We just managed to get into this harbour. We had no thought for food though we were hungry enough, but just came ashore every man and lay down as we were. I was so weary that I fell into a deep sleep: the others brought out my goods from the ship and left them beside me on the sand. They have gone off to Sidon, and here I am left behind, worse luck."

Athena smiled and her bright eyes flashed, and she stroked him with her hand. Now she looked like a tall and majestic woman, clever and intelligent, and she spoke to the point:

"A cunning rogue he would be, master of craft, who would outwit you! Even a god couldn't do it. Irrepressible! everlasting schemer! indefatigable fabulist! Even in your own country you wouldn't desist from your tales and your historiological inventions, which you love from the bottom of your heart.

"But no more of this. We are both clever enough; you are the paragon of mankind at planning and story-telling, and I have a name among the gods for cleverness and intelligence. And you didn't know Pallas Athenaia the daughter of Zeus himself, your faithful stand-by and guardian in all your labours! and it was I who made the Phaiacians kind to you. Well, here I am again, to make plans for you, and to hide your treasures which the generous Phaiacians bestowed upon you—all my doing, let me tell you; and to explain the dangers which fate has waiting for you in your own home. Be patient, for you must; say not one word either to man or woman living, don't tell a soul that you have come back from your wanderings, but suffer all in silence, and put up with the violence of wicked men."

Odysseus was not taken aback, but he answered at once:

"It is a difficult thing, goddess, for a mortal man to know you at sight, even a man of experience; you turn yourself into all sorts of shapes. One thing I do know, that you were gracious to me long ago when we Achaians were fighting at Troy. But after we had sacked the tall city of Priam, and embarked, and God scattered the fleet, I did not see you then, O daughter of Zeus himself! I did not notice you on board my ship when I wanted some one to help me. I had to go drifting about in misery and wretchedness until the gods freed me from my troubles; that was before you encouraged me in the Phaiacian land and led me into the city yourself. Now I implore you by your father—for I do not think this is my beloved Ithaca, but some other country, where I find myself. I think you are only making fun of me to bewilder my mind. Tell me if this is really Ithaca my home."

Athena answered with flashing eyes:

"Ah, you are always the same, no one can catch you napping; and that is why I cannot desert you in misfortune, because you are so charming and discreet and always ready for anything. Any other man after those long wanderings would have been eager to see home and wife and children; you do not choose to ask anything of any one until you make sure of your wife by your own observation—and she, let me tell you, just stays at home, while she weeps the nights and days away.

"But I never doubted, I knew quite well that you would return at last after losing all your men. The truth is, I did not wish to quarrel with Poseidon, who is my father's own brother, and he was furious because you blinded his son. Look here, I will show you the landscape of Ithaca, and then you will believe me. This is the harbour of Phorcys the Old Man of the Sea; this is the olive tree with its long leaves; this is the vaulted cave where you have offered so many solemn sacrifices to the nymphs; there is Neriton hill covered with woods."

With these words the goddess dispersed the mist, and the land became visible. And Odysseus was filled with joy after all his troubles, and kissed the fruitful earth. Then he lifted up his hands and uttered a prayer to the nymphs:

"Naiad nymphs, O daughters of Zeus! I thought I was never again to see you; but now accept my greeting and my loving prayers. I will make my offerings also as I used to do, if the guiding daughter of Zeus graciously allows me to live and my son to grow."

Athena answered him: "Take courage, do not let that trouble you. But now let us put away these treasures far within the sacred cave, that they may remain in safety. We will consider between us how to manage for the best."

The goddess entered the dark cave, and searched about for hiding-places; while Odysseus brought up the stuff, gold and bronze and clothing, which the Phaiacians had given him. All this they stowed away carefully, and Pallas Athenaia daughter of Zeus Almighty herself placed a stone before the mouth.

Then the two sat down under the olive tree, and discussed how to make an end to the riotous gallants. Athena began by saying:

"Prince Laërtiadês, you are a man never baffled, and now is the time to consider how you may lay hands on those shameless men, who for three years have been lording it in your house, and paying court to your incomparable wife!

She longs continually for your return, keeps them in hope, makes promises to each, proposes this and that, while she has quite other things in her heart."

Odysseus said:

"I do declare I should have met the same cruel fate as Agamemnon Atreidês in my own house, if you had not told me clearly what has been going on, my goddess. Come on, weave me a plan to punish them; stand by my side, give me unfailing courage, as when we tore the pretty veil from Troy's head. If you stand by me in earnest, Brighteyes, I could fight three hundred men, with you my queen and goddess, so long as you would really help me."

Athena said to this:

"Of course, I will stand by you; I will not forget you when we are about this business. I think those men who woo your wife and devour your wealth will soon bedabble the floor with their own blood and brains!

"Now then, I will disguise you so that no one will be able to know you. I will shrivel up the sound flesh of that muscular body, I will sweep off the brown crop from your head, I will wrinkle up those beautiful eyes, I will give you rags to wear which any one would be sick to see on a human being, and you shall seem like a shabby vagabond to the proud gallants, and even your own wife and son.

"But you must first pay a visit to the old man who looks after your pigs; he is always loyal to you, loves your son and your faithful Penelopeia. You will find him among his pigs. They feed near the Raven's Rock [1] and Arethusa Spring, with plenty of acorns to eat and clear water to drink, which makes a good fat pig. Stay with him there and let him talk, while I go to Lacedaimon, and bring back Telemachos, yes Odysseus, your own son from the land of handsome women.[2] He has gone to the lawns of Lacedaimon to ask Menelaos about you, and to find out whether you are still alive."

Odysseus very naturally asked:

"And why on earth didn't you tell him, since you knew all about it? Did you want him to see how *he* likes drifting over the sea in dispair? The sea is barren enough, and these men are devouring his wealth all the time."

Athena replied:

[1] The Raven's Rock still bears that name in Ithaca.

[2] She seems to suggest that Telemachos may be a regular lad in the land of pretty girls. Odysseus gives a start at the name of Telemachos. He is not taken in, but sees the weak point. How neatly he reminds her that she let him go drifting on the sea.

"Now don't worry too much about him. I went there with him myself, that he might win some credit in the world. There's nothing the matter with him; he is staying peacefully in the palace of Atreidês, living in luxury. It is true there are some young fellows waiting for him in a ship, intending to murder him before he gets home. But I don't think that will happen. The men who are devouring his wealth will be dead and buried before that."

As she said this, Athena passed her rod over Odysseus. She withered the sound flesh of his muscular body, she swept the flaxen crop from his head, she made the skin of every limb like the skin of an old man, she wrinkled up his beautiful eyes, she changed his clothes into a shirt and a lot of filthy old rags begrimed with foul-reeking smoke; upon this she threw a big hartskin with the hair worn off, and she gave him a stick and a coarse bag full of holes with a twisted cord to carry it.

BOOK XIV

Odysseus and the Swineherd

So THE PAIR FINISHED THEIR PLAN AND PARTED. SHE SET off at once for sunny Lacedaimon to fetch his boy for Odysseus; he entered upon a stony path which led from the harbour, through the woods and over the hilltops. Athena had shown him this way to find the honest swineherd, who cared most for his master's wealth out of all the servants of Odyesseus.

He found the man sitting under the porch in front of his enclosure, round which a high wall had been built. It stood in an open space, a great wide place with a clearing all round it. The swineherd had built this himself for the pigs since his master had gone away, and his mistress and old Laertês had nothing to do with it. It was made of huge unshaped stones, with prickly pear planted along the top. Outside this was a palisade carried all round, made of logs set upright together, and the outer part split off to leave only the black heart-of-oak. Within the enclosure were twelve pens close together for the sows, fifty sows in each pen with their litter, lying on the ground. The boars lay outside, and they were not nearly so many; for my lords the gallants kept thinning them out .The swineherd had to send in always the best of the fat hogs, but there were three hundred and fifty left. Four dogs always lay with them which the swineherd had bred, as savage as wild beasts.

Just then the swineherd was cutting a pair of shoes out of a prime piece of leather, and fitting them to his feet; the other men had gone off in different directions with droves of boars, that is, three of them, for he had been obliged to send in the fourth with a hog to satisfy the appetite of the boisterous company.

Suddenly the dogs caught sight of Odysseus. They were champion barkers [1]—they set up a howl, and at him! But Odysseus knew the trick, sat on the ground and dropt his cudgel. Even then he might have been roughly treated outside his own pigfold, but the swineherd took a hand—dropt

---

[1] This is one of the poet's parodies: ὑλακόμωροι like ἐγχεσίμωροι, "champion spearmen."

his leather and ran to kick away the dogs, shouting and shoo-ing them off in all directions with the help of a shower of stones. Then he spoke to his master:

"Well, gaffer, that was a nice chance; the dogs would a done for thee in a twink, and then tha'd a blamed me. Aye, the gods have given me many a moan and groan already. A rare fine master I have to mourn, and here I bide, fattenen my hogs for a lot of foreigners; and the master may be lacken a bit to eat, knocken about in cities and countries where they don't speak our language, if so be he is alive and sees the light of the sun. But come along, gaffer, into the hut; there's bread and wine to fill thi belly, then tha'lt tell me where tha comes from and what thi troubles have been."

So saying, the swineherd led him into the hut, and made him sit down. He laid a pile of thick twigs and spread over them the dark skin of a wild goat. Odysseus was right glad at this welcome, and he said to the man, "I pray that Zeus and all the gods of heaven may grant you your heart's desire, for this kind welcome of me."

Eumaios answered:

"Man alive, it is not my way to slight a stranger, though he were more of a shally-go-naked than thisen! God sends the stranger and the beggarman, we gladly give not much but all we can; donta look for much when the hands are all afeard of new masters. Sure enough the gods have tied up his home-comen, or a would have loved me well and given me summat of my own, as a master will do when he has a mind to the man, a house and a bit of land and a wife that might take her pick, when a man works hard and has the blessen of God on his work, as my work here is blessed. So my master would have made me rich if he had stayed here to grow old; but he is dead! I wish Helen had died first and been wiped out with all her kith and kin, for she brought low many a man. Master himself went to the war at Ilion, with Agamemnon, to pay 'em out."

As he said this, he tightened his belt and tucked in his shirt, and went to the pens where the pigs were kept. He chose two and killed them, singed them, chopt them up, ran spits through the bits; they were soon grilled, and he served up all hot on the spits and laid it before Odysseus, and sprinkled white barley-meal over. Next he mixed a delicious draught of wine in an ivy-wood cup, and sat down opposite and urged him to set to:

"Eat away, stranger, it's hind's fare, just young porkers, but the fat boars go down for my lords to eat, who have not the fear of God before 'em or pity in their hearts. Well, the blessed gods love not reckless deeds, but they honour justice and uprightness. Why, even cruel men who invade a foreign land, if Zeus gives 'm spoil, when they have loaded their ships and turn homewards, even they have a mighty fear of God in their hearts. But these men—be sure they know the master is dead, poor soul, they have heard some voice from God, that they won't do their wooen decently, or else go home, but there they sit coolly champen up his flocks and herds, it's too bad, no stinten there! Every single night and day that God gives us, they kill not one beast, or two only; and the wine they waste, it's too bad, broachen and broachen! Once a had a champion fortune; not a soul had so much, none of the great squires on the mainland, not to say Ithaca; twenty of those chaps together couldn't match him. I'll just count the tale over, and tha'lt see.

"Twelve herds on the mainland, as many flocks of sheep, as many drift of swine, as many solid flocks of goats, looked after by foreigners or his own hinds. And here, eleven solid flocks of goats, feeden at the ends of the island, and good men to watch them. Every man of 'em drives in a beast every day, has to pick out the best of 'em rare and fat. Then here am I with these pigs to guard and watch; I have to choose the best one and send him in."

While the man was speaking, Odysseus was making a hearty meal with a good appetite, but he said nothing, only brooded over his revenge. When he had finished, the swineherd filled the cup he used to drink from, and handed it brimming over to Odysseus, who received it gladly, and asked him a plain question:

"My friend, who was it bought you and paid for you, this man of substance and power as you describe him? You say he died to take toll for Agamemnon. Tell me, perhaps I may know him, if he is a man like that. God knows whether I have seen him, for I have travelled far; but I may be able to tell you something."

The honest swineherd answered:

"No, no, gaffer, no traveller who brought news of that man could make his wife and son believe it. They are all just vagrom men who want what they can get, all liars, who will not tell the truth. Every vagabond who comes to our country goes to the mistress with his false lies; she takes him in, and treats him well, and asks all the ins and outs, and then down come the tears in a flood, as a woman will do when her husband dies abroad. Tha be'st like the rest, gaffer, soon make up a good yarn, if some one gave tha a shirt and coat to wear.

"As for him, his soul has left him by this time, dogs and carrion birds will have torn skin from bone, or he has been food for fishes in the sea, and his bones lie on the shore buried in sand. So we have lost him over there, and he has left trouble for his friends, most of all for me; I shall never find so kind a master, wherever I go, not even if I go back to my father and mother, to the house where I was born and brought up. Indeed I do not mourn so much for them as for him, though I long to see 'em again and my native land, but I do miss Odysseus since he went away. I don't like to speak his name, man, although he is absent, but I call him 'his honour,' even when he is far away."

Odyssesus heard this, and showed no sign, but said to him:

"Since you will have none of it, my friend, and say that man will never come, and refuse to believe anything, I will not just tell you so, I will swear it—Odysseus will return! Let me have my reward for good news when he shall come to his own house, and not before—I would not take it if you offered it, though I am poor enough. I hate that man like the gates of hell who tells a lie because he is penniless. O Zeus! be witness now, first of all gods! and the guest's table, and the hearth of Odysseus, without stain and without reproach, to which hearth I come for refuge! I swear that all will come to pass as I declare. Within this very lichtgang Odysseus will return, as the old moon is waning and the new moon is rising;[1] and he shall take vengeance upon all who here dishonour his wife and his proud son."

The swineherd replied:

"No, gaffer, I will never pay tha that reward for good news, and Odysseus will never again return home. But sit quiet and drink, and let us talk of summat else, donta mind me of this; my heart is heavy and sad when any one minds me of my dear master. Never mind the oath, but may Odysseus return as I only wish he would, and so does my lady and old Laërtês and that grand boy Telemachos.

"Aye, 'tis that boy I'm sorry for; can't get him out of my mind, his son Telemachos: grew up tall like a young tree,

---

[1] The poet uses a very old word, otherwise unknown (except in later imitations), which I have translated literally. It might mean day, month, or year, and was generally explained as year in antiquity; but month suits the passage better, and so it is interpreted by Dion Chrysostom, *Venator*, vii. 84. In prehistoric times, the important period was not the year, but the month; the changing light of the moon.

God be blessed! and I thought a would be as fine as his
father, when a grew up, handsome and well-grown, a master-
piece. But some god must have touched his wits, or some man
maybe, and off a went to Pylos for news of his father. The
grand come-marry-me-quicks are lying for him on his way
home; what they want is to wipe out the whole family of
Arceisios from Ithaca.

"Well, never mind that boy, he may be caught, he may
escape, Cronion may hold a hand over him. Come now, gaffer,
tell us thi own troubles, and first answer me this and make
my mind clear about thiself. Who ista, where dosta come
from, what ship brought thee here, how came it to put in at
Ithaca, who were they at all? I don't suppose tha's walked all
the way here."

To this Odysseus answered:

"Very well, I will tell you the whole story. But give us a
year's provisions in your hut, food to eat and good wine to
drink, let us stay quietly here and others do the work, it
would not be easy to finish my story in the time, or tell all
the toiling and moiling I have had by God's decree.

"I am proud to claim my breeding from the wide plains
of Crete. My father was a rich man. Many other sons were
born and bred in his house, sons of his lawful wife; but my
mother was a purchased slave, yet my father, Castor Hyla-
cidês, gave me a place equal to his lawfully begotten sons.
At that time my father was honoured like a god among
the Cretans, for his happiness and riches and his splendid
sons. But death carried him away to the house of Hadês,
and his proud sons cast lots for his wealth and divided it
amongst them; they gave me a very small share with a house.

"I married a wife from a rich family, won by my own
merits, for I was no weakling or shirk-battle; but all that is
gone now, although I think you may still guess the corn
from the stubble; indeed, I have had misfortune in abundance.
Courage I certainly had from Arês and Athena, and strength
to break my foes; when I used to pick the best men for
ambush, and planned some deadly stroke, my firm spirit
never thought of death, but I would leap to the front spear
in hand and down my man, unless he could show a clean
pair of heels. War was my line, not work or housekeeping
and a fine family; what I liked were ships and oars and
battles and fine smooth javelins and arrows, dangerous things
like those, which make other people shudder.

"But I suppose I liked what God made me like; one likes
this and one likes that. For before the Achaians sailed for

Troy, nine times I commanded a fleet against foreign enemies, and I won a great deal of spoil. I had my choice first as commander, and took whatever I wanted, and after that my share, a lot more; soon my house grew powerful, and I was feared and respected among the Cretans. But when Zeus Allseeing ordained that dreadful enterprise which brought low so many men, they appointed me and the illustrious Idomeneus to command their fleet against Ilion; there was no remedy, go we must—public opinion was too much for us.

"There we Achaians waged war for nine years; in the tenth year we sacked Priam's city and set out for home, but God scattered our ships. Then Zeus in his wisdom had suffering in store for me. One month only I was happy with wife and children and home; then I took it into my head to lead a fleet against Egypt, crack ships and crews too good for this world. We had nine ships, and all soon filled up.

"The men feasted well for six days. I provided plenty of animals for sacrifice and food. On the seventh day we embarked, and left Crete with a fair north wind blowing free, running as easily as if we were running down a river. Nothing happened to any of the ships; we sat tight, safe and sound, not a sick man in the fleet, while wind and pilots kept a straight path. In five days we arrived at the noble river Aigyptos, and there I lay to.

"I left the men to defend the ships, and sent spies to find out what they could; but they went ravaging about at their own sweet will, pillaging the countryside, killing the men and carrying off the women and children. Soon the news reached the city. The people heard a hue and cry at dawn, and came running out; the whole plain was full of men and horses and flashing armour. Zeus Thunderer sent a panic upon my men, and they showed no fight, for ruin and destruction were all around. Many of us were killed, the rest carried off to be slaves.

"Then Zeus himself put a plan into my head—how I wish I had been killed there in Egypt! but there was more trouble waiting for me. I threw off the helmet from my head and the shield from my shoulders, and dropt my spear, and ran to meet the king's chariot; I clasped his knees and kissed them, and he took pity and saved me, and took me home in his chariot, miserable enough. Many a man rushed at me levelling his spear to kill me, for they were greatly infuriated; but he kept me safe and respected the wrath of Zeus, who is the stranger's god, and is angry at evil deeds.

"There I stayed seven years, and gathered a good deal of

wealth among the Egyptians, for they all gave me something.
But when the eighth year came rolling round, a Phoinician
man turned up, a cheat and liar, one of those nip-screws,
one who had done plenty of mischief in the world already.
He cajoled me by his cunning to go with him to Phoinicia,
where his house and property lay. I stayed with him for a
full year. But when the months and days had passed and
the seasons came round with another rolling year, he took
me on board a ship for a voyage to Libya, pretending falsely
that he wished me to be partner in the cargo, but what he
meant was to sell me for a handsome price when he got
there. I went with him because I must, although I had my
suspicions.

"The ship ran before a fair wind, across the open sea to
the windward of Crete; but Zeus meant to destroy them!
When we had left Crete behind and were out of sight of
land, only sea and sky to be seen, Cronion brought a black
cloud over the ship, and the sea grew dark beneath it. Then
Zeus thundered and lightened together and struck the ship;
her timbers all shivered at the stroke, and the place was
filled with sulphur. All on board were cast into the sea. They
were carried over the black waters bobbing about on the
waves like so many black crows; it was God's will that they
should never see home again.

"I was in a bad way, but Zeus himself put the ship's mast
in my hands, a huge pole, to save me again from death.
With my arms round this I drifted before the accursed winds.
Nine days I drifted; on the tenth dark night I was thrown up
by a great wave on the Thesprotian shore. There the king,
Pheidon, entertained me without payment; for his son hap-
pened to find me worn out with exposure and hardship; he
offered me his hand, and raised me up,[1] and took me home
to his father, and gave me a shirt and cloak to wear.

"There I heard of Odysseus. The king said he had enter-
tained him as a guest on his way home, and showed me a
heap of choice things which Odysseus had brought, bronze
and gold and wrought iron; there were treasures enough in
that mansion to support Odysseus and his family for ten
generations. The king said he had gone to Dodona that he
might learn the will of Zeus from the great oak, and find
out how he ought to return to Ithaca after his long absence,
whether openly or secretly. And he swore a solemn oath in
my presence, as he poured a libation in his own house,

---

[1] A formal acceptance of the duties of hospitality.

that a ship was launched and crew ready to carry him safe home to his native land.

"But the King said good-bye to me first, for a Thesprotian ship happened to come in which was bound for wheat-bearing Dulichion. He gave the men careful instructions to see me safe to King Acastos. But it pleased them to plan mischief against me, that I might have more trouble. When the ship was out at sea and far from the land, they prepared me for the day of slavery. They tore off my cloak and shirt, and threw me a dirty shirt instead and a lot of rags, full of holes as you see with your own eyes, and at evening they reached the fields of Ithaca. Then they tied me up tight with twisted ropes, and left me on board while they went ashore and had a hearty meal on the beach. God unwound my ropes easily enough; I wrapt my head in my rags and slipped down the lading-plank, breasted the sea, paddling away with both hands, and soon got ashore a good way off. Then I climbed into a coppice of flowering shrubs, and lay there in hiding. The sailors ran shouting about till they thought it no use to hunt any further, then they went back on board. The gods hid me easily; it was their doing, and they have led me to the croft of an understanding man. Sure enough it is not my fate to die yet."

Eumaios answered:

"Poor soul, tha's moved my heart by that long story of sufferens and wanderens. But tha'rt wrong in one thing, I think, and that wilt not make me believe all that about Odysseus. Why must a man like thee tell a lot of lies for nowt? I know all about my master's return myself; I know all the gods have a grudge against him, no doubt about that, or they would have let the Trojans kill him, or let him die in his friends' arms, after he had wound up the war. Now there's never a word of him, the snatcher-birds have snatched him up.

"And I keep out of the way with my pigs; never go to town, unless my wise mistress sends for me, when news comes from somewhere. Then they all sit round, and ask all the ins and outs, whether sorry or glad, whether they want the master to come back, or want to go on eaten up his goods for nowt.

"But I don't care to ask any questions, ever since that Aitolian man took me in with his yarn, the man who killed somebody, and wandered all over the world, and came to my place. He said he had seen him in Crete, where Idomeneus put him up; he was menden his ships which had been smashed in a storm. He said a would come either that sum-

mer or in the autumn, had plenty of stuff with him and
champion crews. Donta be like him, gaffer many-troubles,
now God has brought thee up to my door, donta wheedle
me with lies; that won't make me pity thee and treat thee
well; I do it because I fear the god of strangers and I am
sorry for thisen."

Odysseus answered:

"You are a most unbelieving sort of fellow, I declare,
when you won't believe me on my oath. All right, let's make
a bargain; witness on both sides, the gods of Olympos; time,
by and by. If your master comes back to this house, you
shall find me a coat and shirt and give me a passage to
Dulichion, where I have a mind to be. If your master does
not come, set the men on me and throw me over the cliff,
to warn other beggars not to deceive."

My lord the pigman answered:

"My word, I should get myself a good name for hospitality
in the world, now and evermore! First invite thee in and
give thee food, then kill thee and bundle thee over the cliff!
I should have to look sharp and make my peace with God!
But now it is time for supper. I hope my fellows will soon be
in, and we can make a good square meal."

As they were talking together the men were coming in
with their hogs. They shut up the sows in the pens, and a
rare noise they made as they went to bed. My lord the
pigmen called out to his companions, "Sitha, bring in the
best of yon hogs, I want to kill one for a stranger who has
come from foreign parts, and we shall have some good our-
selves, after all our toilen and moilen with the tuskers while
other people eat our labour scot-free."

He chopt up some wood with pitiless blade [1] as he spoke,
and the others brought in a fine fat boar, a five-year-old. They
soon set him beside the hearth, and the swineherd did not
forget the immortals, for he had a pious heart. He cut off
the firstling hairs of the tusker, and cast them into the fire,
as he prayed to All Gods that Odysseus might return to his
own home—after all, he was equal to anything. He picked up
a billet of oak which he had left while splitting, and stunned
the boar: the others cut his throat and singed him.

They soon carved him up, and the swineherd took the first

---

[1] Here, as often, Homer is poking fun at the poetical tags. He uses
one phrase which belongs to the battlefield, like "cold steel," and
another which he has used in the *Iliad* better suited to beef than
pork. So he calls the swineherd Dios, as if he were a prince, "My
lord the pigman."

slices from all the limbs and covered them with fat in due
form. These they cast into the fire, and sprinkled the white
meal over; then they sliced up the rest and put all on the
spits, broiled it to a turn, took it off, laid it on platters;
the swineherd got up and did the carving, for he knew the
proper thing to do.

He divided all into seven portions: one he set aside for the
Nymphs and Hermês Maia's son, with a prayer, the others
he served one to each. But Odysseus had the honour of the
tusker's long chine, which made the master's heart proud.
Then Odysseus said to him:

"Eumaios, I pray Zeus may bless you as I do, for the
honour you have done to a ragged stranger with these good
things."

Eumaios answered: "Eat away, dear heart alive, and enjoy
what we have to offer. The Lord gives and the Lord takes
away, as it pleases him, for he can do all things."

So saying, he consecrated the firstling-bits to the deathless
gods, and the first drops of wine, then handed the cup to the
victor of Troy, and he sat down before his plate. The bread
was taken round by Mesaulios,—a man whom the swineherd
had bought since his master went away, on his own account,
nothing to do with the mistress and old Laërtês; he got him
from the Taphians and paid out of his own savings. Then they
helped themselves to the good things that were before them.
When all had had enough, Mesaulios cleared away the bread,
and they prepared to lie down after the hearty meal.

It was a rough night, in the moon's dark time; the rain
fell all night long with a high west wind, which always
brings wet. Odysseus thought he would try whether the swine-
herd could take a hint, and lend him his own cloak, or tell
one of the men to lend his, since he was mighty fond of his
guest. So he said:

"I say, Eumaios, and you other good fellows, I want some-
thing, and I must let it out; more wine, less wits, you know;
wine makes a man sing even if he is a rare scholar, makes
him titter and chuckle, aye, makes him dance a jig, and
makes him blurt out what were better kept to himself.

"Well, now I've begun my croak, I'll just go on. I wish I
were young and strong and full of go as I was when we laid
that ambush outside Troy! Odysseus was in command with
his grace King Menelaos, and I was third; had to obey orders,
you see. When we came to the place near to the city walls,
we crawled under a lot of thick bushes among the reeds of a
marsh, and there we lay in our armour. It was a rough night,

for the north wind had fallen and brought frost, there was
snow falling like rime, very cold, and the ice formed over
our shields. All the others had cloaks and jerkins, and slept
quietly with the shields over their shoulders; but I had been
fool enough to leave my cloak behind, as I didn't think I
should freeze even like that, and I had nothing but my shield
and belly-band.

"In the third watch of the night, when the stars had turned
their course, I nudged Odysseus with my elbow as he lay
beside me, and he was awake in an instant; then I said, 'Prince
Odysseus, you can always get a man out of a hole—the
cold is too much for me, I shall soon be no longer in the land
of the living. I have no cloak, I was such a damned fool that
I came away with only my jerkin, and now I'm done for.' He
had a plan ready at once, a rare one he was for planning as
well as fighting! He whispered to me, 'Quiet now, or they'll
hear.' Then he lifted his head on his elbow and said aloud, 'I
say, friends, God has sent me a dream. We are a terrible way
off from the ships, and I wish some one would go and ask
my lord Agamemnon if he would send us a few more men.' A
man jumped up at once. Andraimon's Thoas he was—threw
off his fine cloak, and away to the ships at the double. I lay
snug under his cloak until daylight did appear. I wish I were
young and strong as I was then!"

Eumaios answered: "That's a good yarn, gaffer, very much
to the point, and tha'lt not lose by it. Tha'lt not lack clothes
or anything else that a poor man might expect from a friend
in need, for to-night, that is; to-morrow tha must rub along
with thi own rags. We have no great stock of cloaks here or
change of shirts, one man one cloak is our rule."

As he spoke, he jumped up and laid a bed for him near the
fire, a heap of sheepskins and goatskins, and there Odysseus lay
down; the swineherd covered him with a large thick cloak, his
own special reserve, which he kept for terrible cold weather.

There Odysseus slept, and the young men lay round him.
But the swineherd did not choose to lie anywhere apart from
his pigs, so he made his preparations outside. Odysseus was
pleased that he was so careful of his master's property when
the master was not there. First Eumaios slung a sword over
his strong shoulders, then threw over him a heavy cloak to
keep off the wind, and upon it a fleecy goatskin, lastly chose a
sharp javelin to defend him against man or dog. Then he went
to lie where the tusker boars were sleeping, under a rock
which sheltered them from the north wind.

BOOK XV
How Telemachos Sailed Back to Ithaca

So PALLAS ATHENA WENT ON HER WAY TO LACEDAIMON, to remind Telemachos that it was high time to return. She found him and Nestor's son sleeping in the open gallery before the mansion of Menelaos; at least, one of them was sound asleep, but Telemachos was too anxious about his father, and he had been restless all night.

Athena came to his side, and said, "Don't dally in this valley, Telemachos, I tell 'ee! [1] Remember your estates and the bullies in your house! They will eat everything up among them, while you are wasting your pains on this journey. You must take leave of Menelaos, if you want to find your dear mother still in your house; for her father and brothers are urging her to marry Eurymachos. He is easily first in the matter of bridal gifts, he is just piling them up. Take care that she does not take something with her that you would not like to lose.

"You know what a woman's mind is like; she wishes to enrich the man who marries her, but as for the other husband and his children, once he is dead she forgets them all and never asks about them. The best thing you can do is to go back, and put everything in the hands of one of the women, whichever you think the best, until the gods provide you a good capable wife.

"There is something else I want you to know—don't forget it. The leading men of that company are lying in wait for you in the strait between Ithaca and Samos, and they mean to kill you before you can get home. But I don't think they will do it; before that can happen, the earth will cover some of those men who are devouring your substance. You must keep your ship away from the islands, and go on through the night; the god who protects you and saves you will send a fair following wind.

"And as soon as you first touch the shore of Ithaca, leave the ship and all the crew to go on to the town, but land your-

---

[1] This is a pun on his name. You may be Τηλέμαχος the fighting man, but you should not be Τηλάλαλος the loafing man and Τηΰσιος the feckless man as well.

self and go first to the swineherd in charge of your hogs,
who is true and faithful to you. Stay the night there; send
him into the town, and let him tell your mother, who is a
sensible woman, that you have come back from Pylos safe
and sound."

As soon as Athena had said this, she returned to high
Olympos. Telemachos turned to his friend sleeping soundly in
his bed, and stirred him up with his foot, saying, "Get up,
Master Peisistratos! Bring along the horses, and let us be off!"

Peisistratos answered:

"My dear man, why all this hurry? We can't travel at night
in the darkness; it will be morning soon. At least wait till his
Grace the royal champion Menelaos can bring his presents,
and put them in the car, and bid us an affectionate farewell
before we go. That's what a guest remembers to his dying
day, when a hospitable man has been kind to him."

As he spoke, the dawn rose enthroned in gold. And there
was the royal champion himself coming out of bed already,
and Helen still asleep! When Telemachos saw him, he lost no
time, but put on his tunic and threw the wrap over his sturdy
shoulders, and went out to greet him. He said:

"My lord King Menelaos, I beg you let me take my leave
at once, for I desire most earnestly to go home at once."

The king replied:

"My dear Telemachos, I am not the man to delay you if
you wish to go. I think it most improper that any one in the
place of a host should go too far in his likes and too far in his
dislikes. The best rule is moderation in all things. You may
take it that it is equally bad manners to press your guest to go
if he wants to stay, and to stay if he wants to go. Yes, feed
him if he wants to stay, speed him if he'd go away.[1]

"Still, you might stay while I fetch you my parting gifts
and pack them in the car, something nice, you haven't seen
it yet, and let me tell the women to get you a good breakfast
in hall. There are two good reasons for that: it is a proper
attention on my part, and it will do you good to have a good
feed before you go on a long journey to the ends of the earth.
But if you will go trapesing all over the country, all right,
only let me come too, I will yoke up, and I'll introduce you to
the various towns. No one shall let us go just as we came,
something he shall give us to take back home, say a bronze
tripod or cauldron, or a pair of mules or a gold cup."

---

[1] This line, called an interpolation by the editors, is exactly in
keeping with the speaker's character. He cannot even keep his tags
out of his prayers, as we see in the *Iliad*.

Telemachos answered politely:

"My lord King Menelaos, with your Grace's leave, I wish to return home at once, for I left no guardian behind me to look after the estate. I have my fears that in seeking for my noble father I may be lost myself, or at least something worth keeping may be lost from my house."

When the great champion heard this, at once he told his wife and servants to get ready a good breakfast in hall. Eteoneus Boethoïdes was up already and waiting, for he lived close by. Menelaos told him to light the fire and grill something, and he got to work at once. The king went down himself to the vaults, not alone, for Helen and Megapenthês went with him. When they reached the treasure-chamber, the king chose a two-handled cup, and told his son Megapenthês to take a silver mixing-bowl. Helen was at her coffers, where she kept the robes she had made herself, covered with beautiful embroidery. She chose out the largest of these, which had the finest work on it, and shone like a star; it lay right at the bottom. Then they all came back to Telemachos, and Menelaos said:

"Now then, Telemachos, I beseech Zeus the loud-thundering lord of Hera to fulfill your heart's desire! And I will offer you the finest and most precious of all my treasures. It is a mixing-bowl of solid silver, the lips finished off with gold, a genuine Hephaistos: Phaidimos gave it to me when I stayed in his house on my way home; he is the king of Sidon, you must know. And now I offer it to you."

With these words he handed the cup to him, and Megapenthês placed before him the splendid silver mixing-bowl. Lovely Helen was beside him with her robe, and she said:

"I also bring you this gift, dear boy; something to remind you of Helen, who made it with her own hands. Keep it until your wedding day, and on that happy day give it to your wife. Until then let your mother keep it for you. I pray that you may return safe to your home and your native land!"

So she laid the robe in his hands, and he received it beaming with joy. Peisistratos took all the gifts and packed them into the basket, gazing at them with admiration.

Then Menelaos led them into the hall, and they took their places, while a maid brought the hand-wash in a golden jug and poured it over their hands into a silver basin as usual. The dignified housekeeper brought bread, and Boethoïdês served the meat, and the son of Menelaos poured the wine. They helped themselves to the good things that were set before them; and when they had taken enough, Telemachos and

Peisistratos yoked the horses and got in themselves. As they moved away from the portal, Menelaos went after them holding in his right hand a golden cup full of honey-hearted wine, that they might pour the libation before they started. He stood before the horses and pledged his guests, saying, "Farewell, my lads, give my greetings to King Nestor. Indeed, he was kind as a father to me when we Achaians were in camp before Troy."

Telemachos answered politely:

"You may be sure of that, my lord King, we will give him your message. I wish I were so sure of finding Odysseus in Ithaca to hear about it when I get there, as I am sure you have treated me handsomely in every way and given me grand treasure to take home with me."

As he uttered these words, a good omen came: a bird flew over to the right, an eagle carrying in his claws a huge white goose which he had caught up from a farmyard, and there were the men and women following with shouts. The eagle passed close to them and shot over in front of the horses towards the right. At that sight all felt a deep glow of satisfaction, but Peisistratos was the first to speak:

"What do you think, King Menelaos? Was that omen intended for us two, or just for you?"

Our champion Menelaos did not know quite what to say, or how he should interpret this omen properly; but Helen did not leave him time to answer, she spoke up herself.

"Let me speak, and I will utter the words of prophecy which the immortals put into my heart, which I believe will come true. As that bird has come from his native mountains and caught up this goose from the house where it was bred, so Odysseus after much tribulation and many wanderings shall come to his house and take his vengeance; or perhaps he is at home already, and laying plans for the destruction of all those men."

Telemachos answered at once, "So may Zeus grant it to be, the loud-thundering lord of Hera! Then I will offer thanks to you also in my own place, as if you also were a god!"

As he spoke, he touched up the horses, and they galloped on through the city in fine fettle. So all day long they kept the yoke dancing on their necks.

The sun went down, and all the roads were darkened; and they came to Pherai and the house of Dioclês: he was the son of Ortilochos, whose father was the river-god Alpheios. There they spent the night, and their host gave them gifts as a host ought to do.

When the rosy fingers of Dawn showed through the mists, they yoked their horses and got into their car and drove away from the portal of the echoing gallery. Peisistratos touched up the horses, and they flew along with a will. Soon they reached the tall fortress of Pylos, and then Telemachos said to his companion:

"Nestoridês, old fellow, will you do something for me? Say yes! We call ourselves friends by our fathers' friendship, and we are both young men: this journey will make us better friends than ever. Don't drive past my ship, there's a good fellow; leave me here, or the old gentleman will delay me out of pure good nature, but I simply must hurry on."

The young man mused a moment how he could oblige his friend without forgetting his duty. It seemed best on the whole to do as he was asked, so he turned the horses towards the seashore. Then he took out the treasures, the robe and the gold which Menelaos had given, and put them on board, and without any shilly-shallying he bade his friend make haste:

"Look sharp now, on board with you, and call your men. Get it done before I can go and tell the news to the old gentleman. I understand his masterful ways quite well. He'll never let you go, he'll come down here himself and insist, he will not go back without you. An angry man he will be, that is certain."

With these words he drove off towards the city, and soon found himself at home. But Telemachos urged his men to hurry: "In with the gear, you men, in with yourselves, and let us be off."

They lost no time in obeying: in a trice they were on their benches.

While he was busy with this, and offering prayer and sacrifice to Athena beside the ship, a man suddenly appeared. He came from a far country, banished from Argos for killing some one.

He was a prophet who traced his descent from Melampus. His ancestor had been settled in Pylos, "the mother of sheep," as men called it. He was a rich man, and lived in a splendid mansion; but he had been obliged to leave the country and seek another home for fear of Neleus: and that proud imperious prince seized his great property, and kept it for a whole year.

Meanwhile he was himself kept a prisoner in the house of Phylacos. That was a cruel imprisonment for him, full of humiliation; and it all came from the daughter of Neleus, and

the blind infatuation which the destroying Avenger brought
upon the father. However, he escaped death: he drove the
cows from Phylacê to Pylos, and made King Neleus pay for
his disgraceful doings, and married the girl to his brother.[1]

But he went abroad himself to Argos, for there he was des-
tined to live as ruler over that great nation of horsemen.
There he married a wife, and built a great palace, and had two
strong sons, Antiphatês and Mantios. Antiphatês was the
father of Oïclês, and Oïclês the father of Amphiraraos,
the man who collected the famous army against Thebes, one
who was very dear to Zeus Almighty and Apollo; but he did
not set foot on the threshold of old age, for he perished at
Thebes to satisfy a greedy woman.[2] His sons were Alcmaion
and Amphilochos. Mantios was the father of Polypheidês
and Cleitos. Of these Cleitos was carried off for his beauty by
Eos Goldenthrone, and taken to be among the immortals:
Polypheidês by Apollo's grace became the greatest prophet
in the world after Amphiaraos died. He quarrelled with his
father and went away to Hyperesia, where he was all-the-
world's prophet as long as he lived.

It was the son of this man who appeared before Telema-
chos, as I have said: his name was Theoclymenos. He found
Telemachos in the midst of his prayer beside the ship, and
cried out to him in plain words:

"My friend, as I find you offering sacrifice in this place, by
your sacrifice I adjure you, and by the god, nay by your own
head and your companions, tell me truly and hide it not—
Who are you, what is your country and your family?"

Telemachos answered:

"Very well, sir, I will tell you all you ask. I come from
Ithaca, my father is Odysseus, as surely as there ever was
such a man! but now he is lost, to my great sorrow. For that
reason I provided this ship and crew, and came to find out
why he is so long away."

The prophet answered:

"I had to leave my country like you. I killed a man of my
own kin: there are many brothers and kinsmen of his in

[1] Pera was the daughter of Neleus. She was not to marry unless
the bridegroom could present the cows of Iphiclos brought from
Phylacê. Melampus tried to carry them off, but he was caught and
imprisoned, and Neleus seized his property. Melampus made friends
with Iphiclos by his gift of divination, and the cows were given to
him. He gave them to his brother, who married the princess.

[2] His wife Eriphylê was bribed with a necklace to persuade him to
join the expedition, which he knew would fail.

Argos, men of great power in the nation. I had to take flight
from them, or I was a dead man: it seems I was destined to
be a wanderer on the face of the earth. Now I beg you take
me on board, since I am a fugitive and your suppliant, or they
will kill me: I am sure they are on my track."

Telemachos answered:

"I will not drive you from my ship, since you desire to
join us. So come along; when we arrive, you shall have the
best entertainment we can give."

He took the spear from the man's hand and laid it upon the
deck; then he went on board himself and sat down on the
after-deck, with Theoclymenos at his side. The hawsers were
cast off; Telemachos gave the word, and the men quickly
stept the mast and made fast the forestays, and hoisted the
sail by its ropes of twisted leather. Athena sent a following
wind, which went fanning them briskly along, to bring the
ship over the salt sea to her goal.

The sun set, and all the ways were darkened: and the ship
stood for Pheai running before the wind. Past Crunoi and
Chalcis they sailed, and past Elis, where the Epeians hold the
country. From thence Telemachos set his course for the
points of the islands, turning over in his mind the chances of
life or death.

Meanwhile in the hut Odysseus and the swineherd were
supping, and the other men with them. When they had fin-
ished, Odysseus spoke to Eumaios, for he wanted to see
whether he would invite him hospitably to stay in the hut or
send him down to the city.

"Look here, Eumaios," he said, "and you other men. To-
morrow morning I want to go and beg in the town, for I don't
like to be a burden on you all. Now then, advise me, and give
me a guide to show the way; but I must go about the town by
myself, to crave a cup and a crust.

"I should like also to find the house of Odysseus, and tell
my news to the noble lady, and have a try at those high and
mighty bridegrooms-to-be; perhaps they will give me a meal,
for they live on the fat of the land. I should be quite ready to
turn a hand to anything they want doing. For I tell you one
thing, and don't you forget it: by favour of God's messenger
Hermês, who bestows grace and glory on all the works of
man, there's not a man alive who comes near me for hard
work, piling up a good fire, chopping dry wood, carving and
cooking and serving wine, all that common men do for the
gentry."

Eumaios flared up at this, and said:

"Mercy on us, my good soul, what on earth put that into thi head? 'Tis asking for certain death then and there, if tha'rt set on goen among those fellows! Why, their violence and outrage cries out to the brazen sky! Their servants are not a bit like thee. Young men, drest up fair and smart, sleek heads and pretty faces, that's what their servants be. Polished tables loaded wi' bread and meat and wine! No, no, stay here. Nobody minds tha here, neither I nor my friends. Then if the master's son comes along, he'll give tha a coat and shirt to wear, and help tha wherever tha'd fain go."

Odysseus answered:

"May Father Zeus bless you as I do, Eumaios, for giving a rest to my wanderings and my heavy troubles. There's no worse life for a man than to tramp it. It's this damned belly that gives a man his worst troubles.

"Well, since you want me to stay here and wait for the young man, be so kind as to tell me about your master's mother, and his father, who were on the threshold of old age when he left: are they still alive, do they still see the light of the sun? or are they dead and buried?"

The swineherd answered:

"Very well, tha shall have the whole story from end to end. Laërtês is still alive, but every day he prays that his spirit may leave his old body: for he is terribly afflicted by his son's goen away, and the death of his own true wife, which was a cruel blow for him and made him old before his time. She died o' grieven for that famous son of hers, poor soul. I hope no one near and dear to me may have such a death. As long as she lived for all her sorrow, I'd gladly go and ask after her, and hear the news, by reason she bred me up herself along with her own little maid Ctimenê, her youngest—the picture of health she was in her long frock! Yes, we grew up together, and I was most one of the family. But when we both began to grow up, as happy as the day was long, they married her away into Samê, and what thousands of presents there was! The lady drest me up fine in a new coat and shirt and a new pair o' boots, and sent me on the farm, but in her heart she loved me more than ever.

"How I miss all that now! although for mysen the blessed gods give increase to the work which I do: it brings me food and drink and summat for those that have a claim on me. But the mistress has no comfortable word or deed for me now, since trouble has fallen upon the house, rude and violent men are there. Yet servants do greatly desire to speak before the mistress, and hear all the news, and have summat to eat and

drink, and then summat to take home with them: those things
do warm their hearts."

Odysseus answered:

"Upon my word, swineherd, you must have travelled far
from your own country and your parents when you were a
little tot! Tell me the whole story, please. Was it a great wide
city you lived in with your father and mother in a big house?
did the enemy take it and carry you off? or were you alone,
looking after sheep or cattle, and the pirates sailed away with
you and sold you into this man's house for a good price?"

Then Eumaios told his story:

"Th'art my guest," he said, "and tha shall hear the story of
my life. Hearken now quietly, and I hope it may please tha;
there's sleep and there's talk for them that list. But sit tha
down and drink thi liquor. The nights are terrible long: there's
no sense in turning in too early: too much sleep is a nuisance.
You other fellows may go out and sleep if you like, and in the
mornen have a feed and drive out the master's pigs. We two
will stay in the hut; we'll eat and drink and cheer us up by
tellen our tales of sorrow, as we call 'em to mind. There is a
comfort even in trouble when it's over and done with, if a
man has suffered much and travelled far. Very well, tha shall
have the whole yarn.

"There is an island called Syriê, if th'ever heard tell of it,
above Ortygia, near the sun's turnen-points: not so very rich,
but a good place, good for cattle and sheep, plenty of wine,
plenty of wheat. The people don't know what hunger is, and
as for disease, none ever comes near there to plague poor
mortals; but when folks grow old in that country Apollo
comes with Artemis, a carries his silver bow, and a shoots 'em
with his gentle shafts and kills 'em. There are two cities, half
the island with each, and my father was king of both; his
name was Ctesios Ormenidês, and a heavenly man he was.

"A ship came there with a crew of seafaren Phoinicians,
those nip-screws, with a cargo of trinkets in thousands. There
was a Phoinician wench in my father's house, a big bouncen
creature and clever at all sorts of work, and those cunning
swindlers befooled her. She was at her washen near the ship,
and one of them lay with her; huggen and kissen will befool
any female woman, clever or no. Well, he up and asks her
who she was and where she came from. 'I come from Sidon,'
says she, 'a wealthy city, and my father was Arybas, a man
rollen in riches. A gang of Taphian pirates caught me comen
in from the country, and carried me off, and brought me here,
and sold me into that man's house,' says she, pointing to the

roof of my father's great house, 'and they made him pay a good price.'

"The man said, 'Well then, wad tha come back with us, to see thi father and mother and their great house? They are still alive and wealthy, they say.'

"The woman answered, 'Yes, I might do that, if you will all swear an oath to take me home safe and sound.'

"All the lads took the oath as she told 'em, and after that the woman said, 'Now, keep a still tongue; if you meet me in the road or at the fountain, not one word to me. Some one may go and tell the old man, he might suspect summat and tie me tight and fasten me up, and plan some mischief against you. Keep our talk to yourselves, hurry up with your chafferen: and when you have got plenty of stuff on board, send a message up to the house at once, for I will bring with me any gold I can lay my hands on.

" 'I could bring you summat else to pay my passage, and glad to do it. I have to look after the gentleman's little boy, just as canny a brat as can be, trots about with me everywhere out of doors: I could bring him aboard with me, and you might get a grand price for him, if you sell him somewhere in foreign parts.'

"So that was her notion, and back she went to the great house. The foreigners remained a whole year with us, and got their ship full of stuff by traden. When the ship was reet full up and ready to go, they sent some one to tell the wench.

"He was a very shrewd lad who came to our house, and he brought a necklace of gold and amber beads. All the maids were in hall, and my mother too, fingeren it, passen it round, staren with all their eyes, bargainen: while this was goen on, the man quietly nods to that wench, gives her a nod, and away a goes back to the ship, she clips me by the hand and takes me out. In the fore-hall she found tables with cups on 'em: there had been a dinner for some people who had been busy with my father, and they had gone on to the parliament place. In a twink she picks up three cups, hides 'em in her bosom and carries them out; I followed like a little innocent.

"The sun went down, and all the roads became dark; and we reached the harbour. There were the Phoinicians with their ship: they took us on board, and away they sailed over the sea; Zeus sent 'em a fair wind. Six days and six nights we sailed: when the seventh day came, Artemis Archeress shot the wench, and down she went plump into the bilge like a sea-diver. They threw her overboard for seals and fishes to play with, and I was left unhappy. Wind and water carried them to Ithaca, and then Laërtês bought me. That is how I came to set eyes on this country."

Odysseus said:

"You have moved me deeply by your story, Eumaios: you have indeed suffered great trouble. But Zeus has given you good with the evil, there is no doubt about that: after those dangers you have come into the hands of a kind master, who gives you food and drink generously, and you have a good living. But look at me: I have travelled all over the world, and this is what I have come to."

They went on so long talking together, that when they did go to sleep there was not much of the night left. Soon Dawn came in all her majesty, and with the dawn Telemachos reached the land. The men furled sail and let down the mast smartly, and paddled into the roadstead. They dropt the anchoring-stones and made fast the moorings from the shore; then disembarked and prepared their meal on the beach, with good wine to wash it down. When they had had enough, Telemachos gave them his directions. "You sail on to the city, and I will find my way to the herdsmen on the farm: in the evening, when I have taken a look round the place, I will come down to the city myself. To-morrow I will invite you to your way-feast, a good spread of vittles and drink of the best."

Then the prophet Theoclymenos asked:

"And where shall I go, my son? Which of the lords of rocky Ithaca will give me shelter? Am I to go straight to your mother's house and yours?"

Telemachos knew that would not do, and he answered:

"I would have invited you at once to our house, for there is no lack of entertainment there; but as things are you would not be comfortable by yourself, since I shall be away and my mother will not see you. She does not often appear when those men are present; she keeps clear of them and goes on with her weaving in her own rooms. But I will tell you a good fellow to go to, Eurymachos o' Polybos, the notable son of a wise father, a man whom the Ithacans now respect very highly: he is by far the best man, and most earnest to win my mother and to hold the honours of Odysseus. But Zeus Olympian in the heavens knows whether he will bring the day of reckoning upon them before it comes to a marriage!"

At the moment when he said this a lucky bird appeared, a falcon towards the right, that swift messenger of Apollo: he held a dove and tore it with his talons, and the feathers fell in a shower between the ship and Telemachos. Theoclymenos drew him apart and said, as he grasped his hand:

"Telemachos, not without God that bird came flying towards the right. I knew it was an omen as soon as I saw it. None is more royal than yours of all the families in Ithaca, and you shall be strong for ever."

Telemachos answered:

"My guest, I pray that these words may be fulfilled: then you would soon see friendship and generous gifts from me, enough to make any one envy you."

Then he called his trusty companion Peiraios, and said:

"Peiraios Clytidês, of all our crew you are always most ready to do me a good turn—now then, please take this stranger to your house and entertain him handsomely until I come."

Peiraios answered. "Why, of course, I will look after him however long you stay; he shall lack nothing that a guest ought to have."

With these words he went on board, and called for the rest to come aboard and cast loose. They were soon in their places by the oars.

But Telemachos put on his boots, and took his sharp spear from the deck: the hawsers were cast loose, the crew pushed off and set their course for the city, as Telemachos had told them to do. Then Telemachos marched away at a round pace, and came at last to the enclosure with its thousands of sows, and the honest swineherd sleeping beside them, so faithful to his masters.

BOOK XVI

How Telemachos Met His Father

BY THIS TIME DAY HAD DAWNED. ODYSSEUS AND THE swineherd were in the hut, lighting the fire and getting ready their breakfast; the men had been sent out with the boars in droves; and there were the champion barkers, wagging their tails and jumping about Telemachos, not one bark out of the four of them. Odysseus heard them pattering about and fawning on him, and understood it at once, as he called out:

"Eumaios! Here will be one of your mates, or some one you know, for the dogs are not barking but fawning upon him: I can hear the patter of their feet."

Before he had finished, his own son stood in the porch. The swineherd jumped up in amazement, and the cups fell from his hands—he was just then mixing the wine. He ran to his young master, and kissed his head, and both his beautiful eyes, and both hands: and tears ran down his cheeks. As a father fondles the son whom he dearly loves, when he returns from a far country after ten long years, his only son well-beloved for whose sake he has suffered much, so the faithful swineherd threw his arms round the noble boy, and kissed him all over as one come back from the dead: then sobbing for joy he spoke from the bottom of his heart:

"Hasta come, Telemachos, blessed light o' my eyes! I thowt never to see thee more, sin tha gaed to Pylos in yon ship. Come tha reet in, my son, that I am warm my heart wi' gazen at the traveller new come fro foreign parts. Tha doesna come oft to the farms, tha keeps close in the city: well, every man to his taste, if tha like looken at yon murderous mob of marry-come-quicks."

Telemachos answered:

"That I will, daddy! Just to see you I came here, and to ask the news. Is my mother still in the house, or has somebody married her? Is my father's bed buried in cobwebs for lack of sleepers?"

The swineherd answered:

"Still in the house? I should think she is! patient as ever, but her nights and days are taen up with grieven and greeten."

Then he took the spear from the hand of Telemachos, and the young man passed in over the threshold. As he entered,

181

his father Odysseus rose from the seat to make room for him, but Telemachos checked him, and said:

"Stay where you are, stranger, we can find another seat in our hut; there's a man here to provide one."

Odysseus sat down again, and the swineherd made a pile of green twigs for Telemachos, and spread a fleece on the top; there the son of Odysseus sat down. The swineherd set before them trenchers of the roast meat which remained over from yesterday, and heaps of bread in baskets, and filled the ivy-wood mug with delicious wine. Then he sat himself opposite to Odysseus. They helped themselves to the vittles; and when they had taken enough, Telemachos asked the swineherd:

"Daddy, where does this stranger come from? How was it the sailors brought him to Ithaca, and who were they at all? I don't suppose he walked all the way here."

Eumaios answered:

"I will tell thee the truth about it, lad. Crete is the home of his family, so he says; he has been knocken about all over the world, a wanderer, that was the destiny which God spun for him. Just now he has given the slip to a lot of Thesprotians, and found his way to my hut. So I put him in thi hands. Do with him as tha will: he claims refuge with thee."

Telemachos answered:

"Ah, Eumaios, you cut me to the heart. Tell me how I can receive the stranger under my roof! I am young, and I cannot yet trust my hands, and stand up to a man if he wants to pick a quarrel. My mother is of two minds; she does not know whether to stay at home with me and look after the house, and respect her husband's bed and people's talk, or to give herself to the best man who woos her and offers the most.

"But now about the stranger; since he has taken refuge with you, I will give him a good coat and shirt to wear, and a sharp sword, and a pair of shoes for his feet, and help him on his way wherever he has a mind to go. Or if you like, keep him here and look after him yourself. Then I'll send up the clothes, and all the bread he wants, and he shall not be a burden on you and your men. But I would not have him come among the pretenders. They are really too violent and outrageous! I am afraid they will make game of him, and that will be a dreadful humiliation for me. One against many is done—many's too many for one!"

Odysseus, ever patient, said to this:

"My friend, since I hope it may be allowed me to answer you myself, I declare it tears my heart to hear you say that, about those marriage-pretenders and their outrageous doings, flouting you in your own house, a gentleman like you! What is the reason? Are you a consenter to their tyranny? Are you in bad favour with the people from some ugly rumour? Are your brothers to blame, instead of defending you as a man might fairly expect, even in a dangerous quarrel?

"I only wish I were as young as you are, in my present temper, if I were a son of the admirable Odysseus or even himself—for there is room for hope yet, then let one of your foreigners cut off my head on the spot, if I wouldn't march into the hall of Odysseus Laërtiadês and make them all rue the day! Even if they should be too many for me, and got the better of me by their numbers, I would choose to die in my own hall rather than to look on for ever at such disgraceful doings—strangers maltreated, maids pulled about all over the house, wine poured out in fountains, bread simply wasted and thrown away, interminable, no end to the business."

Telemachos answered his questions:

"I will tell you the whole thing, stranger. I am not in bad favour with the people. No brothers are to blame, or refuse to defend me as a man might fairly expect even in a danger-ous quarrel. The truth is, Cronion has made our family go by ones; Laërtês was the only son of Arceisios, Odysseus was the only son of Laërtês, I am the only son of Odysseus, and he went and left me behind and had no joy of me.

"That's why these thousands of enemies are in the house now. For all the best men in the island, the princes of Dulichion and Samê and woody Zacynthos, and all the powerful nobles of my own rocky Ithaca, every one of them would marry my mother, and they are ruining the place. She does not refuse this hateful marriage, but she cannot make an end of it; meanwhile they are eating us out of house and home, and I daresay they will tear me to pieces myself. But of course, all that lies on the knees of the gods.—Daddy, hurry up and go to your mistress, and tell her I am back from Pylos safe. I will stay here; you be sure to come straight back, and see that she is alone when you tell her; don't let another soul hear, for there are many plotting harm against me."

The swineherd said:

"I see, I understand, I have some sense in my head. But lookee now, just answer me this: shall I go the same way to tell Laërtês? Poor old man, he was always grieven for Odysseus, still he used to look after his farm, and eat and drink in the house with his servants when he felt like it; but since tha gaed away to Pylos, they say he will not eat and drink any more, or look after the farm, but there a sits mournen and lamenten, till the flesh is wasten off his bones."

Telemachos answered:

"That's a pity, but still we'll leave him alone, although we are sorry for him. If wishings were gettings, the first thing we would choose is my father's return. You just give your message and come back, and don't go trapesing over the fields to find him. You can tell mother to send the housewife at once, and secretly; she can tell the old man."

So he packed off the swineherd, who put on his boots and set out for town. Athena did not fail to see him go; at once she approached, in the form of a woman, a fine tall woman, one quick and handy and well up to her work. She showed herself just outside of the enclosure. She stood right opposite the door, but Telemachos did not see her; for gods do not show themselves manifestly to every one. Odysseus saw her, and so did the dogs, but they did not bark; they only whimpered and slunk back to the other side of the barton. She signed to him with her brows; he took note of it, and stept out of the room along the enclosing wall, and stood before her. Athena said to him:

"Prince Laërtiadês, you are a man ever ready! now is the time to speak to your son! Hide nothing from him, contrive with him death and destruction for the pretenders, and then return to the town. I will not be far from you and your son in the thick of the fight."

Then Athena stroked him with her golden rod. She clothed him in spotless raiment, and made him the picture of youth and strength; once more he was dark and tanned, his cheeks filled out, a dark beard covered his chin.

When her work was done, she departed. Odysseus went into the hut, and his son was filled with amazement; he was afraid, and turned his eyes aside, uncertain whether it might be some god. Then he spoke, plainly and to the point:

"You look different now, stranger, from what you were before; your clothes are changed, your colour is not the same. Surely you are one of the gods who rule the broad heavens! Be gracious, that we may do sacrifice to thee, and make offerings of wrought gold; spare us, good Lord!"

Odysseus answered out of his patient heart:

"I tell you, I am no god; why do you rank me with the immortals? No, I am your father, for whom you have mourned so long and put up with the wrongs and violence of men."

Saying this he kissed his son, and let the tears run freely down his cheeks; until that hour he had always held them back. But Telemachos could not yet believe it was his father, and he said once again:

"Oh no, you are not Odysseus my father, but some being more than man come to bewitch me and to make my grief greater than it was. It is impossible that a mortal man could have contrived all this by his own power, no one but very God could make one young or old at will, but it is easy for him. Why, a moment ago you were old and dressed in rags; now you are like one of the gods who rule the broad heavens!"

Odysseus answered:

"My son, it is your own father at home once more, and that is nothing to astound you or make you wonder overmuch. I tell you truly, that no other Odysseus will ever come here; but only I as you see me, after many sufferings and many wanderings, returned after twenty long years to my native land. This indeed is the doing of Athena the Queen of Victory; she has made me such as I am, for it is her will and she has the power—now a beggar, now a young man in handsome dress. It is easy for the gods who rule the broad heavens both to exalt a mortal man and to bring him low."

He sat down, and Telemachos threw his arms round his noble father and burst into tears. They sat throbbing and shaking in the relief from that long strain, like a pair of sea-eagles robbed of their young before they are feathered, who quiver and shake as they utter their shrill cries. So they would have remained until the sun went down, but Telemachos suddenly said to his father:

"What ship brought you to Ithaca, my dear father? Who were the crew? I don't suppose you walked all the way!"

Then Odysseus answered:

"Well, my boy, I will tell you the whole story. Those famous seamen the Phaiacians brought me here; you know they are always ready to help a traveller on his way. I slept all through the voyage, and I was asleep when they put me ashore in Ithaca. They gave me splendid treasures, bronze and gold and plenty of woven stuffs. All these lie in a cave, by the grace of God; and now I have come to this place at the bidding of Athena, that we may make our plans for the death of our enemies. Now then, count over the men for me, and tell me how many they are, and who they are; then I will consider carefully whether we two can face them alone, or if we should look for helpers."

Telemachos answered:

"My father, I have always heard great things of you, both your strength in fight and your wisdom; but this is something too big. I am astounded at the thought! It is utterly impossible that two men could fight such a host, and all strong men! They are not just ten or twenty, but many more; listen now, and you can count them up.

"From Dulichion two and fifty lads, picked men, with six servants; from Samê four and twenty young fellows; twenty lads from Zacynthos, and twelve from Ithaca itself, the best in the island, and they have with them Medon the marshal and a fine singing-man and a couple of good carvers. If we attack them all together in hall, I am afraid you might bitterly rue your day of vengeance. If you can think of some one to help us two, do think who would be a faithful and willing ally."

Odysseus answered:

"Very well, see what you say to this. Do you think Athena will be enough for us, with Father Zeus? or must I think of some one else to help us?"

Telemachos answered: "That's two more certainly, and good ones, although they do live high up in the clouds. They do rule over all men, and the gods too."

Odysseus answered:

"Those two more certainly will not be long absent from the fierce battle, when we and my supplanters meet and fight it out between us.

"But now, you must go home at dawn and mix with them all as usual; I will come later. The swineherd shall bring me like some wretched old beggar. If they insult me when I get there, you must harden your heart to see it, even if they drag me out by the legs or throw things at me—just look on and control yourself. But you may ask them not to be fools if you can speak politely. They will not listen to you, I am sure of that, for the day of their fate is at hand.

"Another thing I want you to remember carefully. When Athena in her wisdom shall reveal to me that the time has come, I will give you a nod, so be on the look-out; then take away all the weapons and shields which hang about in the hall, and pack them into the corner of one of the rooms upstairs, every one, don't leave one behind. If any of them ask what has become of the stuff, speak politely and say, 'I have put them away out of the smoke. Even now they are by no means the same as when my father left them; all the smoke from the fire has quite spoilt them. And there is something else you mustn't forget, I have just thought of it. You may take a drop too much and quarrel, you may make a mess of your supper and your wedding together! You know the saying, Bare steel in sight draws men to fight.'—But you may leave enough for us two alone, two swords and two spears and a couple of leather shields, handy if we want them.

"As for the others, Pallas Athenaia and Zeus Allwise will keep their minds at rest. Another thing you must be careful to remember; as you are my true son and my own flesh and blood, let not one single soul know that Odysseus has come home, not even Laërtês, not the swineherd, none of the servants, not your mother herself, only you and me, and we will find out the temper of the women, and try some of the farm hands; we'll see if some one somewhere fears and respects us; we'll see who cares nothing and only despises you for a boy."

His son answered:

"My father, time will show what my spirit is: indeed there is no slackness in me. But I must say I don't think that will be of much use to either of us; you must judge, of course. You will waste a great deal of time in going round the farms and having a try at each man, and all the while those others are in the house, battening on our goods like brigands, and sparing nothing. I should recommend you to find out which of the women disgrace you, and which are innocent; but I don't think I would go round to all the crofts and shanties and explore. Leave that for afterwards, if in sober truth you have a sign from Zeus Almighty."

While these two were talking, the ship which had brought Telemachos from Pylos arrived at the town of Ithaca. When they were safe inside the harbour, they beached the ship; the servants carried out all the gear and took the king's gifts to the house of Clytios. A message was sent to Odysseus' house to inform Penelopeia that Telemachos was in the country, but that he had sent on the ship to town to save his mother any alarm.

This messenger met the swineherd bound on the same errand to Penelopeia. When they reached the master's house, the crier spoke out before all the household, "My lady, your son has just arrived." But the swineherd took her apart, and told her everything her son had bidden him tell. As soon as his errand was done, he left the mansion and returned to his swine.

But the pretenders were utterly cast down by this blow. They left the hall and passed along the courtyard wall to the gateway, where they held a sitting. Eurymachos spoke first, and said:

"My friends, Telemachos has succeeded in his great deed of defiance, this journey of his, which we thought would never come off. Let us launch the best ship we can find, and collect a crew, and send them off at full speed to tell those fellows to come home quickly."

Before he had quite finished, Amphinomos turned on his seat and spied a ship, already within the harbour, men furling sails and men still holding the oars. He laughed merrily, and called out:

"There's no need to send a messenger now; here they are! Some god told them, or they saw the ship sailing past and could not catch her."

They all got up and went down to the shore. They helped to beach the ship, and the serving men carried out the gear. Then they all went to the market-place, where they kept together and let no one else join them, young or old. Antinoös now addressed them:

"Damn it all," he said, "see how the gods have saved this man from destruction! All day long we had spies posted on the windy heights, relieving each other, when the sun set. We never passed a night on land, but kept our ship afloat and cruised about all night, watching for Telemachos, to catch him before he could come in!

"Well, this time a special providence has brought him home, but don't let him escape! We must find some way to kill him here, for I don't think we shall do our business while he is alive. He certainly has brains and intelligence, and the people are not at all in our favour now. Look alive, before he summons the country to a meeting—I am sure nothing will stop him, he will get on his feet and proclaim to the whole nation that we plotted his murder and couldn't catch him! They won't like to hear of violence; I am afraid they will be violent themselves and kick us out of the country, and then, it's off we go to banishment.

"Let's be ready, then, and catch him in the country on his way to town. We can keep his goods and chattels, and divide them fairly amongst ourselves, but let his mother and her husband have the house.—Well, if you don't like that plan, if you prefer to let him live and enjoy his father's wealth, suppose we give up living here on the fat of the land all together; and let each man do his wooing from his own house with gifts and pleadings. Let her marry the man that offers the most and has the luck."

A dead silence followed this speech. At last Amphinomos spoke. This was a notable man; his father was Prince Nisos

Aretiadês, and he was the chief of the pretenders from the meadows and wheatlands of Dulichion. His manners pleased Penelopeia more than any of the others did, for he was a goodhearted fellow. This man then rose, and said:

"My friends, I should not be willing to kill Telemachos. It is a dangerous thing to kill one of a princely race. But first let us inquire the will of God. If the oracles of Zeus most high consent I will kill him myself, and bid the others join; but if the gods forbid, I bid you have done."

They all agreed to what Amphinomos proposed; then they broke up and returned to the house of Odysseus, and dispersed to their usual seats.

But Penelopeia had her own thoughts on these matters, and she was a wise woman. She resolved to appear before these wild and violent men. For she had learnt in the house about the plot against her son's life; you remember that Medon overheard the plot, and told her. So she came down to hall with her women, a lovely creature, and stood beside the doorpost of the great chamber, holding her shimmering veil before her cheeks; then she reproached Antinoös, whom she called by name:

"Antinoös! Man of violence! Conspirator! And yet they say that of all the men of your age in this country you have the ripest wisdom and the most eloquent speech! You have proved to be not at all like that, Madman, how dare you scheme to murder Telemachos? Do you not respect those who appeal to the protection of Zeus? Indeed it is not decent for men to be treacherous to one another. Do you not know how your own father once came here for refuge in fear of his people? Yes, they were terribly enraged against him, because he had joined the Taphian pirates to harry the Thesprotians, and they are allies of ours. So the people were ready to destroy him and tear out his heart, and to swallow up all his rich possessions; but Odysseus held them back; Odysseus checked them when they were all eagerness.

"And now you are swallowing up the house of Odysseus, and pay no price! You propose to marry the wife of Odysseus! You murder the son of Odysseus, and plunge me into the depths of sorrow! I charge you to cease, and tell your friends to do the same."

Antinoös said nothing; but Eurymachos had the face to answer:

"That is wisely said, Penelopeia, and we do not forget whose daughter you are. But take courage, let no such thoughts disturb your mind. That man lives not and never

shall be bred or born, who shall lay hand on your son Tele-
machos, while I live and see the light upon this earth. I de-
clare solemnly, and I am a man of my word; the spear shall
suddenly drink that man's blood—our spear, I should say;
for I too was dandled many a time on your husband's knees,
and the hero who sacked Ilion would pop a bit of meat into
my fingers and a drop of wine into my mouth. Therefore I
love Telemachos more than any man living, and I tell you
there is no need to fear death for him, at our hands at least.
What comes from God none can avoid."

He said this to quiet her, but all the while he was himself
plotting the murder of that very son.

So she retired to her chamber, and mourned for the hus-
band whom she loved, until Athena shed sweet sleep on her
eyelids.

In the evening the swineherd returned to Odysseus and his
son. They had killed a yearling hog for supper, and they were
busy about that. Athena came near, and with a tap of her
staff made Odysseus an old man again, clad in mucky rags;
for she did not wish the swineherd to know him. The man
would never keep the secret, off he would go and blurt it
out to Penelopeia.

As he came up, Telemachos hailed him:

"So you are back, Eumaios. What is the talk about town?
Have the heroes come home already from their lurking-hole,
or are they still on the watch for me on the way home?"

Eumaios answered:

"Nay, I took no trouble to ask about them in town: I meant
to give my message and come back here as quick as I could.
But a runner caught me up coming from his friends, and he
gave the first news to thi mother. Aye, I know summat else,
too, which I saw him with my own eyes. On my way, just as
I was over the city, by Hermês' Hill, I saw a ship comen into
harbour. It was full of men, a regular cargo of shields and
sharp spears. I thought it wad be those men, but I don't
know."

Telemachos glanced at his father with a smile, but he
did not let the man see.

When they had finished their preparations, they had supper,
and there was plenty for all. They ate and they drank, and
when they had taken enough they went to bed, and thankful
they were for the gift of sleep.

BOOK XVII
How Odysseus Returned to His Own Home

WHEN THE FIRST ROSY FINGERS OF LIGHT APPEARED IN the morning, young Telemachos lost no time in putting on his boots for the journey to town. Then he took up the good spear that fitted his grip so well, and called out to the swineherd:

"Daddy, I'm off to town. I must show myself to my mother: I'm sure she will never stop weeping and wailing until she sees my own self. Now then, listen to me. Take this poor devil to town and let him beg for his dinner. Any charitable soul will give him a cup and a crust: I can't carry the whole world on my back when I have troubles enough of my own. The stranger may be as angry as he likes, and much good will it do him: I am a plain man and say what I mean."

Odysseus answered:

"My friend, I have no wish to be kept here. A begger's business is to beg for a bite, whether in town or country: any charitable soul will give. I am not of an age to hang about a farm at the beck and call of some jack-in-office. You go on and this man will bring me as you say, as soon as I have warmed myself at the fire and the day gets a bit hotter. These are a terrible lot of rags I have, the early frost may be too much for me; and you say the town is a good way off."

Telemachos passed through the barton, and went off at a rattling pace, with his mind full of the coming fight. When at last he reached the great house, he stood his spear by the pillar and went in over the doorstone.

Nurse Eurycleia was there spreading the sheepskins over the chairs, and she was the first to see him. She ran to him straight and cried over him: all the other women of the household crowded round, kissing and fondling his head and shoulders. Then Penelopeia came down herself, looking like Artemis or golden Aphrodite, and threw her arms about her darling son, cried over him too, kissed his head and both his beautiful eyes, and said through her tears:

"So you have come back, Telemachos, light of my eyes! I never thought to see you again after you went over the sea to Pylos, secretly, without my consent, to seek news of your father. Now tell me, what did you hear?"

Telemachos answered, "My dear mother, don't let us

have any crying, please; don't harrow my feelings, even if I
have escaped death. Take a bath and put on clean linen, and
vow a solemn sacrifice to All Gods if Zeus will grant us a day
of reckoning. Now I am going down to the market to bring
home a guest who came with me from those parts. I sent him
ahead with the others, and I told Peiraios to take him to his
house and entertain him properly until I should come."

That was what he said; but that arrow missed the mark—
she knew not what he meant.[1] Then she bathed and put on
clean linen, and vowed a solemn sacrifice to All Gods, if
Zeus would grant a day of reckoning.

But Telemachos went out, spear in hand, and his two dogs
went dancing round him. He was full of enchanting grace by
power of Athena, and every one stared at him as he walked
along. All the pretenders crowded about him with pleasant
speeches, but there was hatred in their secret hearts. He kept
clear of the crowd, however, and seeing a group of his
father's old friends, Mentor and Antiphas and Halithersês,
he went and sat down beside them to answer all their ques-
tions.

By and by Peiraios came along the street to the market,
bringing his guest. Telemachos lost no time in joining him:
and Peiraios began,

"I say, Telemachos, be quick and send some of your maids
to my house, and let me hand over the gifts you had from
Menelaos."

Telemachos said:

"Ah, my dear fellow, we don't know yet how things will
go. If those headstrong men kill me secretly in the house
and divide all my father's goods among them, I prefer you
to have the things rather than one of them. But if I can
manage to destroy those men, you may bring the goods to
me, and I shall be as glad as yourself."

Then he took home the unfortunate stranger; and when
they got there, rugs were spread over the seats and he was
taken to the bathroom. After the maids had given him a bath
and a good rub down with oil, they gave him a change of
clothing and brought him to a seat in the hall. The attendant
poured him a handwash from a golden jug into a silver
basin, and then placed a table beside him. The housewife
brought bread and set dishes of food on the table; there was

[1] See J. A. K. Thomson, in *Classical Quarterly*, vol. xxx, page 1. The
winged or feathered arrow flies straight, unfeathered it wobbles and does
not hit the mark.

no stinting in that place. Penelopeia sat opposite with her seat against a pillar, spinning her fine thread. They helped themselves to the good things that were set before them, and when they had had enough, Penelopeia said:

"My son, I think I will go up to my room and lie down on my bed of sorrow, which has been always drowned in my tears since Odysseus left us for Ilion with the royal princes. And you would not condescend to tell me plainly if you heard anything of your father, before all these rough men came in!"

Telemachos answered:

"Well, mother, I will tell you all about it. We went to Pylos, and found King Nestor. He treated me handsomely in his great house, as a father would treat his own son who had returned after a long time from foreign parts. Yes, he treated me handsomely, and his noble sons did the same. But he had not a word to tell me of my unhappy father, did not know if he were dead or alive, so he lent me carriage and horses and sent me to his Grace King Menelaos.

"There I saw that very identical Helen who was the cause of that dreadful war about Troy, by the will of heaven. Menelaos asked me at once what brought me to sunny Lacedaimon, and I told him the whole story. This made him cry out. 'Upon my word,' says he, 'they are a lot of cowards who want to lie in the bed of a strong man! It is like a deer who lays her new-born sucklings to sleep in a lion's den, while she ranges hills and dales for her food: then the lion comes back to his lair and tears them to pieces, both dam and fawns. So Odysseus will come back and tear these men to pieces. O Father Zeus,' he went on, 'and Athenaia and Apollo! If he could only be like what he was long ago in Lesbos, when he up and wrestled a bout with Philomeleidês, and threw him heavily to the delight of the nation! May Odysseus be like that when he meets these violent men! Short shrift would be theirs, they would be sorry they ever wanted to marry! As to your questions, I would not shirk them or try to deceive you, but I will just tell you what the truthful Old Man of the Sea told me, I will not hide or conceal anything. He said he had seen him in an island very unhappy, in the house of a nymph Calypso, who is keeping him there by force; he cannot return to his native land, for he has neither men nor galleys to convey him over the broad back of the sea.'

"That is what his Grace King Menelaos told me. When that was all done, I came back. The immortals granted me a fair wind, and brought me safely home."

This tale moved her to the depths of her heart. Then the prophet Theoclymenos broke in:

"Honoured lady of Odysseus Laërtiadês! indeed he does not know the truth: but pay heed to what I say, for I will reveal it to you and hide nothing. O Zeus bear witness, first of all the gods! and this hospitable table, and the hearth of Odysseus where I take refuge, that Odysseus is verily now in his native land, resting or walking, and inquiring of all these evil transactions; indeed he is, and he is planning the doom of these men. That follows from the omen I noticed while I sat on board the ship, as I told Telemachos at the time."

Penelopeia said:

"I pray, sir, that your words may be fulfilled. You would soon know my gratitude, and you should have bounty enough from me to make others envy you!"

While these three were talking together, the intruders were amusing themselves as usual in the courtyard before the hall, putting the weight or casting javelins at the mark, bold and defiant. At that moment out came Medon, who was their favourite servitor and always attended them in hall, and he called to them:

"Come along, lads! now you've all had a good game, let us think about dinner. Come along—dinner at noon is none too soon!"

They all jumped up and followed. Into the hall they ran, and spread the rugs over the seats. They killed the big sheep and fat rams, killed the plump hogs and an ox from the herd, got ready their dinner.

While this was going on, Odysseus and the swineherd were about their journey to town. The swineherd began by saying:

"I see tha'rt eager to go into the city to-day, as my master said—though for mysen I would rather leave thee here to take care of the pens; but I respect him and fear him, and he would scold me sure enough, masters have a rough side to their tongues. Come along, then, let us start. Already the day is pretty well done, and it gets cold towards evening."

Odysseus answered:

"I see, I understand, I have some sense in my head. Let us start, you go in front and show the way. But if you have a good staff ready cut, let me have it to lean on, for you say it is a rare rough road."

So he threw over his shoulders the musty old ragged bag, and let it hang by the cord; Eumaios gave him a stout stick. Then they started, and left the place to the dogs and hinds.

The swineherd led: and behind him, like a miserable beggar, an old man huddled in rags and leaning upon a staff, the master returned to his own home.

On they marched down the rocky path, until not far from the city they reached a spring of clear water, which fell into a basin of wrought stone: it was built by three brothers, Ithacos, Neritos, and Polyctor, and the townspeople used to draw their water there. A clump of poplars grew all round their beloved water, and the cool water fell from high up the rock in a cascade. Above it was built an altar for the nymphs, where all wayfarers made their offerings.

At this place they were met by a man driving the best goats of the different flocks for the gluttons' dinner. His name was Melanthios o' Dolios, and two hinds were with him. As soon as he saw the two men, he broke into taunts and foul language, which made Odysseus indignant.

"Here's a procession! Rags in the rear, and tatters in the van! It's always like to like, as the proverb says. Where did you pick up this dirty pig, you dirty pig-man? The beggar, this nuisance, this spoil-sport? He'll stand and rub shoulders on many a door-post, begging for scraps—he's not the sort that goes begging for my lord's guest-gifts.[1] Give me the man to look after a steading, or sweep out a sty, and carry a load of greenstuff for the kids; he might drink buttermilk till a got a good fat thigh. But this man has learnt only how to do mischief; he won't do honest work, he'll only go cringing about the town, and begging for something to feed his greedy belly. I'll tell you one thing, and that you'll find true. If he pays a visit to Odysseus' house, he'll find a shower of footstools flying about his ears and barking his ribs! He will be pelted out of the place!"

As he spoke, the fool landed him a kick on the hip: but Odysseus stood firm as a rock, and it did not move him an inch. He thought for a moment that he would kill the man with a blow of his staff, or lift him by the waist and dash his head on the ground: yet he controlled himself and bore it. But the swineherd rated the man, when he heard all this: he held up his hands to heaven and lifted up his voice in prayer:

"O ye nymphs of the fountain, O ye daughters of Zeus! If ever Odysseus made burnt offering to you, grant me this grace, that that man may return and providence may bring

[1] Not a gentleman who would receive a grand parting gift. From the base man's point of view that is only another kind of beggar.

him home!—Then, man, he would tear all the pomps and fripperies off thi back, and tha'd not go flaunten it through the streets while the herdsmen play the devil with thi sheep!"

Melanthios the goatherd answered:

"Bless us all, how the son of a bitch does talk. What malice is in his mind! I'll bundle him on board ship one fine day, and carry him a long way from Ithaca, and make good profit out of him. I only wish Apollo would shoot Telemachos with his silver bow, or the fine gentlemen would make an end of him, as surely as Odysseus is dead far away and will never come home!"

With this he left them plodding along, while he made haste to his master's house and joined the company in hall. He sat down opposite to Eurymachos, who favoured him particularly. The servants brought him food, and the house-wife bread, as usual.

By this time Odysseus and the swineherd had reached the place. They stood still, and the music of a harp came to their ears, for Phemios had just begun to sing. Odysseus took the other by the hand, and said:

"Eumaios, surely this is the great house of Odysseus! it is easy to see that this is no common place. Building upon building, courtyard with wall and coping complete, strong double doors—no one could turn up his nose at a place like this. I notice that there is a large company at table in there, for I can smell the food, and there is the sound of a harp; and by heaven's decree, no harp without a dinner."

Eumaios answered:

"Tha's seen that easily enough, for tha'rt no fool. But now let us decide what to do. Wilta go into the house first and join the company, and leave me here? or sooner stay thee here and I will go first? Donta be long about it, or some one may see thee outside and drive thee away with stones, so be careful."

Odysseus answered patiently:

"I see, I understand, I have some sense in my head. You go first, and I'll stay here. I am not unacquainted with hard knocks and volleys. My heart is hardy, for I have suffered much on the seas and the battlefield: this will be only something more. But a ravenous belly cannot be hid, damn the thing. It gives a world of trouble to men, makes them fit out fleets of ships and scour the barren sea, to bring misery on their enemies."

As they were talking together, a hound that was lying there lifted his head and pricked up his ears. This was Argos, whom

Odysseus himself had bred and trained: but he had not had much good of him before he went away to the war. Formerly the young men used to take him out to hunt wild goats or hares or deer: but there he was, lying neglected, his master gone, on the midden, where the mule-dung and cow-dung was heaped in front of the gates ready to be carted out to the fields. There lay Argos the hound, covered with vermin. When he knew that it was his old master near him, he wagged his tail and dropped both his ears; but he could not move to approach him. Odysseus saw, and secretly wiped a tear from his eye so that Eumaios did not notice: then he said to him:

"Eumaios, I am surprised to see this hound lying on a dung-heap. He looks a fine animal, but of course I don't know if he has speed to match his looks, or if he is just one of those tabledogs a man keeps, something for the master to show off."

Eumaios answered:

"Eh well, to be sure his master is dead and far away. If his looks and his powers were now what they were when the master went away and left him, tha'd see his big strength and speed! Never a beast could escape him in the deep forest when he was on the track, for he was a prime tracker. But now he has fallen on bad times: his master has perished far from his native land, and the women care nowt and do nowt for him. That's like your serfs; when the master's hand is gone, they'll not do an honest day's work. Aye, Zeus Allwise takes away half the good of a man when the day of slavery catches him."

So saying he entered the well-built mansion, and made straight for the riotous pretenders in hall. But Argos passed into the darkness of death, now that he had seen his master once more after twenty years.

Telemachos saw the swineherd coming before any of the others, and at once gave a nod to call him. The man looked round, and picked up a seat which lay near where the carver used to sit when he was serving out meat to the company. He carried this to the table where Telemachos sat, and took his place opposite. The servitor brought him bread and a plate of meat.

Close upon him Odysseus entered his own home, like a miserable beggar, an old man leaning upon a staff, and clothed in rags. He sat down on the wooden floor inside the doorway, supporting himself on the doorpost of cypress-wood, which some craftsman had pared and polished so well and made straight as a plumb-line.

Telemachos called to Eumaios; and taking a whole loaf out of the basket, with as much meat as his hands could hold, he said to him:

"Here, take this and give it to the stranger, and bid him go round the tables and ask a dole of every one. When want is by you mustn't be shy!"

The swineherd went as he was told, and said:

"Telemachos sends this, stranger, and bids tha go round the tables and ask a dole of every one. He says, when want is by tha musna be shy."

Odysseus said, "O Lord Zeus! grant that Telemachos may be happy in the world, and may he gain all that his heart desires!"

Then he received the food in both hands and laid it down before his feet upon that dirty bag, and ate while the minstrel sang. As he ended his meal the singer ended his song, and the unwelcome visitors made a great noise through the hall.

Athena stood near Odysseus, and whispered that he should go round and beg bread of the company, to learn who were decent men and who were lawless: but she was not to save any of them in that way. So he went round the company rightways, and held out his hand in all directions as if he were really an old beggar.

They were sorry for him and gave: they were surprised also, and asked each other who the man could be, and where he came from. Then Melanthios the goatherd up and spoke, and says he:

"Gentlemen who are courting our illustrious lady, I can tell you about this stranger. I have seen him before. The swineherd was bringing him along, but I don't know exactly what part of the world he comes from."

At this Antinoös began to rate the swineherd:

"O you notorious swineherd! what made you bring this fellow to town? Haven't we vagrants enough and beggars enough, confound them, a perfect nuisance at dinner-time? Aren't you content that they come here in crowds and eat your master's substance, but you must invite another besides?"

Eumaios the swineherd said:

"Maybe tha'rt one of the gentry, sir, but that's not the reet of it. Who ever goes himself and invites a stranger from abroad? unless it be one who serves the public, such as a prophet or a physician or a clever craftsman, or it may be a heavenly singer to give pleasure at a feast. Men like these are invited all the world over; but no one would invite a

beggar to burden hissen with. But tha'rt always the most harsh
of all the company to my master's servants, and especially to
me. But I don't care, so long as my gracious mistress lives in
the place and my noble young master Telemachos."

Telemachos said to him:

"Be quiet, don't talk so much. That's his way, to provoke
us always with hard words, and he makes the others do the
same."

Then he told Antinoös what he thought of him:

"How kind you are to me, Antinoös! You might be a
father teaching his son, when you tell me to chase the stran-
ger out of the house, and let might be right! God forbid!
Give him something: I don't grudge it, I tell you to give! In
this matter pay no attention to my mother or any of the
servants about the house. But that is not your way. You like
eating better than giving."

Antinoös answered:

"What a lofty oration! what an exhibition of temper! If all
the rest us would give as much as I do, this house would see
no more of him for three months to come!"

His feet were resting on a stool under the table: And as he
spoke, he stooped and pushed it up so as to show it over the
top. But the others all gave something; the beggar filled his
bag with bread and meat, and it seemed likely he would have
his taste of all the men scot-free before he went out. But when
he came round to Antinoös, he said to him:

"Give, my friend; you seem to me no common man, but
the highest in the nation, for you look like a prince. Then you
ought to give even more than others, and I will sing your
praises over the wide world. I once had estates myself in the
world; I lived happy in a rich house, and often gave to a
homeless man, whoever he was and whatever he needed. I
had serfs in thousands, and everything else by which men
live well and get the name of riches.

"But Cronion ruined me—such was his will, no doubt; he
tempted me to lead a raid of pirates upon Egypt, all that long
way, that I might come to destruction. I moored my ships in
the river Aigyptos, and directed the men to stay by the
ships on guard while I sent scouts to different places of view.
But the scouting parties ran wild and let themselves go, scour-
ing the countryside, destroying the fine crops, carrying off
women and children, killing the men. Soon the news came to
the city; at dawn they all sallied out, and soon the whole
plain was covered with men and horses and the glittering of
arms. Then Zeus Thunderer sent a panic among my men,

and not one would stand to strike a blow; death and destruction was all around. There the enemy killed many of us with cold steel, and others they took alive to be their slaves. But they gave me to some friend who met them; he was Dmetor Iasidês, the king of Cyprus and he carried me to Cyprus. From Cyprus I am now come to this place, one trouble after another."

Antinoös said:

"What bad luck has brought this nuisance to spoil our dinner? Just stand clear, will you, and get away from my table, or you may wish you were back again in Egypt or Cyprus! What a bold-faced shameless beggar it is! You stand by each man, one after the other, and they don't care what they give; there's no need to be stingy, why should they have mercy on other men's goods when there's plenty here?"

Odysseus said:

"Upon my word, your heart's not like your looks! You wouldn't give a grain of salt to your own housekeeper out of the pantry, if you sit by another man's table, and can't let yourself stretch out a hand and give me a bit of bread. There's plenty here!"

Then he moved away. This put Antinoös in a fit of rage; he frowned, and said straight out:

"You shan't leave this hall with a sound skin after that piece of rudeness!" Then picking up the footstool, he threw it, and hit him full on the back under the right shoulder.

But Odysseus stood firm as a rock; the blow did not move him, he only threw back his head silently, and brooded over his vengeance. Once more he took his seat by the threshold, and laid down the bag full of doles. Then he called out to the company:

"Hear me, you gentlemen who pay court to the illustrious lady, and let me say what is upon my mind. There is really no resentment or bitterness in a man's mind when he is struck in defending his own goods or cattle or sheep; but Antinoös has hit me in a base cause, the Belly, damn it! which brings many troubles upon mankind! Now if there are gods and avengers for beggar men, may Antinoös come to burying before he comes to marrying!"

Antinoös answered, very little like his father's sweet reasonableness: [1]

"Sit quiet and eat, stranger, or go somewhere else. If you

[1] He was the son of Eupeithes, "the Soft Persuader," whose name is brought in here with a touch of irony.

go on talking like that, the young men will drag you out by a leg or an arm, and strip the skin off your body."

This was too much for the others, rough and rude as they were; they resented it strongly, and one or another would say:

"You ought not to have hit the poor vagrant, Antinoös."

"Curse it all, man, suppose there really is a god in heaven!"

"Sometimes gods make themselves like strangers from foreign lands, all sorts and conditions of men, and visit the cities of mankind to watch their doings and to see whether they are good or evil!" [1]

Antinoös took no notice. But Telemachos nursed bitter resentment in his heart for that blow. Yet he did not shed a tear, only shook his head silently and brooded over his vengeance.

When Penelopeia heard of the blow in hall, she said to her women, "So may Archer Apollo strike him!" And the housewife Eurynomê added, "O that our prayers might be fulfilled! Then not one of them would see morning dawn!" And Penelopeia said to her, "Nurse, they are all hateful and full of evil thoughts, but Antinoös is most like black death. A poor stranger comes begging bread of those men; it is not his fault, he is destitute. All the others give him something, but this man throws the footstool at him and hits him!"

So she talked with her maids in her own room, while Odysseus was having his meal. By and by she sent for the swineherd, and said to him:

"Go, my good Eumaios, run and tell the stranger to come here. I want to bid him welcome, and to ask if he ever heard or saw anything of my husband. He seems like a great traveller."

Eumaios answered:

"O my lady! if they would not make all that noise down there, what stories he do tell! he would bewitch the heart in thee! Three nights on end I had him, three days I kept him in my hut, for I was the first he come to after escapen from that ship; and a haen't yet come to the end of his tale of tribulation. It's like one of those singers who learn their lovely songs from heaven; he sings, and they all stare at him, and listen hard, and never want him to stop; he bewitched me just like that in my lodgen. Says he is a friend of the master's family, and lives in Crete where the house of Minos rules. So he started from Crete, and got as far as this after great hard-

[1] These are three independent outcries; there should be a stop after 484.

ships, rollen on and on and on; sticks to it that he had heard of the master close by, in Thesprotia, and alive too; the master has a cargo of treasures to bring home."

Penelopeia said at once:

"Go and fetch him, I want him to tell me face to face. As for those men—let them have their jollification, let them play outside or here in the house. They are merry enough, and why not? Their own stores and cellars are full of bread and drink! nobody touches it but the servants, while their masters haunt our house every day, killing oxen and fat sheep and goats, feasting and drinking our fine wine recklessly. And so it all goes; for there is no man like Odysseus at the head, to drive this curse from the house. If only Odysseus would come back to his own country, he and his son would soon punish the men!"

As she uttered these words, Telemachos gave a loud sneeze which made the room ring again. Penelopeia laughed aloud, and cried out point blank:

"Go, go, call the stranger, bring him to me! Don't you see how my son gave a loud sneeze right upon my words! That means that death will come upon all the intruders, yes all, not one shall escape! And mark this: if I find that the man is telling the truth, I will fit him out with fine clothes to wear."

The swineherd went off as he was told, and cried out point blank to Odysseus:

"Gaffer, the mistress wants tha, the young master's mother. Tha knows sh'as a mind to hear about the master, poor dear. And if she finds tha tellen the truth, tha'lt get a fine rig-out, and high time too. And the freedom of the town to go a-beggen and fill thi belly, for any charitable soul to give what a will."

Odysseus, patient as ever, replied:

"By and by, Eumaios; I will tell everything honestly to your noble lady, for I know all about him, and we have endured the same hardships. But I fear this mob of dangerous men, whose violence and presumption affront the brazen sky! You saw just now how that man struck me a painful blow, when I was only walking about the hall and doing no harm; Telemachos did nothing to stop him, nor did any one else. Now then, tell the lady to wait in her room until sunset, although she is anxious, of course; then let her ask me about her husband's return while she sits quietly by the fire. I am not properly dressed, as you know yourself, for I appealed first to you."

Eumaios came back with his message, and as he stept over the threshold, Penelopeia said:

"You haven't brought him then, Eumaios? What has the man in his head? Is he afraid of ill treatment, or just shy of being seen in the house? Shy beggar is bad beggar!"

Eumaios answered:

"He talks good sense, just what any one else would think if a wants to keep clear of rowdy men and their heavy hands. He says, wait till sunset, tha'lt find it better for thi own sake, my lady, to be alone when you have your talk."

Penelopeia said:

"The stranger is no fool; he guesses what may well happen. I don't think there are any other men alive who go on in this wild reckless way."

The honest swineherd had no more to say, so he returned to the dining-hall. There he sought out Telemachos, and told him straight, in a whisper, putting his head close that the others might not hear:

"My honey, I'm going now, to look after my pigs and all that, thy liven and my liven; thy business is here. Take care of thisen first, and donta run into trouble; many of the people bear thee ill-will, and may God blast them before they do any harm!"

Telemachos answered:

"That will be all right, Daddy, but have supper before you go, and to-morrow drive down your pigs. I will manage the rest, with heaven's help."

The swineherd sat down again, and had a hearty meal; then he left the house and went after his swine.

BOOK XVIII

How Odysseus Fought the Sturdy Beggar

IT WAS AFTERNOON BY THIS TIME, AND THE CROWD OF feasters in the hall were making merry with song and dance, when a new visitor appeared. This was the town beggar, who used to go begging about the streets and was well known for his ravenous belly. He was always eating and drinking, but he had neither strength nor guts, although he was a great hulking creature. Arnaios was the name which his mother bestowed on him in the cradle; but all the world called him Iros, because he would run errands for any one who wanted him.[1] This man tried to drive Odysseus out of the house, and flew at him straight with a rude speech:

"Get away from the door, greybeard, unless you want to be dragged out by the leg! Don't you see how they are all squinting at me and telling me to drag you out? I'm wholly ashamed to do it! Up with you, before it comes to fisticuffs!"

Odysseus said with a frown:

"My good man, I do you no harm, and I say no harm; get as much as you like, I don't grudge it to you. There is room here for both, and you need not grudge another man's goods. You seem to be a vagrom man like me; wealth is the gods' gift, of course. Don't say too much about fists, or you may make me angry. I am an old man, but I might colour your face and chest with ruby red. That would save me trouble tomorrow, for I don't think you would put in a second appearance at the hall of Odysseus Laërtiadês."

Iros flew into a rage, and said:

"Damn it all, how the dirty hog's tongue doth run like an old kitchen-wife! I should like to give him a good right and left, and knock out all the teeth from his jaws as if he were a sow in the growing corn! Tuck up now, and let them all see us fight. How could you stand up against a young man?"

While they were prickling and spiking with all their hearts, on the doorstone by the great door, his high-and-mightiness Antinoös heard them. Laughing pleasantly, he called out:

"My friends, here is a real new sport brought by God to our

---

[1] Iris was the gods' messenger, and Iros is the same name with a masculine ending.

very doors for our amusement! The stranger and Iros are spoiling for a fight! Let us match them together at once!"

All the others jumped up laughing, and made a ring about the ragged pair. Then Antinoös said, with his father's soft persuasive tongue:

"Look here, my stout fellows, listen to me. Here are a lot of black puddings by the fire, stuffed with blood and fat, ready for supper. Whichever of these two proves the better man, let him come along and choose the one he likes; he shall always have the right to share a meal with us, and no one else shall be allowed to come in here and beg."

They thought this a capital notion. But Odysseus was never unready, he too had his little plan, and he said:

"My friends, an old man worn out with hardship cannot stand up against a younger man; only that damned belly drives me on to take a good beating. But now you must all swear to me solemnly, that no one shall give me a foul blow to favour Iros and make me lose the battle."

They all swore solemnly to see fair play. This duly done, Telemachos said with great dignity:

"Stranger, if you are determined to stand up bravely and fight this man, you need fear no one else; if any one strikes you, he will find a many's too many for one. I am the host here and I have the support of two princes, Antinoös and Eurymachos, proper men both."

This was approved by all. Then Odysseus tucked up his rags about his middle and showed a fine pair of sturdy thighs, broad shoulders and chest, and strong arms; for Athena was near him, and she filled out his limbs. The young swaggerers were mightily amazed, and one would say to another:

"Our hanger-on will hang-off before long, to judge by the muscles of that thigh under the old man's rags! Well, he asked for it!"

But Iros was in a dreadful state. The servants had to tuck up his clothes for him, and drag him into the ring willy nilly, in such terror that the flesh trembled on his bones. Antinoös did not spare him—

"You had better never have been born or thought of if you tremble like this and shake with fear, a great lout like you, at an old man worn out by hardships! I tell you one thing, and I'll do it too. If he proves the better man, I'll bundle you on board ship across to Catch'im the bogey king,[1] who chops

---

[1] Ἔχετος a comic name, as if ἔχε τόν.

men up into mincemeat; he shall cut off your nose and ears and cods and throw them to the dogs to eat raw."

This made him tremble more than ever. But he was dragged into the ring, and the two men put up their hands. Odysseus considered whether he should hit hard enough to kill on the *spot*, or give him a gentle tap and down him. On the whole he thought the gentle tap would be better, or he might be found out. So when they put up their hands, Iros let drive at the right shoulder, but Odysseus struck the man's neck under the ear and broke his jawbone; the red blood gushed out of his mouth, and he fell in the dust bleating, and gnashed his teeth, drumming with his heels on the ground. The spectators lifted up their hands, and fairly died of laughing. Odysseus dragged the man out by one leg through the fore-hall and into the courtyard near the gate; there he propt him up against the courtyard wall, and put his stick in his hand, and said loudly:

"Sit there now, and keep off the pigs and dogs. Don't set up to be Monarch of all the Beggars, you miserable wretch, or a worse thing may come upon you."

Then he threw his own ragged old rotten bag over the man's shoulders and slung it there by the cord, and back he went to the threshold and sat down. The others went into the hall, roaring with laughter and congratulated the winner:

"May Zeus and All Gods give you the dearest wish of your heart! Now this insatiable beggar will walk in our streets no more! We'll soon bundle him off to Catch'im the bogey king, who chops up men to mince-meat!"

Odysseus was glad of the omen when he heard these words. Then Antinoös himself set down a huge black-pudding by his side stuffed with fat and blood; Amphinomos took a couple of loaves from the basket and brought them too, and then pledged him in a golden cup with pleasant words: "Here's good luck, gaffer Stranger! Happy days to come! You seem to be un-happy enough now."

Odysseus replied:

"Amphinomos, you seem to me a man of good understand-ing, as your father was before you: for I have heard the good repute of Dulichian Nisos as an excellent man and a rich one. Such was your father, and you seem to be courteous in your ways. Then let me say something you will do well to remember. Of all creatures that breathe and move upon the earth, nothing is bred that is weaker than man. He thinks no evil thing can ever come upon him, so long as the gods give him power and his knees are nimble; but when the blessed gods bring sorrow, he has to bear this also, unwillingly yet with patient heart.

"So the spirit of man upon this earth is as the day which the Father of gods and men brings upon him. I myself was once like to be happy amongst men, but I gave way to violent passions and did reckless deeds, trusting to the support of brothers and father. Therefore no man should ever disregard justice, but let him enjoy in silence the gifts which the gods may give him.

"This is in my mind when I see these pretenders to marriage acting so recklessly, wasting the substance and insulting the wife of a man, who I say will not long be absent from his friends and his native land: indeed he is very near. But I pray that providence may take you safely to your home, and not let you meet him when he comes back to his native land. For I think the pretenders and he will not part without bloodshed, when he returns to this house."

So saying, he spilled the sacred drops from the cup, and drank, and returned the cup into the prince's hands. But Amphinomos moved away much disturbed in heart, and drooping his head: for he had a foreboding of evil. Still and all he did not escape death: Athena shackled him also, to fall in fight by the hands and spear of Telemachos.

Now Athena put a new plan into the mind of Penelopeia; to show herself to the pretenders, that she might flutter their hearts and be more valued by husband and son than ever before. She forced a laugh, and said to the housewife:

"Eurynomê, I never had such a wish before, but I have a notion to show myself to those men, much as I hate them. And I should like to warn Telemachos that he had better not go among that rough company; they speak pleasantly, but bad schemes are coming after."

Eurynomê replied:

"That's right, my love. Go and speak a plain word to your boy, let him have it. But first have a bath and give your cheeks a rub down with oil. Don't go out with that tear-bedabbled face; eternal lacrimation is a sorry occupation. Remember how your son is grown up now, and how your greatest prayer always was to see him a bearded man."

Penelopeia said:

"Don't coax me, Eurynomê, though I know it is only your kind heart. I will not bathe or smooth down my face with oil, for all my comeliness is gone; the gods who rule Olympos destroyed it, on the day when my man left and sailed away. But tell Antinoê and Hippodameia to come, that they may attend me in the hall. I will not go among men alone; no modest woman would do that."

So the old woman went to call the maids. Then Athena did her part. She made Penelopeia lie down on her bed and fall into a deep sleep, with every limb and muscle at rest; and as she lay there the goddess instilled her divine gifts, that she might win the admiration of all beholders. First she cleansed the fair face with immortal balm of beauty, such as Cythereia uses when she goes all garlanded to the Graces' lovely dance. Then she made her tall and full and more white than polished ivory. And when her work was done, the waiting women came chattering out of their room. The lady woke up and rubbed her cheeks, saying:

"Ah, that was a soft slumber that made me forget my troubles. O that holy Artemis would grant me at this moment a death soft like that, so that I might no longer waste my days in mourning, no longer miss my dear husband and his incomparable goodness, for there never was a man like him!"

Now she came down from her room, with two maids in waiting. When she reached the company, she stood by the door-post of the great hall, holding the veil shimmering before her cheeks, and one maid stood on each side. The men were thrilled, and their hearts warmed with love, and each man prayed that she might hereafter lie by his side. Then she spoke to her son and said quietly:

"Telemachos, your spirit is not what it used to be. What a boy you were! as clever as could be, and determined! Now you are grown up and come of age, and one who didn't know you might think to look at you that you belong to a great family, for you are a fine big fellow but your spirit is not what it was, and you don't know what is right. See what has been done in this hall, when you let a stranger be maltreated like this! How will it be if the stranger comes to harm by being mishandled in this cruel way while he sits here in our hall? It would be a shame and a disgrace to you in the world!"

Telemachos answered, with his usual good sense:

"Mother dear, I can't be surprised that you are angry. I do notice everything, and I know quite well what is good and what is bad. I was only a child before. But I cannot think always of the right thing to do, for these men fairly daze me; here they sit, on this side and on that side, full of malice, and I have no one to help me. However, that mill between Iros and the stranger did not come off as these men wished; the stranger was the better man. O Father Zeus, Athenaia, Apollo! May these bullies in our house bow their heads in defeat! may they be broken and lie in the courtyard or here in the hall, as surely as Iros lies now beside the gateway with his head lolling like a drunken man, and can't stand up or go home on his feet, because he is wholly broken up!"

As they were talking together, Eurymachos called out to Penelopeia:

"My Lady Penelopeia, if all our nation could see you from north to south, there would be a crowd of new-comers dining here to-morrow and aspiring to your hand! for you are the pearl of women for beauty and intelligence too!"

Penelopeia replied:

"Eurymachos, all my comeliness and beauty, as you call it, the immortal gods took from me when the army embarked for the war, and with them went my husband Odysseus. If that man would come and care for me, I should have a greater and better name in the world. But now I can only mourn for the afflictions which heaven has sent.

"What he said to me when he left his native land was this. He clasped my right hand by the wrist, and said, 'My wife, I do not think all our brave men will come back from Troy safely. They say the Trojans are warriors as we are, lancers and archers and men who can use a horse, such men as can most quickly turn the day in a hard-fought field. So I do not know if God will spare me, or if I shall fall in the Trojan land. I leave you the care of all that is here. Care for my father and mother in this place as you do now, or even more when I am far away; and when you see our son with a beard on his face, leave your house and marry the man of your choice.' And now all is happening as he said. A night will come when that hateful marriage will fall to my lot; and mine is a wretched lot since Zeus took my happiness away. But I have a bitter humiliation to bear. Your way of wooing a wife was never seen before. Those who would win a woman of rank and wealth, vie with one another in offering herds of cattle and flocks of sheep, and feasting the lady's friends, and heaping gifts upon her; they do not devour the wealth of another without compensation."

Odysseus had some comfort now for his patient heart, to see how she attracted their gifts, while she wheedled them with soft words and had quite other thoughts in her mind.

Antinoös saw there was reason in that, as his father's son ought to do: and he answered:

"What you say is true, my Lady Penelopeia, and we should not forget whose daughter you are. Let each bring what he thinks proper, and do you accept our gifts, for it is not fair to refuse a gift. But we will not go back to our lands or anywhere else until you marry one of us."

The others were all content, and each sent a man to bring

their gifts. Antinoös provided a magnificent robe richly em-
broidered: it had golden buckles, a round dozen of them, fitted
with curved clasps. Eurymachos gave a gold chain of fine
workmanship, studded with amber beads and sparkling like
the sun. Eurydamas had a pair of earrings, each with a cluster
of three drops, and a groom to carry each earring: a lovely
pair of trinkets! From the house of Peisandros Polyctoridês
came a servant with a beautiful necklace. So each of them
offered his own fine gift. Then Penelopeia returned to her
chamber, and the women carried away the gifts.

The young men now amused themselves with singing and
dancing, to while away the time until evening; and soon the
darkness came on. Then they placed three braziers in the hall
to give light, and piled round them heaps of good dry sticks,
neatly chopt up for the purpose: in between were torches, and
relays of maids looked after the light. By and by Odysseus
said to the maids:

"My good girls, it's long since you saw your master.—But
now you may go to your quarters, and your gracious mistress.
Sit in her room and make yourselves pleasant, spin the yarn,
card the wool, and I will show a light for all these gentlemen.
If they like to carry on till daylight doth appear, they will not
beat me: I am a patient man."

The girls laughed, and glanced at one another. But one
had a sharp tongue, that cherry-cheeked wench Melantho,
Dolios' daughter: she was a favourite with Penelopeia, who
treated her like her own child, and gave her trinkets to please
her fancy. But she was ungrateful, and cared nothing for her
mistress; indeed, she was the sweetheart of Eurymachos. This
young minx rated Odysseus roundly:

"Well, Mr. Patience, your wits must have been smacked out
of you! Why don't you go and sleep at the smithy,[1] or the
gossips' hostel, instead of giving play to your tongue here be-
fore all these gentlemen, bold as brass? I wonder you aren't
ashamed. The wine has gone to your head, or perhaps you are
always like that with your bibble-babble. Are you above your-
self because you beat Iros the beggar? Take care some one
better than Iros doesn't turn up, to box your ears well for you,
and kick you out of the house in a pretty mess!"

Odysseus frowned at her and said:

"Just wait a minute, you bitch, and I will see what Telem-
achos has to say. When he hears what you have said he'll
soon chop you up into mincemeat!"

[1] Where chance visitors used to go.

This sent them scurrying away, and they fled to their rooms, terrified to death, for they all thought he meant it. But he took his post near the braziers to keep up the light, and watched all the company: his mind was full of other thoughts, which came to pass in due time.

But Athena would not suffer the young bullies to cease from their humiliating insults, for she wished to excite the anger of Odysseus still more. So Eurymachos began to make game of him, and raised a laugh by saying:

"Look here, my good rivals for the great lady's hand! I have just had a happy thought. Shall I tell you what it is? Some kind divinity has sent this man here. At least I think there's a brilliant illumination coming from the top of his head, the torchlight perhaps—for there's not one hair upon it!" And then he called out to Odysseus, "Do you want a job, stranger? What if I take you on? My place is in the country. I'd give you good wages—laying walls and planting trees; you should have your keep all the year round, clothes to wear and boots to tread on. But you have never learned anything but vice: you won't do honest work, only tramp the country to fill your greedy belly."

Odysseus made quite a speech in answer to this:

"Eurymachos," he said, "I should be glad if you and I could have a match in the springtime, when the long days come round. In the hayfield, say, let us have a try; give me a well-curved scythe and you take another, plenty of grass, nothing to eat or drink till it is quite dark. Or what about plowing: the best oxen to be had, a couple of big tawny beasts, the same age and strength, never tired; give them a good feed, and put us on a four-acre field, and let the plow turn up the sods: then you should see if I could run a straight furrow to the end. Or if Cronion should stir up war from some quarter this very day: let me have a shield and a couple of spears and a metal cap to fit over my temples, you should see me fighting in the first rank, and you would have nothing to say about greedy bellies. You are only a bully, and your temper is ungentle: you think yourself great and strong because you mix with a small society of nobodies. But if Odysseus should come back to his native land, those wide portals would give you no room to run out of the door."

At this Eurymachos was infuriated, and scowled at him, as he blurted out:

"Base clown, I'll punish you for talking like that before all this company, bold as brass; I wonder you are not ashamed! The wine has gone to your head, no doubt, or are you always like that with your bibble-babble?"

Then he caught up a footstool to throw; but Odysseus ducked behind the knees of Amphinomos, and the stool hit the man with the wine on the right arm—down went the jug with a bang, and the man fell on his back in the dust yelling. Then there was a great uproar, and cries and exclamations on all sides—

"I wish the stranger had gone tramping to the devil before ever he came here: then we should have been spared this noise. Now we are brawling over a beggar, and there is no pleasure in a good meal, for this is no place for a decent man."

Telemachos now called them to order with dignity:

"Gentlemen, what is this? You are behaving like madmen, and you cannot carry your food and drink quietly. Some malign spirit must be driving you on. You have had a good dinner, now go home and rest when you find it convenient; I chase no man away."

They bit their lips, and heard with surprise how confidently he spoke. Then Amphinomos said:

"My good friends, that is quite fair, and no one has any right to object or to feel annoyed. Don't maltreat the stranger or any one else. Come along now, let the man pour the drops in our cups, that we may do the act of grace and go home to rest. Leave the stranger for Telemachos to look after, according to his duty as host."

They were all well satisfied to do as he said. The mixing bowl was filled by that majestic herald, Mulios of Dulichion, who was a servitor of Amphinomos. He went the round, stopping by each guest to pour in his drops: they spilled the libation in turn, and drank what they wanted, and went away for the night's rest, each man to his own lodging.

BOOK XIX

How the Old Nurse Knew Her Master

So ODYSSEUS WAS LEFT IN THE HALL, BROODING OVER his vengeance with Athena in his thoughts. He spoke at once to Telemachos and gave him clear directions:

"All the arms must be put in the store-room," he said. "If any one misses them and asks questions, answer as civilly as you can, 'I have put them away out of the smoke. You can see now they are not what they were when Odysseus went to Troy; they are quite spoilt by the fumes from the fire. Yes, and there is another thing I have just thought of. Suppose the wine should go into your heads, you may quarrel together and disgrace your dinner and your wooing both! You know the saying: Bare steel in sight draws men to fight!' "

Telemachos listened: and calling his nurse Eurycleia, he said to her:

"Nanny, shut up the women in their rooms, I am going to put away father's fine armoury. All the things are hanging about neglected since he went away, and the smoke is spoiling them. I am not a child now, you know! I want to put them away where the fumes from the fire will not reach them."

The old nurse answered:

"Aye, my love, I only wish tha'd brush up thi wits to take charge of the house and all that's in it! Come now, who shall go fetch a light for thee? The maids might a done it, but they mustn't move out of their rooms!"

The boy said, "This strange man will do. No one shall be idle who touches my ration-basket, if he *has* come from a long way off!"

The nurse did not understand the secret of what he said; but she locked the doors of the women's rooms. Then Odysseus and his son sprang up and carried away helmets and bossy shields and sharp spears; Pallas Athena went before them with a golden lamp, and made a brilliant light. Telemachos said:

"Oh father! here is a wonderful thing which I see with my own eyes! Really and truly I can see the walls of the rooms, and the fine panels and the pine-wood rafters and lofty pillars, all clear to my eyes as if a fire were blazing! Surely one of the gods who rule the broad heavens is in this place!"

Odysseus answered:

"Be silent, check your fancies and ask no questions. This is the way of the gods who rule Olympos. Now go and lie down; leave me alone here, for I want to tease the maids and your mother a little more, and she will ask me everything amid showers of tears."

So Telemachos went along under the torchlight to lie down in his own room, where he always used to rest. There he remained until dawn; but Odysseus was left in the hall brooding over his vengeance, and thinking of Athena's promise.

Now Penelopeia came from her chamber, beautiful as Artemis or golden Aphroditê. A fine couch was put ready for her, a work of Icmalios the master craftsman, inlaid with spirals of ivory and silver; it had a foot-rest attached, and a thick fleece was laid upon it. There sat Penelopeia, while the maids came in and cleared away bread and tables and cups. They emptied the braziers on the floor, and filled them again with wood, for light and warmth. Then Melantho rated Odysseus once more:

"Still here, you stranger? Going to make yourself a nuisance all night, rolling about the house and ogling the women? Get out of this, you creature, and be thankful for your dinner, or a firebrand shall help you on your way!"

Odysseus frowned and said:

"My good woman, why do you attack me with such bitterness? Because I am dirty and ragged and go begging about the town? I can't help that. Beggars and vagrants are all like that. I had once a house of my very own in the world, I was happy and rich, and often gave to a homeless man, whoever he might be and whatever he wanted. I had my thousands of serfs, and plenty of all that men enjoy when they have the name of riches. But Zeus Cronion brought me to ruin, for that was his will, no doubt. Some day maybe you will lose all the finery which now marks you out from the others. Maybe your mistress will take offence and vent her anger upon you; or Odysseus may come home, for there is room for hope still. But if he is really dead, if he will never come back, his son is here now, his son Telemachos, by Apollo's grace, and like his father. He will not fail to see it if one of the women takes liberties, for he is a man now."

Penelopeia heard this, and scolded the woman:

"You may be sure, you bold girl, that I notice your impudence. You shall wipe it off on your own head! You know perfectly well, I told you myself, that I was going to question the stranger here in the hall about my husband; for I am sorely distressed."

Then she called to the housewife:

"Eurynomê, fetch a chair and lay a rug on it for the stranger; let him sit there and tell his tale and listen to me, for I want to question him."

The housewife hurried off and brought the chair and the rug, and Odysseus patiently seated himself. Then Penelopeia spoke:

"Stranger," she said, "I will begin myself by asking you this question: Who are you? What is your country and your family?"

Odysseus must have all his wits about him now. He began as follows:

"My lady, no one in this wide world could find fault with you. Your name resounds to the heavens, like the fame of a noble king, a god-fearing man who rules over a mighty nation and upholds justice, while the black soil yields him barley and wheat, his trees are heavy with fruit, the sheep wean their young unfailing, the sea provides fish; for he is a good ruler, and the people prosper under him. Then ask me anything else you will, now I am in your house; but do not ask my family and my country, and fill my heart yet more with sorrow when I remember. I am a man of many sorrows, but I must not sit grieving and lamenting in another man's house; eternal lacrimation is a sorry occupation. The servants might not like it, nor you perhaps yourself. They might think me a drunken man all afloat in tears."

"Ah no!" said Penelopeia. "All my comeliness and my good looks are gone; the immortals took them from me when the army embarked for the war, and my husband with them. If that man would return and care for me, my name and fame would be better for it.

"But now I am in distress; see what trouble fate has poured upon me! All the chief men of the islands, from Dulichion and Samê and woody Zacynthos, and all my neighbours in Ithaca, want to take me for a wife against my will, and they are wasting my house. So I take no heed of strangers or suppliants, or public heralds with their messages, but I pine away with longing for my husband.

"These men are in a great hurry, but I wind my schemes on my distaff. First there was the shroud. Some kind spirit put it into my head to set up a web on my loom, a great web of my finest thread. Then I said to them, 'My good young men, you want me for a wife now Odysseus is dead, and you are in a hurry: but wait until I finish this cloth, for I don't want to waste the thread I have made for it. This is to be a shroud for my lord Laërtês, when the fate of dolorous death shall take him off. I should be sorry to have a scandal among our women if he should lack a shroud, when he had all those great possessions.'

"After that I used to weave the web in the daytime, but in the night I unravelled it by torchlight. For three years I kept up the pretence, and they believed it: but when the fourth year came round, the maids let out the secret, shameless things who cared nothing! and they came and caught me, and there was a great to-do. So I had to finish that, because I must, not because I would.

"And now I cannot avoid marriage, I cannot think of anything else to try. My parents urge me to marry and have done with it, my son chafes because they are eating everything up; he notices things now, and he is already quite man enough to manage a house which Zeus favours with some credit. But never mind, tell me who you are and where you come from. Your father was not a tree or a stone, as they say."

Odysseus answered:

"Much honoured lady of Odysseus Laërtiadês! must you still ask my father's name? Well, I will tell you. Indeed you will make me more wretched than I was; for that is the way of things, when a man has been away from his native land as long as I have, after wandering all over the world and suffering much tribulation.

"Well, never mind, I will tell you what you ask. There is a land called Crete, lying in the middle of the sea, with nothing but water all round it, and a fine rich place it is. There are ninety cities; the people are infinite in number, and they speak different languages. Some are Achaians; some are Eteocretans, a proud people who claim to be the true Cretan stock; some are Cydonians, and there are Dorians with long flowing hair, and the splendid Pelasgians. One of the cities is Cnossos, a great city where Minos the nine-year king held sway,[1] who whispered sweet nothings in the ear of Zeus. He was the father of proud Deucalion, my father. Deucalion had two sons, myself and Prince Idomeneus, who went in the fleet to Ilion with the royal princes. My

[1] No one knows what this means. The most plausible suggestion is that he held his power for periods of nine years; but it refers to some lost story. Odysseus thus hints that his own story is a fabulous yarn.

own name is known as Aithon, and I was the younger son; my elder brother was the better man.

"In that city I saw Odysseus and entertained him in proper style. He also was on his way to Troy, but the force of the wind drove him out of his course past Malea to Crete. He escaped the storm with difficulty, and managed to get into the dangerous harbour of Amnisos, where is the cave of Eileithyia. Then he went up to the city and asked for Idomeneus, who he said was the honoured friend of his family. But it was already nine or ten days since Idomeneus had sailed for the war; so I took him into my house and entertained him handsomely. I made much of him; I spared nothing of my own store, and I made a public collection of provisions and wine for his fleet, and fat oxen to their hearts' content. They stayed with us twelve days; for they were kept there by a strong north wind—even on shore they could not stand on their feet—the devil was in that wind! The next day the wind fell, and they sailed."

He made his long invention seem just like the truth as he told it; and her tears flowed while she listened. As the snow melts on the mountain tops, which the west wind has brought and the southeast wind has melted, and as it melts the running rivers are filled, so her fair cheeks melted and the tears ran down in sorrow for the husband who was there by her side. Odysseus from his heart pitied his weeping wife, but he kept the eyes under his eyelids hard as horn or iron without a quiver, and stealthily hid his own tears. When she had enjoyed a good cry, she said to him again:

"Now I will give you a test, my good stranger, and see if you really did entertain my husband in your house, as you say. Tell me what clothes he wore, and what he looked like, and who was with him."

Odysseus answered:

"My lady, that is hard to say after all this time. For it is twenty years since he sailed away from my country: but I will tell you what I can see before my mind's eye.

"Odysseus had on a thick purple robe, doubled over; it was fastened by a brooch of wrought gold, with two sheaths for the pins. It had an ornament in front, a dog holding a speckled fawn in his fore-paws, and gripping his struggling prey. It was the wonder of all beholders how he gripped the fawn by the throat, and the fawn struggled with its feet to get free—yet both were made of gold. I noticed the tunic your husband wore, glossy like the skin of a dried onion, and as soft; it shone like the sun! The women could not take their eyes off him.

"But of course there is this to consider—I don't know whether Odysseus wore that dress when he left home. Some one may have given it to him on board, or some stranger, for Odysseus had many friends, and few of the nation were his equals. I gave him myself a sword and a good folding cloak, and a tunic with a fringe; I showed him all possible respect before he departed. Yes, and he had a herald with him, a little older than he was; I will tell you what he was like. He was round-shouldered, dark-skinned, and curly-headed, and his name was Eurybatês. Odysseus paid him greater regard than any of his companions, because he was an honest faithful man."

How well she knew the things which Odysseus described so exactly! She wept again; and when she had enjoyed another good cry, she spoke to him again:

"I was sorry for you before, sir, but now you shall be my friend and my honoured guest in this house. I gave him those clothes myself, just as you describe them, folded them up and brought them out of the store-room, and put in that sparkling brooch to please him: but I shall never welcome him again to his home and his native land! It was an evil day when Odysseus entered the ship which was to carry him to that accursed city which I cannot bear to name!"

Odysseus answered:

"Honoured lady, do not let the tears spoil your beautiful face; do not break your heart for your husband's loss—not that I wonder at it, not at all. Many another woman mourns the loss of the husband of her youth, the beloved father of her children, even if he was one very different from Odysseus—a god among men, as they describe him. Calm yourself, for I have something to tell you, and I will tell it truly without reserve.

"I have heard that Odysseus is already near home, in the Thesprotian country, alive, with a heap of treasure which he has collected on his travels. But he lost his ship and all the crew on his voyage from the island of Thrinacia. Zeus and Helios were angry because his men killed the cattle of the Sun, and so they were all drowned in the deep sea: but he was saved on the ship's keel and cast up on the Phaiacian shore.

"The people of that country are near akin to the gods, and they treated him with a god's honour and heaped their gifts upon him. Indeed they were ready and eager to bring him home safe and sound; Odysseus would have been here long ago, but he thought it better to go farther and gather more before he returned. You know Odysseus is a man full of schemes, always ready to gain an advantage beyond any one in the whole world; there never was his match.

"I will tell you what Pheidon the Thesprotian King told me himself; he swore me an oath with solemn ceremony in his own house, that he had a ship launched and crew ready to see him safe home. But before that happened, I came away in a ship of theirs which chanced to be sailing for Dulichion. Pheidon showed me all that Odysseus had collected; there was treasure belonging to him in the King's palace enough to keep his sons for ten generations. The King said he had gone to Dodona, in order to hear the will of Zeus from the great oak; how he was to manage his return after his long absence, whether to come openly or secretly.

"And so your husband is safe, and he will come soon; he is very near, not far away, and it will not be long before he returns—I will even swear it upon my oath. Zeus first be my witness and this hearth of Odysseus where I take refuge; verily all shall come to pass as I declare. This very lichtgang Odysseus will be here, when the old moon is waning and the new moon is rising."

Then the faithful Penelopeia replied:

"I pray that this may indeed come to pass! Then you would soon see that I am your friend, and you would be rewarded so as to make anyone envy you. But it is too good to be true. My heart tells me that Odysseus will never return, and you will not have my help on your way; for there is no such master now in this house as Odysseus was when he was alive, as sure as ever he was alive—ready to honour a guest without fail, to welcome his coming and to help him on his way.— Now then, you maids! Wash his feet, and lay a bed with blankets and rugs, that he may sleep warm till the golden dawn. And in the morning after a bath and a good rubbing down, let him go in with Telemachos and do justice to a good breakfast in hall. If any one of those men vexes him with his brutality, it shall be the worse for him; he shall not do any good to himself, let him fret and fume as he likes.

"For how can I show you, my guest, whether I am any better than other women in sense and judgment, if I let you sit down dirty and shabby in my house? Short is the span of a man's life. If any one has an unkind heart, and acts unkindly, all men call down curses upon him while he lives, and when he dies all men give him an evil name; but if there is a blameless man with a blameless heart, guests and strangers carry his fame abroad through all the world, and many call him blessed."

Odysseus answered:

"Honoured lady, rugs and blankets are hateful to me ever since I sailed across the sea from the snowy mountains of Crete. I will lie now as I was used to spend my sleepless nights; for many a night have I spent on a rough bed waiting for the dawn. I care nothing for the washing of my feet; no woman shall touch a foot of mine, none of all the servants in your house, unless there is some old woman you can trust, some one who has suffered as much as I have. I would not mind her touching my feet."

Penelopeia replied:

"My dear guest, no one so discreet as you has ever come to my house, of all the visitors who have come from foreign lands. All that you say is right and true, and could not be better. I have an old nurse, a worthy sensible woman, who nursed that unhappy man and dandled him in her arms as a baby; indeed she took him from his mother when he was born! She shall wash your feet, although there's little strength left in her hands. Come here, Eurycleia! get up, you clever old dear, and wash your master's yearsmate! I should not wonder if Odysseus has hands like his and feet like his! Men quickly grow old in evil days."

The old nurse covered her face with her hands, and burst into tears as she cried in lamentable tones:

"Wellaway, my love, and what can I do for thee? Zeus must a hated thee more than any man alive, for all thi god-fearen mind! Never a mortal man so careful to do his service and sacrifice to the Lord of Thunder! and all a prayed for was to live to old age in comfort, and bring up his fine son! But now God has robbed him of his return, alone among 'em all! The women would mock at him also in foreign parts, when a came to a stranger's door, just as these bitches all mock at thee, sir, and that's why tha'd not let 'em touch thee, with their flouts and jeers! But I'm reet willing to do what my lady bids me. I will wash thi feet indeed, for my lady's sake, aye, and thi own sake too, for I am strangely moved; listen now, think of this! Many a way-worn stranger has come to these doors, but I do declare I never set eyes on one so like my master as tha beest, looks and voice and feet and all!"

Odysseus answered, "True, mother, that's what every one says who has seen us both. We are very much like each other, as you have noticed yourself."

The old woman brought a basin and half filled it with cold water, then poured in hot water and got ready to wash his feet. But Odysseus quickly moved away from the fireplace and turned his back to the light, for he had just remembered something; he was afraid she might touch the scar of an old wound, and everything might come out.

This was a wound made by the tusk of a wild boar. Odysseus had gone up Mount Parnassos to visit his mother's father Autolycos and his family. Autolycos was one who could cajole any man alive on his bodily oath. A god gave him this faculty, the god Hermês himself, for he won the god's favour by his burnt offerings of sheep and goats, and therefore the god was glad to befriend him. Autolycos came once on a visit to Ithaca, and found his daughter's son a newborn baby. As he was finishing supper, Eurycleia laid the child on his knees, and said, "do 'ee think of a name, sir, to give thi daughter's son: indeed he is a child of many prayers."

Autolycos answered:

"My son and my daughter, I will tell you what name to give this child. I have been at odds with many in my life on mother earth, both men and women: let his name then be the man of all-odds, Odysseus. For I promise you, that when he grows up and comes to visit his mother's home on Parnassos, where I have a great house full of wealth, I will give him some of it and send him home happy."

That was the reason why Odysseus paid that visit, to get those promised gifts. Autolycos and his sons greeted him with hand-claspings and friendly words; Amphithea, his mother's mother, threw her arms round him and kissed his head and his two beautiful eyes. Autolycos called out for dinner, and his sturdy sons lost no time in bringing a five-year-old bullock; they skinned it and carved it up, and put the pieces neatly upon the spits, broiled the meat to a turn and divided the portions. Then they spent the rest of the day in feasting until sundown, and every one had a good share: when the sun set and darkness came on, they went to bed and enjoyed the blessed gift of sleep.

As soon as the first rosy fingers of dawn showed through the mists, they sallied out to the hunt, men and dogs together, and Odysseus went with them. They climbed the forest-clad hill of Parnassos and soon came into its breezy valleys. The sun had risen out of the smooth surface of the deep-flowing ocean, and it was just touching the fields when the huntsmen came to a glade; the hounds were in front casting for a trail, and the sons of Autolycos behind. Odysseus was close upon the hounds, with a long spear in his hand.

There in a dense thicket lay a great boar: no damp wind was strong enough to blow through that thick scrub, the blazing sun could not pierce it, nor rain drip through, and the ground was buried deep in leaves. The boar was aroused by the trampling of men and dogs; out he came from the bushes and faced them, his neck bristling and his eyes flashing fire. There he stood close to them, and Odysseus in front of the rest ran at him, pointing the spear to deal him a blow; but the boar charged sideways and struck him first, above the knee. The tusk glanced off the bone and cut a long gash through the flesh. Then Odysseus got home on the right shoulder, and the sharp blade ran right through: the boar fell with a grunt, and died.

The young men looked after Odysseus, and bound up the brave boy's wound with care and skill; they stopt the blood with a charm, and brought him back at once to their father's house. Autolycos and the sons of Autolycos nursed him and cured him, and sent him away happy with a heap of handsome gifts to Ithaca. His father and mother were glad to see him again, and asked about the wound; he told the story at length, how he had gone hunting with the young men and a boar had torn him with his tusk.

All this passed through the mind of Odysseus, as the old nurse touched him with the palm of her hand and felt the scar. She knew him! and dropt the leg, which fell in the basin with a clang, so that all the water was spilt. Joy and sorrow together filled her heart, the tears rose in her eyes, her voice choked, but she touched his chin and said, "Surely tha'rt my baby! And I never knew thee till I had felt my master all over!"

As she said this she looked towards Penelopeia, eager to show that her beloved husband was there in the house. But Penelopeia noticed nothing, for Athena had turned her mind far away. Then Odysseus caught hold of the woman's throat with his right hand, and with his left he drew her closer as he whispered:

"Nanny, d'ye want to destroy me? You nursed me at your own breast, and now after sore tribulations, after twenty long years, I have come back to my native land. Well, since you have found me out and that is the will of God—silence! not another soul must know. Or I tell you plainly, and I will do it, too; if God grants me to master these violent men, I will not spare even you my nurse, when I kill the other women in this house."

The faithful old woman answered:

"Eh love, what a thing to say! Tha knowst my temper, stubborn and stiff! I'll be as hard as stone or iron! And hark a minute; when tha'st downed those lordly marry-me-quicks, I'll tell thee over all the women in the house, which of 'em besmirch 'ee and which are innocent."

Odysseus said:

"Why will you talk of them, Nanny? There is no need of that. I will take note of every one of them and find out for myself. You keep a quiet tongue, and leave the rest to God."

The old woman went out to get some more water, for it was all spilt. When the washing and rubbing was done, Odysseus drew his seat nearer the fire to warm himself, and pulled his rags over the scar. Then his faithful wife began to speak.

"My guest," she said, "there is another thing I will ask you on my own account; for it will soon be time to rest, if anyone is not too unhappy to enjoy the sweet boon of sleep. But my lot is infinite mourning. All day long my only pleasure is tears and sorrow, while I look to my work in the house and the servants. And when night comes, and the others take their rest, I lie in my bed with a throbbing heart while sharp cares torment me in my sorrow.

"You know that bird of the greenwood, who was once the daughter of Pandareos, now the nightingale, how lovely is her song in the early springtime; how she sits perched among the thick leaves of a tree and pours out her full notes with many a trill: she is mourning for her dear boy Itylos, King Zethos' son, whom she killed one day herself with a knife and knew it not.

"So my heart is torn in two; I ask myself, Shall I stay with my boy and keep all safe, my possessions, my women, and this great towering house; shall I respect my husband's bed and the people's talk? Or shall I cast in my lot with the best man who offers himself and brings a handsome settlement? So long as my son was a child and careless, he kept me from marrying and leaving my husband's house; but now he is a great boy and quite grown up, see how he begs me to go back where I came from, because he is anxious about his inheritance which these people are eating up.

"But please listen to my dream and say what it means. There are twenty great geese about the place which come out of the water to be fed, and it warms my heart to watch them.

But a great eagle from the mountains swooped down and broke their necks with his curving claws and killed them. There they lay in a heap on the ground, while the eagle soared up into the sky. I shrieked and cried aloud, I mean in my dream, and a crowd of women gathered about me, as I wept bitterly because the eagle had killed my geese. Back came the eagle again and perched on the free end of a roof-beam, and spoke to me with a human voice: 'Take courage, thou daughter of far-famed Icarios! This is no dream, but a waking vision of good which will surely be fulfilled. The geese are those who woo thee, and I who was lately an eagle am now come as thine own husband; and I will bring a dreadful death upon them all.' Then I awoke, and peering about I saw the geese as usual beside their trough pecking away at the wheat-corns."

Odysseus answered:

"My lady, it is impossible to interpret the dream in any other way, since you see Odysseus himself has told you what he means to do. Death is there for your wooers plain to see; they shall all die, and not one shall escape."

Penelopeia said:

"The truth is, we don't know how to deal with dreams; what they tell is uncertain, and they do not all come true. For there are two different gates which let out the shadowy dreams: one is made of horn, one of polished elephant's tooth. The elephant's tooth is full of untruth, so that any dreams which there come through never come true. But carven horn is ne'er forsworn, and if any one has a dream which came by that gate, it tells him the truth. Now I fear this strange dream did not come through the gate of horn. If it were so, welcome indeed it would be to me and my son!

"And I must tell you something more, which I wish you to bear in mind. The evil day is about to dawn which will cut me off from the house of Odysseus. For I mean to set up a contest, those axes which that man used to set up along the hall like trestles for a ship's keel, twelve in a row; then he would stand a good way off and shoot an arrow through. This is the contest I will set up for the company; whoever shall most easily bend the bow with his own hands, and then shoot an arrow right through the twelve axe-heads, I will cast in my lot with him; and I will leave this house of the husband of my youth, this noble place full of abundance, which I think I shall still remember ever in my dreams."

Odysseus answered:

"Noble lady, put off no longer this contest in your house;

for Odysseus will return here ready for all events, before these men shall handle the bow and string it and shoot through the iron heads."

Penelopeia spoke once more, and said:

"My guest, if you would be willing to sit beside me in this hall and comfort me, no sleep would ever fall upon my eyes. But mankind cannot do without sleep altogether; and the gods have given each thing its place in the life of mortal men on mother earth. Well, I will go up to my chamber and lie down once more upon my bed. Indeed it has been a bed of tears for me, ever since Odysseus left me to visit accursed Ilion, which I can hardly bear to name. I will lie down there, and do you lie somewhere in the house; put your things on the ground, or let them lay you a bed."

So saying, she went up to her chamber, and the two waiting-women went with her. Then she lay down mourning still for her dear husband, until Athena cast a deep sleep on her eyelids.

BOOK XX

How God Sent Omens of the Wrath to Come

ODYSSEUS MADE HIS BED IN THE FORE-HALL, AN UN-dressed oxhide with a pile of sheepskins on it—the sheep had gone down the throats of the uninvited guests. Eury-nomê tucked a cloak round him, and he lay there wide awake pondering his plans of vengeance. He heard the women go out giggling and joking to a pair off with their lovers as usual. He felt as fierce as a bitch standing over her litter of pups, snarling and growling at some one she does not know, and ready to fight; so his heart growled in him at their shameless ways. For a while he did not know whether to kill them all, or to let them go for the last dal-liance of their lives. But at last he rated his heart with grim humour:

"Patience my heart! you have been in a worse mess than this, when Goggle-eye gobbled up my companions, the sav-age beast! You were patient then, until my machinations got you out of that den where you expected to die!" His heart came to heel like a hound, patient now until the end.

But his body kept tossing from side to side. He might have been a good fat black-pudding going round in front of a blaz-ing fire, while the cook basted it on the spit to roast it quick-ly. As he rolled over and over, thinking how he could get his hands on that shameless crew, one against many, Athena came down from heaven and stood by his side in the shape of a woman, saying:

"Why are you wakeful, poor fellow? This is your house, your wife is here in the house, and your boy, such as any one might be proud to have for a son."

Odysseus answered the vision:

"Yes, that is true, my goddess, that is quite right. But what puzzles me is this, How can I get my hands on this shameless crew, alone by myself? They always come here in a crowd. And there is another thing worse than that: If I could kill them by the help of Zeus and yourself, how could I escape the blood-feud? I pray you tell me that."

Athena said:

"Incorrigible! Many a man trusts a weaker friend, a mere mortal who has fewer ways to help; but I am a god, and I always protect you in all your dangers. I tell you plainly, if fifty battalions of mortal men stood round us determined to kill, even so you should drive off their flocks and herds! Come, come, sleep away. All this watching and waking tires a man out, and you shall soon be free of your troubles."

While she spoke, his eyelids drooped in sleep, and the goddess returned to Olympos.

But while sleep held him fast, and as it soothed his heavy limbs soothed also his heavy heart, his faithful wife awoke. She sat up on her bed weeping; and when the tears brought some relief, she prayed aloud to Artemis:

"Artemis, queen and goddess, daughter of Zeus! Pierce my heart with an arrow now, and let me die! Or let the storm-wind snatch me up and carry me through the air, and drop me at the mouth of the rolling ocean stream! Did not the storm-wind carry off Pandaroes' girls? The gods destroyed their parents, and they were left orphans. But Aphrodîtê fed them with cheese and sweet honey and delicious wine; Hera gave them beauty and good sense above other women; holy Artemis made them grow tall; Athenaia taught them skill in women's work. Then Aphrodîtê went to the Olympian heights and made her petition to Thundering Zeus, for he knows all things, both what is fated for men and what is not. She begged Zeus to arrange a happy marriage for the girls; and while she was there, the snatchers snatched them away, and delivered them to the cruel avengers to look after.

"If only the Olympians would make away with me so! Or if Artemis would pierce me with her arrows! Let me once more see my husband before my eyes, and then be laid in the earth with my sorrow, but let me not gladden the heart of a lesser man! Sorrow can be endured even when the days are passed in tears with a broken heart, so long as sleep comes in the night: for sleep brings forgetfulness of all things both good and evil as soon as the eyelids close; but I am haunted by cruel dreams. This very night one like him slept by my side, just as he was when he left me that day; and how glad my heart was! I thought it was no vision of my dreams, but flesh and blood at last!"

As she said this, the day dawned in a golden glow. Odysseus heard her sorrowful voice; and in his dreamy half-consciousness, he seemed to see that she knew him and stood by his side. He gathered up his bedding and took it into the hall, where he laid it upon a chair. Then he carried the ox-hide into the courtyard, and lifting up his hands prayed to Zeus:

"O Father Zeus! if it has been the gods' good will to bring me home over sea and land, after visiting me with sore afflictions, let one of those now awakening in this house speak a word of meaning! and here without let Zeus give me a sign!"

Zeus Allwise heard his prayer. At once came a thunderclap from radiant Olympos out of the clouds on high, and brought joy to his heart. The word of portent came from a woman grinding corn in the mill-house close by. Twelve women used to keep the millstones rolling, to grind wheatmeal and barley-meal, the marrow of men's bodies. The others had ground their portion and gone to sleep; but one was still at it, the weakest of them all. Now she stopt her millstone and gave the sign which her master prayed for, crying out:

"O Father Zeus, King of Kings and Lord of Lords! There was a great thunderclap out of a starry sky, with not a cloud to be seen! Truly this is a sign from heaven for some one! Then hear the prayer of a miserable woman like me. May this day's breakfast be the last breakfast these men shall ever eat! See how they have worn me out with heart-breaking toil to grind their barley! Now may this be their last meal!"

Odysseus was glad to hear the words of omen and the clap of thunder. Now he felt sure he should punish the guilty men.

The other women were busy now, and making up the fire on the hearth. Telemachos rose from his bed and dressed. Then he slung the sword over his shoulder, and slipt his lissom feet into his boots, and took a good sharp lance in hand, and as he came out of his room he called to Eurycleia:

"Nanny dear, how did you look after the stranger? Had he bed and food, or was he left to shift for himself? That's mother's way, though she is sensible enough. She makes no end of a fuss of one man and sends another away with contempt, but the better man gets worse treatment."

The wise old woman answered:

"Now don't tha goo to blame when there's no blame due. He sat down, he drank his wine as long as he liked, and said a wasn't hungry, for she asked the question. When he turned his mind to sleep, she bade the maids lay the bed for him, but not he: said a was used to roughing it, wouldn't lie on bed and blankets, but slept on a raw cowhide and sheepskins in the fore-hall. We tucked him in with a wrap."

On hearing this answer Telemachos went through the house still holding the spear, and his two dogs went dancing about

him. He passed out on his way to the market-place, and
Eurycleia called to the maids:

"Wake up, lasses! Get to work and sweep out the place
and sprinkle it, lay the purple rugs on the seats. Some of you
wipe over all the tables with your sponges, and wash out the
mixenbowls and drinken-cups. Some be off to the spring for
water, and don't dawdle on the way. The company will soon
be here, they'll be early enough to-day when they are all
keepen holiday."

The maids were not slow in obeying. Twenty of them set
out for the spring, and the rest made the house tidy. The
men-servants now came in and chopt wood. By and by the
maids came back from the spring, and after them the swine-
herd with three of his best fat pigs. He left the pigs feeding
in their sty, and asked Odysseus quietly:

"Stranger, are the people looking after thee better, or are
they as bad as ever?"

Odysseus answered: "May God punish them for their
outrageous doings in another man's house! They have not a
scrap of shame in them."

As they were talking, Melanthios the goatherd came in
with his best goats for dinner; two underlings were with him.
He tied up the goats under the porch, and at once began
railing at Odysseus:

"I see you're going to be a nuisance again with your
begging, man! You had better get out while you can. I
surmise that we two shall not part without a taste of fisti-
cuffs, for you play the beggar without rhyme or reason. Are
there no other dinner-tables in the town?"

Odysseus made no answer. He threw back his head in si-
lence, and brooded on the wrath to come.

A third man now joined them, Philoitios, an excellent
fellow, bringing a farrow cow and some fat goats. They had
come across by the public ferry. He tied up his animals
under the porch, and turning to the swineherd said:

"Who is this stranger come to our house, swineherd? What
is his nation and family? Where does he come from? Poor
man, a looks like one of the real quality, but surely the gods
do plague unhappy mankind when they spin out trouble even
for the quality!"

As he said this, he offered his hand to Odysseus in greet-
ing, and went on:

"Welcome to thee, father! and good luck to 'ee in days to
come! just now tha'rt far from happy. O Father Zeus! thou
art most cruel of all gods! Men are thy offspring, but thou

hast no pity for them, to bring them acquainted with pain and tribulation!—I fell of a sweat when I saw tha, and the tears came into my eyes, thinking of the master. I doubt not he's drest in rags like thine and wandering through the world, if he is still alive and sees the light of the sun. But if he is dead and gone, alackaday for my good master, who set me over the cattle in Cephallenia when I was a slip of a boy! And now they breed a fair miracle, else how could a man see the broadfaced beasts sprouting up like stalks in a wheatfield! But these foreigners make me drive 'em in for their eating. They care not a jot for the young master here in the house. God's wrath doesn't make them tremble; what they mean is to parcel out all his goods forthwith, now the master is away so long.

"I keep turning it over in my mind; it's a bad job while the son is alive to march off with my cattle to another country and foreign masters, but it fairly makes a man sick to stay here and look after the beasts with foreigners laying down the law. A wretched life! I'd have made off long ago and taken service with some other squire, for life's not worth living here; but I can't help thinking of the poor master, who might come back—who knows? and make a clean sweep of the lot of 'em!"

Odysseus answered:

"Drover, you seem an honest fellow and no fool, and I can see myself that you know what is right and proper. Therefore I tell you and take my solemn oath upon it: Zeus be my witness and this hospitable table, and the hearth of Odysseus to which I have come for protection, that you will be here when Odysseus will return, and you will see with your own eyes the death of those wastrels who lord it in this place!"

The drover replied:

"May Cronion bring it to pass, stranger! Then tha'st know what my strength is, and how my hands play up!"

While they were talking thus, the pretenders were discussing how they could murder Telemachos, but they spied a bird on the left, an eagle flying high with a trembling dove in his claws. So Amphinomos said to the others:

"My friends, this plan will not run smooth, this death for Telemachos. Never mind, don't let us forget our dinner."

This suited them all very well, and they went in. They made the seats and benches comfortable with rugs, and some of them killed the great sheep and goats, others killed the fat pigs and the cow. They broiled the tripes and chitterlings and sent them round, they filled the mixing-bowls with wine, the swineherd served the cups. Bread was brought in baskets by the excellent Philoitois, and Melanthios poured the wine. So the company fell to.

Telemachos carefully chose a place for Odysseus, and put him within the great hall beside the doorstone, with a ramshackle old chair and a small table. He provided him with a plate of tripe and a gold mug full of wine, saying aloud:

"Sit there now among the gentlemen and drink away! I will protect you from rudeness and violence, for this is not a public place, but my father's house, and he got it for me. So I request you, gentlemen, to control your tongues and your hands, if you wish to avoid a quarrel!"

It astonished them all to hear this bold language, and they bit their lips, but Antinoös spoke to his friends:

"That's a rough way of putting it, men," he said, "with a plain threat, but we had better put up with it. Zeus would not allow us, or we should have silenced him by this time, and heard the last of his oratory."

Telemachos took no notice.

All this while the public heralds had been leading the sacrificial victims in procession through the streets; and the people were gathering in the shady grove of Archer Apollo.

In the house of Odysseus, they had broiled the fleshmeat and served it up. There was a famous feast for them all, and Odysseus himself had the same share as the others, by order of his son Telemachos.

But Athena intended to provoke Odysseus yet more, and she would not let the intruders abate their outrageous doings. One of them was a lawless ruffian named Ctesippos, who came from Samê: no doubt he trusted to his huge fortune in paying court to the lady of Ithaca, while her lord was so long away. This man saw his chance, and called out:

"A word in your ears, my bully lads, just a moment! This stranger has had his due share already, like the rest of us; but I will add a parting gift, so that he may be able to tip the bathman or the servants in this lordly hall!" and picking up a cowsfoot out of the basket, he threw it straight at Odysseus. But Odysseus saw it coming, and dodged it neatly by a slight movement of the head. Bang went the hoof against the wall, and Odysseus smiled grimly to himself; but Telemachos said ironically:

"That was a good notion of yours, Ctesippos, to miss him so neatly—but stay, I see he dodged it himself! If not, I would have run you through with my spear, and your father would have been burying you instead of marrying. So I warn

you all not to indulge in violence here. I am no longer a
child, but I see what goes on and know all about it, both good
and bad. We have to put up with this kind of thing, sheep
slaughtered and wine guzzled and bread swallowed down,
because it is hard for one to control many. But I beg you to
stop all this malicious damage. If you really mean to kill me
outright, I should prefer that: it would be much better
to die than to look on every day at violence, strangers knocked
about and women dragged all over the place in this indecent
way."

They had nothing to say to this; but after a long pause
Agelaos Damastoridês said:

"My good friends, that is quite fair and proper, and no
one has any right to object or feel annoyed. Leave the
stranger alone and all the servants in the house of my lord
Odysseus.

"But I should like to say something with all due respect,
to Telemachos and his mother, and I hope they will take it
in a friendly spirit. So long as any real hope was left that
Odysseus would return home, there was no harm in waiting
and refusing those who offered themselves in marriage. That
was much the best thing if Odysseus did return and put in
an appearance; but now it is clear that he will never come.
Just sit down and have a quiet talk with your mother. Tell
her to take the best man who offers and the most liberal, that
you may enjoy your patrimony in peace and plenty, and some
one else may give her a home."

Telemachos answered:

"I swear to you, Agelaos, by Zeus and by the sorrows of
my father, whether he be dead or wandering somewhere far
from Ithaca, that I do not try to delay my mother's mar-
riage! Indeed I beg her to take whom she will, and I offer
any amount by way of dowry. But I should be ashamed to
lay down the law, and turn her out of doors if she does not
want to go: God forbid!"

The gallants roared with laughter to hear this, and could
not stop; for Athena had sent their wits astray. But the laugh
turned into a grimace—and see! Their plates were messed
with blood, tears streamed from their eyes, their minds fore-
boded mourning: Theoclymenos the seer cried aloud:

"Ah, miserable creatures, what is happening to you? Night
is wrapt about your heads and your faces and your bodies
down to the knees, there is a blaze of lamentation, tears roll
down your cheeks, walls and panellings are bedabbled with
blood; the porch is full of phantoms, the courtyard is full of

phantoms, hurrying down to Erebos and the dark; the sun has perished out of the sky, and a thick fog spreads over all."

They laughed loudly to hear this, and Eurymachos said:

"The stranger is dazed because he doesn't know our part of the world. Look sharp, young fellows, take him out and show him the way to the market-place, since he thinks it is night here."

But Theoclymenos answered:

"I didn't ask you for guides, Eurymachos. I have eyes and ears and a good pair of feet, and my mind is all right, nothing wrong there. They will help me out of this place, since I can see woe coming upon you, which not one soul shall escape out of all those who frequent this house, maltreating men and plotting violent deeds."

So saying he walked out of the house, and made his way to Peiraios, who welcomed him gladly.

But the gallants laughed and nodded, and began to tease Telemachos about his guests:

"My dear Telemachos, there never was any one more unlucky in his guests! First you hunt up this vagrant and bring him in, all he wants is something to eat and drink, can't do a stroke of work or trail a pike, he's just a burden to the earth. And here's another gets on his feet and plays the prophet. If you'll follow my advice, it will pay you; let's bundle the pair of them into a ship and send them off to Sicily, where they will fetch a good price."

So they railed unabashed, but Telemachos took no notice of their talk. He looked to his father in silence, biding his time till he should get his hands on the shameless crew.

Penelopeia had put a seat opposite the door, and she heard all that was said. Laughing and talking they got ready for their meal, with vittles of the best in plenty after slaughtering all those animals; but no supper could have been more unpleasant than that which a goddess and a strong man were soon to set before them, in return for their unprovoked machinations.

BOOK XXI

The Contest With the Great Bow

YOU REMEMBER PENELOPEIA'S PLAN TO BRING HER HUS-
band's great bow into the hall, and the axes, and to propose
a shooting-match. Death was the prize, though they knew it
not! Now she climbed the stair to her room and got out the
key of the store-room, a fine key of bronze with a curving
catch and an ivory handle. She passed on with her waiting-
women into the innermost store-room, where her husband's
treasures were kept, bronze and gold and wrought iron.

There was the great bow with a double back-springing
curve, and a quiver full of arrows. All these his magnificent
friend, Iphitos Eurytidês, had given him, when they met
once in Lacedaimon; and this is the story.

They met in the house of Ortilochos in Messenê. Odysseus
had come to demand reparation from the Messenians; for the
Messenians had lifted three hundred sheep out of Ithaca, and
carried them off in their ships, with the shepherds. So Odys-
seus was sent as public envoy all that long way when he was
quite a youth, by his father and the aldermen of Ithaca.

Iphitos was in search of a dozen brood mares which had
been lost along with their mule-foals. In the end these were
the death of him, when he came across that mighty son of
Zeus, that grand fellow Heraclês, a champion if ever there
was one; but Heraclês entertained him as guest, and then
killed him in his own house. A hard man he was, who
cared nothing for the wrath of God or the table of hospital-
ity. So he killed the owner and kept the mares for himself.
Iphitos was inquiring for these mares when he fell in
with Odysseus, and gave him the bow; his brawny father
Eurytos used to carry it, and he left it to his son when he
died. Odysseus gave him a sharp sword and a strong spear to
mark the beginning of their friendship; but they never
sat together at table, for Heraclês killed Iphitos too soon
for that. He was a great noble who gave that bow. Odysseus
never took the bow with him when he went to war across
the sea, but he carried it in his own country, and treasured it
in memory of a well-loved friend. Those were indeed arrows
of sorrow which Penelopeia came to fetch.

So the lady came to the store-room door. There was the

wooden threshold, planed and polished so skilfully by the craftsman and made straight to the line; there were the door-posts, and the pair of shining doors. Quickly she unfastened the thong from the crow-latch, then ran in the key, dropping the prongs exactly into their holes, and shot back the bolt. What a crashing and creaking there was when the key hit the bolt, and the doors flew open! You might have thought it was a bull bellowing in a meadow.[1] She stept upon the high platform, where chests were standing full of scented stuffs; she reached up to the peg, and took off the bow in a shining case. Then she sat down and laid it across her knees, weeping bitterly as she handed her husband's bow. But after she had enjoyed a good cry, she descended to the boisterous company in the great hall, holding in her hand the bow and the quiver with its arrows of sorrow. The attendants fol-lowed, carrying the tray with the master's iron gear for the contest.

Penelopeia stood by the doorpost of the great hall, holding her soft veil in front of her cheeks, and spoke out before them all:

"Hear me, you proud men that seek my hand, you who have laid siege to this house, eating and drinking day after day all this long time while my husband has been absent: and not one word could you say for yourselves, but that you wished to make me your wife! Now then, here is the prize before your eyes, and, here I lay my noble husband's bow. Whoever shall be able most easily to string the bow with his own hands, and shoot through the openings of twelve axes set in a line,[2] he shall win me: I will leave this house of my young married days, so fine and so full of all good things, which I think I shall always remember even in my dreams."

Then she called Eumaios, and told him to carry round the bow and iron stuff. Eumaios took the bow from his

---

[1] This description is a parody. The kind of key described was set with prongs which fell into holes in the bar which held the door, and the most they could do would be a good loud click; but the bar might creak also.

[2] This is the shape of an ancient axe which suits the story.

mistress and tears came into his eyes as he laid it down; tears came into the drover's eyes where he stood, as he saw his master's bow. But Antinoös rated them both, and said:

"A couple of foolish bumpkins, who can't see to-morrow from to-day! You wretches, why do you blubber and harrow your lady's feelings? She has trouble enough as it is, in losing her husband. Sit down quietly to your dinner, or if you want to cry, go outside and leave the bow here to settle our rivalry once and for all; for I don't think it will be easy to bend that fine bow. There is not a man in all this company as good as Odysseus. I have seen him myself, and I remember him well, although I was only a boy."

That is what he said, though he really expected to bend the bow himself and to shoot through the line of axes. But he was to have the first taste of an arrow from Odysseus, the very man he was dishonouring at that moment, and egging on the others to do the same.

At this Telemachos burst out wildly: [1]

"Upon my word, Zeus Cronion has made me crazy! Here is my dear mother, a model of propriety, going to leave this house and take another man, and I just laugh and enjoy it, like a born fool! Come along then, hearties, here is your prize before your eyes, a woman who has not her equal in the whole country, not in Pylos or Argos or Mycenê! But you know that already; what's the good of praising my mother? Come along, no shilly-shally, don't hang back, string the bow and let us see! I think I will just have a try myself. If I can string the bow and shoot a bull's-eye, I shall not mind it a bit if my honoured mother leaves the house and goes off with some one else, when I am left behind quite able to handle my father's gear!"

Then he stood up, and threw off his purple cloak and the sword from his shoulders. First he drew a long trench in the floor, straight to the line, and set up the axes, stamping down the earth to hold them. All were surprised to see how neatly he did it, although he had never seen them before. Then he returned to the doorway and tried the bow. Three times he moved the upper end forward as he strove to string it, three times he gave up. He felt sure he could bend the bow and shoot the shot; but when he had tried the third

[1] The reader should not fail to notice this touch. Telemachos knows that his father is there, and that vengeance is coming and deliverance for his mother; and he is so excited that he must say something. But what he says is just bluster to hide his thoughts.

time, Odysseus made him a sign and he desisted, much against
his will. Then again the brave lad said:

"Bless my soul, I shall turn out to be a weakling and
good for nothing! or perhaps I am still too young, and I
cannot yet trust my hands to defend myself if some one
attacks me. Come along, you stronger men, have a try at the
bow and let us finish this game."

With these words, he put down the bow leaning against the
polished panels of the door, and stood the arrow against the
tip of the bow; then he sat down again. Antinoös said:

"Come up in order all of you, from right to left, beginning
at the place where the man is serving the wine."

They did so; and the first man who came was Leiodês, their
diviner, the son of Wineface Oinops, Leiodês, who always sat
up at the very end of the hall beside the great mixing-bowl.
He was a man who hated all kinds of violence, and resented
their doings. He was the first to take up the bow and arrow;
he stood at the threshold and tried the bow, but he could not
bend it. His soft unpractised hands soon grew tired as he
pulled and pulled, and he said at last:

"I can't bend it, my friends, let some one else take it. This
bow shall destroy many a strong man, since it is better far to
die, than living to miss that which brings us all here together,
waiting and waiting day after day. There is many a man here
now that hopes and desires to wed Penelopeia; but when he
has seen and tried the bow, let him woo some other woman
of our nation and pay his court with gifts. Then the lady will
take the man who offers most, the man who has the luck."

Then he set the bow leaning against the door, and placed
the arrow against the tip, and returned to his seat. But An-
tinoös rated him roundly:

"I never heard such a thing, Leiodês! dreadful nonsense I
call it, and it makes me angry! So this bow shall destroy many
a strong man just because you can't bend it! The fact is your
respected mother did not produce a son fit to draw bows and
shoot arrows. We shall soon find some one else who is man
enough to do it."

Then he called to Melanthios the goatherd: "Hurry up,
you, light a fire in hall and put a good big seat near it with a
fleece to sit on, and then fetch a good chunk of fat from the
pantry. The young fellows can warm the bow and grease it
well, and then we'll finish our game."

Melanthios lost no time in lighting the fire; he set the seat
in place with its fleece, and brought out a good chunk of fat
from the pantry. The young men warmed the bow and had

their try, but no one could bend it, they were far too weak. Antinoös and Eurymachos kept them hard at it; these two were the ringleaders.

Meanwhile the drover and the good old swineherd had gone out together, and Odysseus followed them. As soon as they were outside the gate of the courtyard, Odysseus began to speak to them quietly:

"You, drover, and you, swineherd—I have something to say to you. Or shall I keep it to myself? My mind urges me to speak. What would you do to defend Odysseus, if some providence brought him here, if he should turn up all of a sudden? Would you side with Odysseus or with the others? Tell me the honest truth."

The drover answered at once:

"O Father Zeus, if only tha'd grant this blessing! If only some god might bring that man home at last! Tha'd know then, sir, the strength of my hands!" So also Eumaios prayed to all the gods of heaven that they might bring back Odysseus to his native land.

Odysseus now saw that they were both honest men, and he spoke again and said:

"Here I am in my house, my very self, after sore tribulation, after twenty years returned to my native land. I see that you two alone of all my servants welcome my coming; I have not heard one other pray that I might return. I promise you both on my honour, and I will keep my word: if God shall destroy all these men by my hands, I will find wives for both of you, and give you land and well-built houses close to myself; and you shall be friends and brothers of my son Telemachos. And now I will show you something to prove manifestly who I am and show that you may trust me. Here is the wound which the wild boar made, when I went that time to Parnassos with the sons of Autolycos."

Then he drew back his rags and showed the scar. They examined it closely, and then they threw their arms round his neck and burst into tears, kissing and fondling his head and shoulders. Odysseus also kissed their heads and hands; and they might have gone on till sunset, but he checked them and said:

"That is enough; no more weeping and wailing now, or some one may come out and see us and tell them inside. Go in one at a time, I first and you after. Let this be your signal. They will all refuse to give me the bow and quiver. But you must come down the hall, Eumaios, and put the bow in my hands; and afterwards go and tell the women to bolt the doors of their rooms, and if they hear any noise or tumult of men where we are, not to come out but stay where they are and mind their own business. You, my dear Philoitios, lock the courtyard gate and fasten it with cords, as quick as you can."

Accordingly he went back to the hall and returned to his seat; and the two others came in after him.

By this time Eurymachos was handling the bow, and warming it all round at the fire; but even so he was not able to bend it. He uttered a deep groan of annoyance, and called out:

"Upon my word, I am sorry for myself and for everybody! It is not so much the wedding, though I am sorry enough about that; there are plenty of women to be had in Ithaca and elsewhere. But to think that we can be so much weaker than Prince Odysseus, that we can't bend his bow! That will be no credit to us in future generations!"

Antinoös answered:

"That's all nonsense, Eurymachos, and you know it. To-day is the feast and holiday of the great god in our town; who would trouble about lending bows to-day? Put it aside and never mind. As for the axes, they may be left here, they will take no harm; I don't think any one will march into the hall of my lord Odysseus and pull them up. Come along, let the man pour in our drops; let us honour the gods, and put away bow and arrows. To-morrow tell the goatherd Melanthios to drive down his best goats, and we will offer the rump-slices to Apollo and his bow, and try again at this bow, and finish our game."

All were glad to agree. The marshals brought water for their hands, the boys filled the mixing-bowls to the brim, and served wine to all in due form. When the ceremony was done, and they had eaten and drunk all they wanted, Odysseus spoke according to his secret plan:

"May I be allowed to speak to the gentlemen who are here paying court to the noble lady? But I address myself specially to Eurymachos and my lord Antinoös, since he said the right thing just now, to put away the bow for the present, and leave the rest to God: to-morrow God will give the victory to whom he will. But I beg you to give me the bow, and let me try the strength of my hands; let me see if my muscles are as strong as they once were, or if all my strength is gone through wandering and hardship."

This made them all very angry indeed, for they were afraid he might succeed in bending the bow. Antinoös gave him a sound rating:

"You wretched stranger, you must be out of you mind!

Aren't you satisfied to dine unmolested in the company of gentlemen, and have all you want to eat? Must you listen to our conversation? No other beggar or stranger listens to our conversation. The wine's too good for you, that's it: wine plays the mischief with any one who opens his mouth too wide and swallows too much. Wine fuddled the famous Centaur Eurytion, when he visited the Lapiths in the hall of Peirithoös; when his wits were fuddled with wine, he went mad and raised a riot in the hall of Peirithoös. The guests leapt up in anger and dragged him out, and cut off his nose and ears. So with his fuddled wits away he went, hag-ridden by his own folly and fuddledom. From this came the feud between Centaurs and men, and he brought punishment on himself first by getting drunk. So I prophesy great trouble for you if you bend that bow. You will find no mercy in our town, but we will send you off to Catch'im Echetos, the bogey king who chops men up, and no one will save you from him. Sit quiet and drink, don't quarrel with younger men."

Penelopeia answered him:

"Antinoös, it is not right or fair to deny any guest of Telemachos who may come to this house. If this stranger is strong enough to bend my husband's bow, do you suppose he will take me home and make me his wife? I do not imagine any such thought ever entered his head. None of you need be anxious on that score, for indeed it would be most improper."

Eurymachos answered:

"Make you his wife? No, my dear lady Penelopeia, we never supposed anything so absurd. It was the thought of men and women gossiping, if some common fellow should say—a lot of second-rate specimens want to marry the wife of a real gentleman, and can't bend his bow! and here comes a beggar on the tramp, bends it easily, and shoots straight to the bull's-eye! That sort of thing would get us a bad name."

Penelopeia replied:

"Eurymachos, no good name is possible for those who dishonour the house of a prince and devour his wealth. Then why do you think such a trifle will get you a bad name? This stranger is a fine well-built man, and he says his father was a man of birth and rank. Just give him the bow, and let us see. I tell you plainly, and I will keep my word: if Apollo grants him the honour of bending the bow, I will supply him with an outfit of good clothes, and a spear to keep off dogs and men, and a sharp sword, and boots for his feet, and I will help him on his way wherever he wishes to go."

Telemachos now put in a word:

"My dear mother, no one has a better right than I to give the bow to whom I will, or to refuse it—no great noble of Ithaca or of the islands along the coast; not one of them shall compel me against my will, even if I wish to present the bow and arrows to my guest and let him keep them. I beg you to retire to your rooms; you have your own work, loom and distaff, and the servants to look after. The bow is a man's business, and mine in particular, for I am master in this house."

Penelopeia was surprised, but she admired his spirit, and went back to her room thinking what a man he had become. Upstairs with her waiting-women she spent the time in lamenting her lost husband, until by grace of Athena she fell into a sound sleep.

Now the swineherd had taken up the bow; but as he was carrying it along there was a great outcry among the intruders, shouts and protests—"Where are are you taking that bow, you crazy swineherd, confound you? Your dogs shall tear you to pieces, all alone among your pigs! You bred them, and soon you shall feed them, if Apollo and All Gods are gracious to us!"

The swineherd dropt the bow on the spot; he was terrified by all these men shouting at him. But Telemachos called out from the other side in a threatening voice:

"Daddy, take that bow along; soon you'll be sorry if you listen to these people—or I'll chase you out into the country with a shower of stones; I may be younger, but I am stronger! I wish I were as much stronger than all these gentry. I could soon send them out of the house in a way they wouldn't like, for they are a wicked lot."

This made them all laugh heartily, and put them into a better temper; so the swineherd carried the bow along and put it into the hands of Odysseus. Then he went out and called Eurycleia the nurse, and said to her:

"My good Eurycleia, the young master says tha must shut the doors of your rooms; and if any one hears any noise or riot where we are, they must not come out, but mind their own business."

She did not understand the meaning of his words, but she shut the doors of their quarters.

Quietly Philoitios ran out and locked the courtyard gate. There was a strong ship's hawser under the porch, and he used this to fasten the gate; then he came in again and returned to his seat, with his eyes ever on Odysseus. By this time Odysseus was handling the bow, turning it round and round, and feeling every part, to see if the worms had got into it while its master was abroad. The others were watching him, and one would say with a look at his neighbour: "He seems a bit of a bow-fancier! He knows the points of a bow! I wonder if he has things like that at home. Maybe he thinks of making one: see how he handles it and poises it, the clever old rascal!" Or another, again: "He's welcome to all he'll get by stringing that bow!"

Amid all this talk Odysseus balanced the bow and scanned it over. Then as easily as a skilful musician stretches a new string on his harp, fastening the sheepgut over the pegs at each end, so without an effort Odysseus strung the great bow. Then he took the bow in his right hand, and twanged the string; at his touch it sang a clear note like a swallow. The gallants were dumbfounded, and their skin paled: Zeus gave a loud thunderclap, a manifest sign. And Odysseus was glad that after all his troubles Zeus had shown him a portent, Zeus, the son of Cronos the master-deceiver. He took one sharp arrow, which lay out on the table before him; the others were still in the quiver, but those present were soon to feel them. This he laid on the bridge of the bow, and drew back the string and notches together; still sitting upon his chair as he was, he took aim and let fly. He did not miss: right through the tops of all the axes went the shaft, and clean out at the other end. Then he turned to Telemachos and said:

"Telemachos, your guest is no discredit to you. I wasted no time in stringing the bow, and I did not miss the mark. My strength is yet unbroken, not as these men taunt me in their scorn. But now it is time to prepare supper for the company while the light lasts; after that there will be time for other sport with music and song, for these are the graces of a feast."

Then he signalled with a nod to Telemachos; and Telemachos slung on his sharp sword, and grasped his spear, and took his stand by the seat, the son armed by his father's side.

BOOK XXII

The Battle in the Hall

NOW ODYSSEUS STRIPT OFF HIS RAGS, AND LEAPT UPON the great doorstone, holding the bow and the quiver full of arrows. He spread the arrows before his feet, and called aloud to the company:

"So the great game is played! and now for another mark, which no man has ever hit: I will see if Apollo will hear my prayer and let me strike it."

Then he let fly straight at Aninoös: he was holding a large golden goblet in both hands, and about to lift it for a drink. Bloodshed was not in his thoughts; who could imagine at the festal board, that one man amongst many, even if he were very strong, would bring certain death upon his own head? The arrow struck him in the throat, and the point ran through the soft neck. He sank to the other side, and the goblet dropt from his hands. In an instant a thick jet of blood spouted from his nostrils; he pushed the table away with a quick jerk of his feet, spilling all the vittles on the ground—meat and bread in a mess.

Then there was a great uproar all through the place as they saw the man fall; they leapt up from their seats in excitement and looked all round at the walls, but there was neither sheild nor spear to be seen. They shouted angrily at Odysseus—

"You shall pay for shooting a man! No more games for you: now your death is a safe thing! You have killed the best fellow in Ithaca, and so the vultures shall eat you here!"

They were just guessing—they never dreamt that he intended to kill the man. Poor fools! they did not know that the cords of death were made fast about them all. But Odysseus said with a frowning face:

"Dogs! you thought I would never come back from Troy, so you have been carving up my substance, forcing the women to lie with you, courting my wife before I was dead, not fearing the gods who rule the broad heavens, nor the execration of man which follows you for ever. And now the cords of death are made fast about you all!"

Then pale fear seized upon them. Eurymachos alone dared to answer:

"If you are really Ithacan Odysseus come back, what you

243

have said is just and right. Plenty of wild doings here, plenty more on your farms! But there lies the guilty man, Antinoös, who is answerable for everything. He was the ringleader; a wife was not what he wanted, not so much as something else, which Cronion has not allowed him to do. He wished to murder your son by a secret assault, and to be sole lord and master in this fine country of Ithaca. Now he has his deserts and lies dead. Sir, spare your own people! We will make it all good, all that has been consumed, all the wine that has been drunk in this hall; there shall be a public collection, and each man severally will pay twenty oxen in compensation, and bring gold and bronze to your heart's content. Till that is done no one could blame you for being angry."

Odysseus answered with a frowning face:

"Eurymachos, not if you would give me your whole estates, all you now possess, and more if you could get it, not even so would I stay my hand from killing until every man of you shall have paid in full for his outrageous violence. Now the choice lies before you, fight or flight, if you wish to save your lives; but I do not think any one of you will escape sudden death."

As they listened, their knees gave way beneath them and despair entered their hearts. But Eurymachos once more spoke:

"My friends," he cried out, "this man will not hold his hands—he thinks he is invincible. He has bow and arrows, and he will shoot from the doorway until he has killed us all! Let us fight for it! Draw your swords and put up the tables to fend off his arrows; have at him all together; see if we can't push him away from the door, and get out and make a hue and cry in the town! Then this man will soon shoot his last shot!"

With this he drew a good sharp blade from his side, and leapt at Odysseus with a yell; but on the instant Odysseus let fly an arrow and struck him in the chest by the nipple. The sharp point pierced his liver; down fell the sword from his hand, he doubled up and fell sprawling over a table, vittles and cup went scattering over the floor; he beat his brow on the ground in agony, his feet kicked out and knocked over the chair, and a mist came over his eyes.

Then Amphinomos ran straight at Odysseus, sword in hand, to force his way out of the door. But Telemachos was too quick for him; he cast his spear from behind and struck him between the shoulders—the point came out through his chest, and his face crashed on the ground with a thud. Telemachos leapt back and left the spear in the body; he feared that some one might stab him with a sword, or strike a blow, if he stooped to pull it out. He ran quickly up to his father, and said without wasting words:

"Father, I'll go at once and fetch you a shield and a couple of spears and a helmet to fit your head, and I'll arm myself, and do the same for the drover and the swineherd. We ought to be armed!"

Odysseus answered: "Run and bring them while I have arrows left, or they may crowd me away from the door."

Telemachos went promptly to the store where the arms were kept. He chose four shields and eight spears and four good helmets of bronze with horse-hair plumes; these he brought back at full speed to his father. First he armed himself, then the two men fitted themselves out, and they stood by the indomitable Odysseus.

As long as the arrows lasted Odysseus went on bringing them down one after another. But when the arrows came to an end and he could shoot no more, he leaned his bow on the doorpost and left it standing, then slung the stout shield over his shoulders, and fitted the helmet on his head, where the nodding plume seemed to threaten those who saw it. Lastly, he picked up two sharp-pointed spears.

But there was a door high up in the wall closed by a strong pair of leaves. At the top of the steps the way led through into a passage on the other side.[1] Odysseus had told the swineherd to stand near this door and to keep an eye on it; there was only one way to get there. Now Agelaos had thought of this, and he called out:

"I say, friends, couldn't some one go up to that door, and publish the news and set up a hue and cry on the spot? This man would soon shoot his last shot!"

Melanthios the goatherd answered:

"Impossible, my lord! The courtyard gate is terrible near, and the passage mouth is dangerous; one strong man could easily hold it against many. But look here, I can fetch you arms from the storehouse; I am sure Odysseus and his son put them away there and nowhere else."

Then Melanthios ran up and through the backways of the house into the storeroom, and collected a dozen shields and as many spears and good strong helmets; back he came

[1] The steps are inferred from the story. The words "top threshold of the hall" seem to mean "the top step which was the threshold of the door into the hall." The passage led both to the storerooms and out into the yard.

quickly with them, and distributed them. When Odysseus
saw the men arming themselves and poising the spears he was
quite taken aback; he saw a new danger. So he called out to
Telemachos without wasting words:

"Telemachos! I'm sure one of the women inside is helping
these fellows against us—or else it's Melanthios. That's what
I think."

Telemachos said:

"O father! it is my fault—no one else is to blame! I left the
door of the storeroom open! and they had a better scout than
I was! Eumaios man, go and shut that door, and see if one of
the women is doing this or Melantios Trickson—like father,
like son!"

While they were talking, Melantios went on a second jour-
ney for arms, but Eumaios saw him this time, and said to
Odysseus at his elbow:

"Look there, my beloved lord and master! The man we
guessed at has disappeared again, going to the storehouse. Tell
me what to do—shall I kill him if I can, or bring him here,
and then we can pay him out for his evil doings in thy
house?"

Odysseus answered:

"I and my son can manage to hold off the worst they can
do here. You two just twist his hands and feet behind him and
tie them to a couple of planks, fasten him to a stout rope
and haul him up the pillar to the roof-beams and leave him
there. Let him live, and see how he likes it."

They listened attentively, and did what he told them. To the
storeroom they went; the man was inside hunting for weapons,
but he did not hear them. They stood one on each side of the
door, and as he came out carrying a helmet in one hand and
an old broad shield in the other—it was one which Laërtês
had carried in his young days, covered with mould and dirt,
which lay there with all the seams bursting—they pounced
upon him and caught him, dragged him in by the hair, threw
him on the ground in a great state, twisted his hands and feet
behind him and trussed him up in a very uncomfortable
package according to directions, twisted a rope round him and
hauled him right up the pillar to the roof-beams. There you had
your revenge, friend Eumaios; for you said pleasantly:

"Now you shall watch all night long, Melanthios, with a soft
bed to lie on, as you richly deserve; and you shall not fail to
see Dawn, when she shall appear through the misty air out of
the ocean, upon her golden throne, at the time when you drive
your goats down for the gentlemen's dinner!"

There they left him, strung up in that dreadful bundle. The two put on their armour again, shutting the door, and returned to Odysseus. There they all stood breathing fury, in the doorway four, within the hall many, and good men too. But now Athena came near to them in the likeness of Mentor. Odysseus was cheered by the sight; he guessed it was Athena Captain of Hosts, but he said to her:

"Mentor, stand by me and remember your old comrade who always did the right thing by you.[1] We are yearsmates!"

Then the others raised a loud shout in the hall, and Agelaos Damastoridês called out threateningly:

"Mentor! don't let Odysseus cajole you to fight on his side against us! If you do, I promise you that when we have settled father and son we will kill you too! You will pay with your life for what you mean to do! We will wipe out your people if they try to avenge you, and seize your goods indoors and out and throw them in with the rest. Your sons and daughters shall not live in your house, your worthy wife shall not walk in the town of Ithaca!"

Athena grew hot with anger at this, and taunted Odysseus with angry words:

"You are not the man you were, Odysseus! Where is the courage and strength you showed in that endless conflict, those nine years of battles for beautiful Helen! Many a man you killed in open fight, and by your device the great city of Priam was taken! Now you have come back to hearth and home, why do you grumble to show your strength before a pack of young men in love? Lazy man, stand by my side and see a masterpiece! I will teach you in the face of the enemy what means the gratitude of Mentor Strongi'th'arm!"

But she did not give him overwhelming victory at once, for she wished to prove still further the strength and courage of Odysseus and his doughty son. In the shape of a swallow she flew up to the smoky rafters, and perched there.

The invaders were led now by six men, Agelaos, Eurynomos, Amphimedon, Demoptolemos, Peisandros, and Polybos. They were the best of those who still lived, and they were fighting for their lives; the rest had been brought down or cowed by the arrows flying thick and fast. Agelaos addressed himself to the whole body:

"My friends, now the man will slacken his invincible hands! You see how Mentor went off after a few empty boasts, and

[1] The word used is suitable to sacrifice, and so it suits Athena in her real character.

left them alone there by the door. Now then, don't all throw your spears at once, but let six of us first give a volley, and see if Zeus will grant us to strike down Odysseus and cover ourselves with glory! Never mind the rest once he shall fall!"

So the six volleyed eagerly; but Athena made them all miss. One spear hit the doorpost, one a leaf of the door, a third fell heavily and stuck in the wall; they dodged the others, and Odysseus gave orders in his turn:

"Now my friends, when I give the word let fly at this crowd, who are determined to destroy us after all their unprovoked injuries!"

At the word they all took aim and volleyed. Odysseus hit Demoptolemos, Telemachos Euryadês, the swineherd Elatos, and the drover Peisandros; all fell together and bit the dust, and the others took refuge at the far end of the hall. The four advanced and drew their spears out of the bodies.

Another volley came from the crowd in fury, but Athena made most of them miss. One stuck in the doorpost, one in the door, and a third fell heavily against the wall. However, at last Amphimedon grazed the wrist of Telemachos, cutting the skin, and Ctesippos with his long spear grazed the shoulder of Eumaios over the shield, but the spear passed on and fell to the ground. Then Odysseus and his party volleyed again into the throng; Odysseus hit Eurydamas, Telemachos Amphimedon, the swineherd Polybos. Lastly the drover hit Ctesippos full in the chest, and shouted in triumph:

"One for you, old Braggartson,[1] with your foul tongue! Learn not to boast like a fool, but leave the word to the gods, for they are mightier far! Here's a little tip for you in return for that hoof which you threw at my master Odysseus, when he was begging in the hall!"

Not bad for a drover of horned cattle! Then they came to close fighting. Odysseus wounded Damastoridês with a spearthrust. Telemachos struck Leocritos, running him through the groin and out at the other side, and he fell flat on his face. At that moment Athena lifted her man-shattering ægis-cape, and held it against them from on high: they fell into a panic, and scampered along the hall like a herd of cows, when the darting gadfly attacks them and scatters them in the long days of springtime. The four were after them like vultures that swoop down out of the mountains with curving beaks and hooked claws on a flock of birds; hide as they will, fly-

[1] This name is no doubt invented on the spot; the English names given earlier are also translations of the Greek names.

ing low under the clouds, the vultures are on them, a pounce
and a kill, there is no help and no refuge, and the onlookers
think it fine sport. So these four rushed upon their enemies
spearing men right and left; to every blow a dreadful groan,
and the ground ran with blood.

But Leiodês ran up to Odysseus and threw his arms
round his knees, begging for his life in plain words without
ceremony:

"Spare me, Odysseus, I pray! have mercy upon me! I de-
clare that I never meddled with the women in this house, by
word or deed! no, I tried to stop the others when they did
anything of that sort! But they would not listen to me and
keep their hands from evil, and so their own recklessness
has brought them to a dreadful end! But I am only their
diviner, I have done nothing, and I am to die because there
is no gratitude in the world for good deeds done!"

Odysseus said to him, frowning:

"If you call yourself their diviner, you must have prayed
often enough that I might never be so happy as to return
home, that my beloved wife might go with you and bear
you children. Therefore you shall not escape the terror of
death!" He picked up the sword which Agelaos had dropt
when he was struck down, and drove it through the man's
throat; even while he was speaking his head rolled in the
dust.

But the minstrel had escaped death so far. This was
Phemios Terpiadês, the tuneful son of harmony as his
name denotes; but he had been dragged in by compulsion to
sing for the roistering crew. He was standing close to the
back door, harp in hand, hesitating whether to run out of the
hall and take refuge at the great altar of Zeus built in the
courtyard, where both Laërtês and Odysseus used to sacrifice,
or to run up and clasp the knees of Odysseus Laërtês' son. He
thought it better to throw himself on the mercy of Odysseus.
So he set down his harp on the ground between the mixing-
bowl and the seat of state, and running quickly, clasped the
master's knees and besought him in plain and simple words:

"Spare me, Odysseus, I pray! Have mercy upon me! You
will be sorry afterwards if you kill a singer like me, one
who can sing before God and man! I am self-taught, but
God has planted all manner of songs in my mind. I am fit to
sing before you as before God; then do not be eager to cut
my throat. Your own son Telemachos can tell you that no
will of my own made me come into this house, no desire for
gain: I had to sing to these men at supper because they were

too many for me and too strong, because they compelled me!"

Telemachos was close by his father, and heard this; he said at once:

"Spare him, father, he is innocent, don't strike him; and let us spare Medon the marshal, who used to look after me here when I was a little boy—unless Philoitios or the swineherd has killed him, or he may have come in your way as you went raging through the hall."

Medon heard him! He was there, smart lad, huddled under a chair, rolled up in a new-flayed cowhide, where he had crawled to escape if he could. Now he was out with one leap from under that chair, threw off the hide, dashed up to Telemachos, grasped his knees, cried out simply:

"Here I am, my dear—spare me, sir!—tell the master not to hurt me with that sharp sword! he's almighty now—and those brutes, no wonder a was angry with 'em, devouring his goods in his own house, and thought nothing of thee, lik ethe fools they were!"

Odysseus smiled,[1] and said:

"Cheer up, my son has saved your life. So you shall know, and tell other men, that doing well is far better than doing ill. Now then, you two had better go out of this carnage into the yard, and stay there until I have finished what is left for me to do in this house."

They both went out and sat down by the altar of Zeus, gazing about them and every moment expecting death.

Odysseus looked carefully in every part of the hall, in case any one were still alive and hiding himself from death. But he saw them all lying in heaps amid blood and dust. They were like a great haul of fishes which the fishermen have drawn into a bay with a wide net; they lie on the sand panting for the salt water, while the blazing sun takes away their life. Then at last Odysseus said to Telemachos:

"Go and call Nurse Eurycleia. I have something I want to tell her."

Telemachos went to the women's room, and shaking the door called Eurycleia:

"Wake up now, grandam wife! Wake up, keeper of all the women in this great house! Come this way; my father calls you. He has something which he wants to tell you!"

She had no notion what he meant, but she opened the door and followed him. There she found Odysseus, smothered

---

[1] This is the first time Odysseus has smiled in the whole story.

in blood and filth, cheeks and chest, from head to foot, with a
terrible look on his face; like a lion which has just chawed
up a bullock in the farmyard. When she saw the piles of dead
bodies and streams of blood, she stretched her body for the
women's alleluia at this great victory; but Odysseus checked
her and stopt it, not without difficulty, as he said plainly:

"Keep your joy in your heart, woman; quiet now, no cries
of triumph. It is not decent to boast over slain men. These
have been brought low by God's decree and their own wicked
deeds. They respected none of those who walk on the earth,
neither good men nor bad; therefore their recklessness has
brought them to a dreadful end. Now tell over the
names of the women in this house, and say which disgrace
me and which are innocent."

The old nurse answered:

"Aye, my love, I'll tell thee the truth of it. Fifty
women there are in this house; we have taught 'em all their
work, to card wool and to put up with what a slave must
bear. A dozen of 'em are shameless huzzies, and pay no
respect to me or my lady herself. The young master has but
now grown up, and the mistress wadn't let him give orders to
the women. But I'll just go up the stairs and tell her the
news; she's haven a bit of sleep, thank God!"

Odysseus answered:

"Don't wake her yet. Tell all the women to come here who
have been disgracing themselves."

Then the old woman went out of the hall to summon the
women at once. He called Telemachos and the drover and
swineherd, and told them plainly what they had to do:

"The first thing is to carry out these bodies, and tell the
women to help you, then wipe clean all the chairs and tables
with sponge and water. When you have put the place in order,
drive out the women between the domed house and the
courtyard wall, and run your sword through them; kill them
all, and teach them to forget their secret bussing and cuddling
with these brave gallants."

The women now came in with dreadful wailing and floods
of tears. First they had to carry out the dead bodies, and lay
them along the courtyard wall, packed close together under
the gallery. Odysseus gave them directions and let them
waste no time—they had to obey. Then they cleaned up the
tables and seats with sponges and water. Telemachos and the
two men scraped over the floor with shovels, and the women
cleared out the scrapings. When the great hall was quite in
order, they drove the women outside, and cooped them up in

a narrow space between the doomed house and the wall so that they could not get out. Telemachos had been thinking, and now he said:

"I should not care to give a clean death to these women who have heaped insults on my head, and upon my mother, and slept by the side of those who pretended to her hand."

So he rigged up a ship's hawser, fastening one end to a tall pillar and throwing the other round the dome. A noose was looped round the neck of each, and he pulled it up tight so that their feet would not touch the ground. They were strung up with their heads in a row—a pitiable death to die, no lover's bed indeed! They looked like a lot of thrushes or doves caught in a net when they come to roost in the bushes. Their feet jerked for a little while, but not long.

Melanthios was brought out by the fore-hall and courtyard. His nose and ears and cods were cut off, and thrown to the dogs to eat raw; then hands and feet were cut off to vent their fury.

The work was done. They washed their hands and feet and went into the great house. Then Odysseus called his nurse Eurycleia, and said:

"Bring sulphur and fire, to cleanse the hall and sweeten the air. Then request Penelopeia to come here with her waiting-women; and tell all the other women in the house to come."

Nurse Eurycleia answered:

"Aye, aye, my love, there's nowt amiss wi' that. But let me fetch thee some clean clothes; don't stand there with that bundle of rags on thi broad shoulders! That would be a real shame!"

Odysseus said, "First of all get the fire lighted."

The nurse obediently brought fire and sulphur, and Odysseus smoked the hall well with it, and the fore-hall and the courtyard.

Then the old woman went into the house, to tell the women to make haste and come; and they came from their quarters torch in hand. How they crowded about Odysseus, throwing their arms round him and giving him welcome, and kissing his head and shoulders and holding his hands! He longed to relieve his feelings with tears, for in his heart he knew them all.

BOOK XXIII

How Odysseus Found His Wife Again

AWAY WENT THE OLD WOMAN WITH HER NEWS THAT the master was in the house. She climbed the stairs chuckling to herself, her knees trotted along, her feet tumbled over each other. She leant down over his mistress, and said:

"Wake up, dear love; wake up, Penelopeia! Come and see with thi own eyes what tha's prayed for many a long day! The master has come, he's in the house, better late than never! and he's killed the whole lot of come-marry-me-quicks, who have made themselves a nuisance, and eaten thi vittles, and plagued thi boy!"

Penelopeia was too cautious to believe this. She replied:

"Nanny dear, the gods have made you mad. They can make the wisest of men foolish, and they can give good sense to the weakest mind. They have upset even you, and you are generally sound enough. Why do you mock me? I have trouble as it is, and here you come to tell me this crazy tale, and wake me out of a lovely sleep when my poor eyes were fast closed! I have not had such a sleep since Odysseus went on his voyage to Ilion the accursed, which I cannot endure to name! Go away, do, and get back to your room. If any of my other women had waked me up and told me this tale, I should have sent her off in disgrace, but your age shall protect you."

The old woman answered:

"I don't mock tha, my love, 'tis the truth! The master has come, he's in the house, as I say—that stranger man, the one they all sneered at in hall. Telemachos knew that he was here, so it turned out, but he's a prudent one, hid his father's notions. Punish the men who were above themselves, make 'em pay for their violence, that was *his* mind!"

How glad was Penelopeia! She sprang out of bed, and flung her arms round the old woman's neck: the tears ran down her cheeks, and her words were plain enough now:

"Tell me, Nanny dear, tell me truly, if he is really come home as you say, how did he get his hands on those shameless men alone by himself, and they in a crowd together as they always were?"

The old woman replied:

"I saw nowt and I axt nowt, only I heard a noise while they

were being killed; we got all as far away as we could and sat in the corners and kept the doors locked, scared out of our wits, till thi son called me out of the room; his father wanted me, says he. Then I found the master standen in the middle of the corpses, they were all around him coveren the solid ground, in heaps! It would have warmed thi heart to see it! Now they're all packed together by the courtyard gates, and he's fumen the hall wi' sulphur, and a great big fire blazen, but he sent me to tell thee. Come now, enter into your hearts' delight and be happy together, after all your troubles! Now at last the prayer is answered that was prayed so long. He is alive, he has come himself to his own hearth, he has found thee also and his son in the house; and he has taken vengeance in his own house on all the men who did him wrong!"

Penelopeia said again:

"Nanny dear, don't boast too soon with all that gloating and chuckling! You know how glad we should all be to see him in this house, especially myself and my son; but there is no truth in your story. No, no, it is one of the immortal gods who killed these proud men. He must have been shocked by their heart-breaking violence and evil doings. For they respected no man on earth that ever met them, good or bad, and therefore they have been punished for their reck-lessness. But Odysseus has lost his hope of return far away from this land, he is lost himself."

The old nurse answered:

"My dear love, what a screed to let out o' thi pretty lips! Here's thi man in the house, by the hearthstone, and tha'lt have it he'll never come back home! But thi mind was ever unbelieven. Look now, I'll give thee a plain manifest sign. The wound that the boar gave him with his tusk—I felt it in the washen and wanted to tell thee, but a clips me over the mouth and won't let me utter a word! Aye, he's a clever one, a deep mind a surely has! Come along, I'll lay my life on it; if I deceive thee, burn me alive and welcome!"

Penelopeia, still doubtful, replied:

"Nanny dear, it is hard to understand the counsels of the immortal gods, even if you are a very wise woman. How-ever, let us go to my son. I should like to see the men who plagued me, and the man who slew them."

Saying this she went down the stairs with a heart full of perplexity. Should she keep aloof and question her husband? Should she go to his side and cover head and hands with her kisses?

She passed over the great doorstone into the hall, and seated herself opposite to Odysseus by the wall on one side of the bright fire. He was sitting against a pillar looking down, and wondering whether his brave wife would speak to him when she saw him. But she sat silent a long time as if struck dumb. Again and again she turned her eager eyes and looked hard at his face, but then again she could not know him in those dirty rags. At last Telemachos burst out impatiently:

"My mother—a devil of a mother you are, with your hard heart! Why do you keep all that way from father? Why won't you sit beside him and ask some question or say something? I'm sure no other woman could be so cold and keep her husband at a distance, now he has come home after twenty years and all those terrible dangers! But your heart was always harder than flint."

Penelopeia, still doubtful, answered:

"My boy, my heart is numbed. I cannot speak to him, or ask questions, or look into his face. If he is indeed Odysseus, and this is his house, we shall know each other well enough; there are secrets that we two know and no one else."

Odysseus smiled at this [1]; he answered at once simply and plainly:

"Leave your mother alone, Telemachos, and let her test me: she will soon know me better. Now I am ragged and dirty, she looks down on me and thinks I am not the man. But we have to consider what is best to do next. If you take the life of one man in the community, and he has a number of friends to avenge him afterwards, you must leave your country to escape his kinsmen. But we have destroyed the bulwark of the city, the finest lads in Ithaca. Consider that, if you please!"

Telemachos said with due respect:

"You see to that, dear father. You have your plans ready for everything, as all the world declares, and no man living could challenge you in that."

Odysseus was quite ready, and replied:

"Very well, I will say what I think best. First wash from head to foot, and put on clean clothes, and tell the household women to dress. Let the minstrel take his harp and strike up a cheerful dance, so that the neighbors and those in the street outside may hear it and think there is a wedding. No rumor must go abroad that these men are killed,

---

[1] This is the second time that Odysseus smiles.

until we can get out to the farms and the forests. After that we will consider any plan that the Olympian may put into our minds."

They set about this at once. They bathed and dressed, and the women decked themselves out; the minstrel took up his harp and put them in the mood for merry dance and song. The great hall echoed to the dancing feet of women and men; and those passing by in the street said one to another:

"Ha! some one has married the much-wooed lady! She's a hard one! She didn't break her heart for the husband of her youth! She might have looked after the house till he came back."

They little knew what had happened. Within that house Eurynomê bathed Odysseus and rubbed him down and gave him good clothes. Then he seemed another man, taller and stronger than before, and splendid from head to foot by grace of Athena; his head covered with a thick curly crop like the thick clustering petals of the hyacinth. He was a noble and brilliant figure; you might think of some perfect work of art made by one who is inspired by the divine artists, Hephaistos and Pallas Athena, brilliant with gold over silver. He came out of the bathroom looking more like a god than a man, and returned to his former seat facing his wife. Then he said to her:

"Strange woman! The inscrutable will of God has made your heart unfeeling beyond mortal women. No other wife could endure to keep her husband at a distance, when he has just returned after twenty years of dreadful perils. Very well. Come, Nanny, lay me a bed and I will sleep alone. She has a heart of steel, it is clear."

His clever wife replied:

"Strange man, I am not proud, or contemptuous, or offended, but I know what manner of man you were when you sailed away from Ithaca. Come, Eurycleia, make the bed outside the room which he built himself; put the fine bedstead outside, and lay out the rugs and blankets and fleeces."

This was a little trap for her husband. He burst into a rage: [1]

"Wife, that has cut me to the heart! Who has moved my bed? That would be a difficult job for the best workman, un-

---

[1] This is the first time in all the eventful tale when Odysseus speaks on impulse; he has been prepared for everything, but this unexpected trifle unlocks his heart.

less God himself should come down and move it. It would be easy for God, but no man could easily prize it up, not the strongest man living! There is a great secret in that bed. I made it myself, and no one else touched it. There was a strong young olive tree in full leaf growing in an enclosure, the trunk as thick as a pillar. Round this I built our bridal chamber; I did the whole thing myself, laid the stones and built a good roof over it, jointed the doors and fitted them in their places. After that I cut off the branches and trimmed the trunk from the root up, smoothed it carefully with the adze and made it straight to the line. This tree I made the bedpost. That was the beginning of my bed; I bored holes through it, and fitted the other posts about it, and inlaid the framework with gold and silver and ivory, and I ran through it leather straps coloured purple. Now I have told you my secret. And I don't know if it is still there, wife, or if some one has cut the olive at the root and moved my bed!"

She was conquered, she could hold out no longer when Odysseus told the secret she knew so well. She burst into tears and ran straight to him, throwing her arms about his neck. She kissed his head, and cried:

"Don't be cross with me, my husband, you were always a most understanding man! The gods brought affliction upon us because they grudged us the joy of being young and growing old together! Don't be angry, don't be hurt because I did not take you in my arms as soon as I saw you! My heart has been frozen all this time with a fear that some one would come and deceive me with a false tale; there as so many impostors! [1] But now you have told me the secret of our bed, that settles it. No one else has seen it, only you and I, and my maid Actoris, the one my father gave me when I came to you, who used to keep the door of our room. You have convinced your hard-hearted wife!"

Odysseus was even more deeply moved, and his tears ran as he held her in his arms, the wife of his heart, so faithful and so wise.[2] She felt like a shipwrecked mariner, when the stout ship has been driven before the storm and smashed by the heavy waves, but a few have escaped by swimming. How glad they are to see land at last, to get out of the water and stand upon solid ground all caked with brine! So glad was Penelopeia to see her husband at last; she held her white

---

[1] Lines 218–224 are out of place here; as they were rejected in ancient days by the great critic Aristarchus, I omit them.

[2] This is the second time he has allowed his tears to flow. The first was when he made himself known to his son.

arms close round his neck, and could not let him go. Dawn would have risen upon their tears of joy, but Athena had a thought for them. She held the night in its course and made it long; she kept Dawn on her golden throne at the end of Ocean, so that she could not yoke up her swift pair, Flasher and Flamer, the colts who bring Dawn with her light to mortal men.

At last Odysseus said to his wife:

"Dear wife, we have not yet reached the end of our labours. There still remains a task which I cannot measure, difficult and dangerous, but I must go through to the end. The soul of Teiresias the prophet told me, on the day when I went to house of Hadês and asked his advice for our homeward voyage. But come to our bed, my wife, that we may have the delight of sleeping side by side."

Penelopeia replied:

"The bed is there for you whenever you please, now that God has brought you back to your home and your native land. But since you have thought of it, tell me about this task; I must learn of it some time, and I should rather like to know at once."

Odysseus answered:

"You strange woman! Why do you make me go on talking again? All right, I'll tell you and hide nothing. You will not like it, nor do I like it myself.

"He told me to visit city after city carrying an oar, until I should find people who do not know the sea or eat salt with their food, know nothing (said he) about ships with crimson cheeks, and well-fashioned oars which are like the ship's wingfeathers. Then he told me this for a clear sign, and I tell it to you: Whenever some one should meet me on the road, and say I had a winnowing shovel on my shoulder, I should fix my oar at once in the ground; then sacrifice to Lord Poseidon in due form a bull, a ram, and a boar-pig; and then on returning home I was to prepare a solemn sacrifice in turn to all the gods who rule the broad heavens. I am to live myself with my people happy around me, until I sink under the comfortable burden of years, and death will just come to me gently from the sea. That is what will happen, according to him."

Penelopeia answered with her usual good sense:

"Well, if the gods are to give you such a comfortable burden of old age, there's good hope that you will come safely through your other trials!"

Meanwhile Eurynomê and the old nurse laid the soft bed-

ding under the torchlight. When all was ready, the old nurse
went to rest in her own room; and Eurynomê attended them,
torch in hand, to their chamber, and left them there. With
happy hearts they came to the place where their old bed
was. And Telemachos with the drover and the swineherd
ended their dance, and sent the women away, and went to
rest.

Now all the house was dark, and these two enjoyed at last
the blessing of love. Then they had a delightful talk of the
past. She described what she had gone through; how she had
to look on while that wasteful gang slaughtered all those
cattle and sheep and emptied all those butts of wine, on her
account; Odysseus told what hardships he had endured, and
what trouble he had brought on others. The story delighted
his wife, and she could not close her eyes till she had heard
it all.

He began with the Ciconian battles, and went on to the
Lotus-eaters' country, and what the Cyclops did, and how he
avenged those fine felllows whom the cannibal devoured
without pity; the visit of Aiolos, how kindly he had received
them and helped them on their voyage; but it was not yet his
destiny to reach home—the tempest caught him up again,
and drove him over the sea in distress. Then how he came to
Laistrygonian Telepylos, and the natives destroyed the ships
and their crews. He told of Circê's tricks and devices, and
how he sailed to the mouldering house of Hadês to consult
the soul of Theban Teiresias; how he saw his old comrades,
and the mother who had borne him and brought him up;
how he heard the throbbing notes of the Sirens' song; how he
went on to the Moving Rocks, and dread Charybdis, and
Scylla, whom no man ever escaped unharmed; how his com-
panions slaughtered the Sun's cattle; how Zeus thundering
in the heights struck the ship with a fiery bolt, and his com-
panions were destroyed every one; how he alone escaped,
and came to Ogygia and the nymph Calypso; how she kept
him in her cave and wanted to have him for a husband, how
she cared for him and promised to make him immortal, never
to grow old, but he would never consent; how after great
hardships he reached the Phaiacians, and they treated him
with right royal kindness and conveyed him to Ithaca in one
of their ships, with a heap of gifts, bronze and gold and fine
woven stuffs. This was the end of his tale, for then sleep
pounced upon him, sleep that soothes the heavy limbs and
the heavy heart.

Now came Athena's turn. When she thought Odysseus had

slept long enough by his wife's side, she released golden Dawn from Oceanos to bring light to mortal men.

Odysseus rose from his soft bed, and said:

"My wife, we have had trials enough already, both of us, you mourning and watching for my return, and I held fast by Zeus and all the gods far from the home I craved. And at last we are both in our own bed which we have so long desired! Now you must take care of the house and what is in it, and I must replace what has been wasted and destroyed. The people will repay part, and the rest I will take by force until my pens are full again. But first I will pay a visit to the woodlands and the farm, to see my good father who is troubled on my account. I warn you to be careful, although you are wise enough to understand without that. As soon as the sun rises, every one will hear about the men I have killed in this house; you must keep in your apartments with your women, see nô one, and ask no questions."

He put on his body-armour, then wakened Telemachos and the two men, and made them do the same. When they were all ready, with their weapons in their hands, they opened the gates and Odysseus led them out. It was already light, but Athena hid them in darkness and quickly led them out of the town.

BOOK XXIV

*How Odysseus Found His Old Father and
How the Story Ended*

CYLLENIAN HERMES CAME TO SUMMON THE SOULS OF
the dead men. He held the rod of fine gold with which he
enchants the eyes of men if he will, or awakes those who
sleep; with this he stirred them, and they followed gibbering.
They were like a swarm of bats in the hollows of a great cave,
which hang clinging to one another from the roof, until one
falls out of the chain, and they all fly about gibbering in con-
fusion. So Hermês the Master-trickster led them along the
mouldering road, and they gibbered as they went. Past the
stream of Ocean they went, past the rock of Leucas, past the
gates of the Sun and the realm of dreams; and then they
came to the meadow of asphodel where abide the souls and
phantoms of those whose work is done.

There they found the soul of Achillês Peleïadês, and
Patroclos and the admirable Antilochos, and Aias, noblest
and handsomest of the Danaän host after peerless Achillês.
These were standing together, and the soul of Agamemnon
Atreïdês joined them grieving, with the others who had been
killed beside him in Aigisthos' house. Achillês first addressed
him thus:

"Prince of the house of Atreus, we always thought you the
nearest and dearest of heroes and men to Thundering Zeus;
for you ruled over a host of mighty men in that terrible war
before Troy. And yet it seems you were doomed to perish
before your time, although death comes to every man who is
born. Would that you had met your fate before Troy, still
enjoying that honourable state of royalty; then the whole
Achaian nation would have built you a tomb to keep a glo-
rious memory of you and your son both. But it seems you
were destined to die a most pitiable death."

The soul of Atreïdês answered:

"You are happy, royal prince of the house of Peleus, that
you died at Troy far from Argos in the battlefield, with
friend and foe falling on every side, fighting for your cause.
There you lay in the whirling dust, grand in death as once
grand in life, forgetful of your horsemanship. But we fought
the whole day long, and never would have ended the fight

but that Zeus made an end with a tempest. We carried you off the field and laid you upon a bier; we washed your body with warm water and anointed it with oil; hot tears were shed from many eyes, and the hair was cut from all heads. Your mother came out of the sea with the immortal daughters of the sea, when the tidings reached her. Their loud lamentations resounded over the deep, and trembling took hold of all the Achaian host; they would have leapt up and taken to their ships, had not a wise old man restrained them, Nestor, whose counsel had proved the best many a time before. He spoke to them gently and kindly:

" 'Back, men of Argos! do not run, brave lads of Achaia! His mother has come out of the sea with the immortal daughters of the sea, to visit her dead son!'

"The Achaians took heart and stayed their flight; round about your body stood the daughters of the Old Man of the Sea, wailing lamentably, and clothed in unfading raiment incorruptible. The Nine Muses sang the dirge with their lovely voices, answering each to each in turn. You could not have seen one tearless eye in the host, when all were so deeply moved by that sweet song.

"Seventeen days and seventeen nights we mourned you, mortal men and immortal gods together; on the eighteenth day we gave you to the fire, and slew around you fatted cattle and sheep. You were burnt in raiment of the gods, with honey and oil in abundance; troops of armed warriors marched round the pyre, both horse and footmen with a loud resounding noise. And when the fierce flame had consumed you, next morning we gathered up your whitened bones, and laid them with pure wine and oil in a golden urn which your mother gave us; she said it was the work of famous Hephaistos and a gift from Dionysos. In that urn lie your bones, Achillês, mingled with the bones of Patroclos, your dead friend; in another the bones of Antilochos, whom you honoured above all others after Patroclos died.

"Then all our armed host built for these three a great and notable tomb on a headland of the coast, above the wide Hellespont, to be seen from the sea afar by men who now live and those who shall come after. Your mother gathered fine prizes from the gods, and set them up for a contest of the best men. Often enough you have been at the funeral games of the great, when a king has died and strong young men gird themselves for the prize; but had you seen those prizes, the beautiful prizes which silverfoot Thetis had provided, you would have marvelled indeed, for the gods loved you dearly. And so although you are dead your name is not forgotten, Achillês, but it will be renowned for ever throughout all the world. But as for me, what pleasure have I in this that I wound up the war? For at my return Zeus had ready for me a cruel death, at the hands of Aigisthos and my accursed wife."

While they were conversing, King's Messenger Argeïphontês drew near, leading the souls of those whom Odysseus had killed. The two princes moved towards them, surprised at this sight. Then the soul of King Agamemnon recognized Amphimedon, who had entertained him in Ithaca. He said at once:

"Amphimedon, what disaster has brought you here under the black earth, all picked men and yearsmates? If one were to choose the best men of your city he could make no other choice. Did Poseidon raised a wild storm and a heavy sea and swamp your ships? Did the enemy fall on you ashore while you were cutting out cattle and sheep? Or were they fighting before their walls for their wives and homes? Answer me, for you are my host and friend. Do you not remember how I came to your house, to enlist Odysseus in the war of Menelaos against Ilion? It took us a whole month to cross the broad sea; and it was a hard task to persuade Odysseus, who brought us victory in the end."

The soul of Amphimedon answered:

"I remember all that quite well, royal prince. I will tell you the miserable story of our death as it happened. Odysseus had been long absent, and we were wooing his wife. She hated the thought of marriage, but she would not refuse outright or make an end of the business, because she was planning death and destruction for us. Here is one scheme which came out of her meditations. She set up a great wide web on her loom, and fine stuff it was, and she said to us, 'You lads who seek my hand now that Odysseus is dead, I know you chafe at the delay, but give me time to finish this piece of cloth; I don't want to waste the thread. It is to be a shroud for Laërtês, when all-destroying fate shall carry him off in dolorous death. I do not wish all the women to be shocked if he lies without a shroud, when he had been lord of great possessions.' Our proud hearts consented. Then she used to work at her great web in the daylight, and unravelled it at night by torchlight.

"Thus for three years she managed to deceive the whole nation; but when the seasons came round again in the fourth year, one of her women, who was in the secret, told us, and we caught her unravelling that fine web! So she had to finish it, much against her will. And when she took down her web, and washed it, and showed it to us shining like the sun or the moon, then some devil of a god brought Odysseus from somewhere, and put him on land's end where the swineherd had his place. Then back comes his son from Pylos over the sea, and the two together make their plan for our death.

"First Telemachos came back to town; then the swineherd brought Odysseus clothed in rats, and leaning upon a staff, like some old beggar. There he was, a disgusting sight, and none of us could know who he was, not even the older men; but we received him with rude blows and words, and he puts up with the rude blows and words in his own house, bides his time, if you please, until Zeus Almighty set him to work. Then he and Telemachos carried off all the armour and weapons and locked them up in the storehouse, and the cunning schemer told his wife to bring out the bow and iron axes and propose a contest, which was the beginning of our unfortunate death. None of us could bend the great bow and string it, we were far too weak. But when the bow was on its way to Odysseus, we all shouted out not to give it, whatever he said, only Telemachos would have it so.

"Then Odysseus received the bow; he strung it easily and shot through the axeheads, went and stood in the doorway and spread the arrows before his feet glaring terribly, then shot Antinoös. After that he took aim at the others in turn and shot them down with those arrows of sorrow, and they fell one after another. It was clear that some god helped them; for they now rushed along the hall furiously striking right and left. Hideous cries and groans came as the heads were smashed and all the ground ran with blood.

"That is how we perished, Agamemnon, and our bodies are still lying uncared for in the great house of Odysseus. Our friends do not know yet; they have not yet come to wash the blood from the wounds and lay out the bodies for mourning, which is the honour due unto the dead."

The soul of Agamemnon answered:

"Happy Odysseus, always ready for every danger! what a wife you have won, with a dower of noble gifts; what a true heart and keen intelligence has the incomparable Penelopeia! How well she remembered the husband of her youth! The fame of her virtue shall never be forgot, and the immortals will make upon the earth a lovely song for faithful Penelopeia. How different she is from the daughter of Tyndareos, who concocted a vile plot and murdered the husband of her youth; what a hateful song will be sung of her among men!

and she will bring an evil name upon all women, even such as are good!"

So they conversed in the house of Hadês, in the caverns under the earth.

Meanwhile the others passed through the city, and soon came to the snug farm of Laërtês, which he had made his own by his own hard work. There was his house, and there were sheds all round in which the serfs lived and fed and slept and did what he wanted. Among them was an old Sicilian woman, who looked after the old man carefully when he was in the country.

Here Odysseus gave his directions to the serfs and Telemachos:

"Go indoors, all of you," he said, "and kill the best pig for our dinner. I am going to try if my father will know me when he sees me, or if I have been away too long for that."

Then he handed his arms to the serfs, and they went indoors. Odysseus passed on to the vineyard to make inquiries. He did not find Dolios as he went down into the enclosure, nor any of his sons or underlings, for they had all gone out with the old man to collect stones for a wall round the vineyard. So he found his father alone in the vineyard digging about one of the plants. He had on him a dirty old shirt full of patches, with patched leather gaiters to save his shins from scratches, and leather gauntlets against the brambles. On his head he wore a goatskin hat [1] in the carelessness of his sorrow.

When Odysseus saw him at last, worn with age and full of sorrow, he stood still under a spreading pear-tree and the tears came into his eyes. What should he do? Should he throw his arms around the old man, and kiss him, and tell the whole story of his return, or should he first question him and see what he would say? On the whole it seemed better to try a few words of pleasantry. So he came near.

The old man was stooping down and digging about one of the plants when his son stepped beside him, and said:

"Well done, gaffer! I see you know how to look after an orchard. It is in fine order, and there is not a single tree or plant neglected in the whole place, not a fig-tree, not a vine, not an olive, not a pear, not a herb or vegetable! But don't be offended if I dare to say you are not so well looked after

[1] This exactly describes a very old man, said to be a hundred years old, whom I saw in another island, grubbing about on his little farm. The hat was a plain piece of thin goatskin, scraped smooth, and pressed while hot in the shape of a basin.

yourself. Old age is bad enough, but you are all over dirt and your clothes are no credit to you. If your master neglects you, he can't say you are an idler. But there is nothing of the slave in your looks, you are more like one of the quality; more like one who would have a bath and a good dinner and soft sleep, as an old man ought to have.

"Tell me now, just to satisfy my curiosity. Who is your master? Whose orchard is this? There is something else too I want to know: is this really Ithaca, as that fellow I met just now said it was? He didn't seem to be quite all there, wouldn't answer questions or listen to what I had to say, when I inquired about my old friend, whether he is still in the land of the living, or dead and buried. I tell you this, and don't make any mistake about it: there was a man whom I entertained in my own country—he came to our house, and there never was a foreigner who was more welcome to my house; said he belonged to Ithaca, said his father was Laërtês Arceisiadês. I took him into my house and treated him handsomely, entertainment of the best, the fat of the land, gave him such gifts as a guest ought to have. Seven talents weight of wrought gold I gave him, and a bowl of solid silver with flowers all around, a dozen sheets, a dozen blankets, a dozen fine robes and tunics to match, not to mention four women as clever as you like with their fingers, and good-looking too, at his own choice."

His father answered with tears:

"Stranger, that is the man whose country you have reached to-day; but now violent and riotous men possess it, and so you have wasted all that heap of gifts which you gave him. If you had found him alive in Ithaca, he would have made a good return for your generous gifts and entertained you as handsomely; quite right too, when one has a debt to repay.

"But pray tell me this, and satisfy my curiosity. How long is it since that unhappy man was your guest, my own son, as indeed he was, poor fellow! Ah, the fishes have devoured him somewhere in the deep sea, or he has been the prey of beasts and birds on the land, far from home and friends; his mother and father did not lay him out and lament him,—their own son! nor his precious wife the true-hearted Penelopeia—she did not close his eyes on the bier, her own husband, and lift up her voice in sorrow, as she ought to do as a last honour for the dead.

"But there is something else I want to know. Who are you and what country do you come from? Where does the ship ride which brought you here with your honourable companions? Perhaps it was not your own ship? You are a merchant and a passenger, and they just left you here?"

Odysseus answered:

"Very well, I will satisfy your curiosity. I come from Wanderland, where I have a great estate, and I am the son of Lord Neverstint Griefanpain; my name is Battledown. Ill luck beat me out of my course from Sicania, and brought me here against my will. My ship lies off the farm, and some way from the city. And this is the fifth year since Odysseus left my home and country, unhappy man. Yet indeed there were good birds for him when he went, on the right hand, which made me glad to speed him on his way, and made him glad to go: both our hearts hoped that we should meet again in friendship, and give each other splendid gifts."

When he had spoken, a black cloud of sorrow came over the old man: with both hands he scraped up the grimy dust and poured it over his white head, sobbing. The son's heart was wrung, and bitter passion pressed through his nostrils as he looked upon his dear father. He made one spring at him and threw his arms around the old man, and kissed him, crying out:

"Here he is himself, my father, I am the man you are looking for! After twenty years I have returned to my native land. Weep no more, grieve no more, for I have news—and there is need of haste sure enough! I have killed the men who sought my wife in my own house, and paid them in full for their violence and outrageous deeds!"

Laërtês answered:

"If you are really Odysseus my son come home again, give me a clear sign to prove that you speak the truth."

Odysseus said:

"That wound first of all—look, here it is for you to see! You remember how the boar gashed me with his tusk as I ran on him? You and my mother sent me to her father Autolycos to receive the gifts which he promised me when he stayed with us. Yes, and let me tell you the trees you gave me in this jolly orchard, when I was a little boy, and went round the garden with you and begged for each! We walked among these very trees, you told me their names, every one! Thirteen pear trees you gave me and ten apples, forty figs, rows of vines you promised, fifty of them, bearing at different times through the vintage, with grapes of all sorts, whenever Zeus made them heavy in the season of the year!"

The old man's knees crickled under him, and his heart

melted, as he heard the signs recounted which he knew so well; he laid his arms about his son's neck, and Odysseus held him fainting. But when he had recovered and come to himself, once more he spoke, and said:

"O Father Zeus! Verily ye gods are still abiding in broad Olympos, if indeed these evil men have paid for their violence! But now I am terribly afraid that soon all Ithaca will be here in force, and they may send summons to the Cephallenian cities."

But Odysseus answered:

"Courage, let not that thought trouble you. But now let us return to your house near the orchard. I sent Telemachos ahead with the drover and swineherd, to get dinner for us as soon as they could."

They set out at once for the homestead; and there they found Telemachos and the two men carving the meat and mixing the wine.

Then the old woman bathed Laërtês and rubbed him down with soft oil, and wrapt a fine robe about him: Athena stood by his side and put fullness into his limbs, so that he seemed stronger and bigger than before. When he came out of the bathroom his son was astonished to see him like one come down from heaven, and he said in plain words:

"My father! Surely one of the immortal gods has made a new man of you, taller and stronger than I saw you before!"

Laërtês answered, full of spirit:

"Ah, by Zeus and Athenaia and Apollo! If I were the man I was when I took Neircon, that strong fortress on the shore of the mainland, when I was lord of the Cephallenians! and if I had been yesterday by your side with armour on my shoulders, to fight with those riotous men! Many a one would I have killed and made your heart glad!"

While they were speaking, the three had finished their task; the meal was ready and they seated themselves about it. As they were about to set to, in came old Dolios with his sons, tired after their work; for their mother had run out in good time to fetch them, that is the old Sicilian woman who used to look after Laërtês so carefully now that he was old. As soon as they saw Odysseus and knew him, they stood there amazed; but Odysseus spoke kindly to them, and said:

"Sit down, gaffer, and don't be astonished. We have been waiting a long time for you, as hungry as we can be."

But Dolios ran straight to him with open arms, and caught the wrist of Odysseus, kissing him, and crying:

"O my dear master! so you have come back, when we never

hoped to see you again! God himself brought you! Bless you and save you, and may God grant you every happiness! Tell me, does my lady know that you have returned, or shall we send a message?"

Odysseus answered, "She knows, already, gaffer; you need not trouble for that."

On hearing this, the old man sat down again; and his sons like him welcomed Odysseus with word and hand, and seated themselves by their father.

While they were busy with their meal, rumour sped all over the city with the news, telling how the pretenders had come to a miserable end. The people on hearing this gathered from all quarters before the house of Odysseus, with groanings and loud uproar. Each family took their own dead, and carried them home for burial; those who came from abroad they sent away in the charge of seamen, each to his own city.

Then they held a meeting of the whole town, and crowded into the market-place sorrowing. Eupeithês first rose to address them, full of indignation and sorrow for his son Antinoös, whom Odysseus had brought down with the first shot. With tears rolling down his cheeks for his son, Eupeithês said:

"My friends, here is a monstrous thing this man has done against our nation! First he goes off with a fleet of ships and a lot of fine fellows, loses the ships, loses the men, and comes back alone: then he kills the best of the Cephallenians. Come now, before he can escape to Pylos or Elis and the Epeians, let us move, or we shall be disgraced for ever! It will be a blot upon us in generations to come if we do not punish the murderers of our sons and brothers! Life would be nothing to me: I would rather die at once and lie in my grave. Move quickly; don't let them steal a march on us and get over the water!"

The people were all filled with pity to see his tears and to hear his words. But suddenly Medon and the minstrel appeared on the outskirts of the crowd. They had just waked up and come straight from the house, and there they were in the midst of them to the amazement of all. Medon spoke up confidently, and said:

"Give me a hearing, men of Ithaca! The hand of God is in this! I saw myself an immortal god standing beside Odysseus, and looking exactly like Mentor! An immortal god now in front of Odysseus and encouraging him, now sweeping through the hall to scare the lady's wooers, and they fell in heaps!"

The listeners went pale with fear. Then spoke the old man Halithersês Mastoridês, who alone could see forward and backward, and he gave them wise advice:

"Hear me, men of Ithaca, for I have something to say. Your own fault has brought this about. You would not listen to me, or to Prince Mentor, when he warned you to restrain your sons from their folly. It is they who did the monstrous thing in the recklessness of their hearts, wasting the goods and dishonouring the wife of a noble man; for they thought he would never return. Then listen to me now, and do as I say: let us make no move, or some one may bring trouble on his own head."

This brought loud cries of applause, and more than half of those present sprang up from their seats; but the others sat still and kept together, for they did not approve the speech but obeyed Monsignor Plausible. These very soon went away for arms and armour: and when they were ready they appeared before the city gate. Eupeithês took the lead, foolish man: he thought to avenge his son's death, but he was destined to find his own death then and there and never to return.

Now Athena was watching, and she said to Zeus Cronion, "Cronidês Almighty, father of us all, let me ask you a question. What plan is hidden deep in your mind? Will you still contrive war upon war, and battle upon battle? Or will you make peace between these two parties?"

Zeus Cloudgatherer answered, "My dear child, why do you ask me such questions? Was not this the plan of your own mind, that Odysseus should come back and punish these men? Do as you like. But I will tell you what seems the right thing. Now that Odysseus has had his vengeance, let them make up the quarrel, and let him continue to be prince as before; but let us pacify the blood-feud for these dead sons and brothers; let them all be friends as before, and let peace and plenty abide with them."

This was just what Athena wanted to do: away she went down from the peaks of Olympos.

Meanwhile Odysseus and his friends had finished their meal, and now he said:

"Some one go out and see if they are coming."

One of Dolios' sons went out of the door, and there he saw the whole body of men close at hand. He turned to Odysseus and said simply:

"Here they are close by! let us arm at once!"

They were soon ready, four led by Odysseus and the six

sons of Dolios; Laërtês and Dolios too armed themselves, warriors perforce. Armed and ready, they issued forth from the door with Odysseus at their head.

Then Athena came near, in the form of Mentor and with Mentor's voice. The sight made Odysseus glad, and he called to his son Telemachos:

"My son, now you have come to the place of battle, where the best men are proved: you will know how not to disgrace your fathers, since our line has been notable over all the earth for courage and valour!"

Telemachos answered:

"You shall see, if you will, my dear father, that my spirit shall bring no disgrace upon your line."

Laërtês was full of joy, and cried out:

"What a day is this, kind gods! I am a happy man. My son and my son's son are rivals in courage!"

Athena came near him, and said:

"Old friend, and dearest of all my comrades, pray to Father Zeus and his fierce-eyed girl, poise your long spear and cast it now!"

She breathed strong passion into him as she spoke: he uttered a prayer to the Daughter of great Zeus, poised and cast his long spear, and struck Eupeithês in his helmet of bronze. Right through the morion it went and the blade came out on the other side: Eupeithês fell in his armour with a crash. Then Odysseus and his brave son fell upon the foremost, and struck them with sword and spear. They would have made an end of them all on the spot, but Athenaia, daughter of Zeus Almighty, lifted her voice and stayed them all:

"Stay your hands from battle, men of Ithaca, be reconciled and let bloodshed cease."

They stood aghast, pale as death; at her voice the weapons slipt from their hands and fell on the ground. All turned and went back to the city, for they did not wish to die. Odysseus shouted loudly and, gathering himself together, he swooped on them like an eagle from the high heaven. But Zeus cast a blazing thunderbolt before the feet of Athena. Then the goddess said to Odysseus, "Odysseus Laërtiadês, prince never unready! Hold your hand, make an end of war and conflict, and fear the wrath of Zeus Cronidês who sees all things."

Odysseus obeyed gladly with all his heart. After this Pallis Athenaia, daughter of Zeus Almighty, in the likeness of Mentor and with Mentor's voice, made peace between both parties and ended the strife for ever.

HOMER'S WORDS

IT IS VERY DIFFICULT TO MAKE REAL TO OURSELVES HOW an old composition sounded to the ears that heard it. As time goes on, and language changes, the words ring up new thoughts and feelings in the hearers, or they are simply not understood: then they are imitated by those who wish to compose in the same style, and bookish dialects grow up. It is always some great genius who shapes the type. Thus Milton shaped the type for blank verse, which was used by his imitators in the eighteenth century, without his genius and without his naturalness; for Milton was firmly based on the natural speech of men about serious subjects. Tyndale and Coverdale in the Scriptures, Cranmer in the Prayer Book, Thomas North, Philemon Holland, Arthur Golding, and a host of others, all wrote, it is true, but wrote as they spoke. Milton sublimated this style, and stiffened it with Latin, but his was a style which rang in the ears of his hearers as a lofty version of their own. Not so with his imitators: these in the eighteenth century, and later in the nineteenth, drew their style from books, not from nature. Even Tennyson did the same, in spite of his delicate ear which found new modulations for the blank verse, and in spite of his true poet's instinct which is shown in the *Northern Farmer,* the *Churchwarden and the Curate,* and other such.

Dryden brought the "poetic" style nearer to nature for his own day, but he also was bookish; and he led up to the convention of the rhymed couplet, which received its final polish in Pope. In this convention, rhetoric took the place of feeling, wit of humour, and the language was such as could be understood only by a society educated on books. Pope would hardly touch an uneducated man. For an educated man his verse is highly entertaining, and often impressive; but it is not natural, it is a work of art.

Shakespeare's style may seem at first hearing to be far removed from natural speech: but it is only old-fashioned. How natural it is, becomes clear, when we remember that he has always been a favourite with all sorts and conditions of men. He wrote to earn a living, not to show his poetical talent. If

he failed to please the common herd, his play was a failure
and his pocket was empty: when he had made his plays, and
they had had their run, he troubled no more about them, but
left them with the company which had paid him and never
thought of a First Folio. I have seen *Hamlet* performed by
strolling players under a tent at a country fair, and heard the
loud comments of the audience. They understood quite
enough of his great speeches without the help of the notes
of Aldis Wright; and in Shakespeare's own day, the exalted
language of these was as familiar in its turns and intonations
as the quips of Lancelot Gobbo. He made a type for tragedy,
which became bookish with Dryden and stage-writers in
general; but the player's instinct kept comedy closer to nature
in the Restoration drama, as it does still in Gilbert and Sul-
livan, and did until lately in the music halls. It is the fault
of modern play-writers that they have forgotten this, and left
nature to the vulgar alone. The style of Shakespeare's great
scenes is exalted, because his mind is exalted; there is noth-
ing in them which a speaker might not have said in prose
if he had been at the same height of feeling and thought.

The same is true of all great literature. Plato's most splen-
did passages might have been spoken, and many probably
were spoken; put into verse, his Myths might have been Pin-
daric Odes, with music and dance to match. There is no
break between the charming bits of talk which he gives and
these great speeches, neither in words nor in style. Just so,
there is nothing in the dialogue of Sophocles which could
not have been spoken in prose, and felt by his contempora-
ries to be natural, although not natural to ribald or base
minds; and a good deal of it—such as the Watchman in the
Antigone—is the speech of the humble man thinking com-
mon thoughts. Even Aeschylus has touches of this, as in
the Watchman of *Agamemnon* and the Nurse of the *Choeph-
oroe;* but his magnificence, his great sounding words, were
rather above the heads of most people, as we learn from
Aristophanes. Euripides as we know tried to be common in
his style—I use the word without disrespect, in its proper
sense—and he even modified his verse, to come nearer to the
rhythms of ordinary speech. We may be quite sure that his
words did not sound to a Greek as Murray's version does
to us:

Orest. Thou art the first that I have known indeed
   True and my friend, and shelterer of my need.
   Thou only, Pylades, of all that knew,

> Hast held Orestes of some worth, all through
> These years of helplessness, wherein I lie
> Downtrodden by the murderer, and *by*
> The murderess, my mother!

Not only *thou* and *thy* are false notes, but the concealed rhyme at once gives an artificial touch. The Greek words sounded more like this:

> Pylades! You are the first in all the world
> That I think faithful and a real true friend:
> The only friend who ever thought Orestes
> Worthy of admiration, having done
> What I have done, to make Aigisthos suffer
> For the vile deed *he* did,—murdered my father,
> With my accursed mother!

Even lyric poetry, with its elaborate conventions of metre, music, and dance, never loses touch with nature. Pindar, the most exalted of the lyrics, loves to drop in a proverb, or a homely word, or a touch of burlesque, which had the piquant effect of a joke from Justice Stareleigh on the bench. Thus he leads off with a glorious roll of distinction for Hagesias of Syracuse (Ol. vi. 1—), and the second half-chorus catches up the first, with some roguish gesture I have no doubt—

> ἴστω γὰρ ἐν τούτῳ πεδίλῳ δαιμόνιον πόδ᾽ ἔχων
>   Σωστράτου υἱός;

all common expressions of everyday life—ἴστω allow me to inform Σωστράτου υἱός the honourable gentleman, with the formal title equivalent to "Mr."—"Allow me to inform the gentleman that his foot fits that boot to a marvel"— that is what the Greek words conveyed to his hearers— δαιμόνιος being a regular term of familiar talk, ὦ δαιμόνιε for example; "the foot fits the boot devilish well" is really the English equivalent. Pindar is not afraid to poke fun at Hieron the tyrant, even while he is urging him to be true to his better self. In the second Pythian (ii. 72), the third triad ends, with a line sung by the whole chorus:

> γένοι᾽ οἷος ἐσσὶ μαθών· καλός τοι πίθων παρὰ παισὶν αἰεί,

and the next strophe opens:

καλός· ὁ δὲ Ῥαδάμανθυς εὖ πέπραγεν,

again a passage with nothing but common words, pointed by
a merry tag:

"Be your true self, you know how: Pretty Poll, they say in
the nursery"—

Then the next strophe answers—

"Yes, Pretty Poll: but Rhadamanthys won his happiness
by doing well."

I have said Pretty Poll instead of Pretty Ape, because one is
natural to us and not the other; but I have given the tone ex-
actly. See what a dramatic point he makes by his proverb.
Again, when he is apologizing for the faults of Damophilos,
and reconciling him with his royal master, against whom he
has been in rebellion, he says (Pyth. iv. 281):

κεῖνος γὰρ ἐν παισὶν νέος,
ἐν δὲ βουλαῖς πρέσβυς, ἐγκύρσαις ἑκατονταετεῖ γενεᾷ—

"the man is a lad among boys, but in counsel he is old,
blessed with the age of a centenarian"—he has been a
rare lad, and sown his wild oats, but he will be a good little
centenarian for the future.

What of Homer then? He comes at the climax of a great
school of epic poets, who had already made a convention of
epic style. They had perfected a lovely model of verse, ca-
pable of infinite variety, never monotonous, but ever
charming to the ear. They had an expressive language, with
inflexions to make clear any meaning, and particles to in-
dicate delicate tones and differences. They could draw upon
a vast vocabulary, which never left them at a loss, which was
so rich that numbers of words were used only once in the
poems—once, when they were wanted, and never again be-
cause they were not. I have noticed that peculiarity in
Greeks I have talked with, fishermen and peasants, unedu-
cated and often unable to read and write; they always had a
rich store of phrases ready, expressing thoughts often subtle
or profound, and when these were wanted in talk, out they
came. Others educated in schools and universities, taught by
books, were generally overflooded with their own verbosity,
and that too when there was no thought to speak of behind

them. I had a good instance of this in the war, when I used to read Greek letters for the postal censor. He sent me once an urgent package, registered, with a demand for immediate translation. It was a folio of many sheets, engrossed in a noble hand, with illuminated capitals and an awe-inspiring seal. When I came to read it, the document turned out to be an appeal from a Greek monk to Kitchener, a Byzantine conglomeration of phrases with as many ancient inflexions as could be got in, but most of it was a flood of words with no connected meaning whatever. There was, however, a thought behind the piece, and quite a simple thought, which could have been expressed on half a sheet of notepaper: it amounted to this, that Kitchener had only to seek an interview with the Kaiser, and tell him what a damn fool he was, and all could be arranged.

But the people who listened to the epic bards were of my other class. They knew nothing of books; they were practical men, educated by life, but keenly alive to beauty, and sensitive to fine art, living amongst fine craftsmen and goldsmiths, delighting in song, and dance, and music, with their minds full of wonderful stories of gods, and dryads, and naiads. They lived in the country, and knew all the sights and sounds of nature and her creatures; they lived in small towns, among fortresses and walls, mansions and temples; they had order and discipline, commerce, law and debate; they were of a keen intelligence, and eager to hear stories of foreign lands; they pondered the meaning of human life, and had already that loathing for cruelty and brutal mockery which marked off the Greek from the barbarian. But there was nothing in them of the prig. They were not ashamed of enjoying themselves; they ate huge meals and drank bowls of wine with as much gusto as Mr. Pickwick, but they knew good wine from bad, and the good was divine—put one cup of wine in twenty of water, and the fragrance filled the room, so that no one wanted to be an abstainer. They were full of merry jests; wit and humour pleased them, and they did not despise a rough practical joke.

The great nobles and princes were Homer's patrons, as they had been of earlier bards from time immemorial. So it was in England, when Caedmon sang in hall; so in Ireland, where every petty chief had his bard, who sang after dinner the great deeds of the princely house. So it is to-day in Arabia, where Lawrence heard the bards singing at the head of the troop the great deeds of their ancestors. "The tribal poets," he says, "would sing us their war-narratives: long traditional forms with stock epithets, stock sentiments, stock incidents, grafted afresh on the efforts of each generation" (*Seven Pillars of Wisdom*). And there is no reason to doubt that Homer's picture of the bard in hall is true to life. Homer sang for a living, as Shakespeare acted for a living. The prince wanted a good story, and he got one; he wanted praise for the great men of old, and he got it; he wanted to hear what his ancestors had done, and he got that too, I have no doubt, which is one reason why we are told exactly what wounds killed what warrior, and how he fell, or how he felled his adversary. Both poets accepted their limitations, and used them, just as the Doric architect did; they did not bother about being better than their ancestors, otherwise they would not have been asked to dinner again. But if they gave what their audience wanted, how much more they gave!

It follows that Homer must have spoken so as to be easily understood. Hearers must have understood at least as much of his words as my holiday-countrymen did of *Hamlet* in the tent, that is, all the general meaning; they may not have understood every word, but they must have understood the general meaning of every sentence, and probably, every phrase. Many of those phrases and turns of expression were traditional, and our first task is to examine, what was traditional, common to Homer with his predecessors.

First of all, the grammar, inflexions, particles, and so forth must have been familiar, that is, Homer must have used the same as his hearers used in speaking. There is no difficulty about that. Highly inflected languages have been transmitted orally for thousands of years. The Lithuanian language is highly inflected; it contains more cases than Sanscrit, which itself contains more cases than Greek: and Lithuanian has no literature—it was not committed to writing until the nineteenth century. Sanscrit was spoken as a vernacular in its richest form before it was arranged in a grammar by Pānini four hundred years B.C. Russian, a most intricate and subtle language, is spoken by millions of illiterate peasants. The languages of American aborigines, far more difficult for us to understand than any language inflected or analytical, are spoken and kept up without the help of writing. The Greek language, as Homer spoke it, was not fixed; it was changing and growing, and we can see the process in such matters as the digamma, the suffixes $-\theta \epsilon \nu$ and $-\delta \epsilon$ and the inflexious -oo and -oιo of the genitive singular. Homer uses the digamma generally where it ought to be, but if he finds it inconvenient, he ignores it—

> When Omer smote is bloomin lyre,
> He'd eard men speak by land an sea;
> An what e thought e might require,
> E went an took—the same as me!

If anyone feels doubt on these points, I can say something to
reassure him. Many years ago, I spent some time in the is-
land of Cos, living amongst the people, travelling about, and
talking to everybody. I collected a large number of tra-
ditional tales and poems, amongst which was a fine poem
called *The Bridge of Camára*, which describes a human sac-
rifice at the building of this old bridge, which still stands in
the island. In this poem there is nothing which cannot be
understood now by the people, although one or two words
are old-fashioned; but the interesting point is that it con-
tains four different forms of the third person plural: two of
the present tense, τρέμουν and πέφτουσι, and two of the past,
ἐχτίζαν and ἐχτίζασι, used for metrical convenience. I know the
colloquial language of Cos quite well, and I find two of
these, -ουνε and -ουσι, used indifferently for the third person
plural in common speech. In the poem there are other varia-
tions of form used for convenience. There is also one phrase
used merely for its sound, in the line—

κεῖνο τὸ τρισκατάρατο, τὸ τρισκαταραμένο°

I shall return to this later. But here is the proof that a va-
riety of forms need cause no inconvenience, and may indeed
reflect the practice of common talk.

So much for the forms. When we examine the words of the
Homeric poems, we find them the natural words for the
things. There is no attempt to heighten the effect by expres-
sions called poetical, as we find in Pope with his nymphs
and swains, and in the pompous paraphrases used for simple
things by other poets.

> "The wooden guardian of our privacy
> Quick on its axle turn."

> [Shut the door]

> "Bring forth some remnant of Promethean theft,
> Quick to expand th' inclement air congeal'd
> By Boreas' rude breath."

> [Light the fire]

> "Apply thine engine to the spongy door,

Set Bacchus from his glassy prison free,
                    [Uncork the bottle]
And strip white Ceres of her nut-brown coat."
                    [Uncrust the bread]

There is nothing of that sort in Homer, and no catch-phrases
worn dim by use: blissful ignorance, French leave, mortal
coil, left him severely alone, and so forth.

There is, however, one class of words which is tradition-
al, the stock epithets—μερόπων ἀνθρώπων, εἰλίποδας ἕλικας βοῦς,
οἴνοπα πόντον, δολιχόσκιον ἔγχος, νῆας ἐΐσας, and descriptions of
human beings, as πεπνυμένος, περίφρων, ἀμύμων, ἱππόδαμος, δῖα
θεάων (and δῖος in many contexts), ὄρχαμε λαῶν, κάρη κομόωντες
Ἀχαιοί. Some of them are applied to particular persons: as
ἱππότα Νέστωρ, νεφεληγερέτα Ζεύς, πολύτλας δῖος Ὀδυσσεύς, βοὴν
ἀγαθὸς Μενέλαος. There are also accepted phrases which describe
common things: as ἔπος φύγεν ἕρκος ὀδόντων, περιπλομένων
ἐνιαυτῶν, ἀλλ' ἄγε μοι τόδε εἰπὲ καὶ ἀτρεκέως κατάλεξον, λύτο
γούνατα καὶ φίλον ἦτορ, and the ever beautiful ἦμος ἠριγένεια
φάνη ῥοδοδάκτυλος ἠώς. None of them are worn out by
use; they all mean exactly what they say, and if people mean
the same thing, why not use the same words?

Many of these are traditional, there is no doubt. One in
fact, δολιχόσκιον ἔγχος, goes back to a prehistoric time be-
fore the division of that great race which invented the parent
language. It occurs in the Zend-Avesta in the form
dareghaarstaya, "long-shafted," of which the first part is
the proper equivalent of δολιχός, but the second, which
should be in Greek ὄρστιος, has no kindred in Greek, and
has been therefore confused with σκιά; δολιχόσκιος, in fact,
is a Greek blunder, like the English Jerusalem artichoke.
Even if it is thought too much to infer that there was epic
poetry in that far-off age, yet certainly the parent race in-
vented quantitative verse, and there are many resemblances
between Greek metres and Sanscrit, not to mention the mu-
sical accent which is common to both. Thus δολιχόσκιος has
a pedigree of a thousand years before Homer: for the
earliest Zend belongs to about 1400 B.C., and who knows
how many centuries must be allowed to reach the meeting-
point of the two languages? The other Homeric puzzles,
μερόπων ἀνδρῶν and οἴνοπα πόντον, for example, may be the result

of similar misunderstandings. However, the audience got a reasonable meaning from them, and they did not trouble about the etymology.

These phrases and epithets were useful to the poets, as helping to round off a line; and that is how Homer uses them. They are a help to the ear, and really nothing more, just like the line I quoted from the modern Greek ballad; but they give real pleasure to the ear, just as a rhyme does to us, because most of them have a beautiful sound, and they give a feeling that we have come to the end of something. But if Homer took over the whole lot of them bodily, together with many more which I have not quoted, that is nothing; they are only the machinery of the verse, and what the machine carries is the thing. If you notice how Homer applies them, you will see that he never forgets what they mean, and that he does not use too many. The Sanscrit epic style has also great numbers of stock epithets, but they are strung on by the dozen, just to fill up the verse, without disguise, and without mercy for the hearer, nor are they always suitable. Homer generally uses his with point. Thus δῖος or διοτρεφής implies not only divinity, but royalty, which comes by divine right, and it is suitable for a great noble. Homer is very apt in his use of tags like πεπνυμένος, when someone shows tact and good form. But sometimes I suspect him of a sly twinkle in his eye, and I cannot help thinking the company laughed when he introduced Eumaios as δῖος ὑφορβός, pigman by divine right. There is also a butler hero (*Od.* xviii. 423) τοῖσιν δὲ κρητῆρα κεράσσατο Μούλιος ἥρως. In the same way there is humour when Homer suggests that ἱερὸν μένος 'Αντινόοιο (*Od.* xviii. 34) was not too high and mighty to offer a sausage as a prize for the boxing-match.

The effect on the ear of these stock phrases can be heard in English. Bunyan uses them in the *Holy War*, where the town of Mansoul tolls at the end of sentence after sentence. Take the following passage, and note that after the first time the name of Mansoul could be omitted without hurting the sense: "But to leave her Recorder, and to come to my Lord Will-be-will, another of the gentry of the famous town of Mansoul. This Will-be-will was as highborn as any man in Mansoul, and was as much, if not more, a freeholder than many of them were; besides, if I remember my tale aright, he had some privileges peculiar to himself in the famous town of Mansoul . . . Whether he was proud of his estate, privileges, strength or what (but sure it was through pride of something), he scorns now to be a slave in Mansoul. . . . When the tyrant therefore perceived the willingness of my lord to serve him, and that his mind stood bending that way, he forthwith made him the captain of the castle, governor of the wall, and keeper of the gates of Mansoul; yea, there was a clause in his commission, that nothing without him should be done in all the town of Mansoul. So that now, next to Diabolus himself, who but my Lord Will-be-will in all the town of Mansoul! nor could anything now be done, but at his will and pleasure, throughout the town of Mansoul" (Bunyan's *Holy War*, p. 28. Dent).

So it resounds all through: the famous town of Mansoul, the once famous but now perishing town of Mansoul, the misery of Mansoul, the losing of Mansoul, the wall of the town of Mansoul, show yourselves stout and valiant men of Mansoul, my lion-like men of Mansoul, his servants and vassals in Mansoul, go down and deliver Mansoul, I have a word to the town of Mansoul, to the besotted town of Mansoul, O unhappy town of Mansoul. And then the Prince comes, and the rhythm changes (p. 100)—

"O unhappy town of Mansoul! I cannot but be touched with pity and compassion for thee. . . . Poor Mansoul! what shall I do unto thee? Shall I save thee? Shall I destroy thee? What shall I do unto thee? Shall I fall upon thee, and grind thee to powder, or make thee a monument of the richest grace? What shall I do unto thee? Hearken therefore, thou town of Mansoul, hearken to my word, and thou shalt live. I am merciful, Mansoul, and thou shalt find me so. Shut me not out of thy gates."

When at last the people receive their envoys back, the old funereal toll is still in their words (p. 144):

"So soon as they were come to Eye-gate, the poor and tottering town of Mansoul adventured to give a shout; and they gave such a shout as made the captains in the Prince's army leap at the sound thereof. Alas for them, poor hearts! who could blame them, since their dead friends were come to life again? for it was to them as life from the dead, to see the ancients of the town of Mansoul shine in such splendour. They looked for nothing but the axe and the block; but behold, joy and gladness, comfort and consolation, and such melodious notes attending them, that was sufficient to make a sick man well.

"So when they came up, they saluted each other with 'Welcome! welcome! and blessed be he that has spared you!' They added also, 'We see it is well with you; but how must it go

with the town of Mansoul? And will it go well with the town
of Mansoul?' said they. Then answered them the Recorder
and my Lord Mayor, 'Oh, tidings! glad tidings! good tidings
of good, and of great joy to the town of Mansoul!' Then they
gave another shout, that made the earth to ring again. . . .

" 'Pardon, pardon, pardon for Mansoul! and this shall
Mansoul know to-morrow.' Then he commanded, and they
went and summoned Mansoul to meet together in the market-
place to-morrow, there to hear their general pardon read.

"But who can think what a turn, what a change, what an
alteration this hint of things did make in the counte-
nance of the town of Mansoul! No man of Mansoul could
sleep that night for joy; in every house there was joy and
music, singing and making merry: telling and hearing of
Mansoul; happiness was the all that Mansoul had to do; and
this was the burden of all their song, 'Oh! more of this at the
rising of the sun! more of this to-morrow!' "

So, with the good news, the rhythm changes too, Mansoul is
no longer a tolling bell at the end of each sentence; it is
swallowed up in pipes and tabors and the merry-making of
the morrow.

Titles like ὕπατε κρειόντων, ὄρχαμε λαῶν, μέγα κῦδος Ἀχαιῶν,
are used as a polite mode of address, your Majesty, your Grace;
they give an air of formality. The same is true of patronymics.
The formal style of a reek was A son of B from C, Δημοσθένης
Δημοσθένους Παιανιεύς; and where Menelaos is called Ἀτρεΐδης
Μενέλαος, that is as much as to say King Menelaos: ὦ Νέστορ
Πηληιάδη, μέγα κῦδος Ἀχαιῶν, is your Majesty King Nestor;
the family name gives his title to royalty. With lesser men, the
family name gives his title to gentle blood. Odysseus introduces
himself, εἴμ' Ὀδυσεὺς Λαερτιάδης, "I am Odysseus Laertison, Es-
quire." Antinoos addresses his hostess, in the same formal way,
κούρη Ἰκαρίοιο, περίφρον Πηνελόπεια, "My lady Penelopeia
Hickson," if I may put it so. But the patronymic when used alone
has something friendly and familiar about it. When Telemachos
sees the palace of Menelaos, he whispers to his friend, φράζεο
Νεστορίδη, τῷ ἐμῷ κεχαρισμένε θυμῷ, χαλκοῦ τε στεροπήν —
"Just look, dear old boy, did you ever see such a splendid pal-
ace?" When Telemachos wakes up his friend, he shakes him, and
gives him his full title, ἔγρεο, Νεστορίδη Πεισίστρατε— "Now
then Mr. Peisistratos, wake up!" But when he tries to coax him

not to go back home, and so make more delay, he says Νεστορίδη,
πῶς κέν μοι ὑποσχεμένος τελέσειας μῦθον ἐμόν; "I say old fellow,
do be kind and keep your promise to me." These patronymics
nearly always have a real point. Iros the beggar, of course, has
no patronymic, no formal style; he has a true name, Arnaios, but
everyone calls him by a nickname. On the other hand, Eurycleia,
the old nurse, is no upstart; she has a pedigree, two generations
in fact of good blood, Εὐρύκλεια Ὦπος θυγατὴρ Πεισηνορίδαο,
daughter of Ops the son of Peisenor, as much as to hint that she
is going to be somebody in the narrative. Eumaios on the other
hand has no formal style, though he was a gentleman born; but
he was a foreigner and a bought slave. Perhaps Homer meant
more than appears when he called him δῖος, for the changes and
chances of mortal life were never absent from his thoughts. See
how neatly also Homer plays on the family name of Antinoos.
He is introduced formally as Εὐπείθεος υἱός, the son of Mr. Good
Reason, as Bunyan might have called him, when he makes his
first bullying speech to Telemachos (Od. i. 383); and in the last
scenes, when there is little enough of goodness or reason, we
hear the same gentle reminder how he falls short of his family
tradition. The treacherous servant who helped the intruders, and
brought them arms, was Melanthios Trickson, Δολίοιο Μελανθεύς
(xxii. 159). When Odysseus seeks out his old father, he intro-
duces himself with a string of invented names:

> εἰμὶ μὲν ἐξ Ἀλύβαντος, ὅθι κλυτὰ δώματα ναίω,
> υἱὸς Ἀφείδαντος Πολυπημονίδαο ἄνακτος·
> αὐτὰρ ἐμοί γ' ὄνομ' ἐστὶν Ἐπήριτος.

(xxiv. 304)

"I come from Wanderland, where I have a good estate, and
I am the son of my Lord Neverstint Griefanpain: my
name is Battledown."

But the poet's masterpiece of mischief is at the games of the
seafaring Phaiacians, where he rolls out a catalogue of very
suitable names (viii. III.):

> ὦρτο μὲν Ἀκρόνεώς τε καὶ Ὠκύαλος καὶ Ἐλαστρεύς
> Ναυτεύς τε Πρυμνεύς τε καὶ Ἀγχίαλος καὶ Ἐρετμεύς
> Ποντεύς τε Πρῳρεύς τε, Θόων Ἀναβησίνεώς τε
> Ἀμφίαλός θ' υἱὸς Πολυνήου Τεκτονίδαο·
> ἂν δὲ καὶ Εὐρύαλος βροτολοιγῷ ἶσος Ἄρηι,
> Ναυβολίδης, ὃς ἄριστος ἔην εἶδός τε δέμας τε
> πάντων Φαιήκων μετ' ἀμύμονα Λαοδάμαντα.

"Topship and Quicksea and Driver, Seaman and Poopman, Beacher and Oarsman, Deepsea and Lookout, Goahead and Upaboard; there was Seagirt the son of Manyclipper Shipwrightson; there was Broadsea the very spit of bloody Ares himself, and Admiraltides, the finest man in stature and strength after the admirable Laodamas."

Who could fail to hear the echoes of the *Iliad* in this, and especially—

Νιρεὺς ὃς κάλλιστος ἀνὴρ ὑπὸ Ἴλιον ἦλθε
τῶν ἄλλων Δαναῶν μετ' ἀμύμονα Πηλεΐωνα·

(ii. 673)

Αἴας ὃς περὶ μὲν εἶδος, περὶ δ' ἔργα τέτυκτο
τῶν ἄλλων Δαναῶν μετ' ἀμύμονα Πηλεΐωνα

(xvii. 279)

Indeed the poet makes amends for this parody at the end of the *Odyssey*, when he says in the familiar words (xxiv. 17):

Αἴαντός θ' ὃς ἄριστος ἔην εἶδός τε δέμας τε
τῶν ἄλλων Δαναῶν μετ' ἀμύμονα Πηλεΐωνα.

In another place he speaks of Scylla, with a voice like a puppydog, but a horrible monster (xii. 87):

αὐτὴ δ' αὖτε πέλωρ κακόν· οὐδέ κέ τίς μιν
γηθήσειεν ἰδών, οὐ δ' εἰ θεὸς ἀντιάσειε,

"No one would be happy to see her, not even if a god should meet her"—an obvious *non sequitur*, and obviously a sly hit at the epic tag. And is there not mischief in the picture of the wedding gift of Eurydamas (xviii. 297)?—

ἕρματα δ' Εὐρυδάμαντι δύω θεράποντες ἔνεικαν
τρίγληνα μορόεντα, χάρις δ' ἀπελάμπετο πολλή—

a magnificent pair of ear-rings, and one groom to carry each! And the champion lancers of the *Iliad*, ἐγχεσίμωροι become champion barkers in the *Odyssey*, ὑλακόμωροι, when the dogs nearly did for Odysseus.

All this bears out the ancient tradition, that the *Odyssey* was a work of Homer's old age, when long experience had taught him that no man can look on the world with sanity

unless he sees life through a glow of sympathetic humour;
and so he laughs at himself.

There seem to be also a few very ancient verses embedded
in the poems, naturally enough, just as Virgil embedded his
bits of Ennius. The most striking are the description of
Dodonaean Zeus (Il. xvi. 233):

Ζεῦ ἄνα Δωδωναῖε Πελασγικέ, τηλόθι ναίων,
Δωδώνης μεδέων δυσχειμέρου, ἀμφὶ δὲ Σελλοὶ
σοὶ ναίουσ' ὑποφῆται ἀνιπτόδες χαμαιεῦναι.

And finally the verse which Odysseus quotes may be an
ancient tag with his name substituted for another:

τοῦδ' αὐτοῦ λυκάβαντος ἐλεύσεται ἐνθάδ' Ὀδυσσεύς;

for it contains a word otherwise unknown, and of unknown
meaning, λυκάβας, apparently the lichtgang, that is day, month,
or year as you please. The meaning suitable to the story is
month, and that is how Dion interpreted it; but Odysseus did
not want its meaning to be too clear. However, such matters
are of small importance to us.

I come now to consider how the words and style of Homer
are related to the speech of his day: and first of all, notice
how many words are taken directly from the common man's
lips, the vivid images which he uses naturally to describe
what he sees. Even the commentators can see these: "The
word is doubtless colloquial," says Munro, regretfully, "like
so much of the vocabulary of the Odyssey" (on xiv. 512).
This is where Odysseus tells his neat little tale of the ambush
before Troy, and how he got a cloak to cover him. "I have
something I want to say," he begins, "the wine has made me
bold, as it often makes a decent man sing a stave and dance
a jig. Well, now I have made my croak (ἀνέκραγον, 467),
I will just go on." Then he gives a broad hint that he would
like a warm cloak. Eumaios answers, "That's a good tale,
and you shall have a cloak to-night, but to-morrow you must
just rub along with your rags—you must sport your rags"
(512):

ἀτὰρ ἠῶθέν γε τὰ σὰ ῥάκεα δνοπαλίξεις

The Iliad has this word once (iv. 472), of a crowd shoulder-
ing each other about (ἀνὴρ δ' ἄνδρ' ἐδνοπάλιζεν). Then again: "I
am the daughter of Arybas, a man rolling in riches" (xv. 426):

κούρη δ' εἰμ' Ἀρύβαντος ἐγὼ ῥυδὸν† ἀφνειοῖο.

Eumaios describes his visitor as a man who has knocked about in foreign parts (xvi. 63):

φησὶ δὲ πολλὰ βροτῶν ἐπὶ ἄστεα δινηθῆναι,

as Melantho the pert maid rails at her master (xix. 66):

ξεῖν', ἔτι καὶ νῦν ἐνθάδ' ἀνιήσεις διὰ νύκτα
δινεύων κατὰ οἶκον, ὀπιπεύσεις δὲ γυναῖκας;

"Are you going to be a nuisance all night, rolling about the house, and ogling the girls?" Iros the beggar says: "Can't you see how they all squint at me and tell me to kick you out?"—

οὐκ ἀΐεις ὅτι δή μοι ἐπιλλίζουσιν† ἅπαντες
ἐλκέμεναι δὲ κέλονται;

(xviii. 11)

Odysseus is afraid the servants "may think me all afloat in tears because I am drunk" (xix. 122):

φῇ δὲ δακρυπλώειν† βεβαρηότα με φρένας οἴνῳ.

There are several countryman's words in the garden scene where Odysseus meets his father, used there only as, λίστρον† a shovel, λιστρεύω† to dig about. Achilles himself, always a downright speaker, speaks before the assembly in the last tragic scenes of the *Iliad*, when he has allowed himself to be reconciled; the rest are all solemn and formal, but he cuts them short (*Il.* xix. 149), "Many thanks for your gifts, but it is time for battle now, we must not stay jabber-winding here":

οὐ γὰρ χρὴ κλοτοπεύειν† ἐνθάδ' ἐόντας
οὐδὲ διατρίβειν.

The wicked nurse leads her master's little boy "trotting along at her heels" (xv. 450):

παῖδα γὰρ ἀνδρὸς ἑῆος ἐνὶ μεγάροις ἀτιτάλλω,
κερδάλεον μάλα τοῖον, ἅμα τροχάοντα† θύραζε,

† The words with this mark are used only once in Homer.

a whole sentence taken straight from the wench's lips, with
τοῖος in the colloquial sense of "just," like the classical οὕτως[2]—
—"There's the gentleman's son, my nursling, just a cunning
little dear, goes trotting out for walks with me." Then again,
Iros and Odysseus were quarrelling together, "prickling and
spiking with all their hearts" (xviii. 33).

> οὐδοῦ ἔπι ζεστοῦ πανθυμαδὸν ὀκριόωντο.†

The faithful drover's cattle sprouted up like a field of corn
(xx. 211):

> νῦν δ' οἱ μὲν γίγνονται ἀθέσφατοι, οὐδέ κεν ἄλλως
> ἀνδρί γ' ὑποσταχύοιτο† βοῶν γένος εὐρυμετώπων—

"now they breed a fair miracle,[2] else you couldn't find the
the broad-faced beasts sprouting up like stalks in a wheat-
field." A vivid picture of a herd in the field with their horns
sticking up. And the swineherd uses what was obviously a
countryman's words when he speaks of the droves of swine
and his solid flocks of goats (xiv. 101):

> τόσσα συῶν συβόσια, τόσ' αἰπόλια πλατέ' αἰγῶν.

Most of these words occur only once; others which are more
commonplace are no less striking: as τυτθὰ βαλὼν κεάσαιμι (xii.
388), "smash it to smithereens"; τυτθὸς ἐών, "when I was a little
tot" (xv. 381); λαρὸν δόρπον, "a good square meal" (xiv. 408);
φῶτες (viii. 218; xiv. 98), "fellows" (a word which always
carries a familiar touch in Greek literature): the adverbs in
-δον, ὃς ἄν μιν χανδὸν ἔλῃ, μηδ' αἴσιμα πίνῃ (xxi. 294), to
drink your wine open-throated, or—

> ἀλλὰ παρὲξ εἴποιμι παρακλιδόν,   οὐκ ἂν ἔγωγε

(xvii. 138)

"I will not talk aside, shuffle, and shirk your questions"; or
expressions like

> πολλὰ δ' ἄναντα κάταντα πάραντά τε δόχμιά τ' ἦλθον,

(Il. xxiii. 116)

---

[1] Compare St. John iv. 6, Ἰησοῦς. . . ἐκαθέζετο οὕτως ἐπὶ ἰῇ πηγῇ,
"he just sat down by the well."

[2] ἀθέσφατοι is also colloquial.

"Here come the logs in plenty, upalong downalong offalong and crosswise." But all Homer's own words are alive, no poetical drapery to hide the things, no affectation, nothing conventional or bookish. He is like Chaucer.

The same is true of longer phrases. There are pithy sayings or proverbs: "When want is by you mustn't be shy" (*Od.* xvii. 347); "the steel in sight draws men to fight" (xix. 13); "who touches my ration-basket must earn his keep" (xix. 28); "to die with a mouthful of salt water" (xii. 350). There are local sayings; obviously it was a regular gambit among the islanders, "What ship brought you here? I don't think you walked all the way" (i. 173):

οὐ μὲν γάρ τί σε πεζὸν ὀίομαι ἐνθάδ' ἱκέσθαι.

The most notable is one which seems to be a special turn of speech in Ithaca. Telemachos gives instructions to Eumaios; "Look sharp, daddy, tell my mother that I am safe, and then come back; take care not to say a word to anyone else." He answers, "I know, I understand, I have some sense in my head (xvi. 136):

γιγνώσκω, φρονέω, τά γε δὴ νοέοντι κελεύεις.

Was not this a familiar sound to Odysseus, and one he had not heard for twenty years? He does not forget it; but in the morning, when the swineherd says, "Now let's be off, we must do what the young master says, for masters have a rough side to their tongue: come along, it will be cold in the evening," Odysseus replies, "I know, I understand, I have some sense in my head" (xvii. 192). And when they see the great house, and Eumaios warns him not to linger, or else he might be knocked about, Odysseus says again, "I know, I understand, I have some sense in my head." How natural again is the scene where Thetis visits Hepaistos. His wife, Charis, sees her, and runs out to embrace her (*Il.* xviii. 385):

τίπτε, Θέτι τανύπεπλε, ἱκάνεις ἡμέτερον δῶ,
αἰδοίη τε φίλη τε; πάρος γε μὲν οὔ τι θαμίζεις.
ἀλλ' ἕπεο προτέρω, ἵνα τοι πὰρ ξείνια θείω.

Every word, except perhaps τανύπεπλε (but who knows?) is exactly what we should expect a Greek woman to say, even to the colloquial τίπτε and δῶ: "My dear, what brings you to our humble home? This is an honour! and I *am* glad to see

you. You do not often pay me a visit. Do come in, and let
me give you a cup of tea." The same expressions are used
by Calypso to Hermes (*Od.* v. 88). Even the word for "come
in," ἔπεο προτέρω, was the regular one, which has lasted
down to the present day. If you knock at a Greek door, you
hear the word μπρός, which is an abbreviation of πρόσω, the
last syllable dropping when the accent on πρόσω became stress.
Charis uses the same to summon her man (*Il.* xviii. 392):

Ἥφαιστε, πρόμολ᾽ ὧδε· Θέτις νύ τι σεῖο χατίζει,

"Husband, come in here! Thetis wants something from you."
Curiously enough, the Indians used the same prefix for their
word "come in," *pravica* (pra= πρό), so our prehistoric an-
cestors seven thousand years ago may have said *pro* to invite
their guests.

There is the same natural simplicity in what Odysseus says
to the Cyclops, which has the very same intonations (if you
speak the accents) as a nurse might use in coaxing a child
(ix. 347):

Κύκλωψ, τῆ, πίε οἶνον, ἐπεὶ φάγες ἀνδρόμεα κρέα—

"Cýclops, hêre, háve a whísky, after your nice meal! Say
when!"
"Dárling, do take your grúel"—
And the monster forgets all his blusterings, and even says
πρόφρων, "If you please," like a good boy,

δός μοι ἔτι πρόφρων, καί μοι τεὸν οὔνομα εἰπὲ
αὐτίκα νῦν, ἵνα τοι δῶ ξείνιον, ᾧ κε σὺ χαίρῃς—

"One more, please! and tell me your name now this in-
stant,
and I'll give you something you'll like!"
So it is with all the talk of humble people: the railing
lady's-maid, the coarse goatherd, the old nurse, the old
swineherd, all speak in natural words, and their way of
thinking and speaking is true to their characters. In higher
life there is more formality, of course. The public speakers
in both *Iliad* and *Odyssey* have to conform to custom, but
most of the formality consists in the mode of address, which
has been already examined. Once they get under way, each
man is himself. It is remarkable indeed how Achilles and
Agamemnon show what manner of men they are at once,

and continue to show it; and no less the speakers in the Ithacan meetings, although they are less important in the story.

But the gods in heaven are Homer's triumph in the matter of conversation. Each god, like the men, shows what manner of god he is; and the scenes are full of delicate comedy, which gives the relief necessary for the grim stories. The gods are really the most human of Homer's creations, and there is plenty of variety in their setting.

Look at the first scene in the *Odyssey;* a family conclave, with Zeus in the chair (i. 32). He breaks out in his usual blunt style, using the simplest everyday phrase, which Homer might have used if he had a bad egg for breakfast: "Damn it all, just see how men always put the blame on us gods! And they have only their own folly to thank if they suffer more than they need. Here's Aigisthos—he need not have made a match of it with the prince's wedded wife, and killed the prince himself when he came home. He knew it was certain death, for we gave him full warning, sent my King's messenger to command him not to kill this man or to make love to his wife, or else Orestes would pay him out. Hermes told him, but he would not listen, and now he has paid in a lump sum."

Athena answers in quite different style, with all the formalities of a public meeting. "Cronides, father of us all, King of Kings and Lord of Lords! that man richly deserved his fate, and I hope anyone else who does things like that may suffer the same! But have you forgotten poor Odysseus? He has done no wrong, quite the contrary, but see how he is kept prisoner by that witch Calypso! And you care nothing about it, Olympian. Didn't he do his pious duty to you with all those sacrifices? Why are you so angry with Odysseus? It seems odd indeed to me!" She is quite in earnest; she is too angry herself to jest, but she does make a pun, and hopes it will sting him.

The pun which Athena made to sting Zeus (*Od.* i. 62) is not alone. Everyone makes puns on Odysseus; in fact, his name originally came from a pun. Grandfather Autolycos happened to visit Ithaca at the time when the boy was born. Eurycleia laid the baby upon his knees after dinner, and said, "Do'ee now find a name for the boy thyself, sir; he is the child of many prayers!"—The only son, you remember, as Telemachos has told us: "In our family, we go by ones; I am the only son of my father, and he was the only son of Laertes." But Autolycos was not in a praying humour, he was his own cynical self, and what he said was this: "My son and my daughter, I will tell you what name to give to this child. I have been at odds with many in the course of my life, both men and women: let his name therefore be Odysseus, the man of all odds." And when the goddess Eidothea sees him struggling in the water, and offers him her enchanted veil to help him, she begins with the usual jest: "Poor fellow, how odd-I-see you Od-ysseus! Why is the Earthshaker so furious against you?" (v. 339). Athena plays the same game with Telemachos, when he dallies in Lacedaimon (xv. 10)—

Τηλέμαχ᾽, οὐκέτι καλὰ δόμων ἄπο .τῆλ᾽ ἀλάλησαι—

"Don't dally in this valley, Telemachos, I tell 'ee," you are just a far-straggler instead of a far-warrior, Τηλάλαλος rather than Τηλέμαχος.

Now we return to Olympos. Zeus keeps the homely touch: "My dear child, what a thing to say! How could I ever forget Odysseus? It's Poseidon who hates him and will go on hating him, because he blinded his son Polyphemos. Poseidon does not kill him, but keeps him wandering about and won't let him go home. Let us see if we can find how to soften him. Surely he will not be able to keep up a grudge all by himself, if the rest of us disapprove!"

Then Athena proposes her motion, with the same formality as before: "Cronides our Father, King of Kings and Lord of Lords! If the immortals approve my proposal, let us despatch Hermes King's Messenger to Ogygia, and declare to Calypso our unchangeable will, that Odysseus shall return home."

Her proposal was carried, and we know what followed then: how Odysseus made his voyage; how Poseidon came back from his week-end with the Ethiopians, and saw him; the storm, and how he was finally brought home to Ithaca. Then Poseidon, in high dudgeon, came to ask Zeus what he really meant (xiii. 128): "Father Zeus, I see I shall have no honour in heaven, when mortal men care nothing for me! I thought it was agreed that Odysseus should be miserable until he returned home, though I did not stop his return altogether because you had promised it. And now see how these Phaiacians have landed him safe and sound, with heaps of wealth, more than he would have had if he had carried home the spoils of Troy!"

Zeus, blunt as ever, retorts: "Bless my soul, Earthshaker,

don't talk like that. The gods do not dishonour you. It would be too bad to bombard our eldest and best with insults! If any *man* does not respect you, you can make him pay for it. Do what you like, what pleases you, pleases me."

Poseidon answered: "That is what I should have done at once, Thundercloud, but I always have a wholesome fear of your temper, and I do my best to avoid it. Now then, what I should like to do is this: to smash that fine ship on the way back, and make an end of their escorting people home, and to raise a ring of high mountains about the city."

Zeus answered: "Gentle creature! My temper thinks the best thing to be this. Wait until the ship is running in, and the whole population gazing at the sight, and then turn it into stone close to the shore; then raise a ring of high mountains about the city."

Notice how the titles are used alone, as a familiar address, with the same tone as the mortal man's patronymic alone; and how Zeus plays on Poseidon's words, like one bantering an angry brother. In this translation I have kept close to the original, even closer than the most unpretending translation I can find, which renders the first words of the last two speeches thus:

"P. I ever dread and avoid thy wrath.
  Z. Friend, hear what seems best in my sight."

The Greek has one word, θυμός, which I render by "temper," and the translation misses the play on that word altogether. It also translates the gods' titles, the friendly address as I take it, by stiff phrases, "thou shaker of earth," "thou god of the dark clouds," when the Greek has no god at all; the vivid saying "to bombard with insults" is softened into "assail with dishonour," the image being lost; and ὦ πέπον is a phrase used to stir up a lazy man, to suggest slackness—"O softy" it means, literally "O ripe one:"

Αἶαν, δεῦρο, πέπον, περὶ Πατρόκλοιο θανόντος
σπεύσομεν . . .   (*II.* xvii. 120)
ἀλλ' ἄγε δεῦρο πέπον, παρ' ἐμ' ἵστασο . . .   (179)
ὦ πέπον, ὦ Μενέλαε διοτρεφές . .   (238)

all in the same battle-scene; and the Cyclops to his pet ram, who says in plain words what the meaning is (*Od.* ix. 447, cp. xxii. 233):

κριὲ πέπον, τί μοι ὧδε διὰ σπέος ἔσσεο μήλων ὕστατος;

"Lazy ram, why are you out last to-day?" Read the passage

once more, and hear how a simple version, without ornament
or disguise, gives just the tones of life. So it is always in
Homer: be simple, and you get both life and truth—al-
though you lose the incomparable music, which no trans-
lation can keep. Why, Homer gives pleasure even by the way
he tells us. "then Zeus says, says he":

τὸν δ' ἀπομειβόμενος προσέφη νεφεληγερέτα Ζεύς.

Take again the domestic scene after Hera has played one
of her tricks upon Zeus. While he sleeps, Hypnos takes her
message to Poseidon, and tells him to go ahead; the Grecians
are rallied, and drive their enemies back. But when Zeus
awoke, he fell into a royal rage (*Il.* xv. 14). Easy-going as he
was, he drew the line somewhere; and when he was really
angry, as Homer tells us, he could knock the gods all over
the place. He says: "This is one of your mean tricks, Hera,
you mischief-maker! Well, you shall be the first to repent it,
when I get my hands on you! Don't you remember how I
hung you out over the edge of Olympos by your arms, with a
big stone fastened to each foot?" Hera shivered, and said,
"I swear by Earth and Heaven and the water of Styx, by
your head and our marriage bed, it is not my doing that
Poseidon is harrying Hector and the Trojans!" This was true
in the letter, for Hypnos had done that part. She goes on,
"It must be his own bad temper, but I would advise him to
follow the path where you lead him, Thundercloud!" Zeus
was mollified at once. He smiled and said, "Ah my dear wife,
if you would only agree with me, Poseidon would soon change
his mind! Well, if you are speaking the truth, go home and
send Iris to me here, and Apollo, and she shall tell Poseidon
to cease fighting and come back home, while Apollo puts
heart again into Hector. The Trojans shall drive their enemies
back upon the ships, Achilles shall send out Patroclos, Hector
shall kill him and my own son Sarpedon too. This will enrage
Achilles, and he shall drive the Trojans back to their walls.
But I forbid all the immortals to take part, until I fulfil the
promise I made to Achilles, when Thetis his mother prayed
me to give him glory."

Hera was thoroughly frightened, but not moved in the
least from her own purposes: that was a vain wish of
Zeus. If only she would agree with him, how happy they
might all be! And how many husbands must have sighed for
the same blessing since Homer's day! Perhaps he may have
hit the nail on the head with some of his great barons, and
one here and there may have taken heart, and followed the

example of Zeus. For the moment, Zeus had his way. Swift as thought, Hera returned to Olympos, as bitter and as obstinate as ever, and there were the immortals all together in hall sitting at breakfast. They rose up and wished her health as she came in. Hera took no notice of them but Themis got up and ran to meet her, disturbed by her gloomy look.

She said simply, without ceremony, "Hera, why have you come? You look scared. I'm sure your lord and master has frightened you!"

Hera said, "My dear creature, don't ask me that!" Notice here a clever touch. A human being in Hera's case would have ἄνθρωπε said "man alive," or ὦ γύναι; but she cannot say that to an immortal. Let us follow Homer's example, and invent an English phrase. Hera said then, "Goddess alive, don't ask me that! You know his temper well enough, high and mighty, unbending. Just sit down and pour out, and let us have a proper breakfast. Then you shall hear, and the rest of the family shall hear, what a wicked thing Zeus proposes to do. I do not think *everybody* will be equally pleased, whether men or gods, if there is anyone who is still cheerful over his meal."

She sat down, having now quite upset the whole company. She laughed with her lips, but there was no warmth on the forehead over her dark brows. She spoke indignantly, so that all around could hear. "We are a lot of children to quarrel with Zeus, just fools! We still think we can stand up to him and stop him, by talking or by force; and he sits by himself and neither heeds nor cares. He says he is far and away strongest and mightiest among us all. So just take whatever he chooses to send you. Already, I think, there is a nasty little parcel for Ares. His son has been killed in battle, the man he loves best, Ascalaphos, at least Ares calls him his son."

At this Ares slapped his sturdy thighs with his two open hands, and cried out in distress, "Now then, Olympians, don't be surprised if I go to the battlefield and avenge my son's death, even if I am to be struck with a thunderbolt and lie in the dust on a heap of bloody corpses!"

Out he went, and called his attendants Terror and Panic to get the horses. Then there would have been another quarrel [1] greater than any Achilles could make, between Zeus

---

[1] μῆτις in allusion to μῆνιν ἄειδε, θεά, Πηληϊάδεω Ἀχιλῆος, the subject of the *Iliad*.

and his family. But Athena was terrified for them all; up she leapt from her seat, and ran out of the door, pulled the helmet off his head and the shield from his shoulders, dragged the spear out of his strong hand, and scolded him roundly: "You're mad, you're crazy, you are lost! What is the good of ears if you cannot hear? Your sense is gone, you don't know where you are! Don't you hear what the queen says, just come from Olympian Zeus? Do you want to run amuck, and then come back here discomfitted, against your will? Do you want to bring ruin upon the rest of us? He will leave Trojans and Greeks on the spot, and then come ramping to Olympos, and grab one after another, guilty or not guilty! Then stop it, I tell you! Don't fly into a rage about your son. Many a man has been killed or will be killed some day, better and stronger than he was. It is a difficult thing to preserve the whole human race!"

As she said this, she led Ares back to his seat. But Hera called Iris and Apollo outside, and told them her message. The battle proceeded as Zeus had foretold; and when the armies were facing each other upon the plain, Zeus summoned all the gods to meet him on the hill of Olympos. He said, "I intend to sit here and watch the fight. The rest of you go down to the battle-field and take sides as you like."

So the gods paired off: Poseidon against Apollo, Athena against Ares, Hera against Artemis, Hermes against Leto, Hephaistos against river Xanthos.

Zeus "laughed for joy" as he saw the gods joining in the strife. Towards the end, Ares finds himself face to face with Athena, and shouts in his rage (*Il*. xxi. 394): "What, again, you dog-fly? gods fight against gods? You egged on Diomede to wound me the other day, and how you shall pay for it!" He struck her aegis-cape with his spear. She gave ground, and picking up a huge jagged stone, she struck Ares upon the neck, and brought him down with a loud crash. She laughed aloud to see his hair dabbled in the dust, and said, "Fool to think you were stronger than I am!" As she turned away, Aphrodite, his lover, came to his help, took him by the hand, and helped him to scramble up, groaning and half-dazed. When Hera saw this, she cried out to Athena, "Bless us, Atrytone, daughter of Zeus almighty! Look—there's that dog-fly again, leading bloody Ares out of the battle! After her!"

Athena joyously ran after her, and struck her on the breast with her open hand; she collapsed, and the pair fell sprawling on the ground. Athena called out in triumph, "So may all those lie that help the Trojans, like this brave and daring pair, Ares and Aphrodite who came to save him! If they were all like these, we should have taken Troy long ago!"

Hera smiled; and Poseidon said to Apollo, "Phoibos, why do we two keep out of it? It would be a shame if we went home without a fight. You begin, since you are the younger. I know more of the world than you do. But indeed you are a fool to fight for people like the Trojans. I built their walls, and you kept their cattle, and at the end of the year the king would not pay us our wages. Have you forgotten all that?"

Apollo said, "Earthshaker, you could not think me sane if I am to fight you for the sake of such paltry creatures as mortals are. Let us stop, and let the others fight."

He turned away, for the truth was, he did not like to fight with his own uncle. But his sister Artemis scolded him: "So you are running away, Shootafar! You let Poseidon call you beaten! What is the good of that bow of yours? Don't let me hear you boasting in future how you will stand up to Poseidon!"

Apollo did not answer; but Queen Hera scolded her, and cried out, "How could you think to stand against me, you shameless bitch? I am no easy enemy, even though you have a bow and arrows. Women find you a lion, no doubt, but you had better go and kill deer on the mountains. But if you want to know something about war, I will show you how much stronger I am."

So with her left hand she caught both the other's wrists, and with her right hand pulled the bow and quiver off her shoulders, and beat them about her ears, smiling, while the other wriggled about, and the arrows dropped down in a shower. The poor thing slipped out underneath and ran away in tears, like a dove fleeing before a falcon. She left the bow and arrows on the ground; Leto her mother picked them up where they lay scattered in the dust, and went after her daughter.

But Artemis ran to the Olympian hall, and fell weeping upon her father's knees. He drew her to him, and said, laughing gently, "Who has done this to you, dear child?" She answered, "Your own wife, father, Queen Hera! She gave me a regular beating, and she is the cause of all these quarrels in the family!"

In these dialogues, and in most of the narrative, I have

used Homer's words. I have left something out, but if you read the Greek words without prejudice, you will see that they are as natural and simple as mine. There is absolutely nothing of poetical embellishment in the words; they are the same words which ordinary human beings would use in these conditions. The Greek is coarse where my words are coarse; and in all I have used only one that has a touch of slang, "ramping," which I chose because the Greek word κυδοιμήσων (*Il.* xv. 136) is not a common one (it occurs only twice) and it has a fine rollicking sound. When real poetry is found in Homer, its beauty belongs to itself; it has nothing to do with special words or forms of speech. So in the simplest English the same nobility and beauty is found when the thing said is noble and beautiful: Bunyan's *Holy War* is full of dignity and splendour, although Bunyan used the speech of the people. But, of course, Homer's own special charm is not here; for that depends wholly on the sound, the lovely inimitable sound of the rolling lines and the reverberating words of the old language.

The intellectual charm of the poem, however, can be given in English. I think I have given some of it, but there is plenty more for all readers to find, for no one has ever studied the effect of the musical accent. One example of what may be found, I have given in the episode of the Cyclops: where, perhaps by accident, the intonation of a line is the same as a coaxing nurse might use to a child. There is something more of that sort to be heard in the passage. Let me read it, and listen whether I have imagined too much (*Od.* ix. 347):

Κύκλωψ, τῆ, πίε οἶνον, ἐπεὶ φάγες ἀνδρομέα κρέα[1]·
ὄφρ' εἰδῇς οἷόν τι ποτὸν τόδε νηῦς ἐκεκεύθει
ἡμετέρη· σοὶ δ' αὖ λοιβὴν φέρον, εἴ μ' ἐλεήσας
οἴκαδε πέμψειας· σὺ δὲ μαίνεαι οὐκέτ' ἀνεκτῶς.
σχέτλιε, πῶς κέν τίς σε καὶ ὕστερον ἄλλος ἵκοιτο
ἀνθρώπων πολέων; ἐπεὶ οὐ κατὰ μοῖραν ἔρεξας.

It does not matter much what the man says; he talks for the sake of talking, to prevent the monster from thinking what he is doing himself. It is a well-known trick of dealers; a man sold me a horse once in that way. And you have all heard a cheap-jack, I dare say. To my ear, the sound of the passage is all coaxing; even when the voice rises on σὺ δὲ μαίνεαι,

[1] See music (*a*), p. 299.

the reproachful words may pass quite unnoticed. Homer goes on:

ὡς ἐφάμην, ὁ δὲ δέκτο καὶ ἔκπιεν

hear the climax as the tone rises—

ἥσατο δ᾽ αἰνῶς
ἡδὺ ποτὸν πίνων, καί μ᾽ ᾔτεε δεύτερον αὖτις·
Δός μοι ἔτι πρόφρων, καί μοι τεὸν οὔνομα εἰπὲ
αὐτίκα νῦν, ἵνα τοι δῶ ξείνιον ᾧ κε σὺ χαίρῃς.
καὶ γὰρ κυκλώπεσσι φέρει ζείδωρος ἄρουρα
οἶνον ἐριστάφυλον, καί σφιν Διὸς ὄμβρος ἀέξει·
ἀλλὰ τόδ᾽ ἀμβροσίης καὶ νέκταρός ἐστιν ἀπορρώξ.
      ὡς ἔφατ᾽ αὐτάρ οἱ αὖτις ἐγὼ πόρον αἴθοπα οἶνον·
τρὶς μὲν ἔδωκα φέρων—

and there are three rising accents—

τρὶς δ᾽ ἔκπιεν ἀφραδίῃσιν.

Then Odysseus tells his name, Οὖτις, and you remember what follows. He sleeps, he is blinded, he wakes and roars for help (401):

οἱ δὲ βοῆς ἀΐοντες ἐφοίτων ἄλλοθεν ἄλλος,
ἱστάμενοι δ᾽ εἴροντο περὶ σπέος ὅττι ἑ κήδοι·

τίπτε τό σόν, Πολύφημ᾽, ἀρημένος ὧδ᾽ ἐβόησας
νύκτα δι᾽ ἀμβροσίην, καὶ ἀΰπνους ἄμμε τίθησθα;
ἦ μή τίς σευ μῆλα βροτῶν ἀέκοντος ἐλαύνει;
ἦ μή τίς σ᾽ αὐτὸν κτείνει δόλῳ ἠὲ βίηφιν;

you hear their rising accents of anxiety.

τοὺς δ᾽ αὖτ᾽ ἐξ ἄντρου προσέφη κρατερὸς Πολύφημος·
ὦ φίλοι, Οὖτίς με κτείνει δόλῳ οὐδὲ βίηφιν.

The neighbours mistake Οὖτις for οὖτις, which a Greek, of course, distinguished easily, but there was some excuse for the savages when their friend was shouting out of a cave:

οἱ δ᾽ ἀπαμειβόμενοι ἔπεα πτερόεντ᾽ ἀγόρευον

they answered plainly and to the point, as this phrase means: and you can now hear four rising tones in succession, expressing their natural indignation:

εἰ μὲν δὴ μή τίς σε βιάζεται οἷον ἐόντα,[1]
νοῦσόν γ' οὔπως ἔστι Διὸς μεγάλοι' ἀλέαθαι,
ἀλλὰ σύ γ' εὔχεο πατρὶ Ποσειδάωνι ἄνακτι.
 ὡς ἄρ' ἔφαν ἀπιόντες, ἐμὸν δ' ἐγέλασσε φίλον κῆρ,
ὡς ὄνομ' ἐξαπάτησεν ἐμὸν καὶ μῆτις ἀμύμων.

I laughed within me, that I had tricked them so well with my noman name and my machinomanations. For we have here not only a play upon Οὖτις and οὔτις, but also μῆτις and μῆτις: my Οὖτις you see is also a μῆτις.

I have noted hundreds of places where the musical accent may mean something; often it is very much to the point. But I have never studied them or brought them under any principles. There is a topic for someone to investigate.

Κύκ - λωψ τῆ πι - ε οἶ - νον (a)

Εἰ μέν δή μή τίς σε βι - ά - ζε - ται. (b)

---

[1] See music (b). It should be noted that the acute is always the same accent. It is printed the reverse way in certain circumstances, but that is a modern innovation. How it came in, I have never been able to discover; it has no ancient authority that I have been able to find.

Pronouncing Index

This index shows the correct quantities of the vowels in the names and an accent ' is placed to suggest how the reader may pronounce them as if English names:

    c always sounded as k.
    ch   "   "   " kh
    a, e, i, o, u as in Italian properly, but they may be sounded as in English (u=oo) for convenience.
    Vowels marked ā, ē, etc., are of double length.
    The mark on ê means that it is not mute, but forms a syllable.

A-chai′-ans.
A′-che-rōn.
A-chil′lēs.
A-ga-mem′-nōn.
A-ge-lā′-os.
Ai-ai′-ā.
Ai′-ās.
Ai-ĕ′-tās.
Ai-gis′-thos.
Ai-gyp′-ti-os.
Ai-gyp′-tos, Egypt.
Ai-o′-li-ā.
Ai-o′-li-dēs.
Ai′-o-los.
Ai′-sōn.
Alc-mai′-ōn.
Alc-mē′-nē.
A-lec′-tōr.
A-lō′-eus.
Al-phei′-os.
am-bro′-si-ā, immortality.
Am′-phi-lo-chos.
Am′-phi-me-dōn.
Am′-phi-no-mos.
Am-phī′-ōn.
Am′-phi-the-ā.
Am-ph-trī′-te.
Am′-phi-trī′-ōn.
A-my-thā′-ōn.
An′-chi-a-los.

An-drai′-mōn.
An′-ti-clos.
An′-ti-lo-chos.
An′-ti-no-os.
An′-ti-o-pē.
An′-ti-phās.
An′-ti-pha-tēs.
An′-ti-phos.
A-phro-dī′-tē.
A-pol′-lō.
Ar-cei′-si-a-dēs.
A′-rēs.
A-rē′-tē.
A-re-thū′-sa.
A-rē′-ti-a-dēs.
A-rē′-tos.
Ar-gei-phon′-tēs or ge-ī-.
Ar′-gos.
A-ri-ad′-nē.
Ar-nai′-os.
Ar-ta′-ci-ê.
Ar′-te-mis.
A′-ry-bās.
A-sō′-pos.
As′-te-ris.
A-thē′-nā, A-thē-nai′-ā.
A′-tlās.
A-tr-ei′-dēs or A-tre′-i-dēs.
A′-treus.
A-trȳ-tō′-nē.

300

304 INDEX

Tĕ-le′-phi-dēs.
Tĕ′-le-phos.
Te′-me-sē.
Te′-ne-dos.
Ter′-pi-a-dēs.
The-o-cly′-me-nos.
Thē′-seus.
Tho′-ās.
Thōn.
Thra-sy-mē′-dēs.
Thrī-na′-ci-ā.

Thy-es′-tēs
Tī-thō′-nos.
Ti′-ty-os.
Trī-to-ge-nei′-ā.
Tȳ-dei′-dēs or Tȳ-de′-i-dēs.
Tyn-da′-re-ōs.
Ty′-rō.

Za-cyn′-thos.
Zē′-thos.
Zeus.